PRELUDE TO APOCALYPSE

He watched his son storm around the trophy room, ripping mounted heads from the wall, smashing at the mute symbols of his father's skill with rapid-firing weapons. His son turned and screamed, "God damn you! What do you expect of me?" But he knew. Even as he asked, he knew what his father's answer would be.

The older man responded truthfully and directly. "I want them dead. I want to rid the world of everybody in the international game. And I expect you to make it happen.

"I want you to fly an air-strike on Arlington National Cemetery. I want the new president and all who attend the funeral to die . . ."

Other Avon Books by
Gregory G. Vanhee

THE SHOOTER

NIGHT STRIKE

GREGORY G. VANHEE

AVON BOOKS NEW YORK

NIGHT STRIKE is an original publication of Avon Books. This work has never before appeared in book form. This work is a novel. Any similarity to actual persons or events is purely coincidental.

AVON BOOKS
A division of
The Hearst Corporation
105 Madison Avenue
New York, New York 10016

To my father, George Joseph Vanhee:
He loved politics,
he loved airplanes,
and he loved women.
He would have loved this book, I think . . .

ACKNOWLEDGMENTS

I wish to extend special thanks to Master Sergeant Sandra Riley, United States Marine Corps, and Rick Bondurant, United States Air Force.

Sandra Riley operates with incredible efficiency and good will out of the Public Affairs Office of the 2nd Marine Aircraft Wing at Cherry Point, North Carolina. Rick Bondurant, Sergeant Riley's Air Force counterpart, operates with equal vigor out of the Public Affairs Office of the 354th Tactical Fighter Wing, Myrtle Beach, South Carolina.

Night Strike, due to its theme, was a difficult book to research. Sandra Riley and Rick Bondurant provided me with all I needed for this task, no matter how unrealistic the request. I sincerely hope they will accept my work for what it is, a novel, and forgive me its faults. I am in their debt. I wear with heartfelt pride their respective unit insignia on my jacket.

Gregory G. Vanhee
Seattle, Washington

PROLOGUE

"You're gonna love this airplane, Colonel." Jonathan Bennett sat in the A-10 cockpit, as the crew chief fussed with his harness, and gave a final wipe of the windscreen, tapping the colonel's helmet with his closed fist. His commanding officer didn't seem to mind the breach of discipline.

"Why am I going to love this airplane, Sergeant?"

"You will love it, sir, because it allows . . . no, it *demands* that you fly it. It's a pilot's aircraft, sir. It's a killer's aircraft. You'll like it, sir."

"Well, let's see, shall we?" The crew chief of the freshly painted A-10, GUNFIGHTER scripted on her nose, climbed down the access ladder, and pulled it away from the plane. The aircraft rolled onto the runway, its pilot hurrying it along. Cleared by the tower, the squadron commander punched the A-10 into the air in 107 feet less than the flight manual stated. Pilot and aircraft were instantly wed . . .

1

SEPTEMBER 1983
WIESBADEN, GERMANY

The A-10, unofficially nicknamed the "Warthog," ripped along the ground, dipping and hugging the terrain, blistering the countryside of the Federal Republic of Germany at 400 plus knots at an altitude of only 150 feet. Occasionally it dipped lower, following the checkerboard squared farmland, once and often ruled and run over by tanks of attacking or defending forces, but always pushed to war by the westward march of Germans, followed by the eastward march of Germans, followed by the reverse. A conquered land of the conquerors, undone by pride and times. The A-10 moved across this centuries-old battlefield with the confidence of a machine built to cross, or defend, any borders.

Operation Cold Fire had been going on for over forty hours, and Colonel Bennett's job for this day was clear. A column of armored vehicles, a mix of tanks and troop carriers immobilized in a heavily defended canyon, was to be destroyed at all costs. The Gunfighter was the lead aircraft in a flight of six A-10s, trailing him by less than 1500 yards, trainlike. If all went as planned, the 354th would chop this column up and leave the battlefield strewn with burning armor and, theoretically, dead troops. It was the colonel's first A-10 command flight and his "train" had no idea of how it would work out. They needn't have worried.

The flight hugged the ground. No. They touched the ground. At the last and best moment, Colonel Bennett's plane popped up, cresting a low hill and flying at the unheard-of altitude for this day of 1200 feet. He checked his HUD target display, lined up the first tank, and touched the trigger of his GAU-8 30mm antitank cannon. A twentieth-century sophisticated copy of the multibarrelled gun of the civil war, it was capable of 3000 rounds of cannon fire per minute. In four short bursts, he destroyed four armored targets and snap-rolled into a deep turn, taking out four more tanks in less than 2.6 seconds of aimed fire. Behind him, the train of five A-10s completed identical passes, banking hard right and skating away at treetop level, following their commander, about whom there could never again be any doubts. The Gunfighter was for real. The armored force, heavily protected by war-games anti-aircraft guns, was destroyed to the last machine. In fact, the tail end A-10s of the Gunfighter's squadron also destroyed two of the available three antiaircraft sites.

Far into the night the burning tanks flickered their souls into the West German skies, slaughtered by the best pilot the U.S.A.F. had ever produced. They were old and used tanks, linked to the ground, empty of combat soldiers who might have fought back, and escaped. Steel hulks, without combatants. Yet with every available advantage, against a new, untested wing commander, they should have suffered less than 20 percent casualties.

The Gunfighter and his mates had destroyed the equivalent of a full Russian tank battalion, and he had not been located until it was too late to counter his attack plan. Jonathan Bennett, former F-16 pilot, had transferred and assumed command of a wing of aircraft that he was born to fly. The F-15 and the F-16 were very fast, darting, diving, sexy aircraft for every top gun in the Air Force. The A-10 Warthog was slow, clumsy, powered by commercial airliner engines, and ugly by any comparison to a true fighter aircraft. It was also the most deadly machine ever designed. It could fight—and defeat—most any advanced, lightning-fast aircraft in the world. NATO hated it. Nobody bought it, except the United States Air Force, and they bought only one version.

Nevertheless, every year, 200 U.S.A.F. pilots tried to transfer to the A-10, officially designated the "Thunderbolt II" but unofficially named "Warthog" by its pilots. Why? Because the A-10 was a pilot's aircraft, and in one punch, pound for pound, the most destructive airplane ever flown. It was suited, temperamentally and offensively, to its new wing commander. Jonathan Bennett had once considered the A-10 a demotion. After Operation Cold Fire in 1983, he thought he had been saved, a pilot matched to his aircraft. A Gunfighter with guns. There were no buttons to push with the A-10. No computers. No fuss. You aimed it and pulled the trigger. What you could see, you could defeat. Baron Manfred von Richthofen would have loved it.

DECEMBER 21, 1987
MARINE CORPS AIR STATION
CHERRY POINT, NORTH CAROLINA

Marine Corps Second Lieutenant Jason Porter Kelly stood at ease in front of his squadron commander's desk, watching the colonel read through his orders.

"Well, Lieutenant Kelly, it says here you did very well in the two-seater. I suppose you're all hot to have a Harrier II all to yourself?"

"Yes, sir. I asked for tactical assignment, sir. I'm very grateful to get it."

"You may not be, Lieutenant Kelly, after you've been here awhile. They call this base the home of the Harrier. My personal license plate for North Carolina reads AV8-TOR. This is a gung-ho, working base. We fly a lot, and we fly hard. In a couple of months, we're going out to Yuma to do some bomb-range work. Let's you and I go out and see what you are best suited for. I want to know if you can fly this thing like the record says you can."

"Now, sir?"

"Why not now?" The colonel's bushy eyebrows arched into a fierce V as he scowled at the young lieutenant in front of him.

"Of course, sir. Now. Why not?"

"That's the ticket. Get your flight suit and meet me out on the line in a quick thirty."

"Yes, sir." Jason Porter Kelly, newly arrived from a training squadron, came to a rigid attention, and saluted his C.O. The salute he received in response was so sharp it made an audible sound in the room. Welcome to Cherry Point, North Carolina, he thought. It's show 'n tell time . . . He got dressed for flight with two minutes to spare.

He found the colonel without difficulty, standing near a pair of Av-8B Harrier IIs, the Marines' newest and certainly their weirdest operational aircraft.

"Lieutenant, you're a member, at least on paper, of VMA-231, the best Marine air unit in the Corps. We are the best because we fly the best. Let's us start our day with a hot little VTO departure. Stay on my wing. I'll head out over Cape Lookout, down the coast to Camp LeJeune, and close the triangle back to the base. We'll see how you fly in the process."

Holy Christ! A vertical takeoff, right out of the chute. His C.O. walked away and climbed the service ladder of his aircraft. Jason turned toward his designated aircraft, and was met by a crisp salute from a sergeant.

"Macklin, sir. John Macklin. I'm your plane captain, sir. Been expecting you."

Jason Kelly received quite a shock when he was handed a white helmet with his name printed on it. As he climbed into the cockpit, he noticed his name stenciled just under the Plexiglas canopy. Expecting him? Wow! A very nice touch.

As he strapped himself in, he heard the colonel's voice, clear and sharp in his headphone. "Are you comfortable, Lieutenant Kelly?"

"Yes, sir," he answered. He felt the sweat gather and roll down his back. Comfortable? Not very.

"Okay. Crank her up. We'll vector up together, whenever you are ready."

He hit the switches, and the Rolls Royce Pegasus engine roared to life. The plane rocked gently as he let it gather power to its full 21,500 pounds of thrust. When he was ready, he saluted his plane captain, on the runway a few yards away, tossed a thumbs-up to the colonel, and moved the engine's swiveling exhaust nozzles to the fully vertical position. The Harrier began to rise, like always. It never ceased to amaze him. Alongside him, the colonel's plane rose also, the blast from the downward-vectored nozzles shooting boiling clouds of dusty air around the two aircraft. Delicately, the two fighters hung over the runway, climbing to 200 feet before the colonel, in the most demanding maneuver required to fly the Harrier, eased the nozzles rearward and his aircraft began the transition from vertical takeoff and hover into normal flight, moving quickly forward and level as it headed out to sea.

Jason Kelly, hanging like an ungainly insect over the base, forgot for the moment where he was, and where he was supposed to be. His aircraft twirled slowly in the air, as if on a record turntable, its raw power held in critical balance by his delicate control.

"Are you coming, Lieutenant, or are you just going to hang there like that?"

His commander's voice penetrated immediately. Jason Kelly, newly added to VMA-231, Cherry Point, North Carolina, shifted the nozzles evenly to the rear, pulling the aircraft into rapid, level flight as the ungainly wheels and wing outriggers pulled back and into their nests. In a little longer than it takes to tell, he accelerated through 300 knots and drilled a hole in the low clouds over the base, bursting into the clear at 2500 feet.

"Airborne, Colonel." Jason could see the colonel's plane directly ahead.

"That's a roger, Lieutenant."

Jason pulled up near the colonel's aircraft, tucked in to about thirty yards and slightly below the colonel's right wingtip.

"Colonel?"

"Yes, Lieutenant?"

"Sorry, sir."

"It's a hell of an airplane, isn't it, Lieutenant?"

"Yes, sir."

The flight was uneventful, but satisfying. When they returned to Cherry Point, the colonel chose to land as they had taken off, vertically. A half mile from the field, Jason selected 40 degrees nozzle deflection, slowing to 140 knots, and then he continued vectoring until the nozzle brought him to a hover stop, 81 degrees down nozzles, arriving at 100 feet over his intended point of landing. Jason deftly controlled the nozzles between the hover stop and the braking stop. As the plane lowered, he gave it a touch of power, to compensate for the ingestion of hot exhaust. When he felt the weight on the landing gear, he slammed the throttle to idle and unvectored the nozzles. In front of him, his plane captain, Sergeant Macklin, waved him forward. He engaged the nosewheel steering and followed the sergeant the twenty yards to "his" AV-8B Harrier II spot on the squadron runway. He shut down and flipped the canopy open as the access ladder was clamped to his aircraft.

Sergeant Macklin, a black cigar locked in his teeth, scrambled up the ladder and handed Jason a cold bottle of beer. Jason Kelly thought it unlikely a beer would ever taste this good again. He had no way of knowing that in the not-too-distant future, he would fly this aircraft against another U.S. pilot in another unusual aircraft and attempt to shoot him down over Washington, D.C., attempting to stop a massacre of monumental proportions.

The aircraft and its pilot, Colonel Jonathan Bennett, were stationed just down the coast at Myrtle Beach, South Carolina. They would never meet, until Jason Kelly tried to blast the colonel from the skies over Arlington National Cemetery.

DAY ONE: WEDNESDAY

THE WHITE HOUSE
WASHINGTON, D.C.
WEDNESDAY, 8:00 A.M.

"Good morning, Mr. President."

"Same to you, Alice. Where's my coffee?" Conrad Wilson Taylor, the President of the United States, stood just inside the door of the Oval Office, wearing shorts and a sweatshirt, a towel draped around his neck. His workday began at 8:30 A.M. His workout on the exercycle began at 7:30, part of a daily ritual, including the byplay with his prim secretary.

"Your coffee, Mr. President, is on the tray next to your desk, where it always is at eight o'clock."

"Right. You do good work, Alice. Keep this up, and you'll pass through your probationary period and be officially a full-time employee." As usual, this brought a rare grin to Ms. Alice Burke. She had been his secretary for twenty-one years. She was the stern keeper of the seal, and he trusted her completely.

The President settled into his chair, sipping his coffee, watching his secretary as she placed two stacks of papers on his desk, one stack "to look into," one to "take care of," as she put it. On a small stand next to his elaborately carved desk was a pile of the morning newspapers, along with an attached typed sheet of Alice's "pertinent" facts she had gleaned for him. The press was led to believe he read all the newspapers, every day.

Conrad Taylor was not a big reader. He was a glib talker, a dreamer of dreams, a visionary, a believer. He had won

9

the election because he had the uncanny ability of convincing the American people to believe what he envisioned as a new generation of true peace. After ten months as President, the heat was on, the honeymoon over. The President wanted a startling new treaty with the Soviets. He had said so during his election campaign. He had meant it. He felt his presidency would rise or fall on the outcome. The attacks on his proposals were growing, and they were full of venom.

"How did Rosemary do?"

"Ms. Hawkins always does well, Mr. President." Alice refused to call the President's National Security Advisor by her first name. Conrad Taylor would have been shocked to realize the depth of his secretary's feelings toward Rosemary Hawkins.

His National Security Advisor was also his lover, and had been for over five years. He thought their love affair was a complete secret, in spite of its duration. It was not a secret to Alice. She hated Rosemary Hawkins. Conrad Taylor had many faults. One of the most damaging was his complete lack of sensitivity about the people around him. It never occurred to him that his trusted secretary would like nothing better than to see Rosemary Hawkins develop a quick, painful, terminal illness.

"Be more specific, Alice. Rosemary gave a speech last night to the National Press Club. It was a biggy, right? So what did they say?"

"Mike Purcell of the *Post* said she had the best legs of any National Security Advisor in his memory."

"Alice!"

"Well, that's what he said. He doesn't like her and he hates you. The general thrust was that she gives good speech."

"Good speech?"

"That's the joke."

"Not funny."

"No, Mr. President, it's not funny. But how can she be taken seriously when she wears a dress slit up to here?"

His secretary's hand waved around vaguely in the area of her pelvis, demonstrating what "up to here" meant.

The President abruptly stood up, thus cutting the usual thirty minutes with his secretary by half. "Who's on my schedule today, Alice?"

"Ms. Hawkins, nine to ten, and the Vice President at lunch."

"Here, in the Oval Office?"

"Yes, sir. You know he likes to spend as much time in here as he can."

"Yes, I know. Pathetic, isn't it? Well, I owe him. He got me elected, so I'll satisfy his little vanities. What else this morning?"

"The Conservative Caucus of America. You gave them an hour. Then, off to Andrews and your speech tonight in New York. That's it."

"Who's coming for the caucus? Which crazy is it this time?"

"Former Governor Bennett, sir. I'd hardly call him a crazy. Nor should you. He has powerful friends, and many of them are in the Senate. He can kill your treaty. You need to sell it to him."

"Alice?"

"Yes, Mr. President?"

"Don't you think you're getting just a little bit pushy?" He left the Oval Office, without an answer to his question.

SUBURBAN MARYLAND
8:00 A.M.

As the limo carrying the President's National Security Advisor pulled away from her suburban Maryland home, Rosemary Hawkins began to read the morning papers, a grim little smile on her face. All the cutesy references about her legs aside, it had been a very effective speech. The sexist jokes were beginning to wear thin, over-

whelmed by her toughness and her message. The message
was peace. Radical peace, but peace. She had timed the
"erector set" comment very well. "We're not talking
erector sets here, we are talking grown-ups playing with
missiles that they can't control. I say . . . the President
says, scrap them all! Unilaterally, if need be. Someone
must lead the way." Heavy stuff. But she had scored. The
morning papers were full of Rosemary Hawkins and her
"erector sets."

Aside from the fact she was an obviously beautiful female, Rosemary Hawkins was as qualified as anyone in
recent history for her job: Chief Advisor to the President
of the United States on Foreign Affairs. She was a graduate of Georgetown University, a glittering example of
what monied education and "breeding" could produce. A
gifted lawyer, specializing in foreign trade problems, representing multinational corporations. A lecturer of high
visibility and stunning competence on history, the military, and political science. A world renowned authority on
diplomatic law, and a regular contributor to scholarly magazines, hammering away at her theme of peace, peace . . .
at whatever cost.

The major plus was she had been the President's lover
for over five years before his election. Her appointment
had caused a fire storm of protest, quickly extinguished by
her obvious qualifications. For ten months, she had spear-
headed the new President's attack on the status quo. The
milk of past foreign policy had curdled. She meant to kick
it over or kill the cows. Translation: Rosemary Hawkins
was a closet socialist. She believed that peace had a price,
and the United States should pay it. She meant for the
United States to abdicate its role in the world, closet itself
behind its coastlines, and dedicate itself to ending hunger
and poverty. It sounded terrific and the newspapers were
full of it.

There was just one hitch, one unspoken truth. Rosemary Hawkins didn't believe a single word she, or her
lover, said. But she would continue to say it, promote it,

carry it forward. She was a politician, with terrific legs, and no scruples whatsoever.

WASHINGTON, D.C.
8:00 A.M.

James Robert Kelly, C.I.A. agent and bon vivant, rolled over in bed and bumped into a vivant he did not recognize. She had at least one good leg, to be sure. The other was tangled in the covers, and might or might not have matched the first. She had blond hair, but not everywhere. She also had bad breath, and that was without dispute. If she had a name, J.R. Kelly couldn't remember it, or for that matter, where in the hell she came from. Or, where he was.

He checked the ceiling, looking for his New Orleans fan. It was there, twirling slowly, ineffectually, but it was definitely there. He was home and could, therefore, throw the unknown good leg out. He pushed the covers off, discovered the terrific first leg matched the second, and somehow, through an alcoholic fog, managed to get both legs wrapped around his face. It was wonderful. It was a great, early morning fuck. For an average-looking, rumpled C.I.A. agent, that wasn't too bad.

CHERRY POINT, NORTH CAROLINA
"HOME OF THE HARRIER"
WEDNESDAY, 8:35 A.M.

Marine Second Lieutenant Jason Porter Kelly, J.R.'s younger brother, was sitting in an AV-8B Harrier jet fighter, waiting for permission to take off from the Marine airbase. He was twenty-two years old, and as straight as Superman. Permission granted, he lifted the Harrier into the air at approximately the same time his older brother vanished headfirst between the slimmest, softest thighs he'd ever encountered. It was debatable which of the two brothers was the happier at the moment. The tower controller began to feed him commands and he eased the Harrier out over the Atlantic, overwhelmed as usual by the pure thrill of flying.

THE VICE PRESIDENT'S RESIDENCE
NAVAL OBSERVATORY HILL
WEDNESDAY, 8:35 A.M.

William Rodgers, the Vice President of the United States, liked to shave. Most men hate this daily ritual, but the Vice President used this everyday chore to think. What he liked to think about the most, was being President. He'd taken the V.P. job because he hoped the President would die. Heart attack. Polio. Burglars. Who cared? He knew the President was younger, but . . . well, it could happen.

In the meantime, he had to apply brakes to this idiot in the White House. Today, at lunch, he would lay out a few lines of thought, to slow the President down a bit. Jesus Christ, the son-of-a-bitch was worse than Chamberlain! In this very morning's paper, there was a devastating cartoon of Conrad Taylor, shown waving a piece of paper declaring "Peace In Our Times" and carrying the pre–World War II symbol of Neville Chamberlain. The umbrella. Except this one was edged in lace and garter belts. A not-very-subtle shot at the President's National Security Advisor. Peace in our times, indeed! The widowed Vice President would lay it on the line with the President. Rosemary Hawkins had to go. If the President of the United States was seen as a parody of the 1930s British appeaser, then it was his duty as Vice President, to speak up. As he shaved, he rehearsed his speech. "Mr. President [cut, nick] I took this job to advise you. Now, I [cut, nick] . . ."

THE WHITE HOUSE
WEDNESDAY, 9:00 A.M.

"Sir?"

The President punched the intercom button, still sipping coffee. "Yes, Alice?"

"Ms. Hawkins is here."

"Fine. Please send her in. And no calls, Alice, unless somebody drops it."

"Drops what, Mr. President?"

"Alice!" The President's voice rose to a near screech.

"Yes, sir. I'll send her right in."

"Good morning, Mr. President." Rosemary Hawkins looked at the President with a zealot's eyes.

"So it is, Rosemary, and good morning yourself. You killed 'em last night, I'm told. 'Erector sets.' Really, Rosemary, who writes your speeches?"

"The same person who writes yours, Conrad." Rosemary Hawkins settled into a large chair opposite the President's desk. When she sat down, she let the wrap skirt she was wearing flip open, exposing her legs and her gartered stockings above her thighs.

"Is there anyone in my administration you don't speak for?" His eyes settled on her legs.

"No, Conrad. Nobody." Her sleek thighs parted, opened.

"I'm horny, Ms. Hawkins. Do you want your President to face the day horny, or satisfied and able to do great things?"

"Mr. President, I want you at your functional best. So why don't you come over here, and 'function' me?" Rosemary Hawkins had less than ten seconds to pull her wrap skirt free of her body before the charismatic, new visions President of the United States had pulled her tiny panties aside and thrust his eloquent tongue into her. His shoulders hunched as he drove forward, her legs locked across his suited shoulders, her eyes open, staring across the top of his desk, into her capital dreams, her future, even as her past opened and flowered under the pressure of his active mouth, and she bit her lip to keep from screaming in triumph.

"How did you do that?"

"What?"

"How did you get me off? I was down on you, if I recall."

"And you were wonderful, Mr. President." Rosemary Hawkins always called him "Mr. President" after they had sex. It seemed appropriate, after all.

"If you want to know, I used my foot this time. Is it sticky down there?" She waved a manicured fingernail in the general direction of his crotch, as she pulled herself out of the chair.

"You know damn well it is!" There were times when she made him feel like a high school sophomore.

"Good. Now, should we get down to the business of running these United States?" The President's National Security Advisor rehooked her garter belt, straightened her wrap skirt, and sat down, her green eyes cool and distant. "Please, Mr. President, let's talk about your speech in New York tonight. And I think we should discuss what you might say to Governor Bennett in the next hour." She looked at him, not a single red hair out of place. The President of the United States tried to shift his penis around inside his damp boxer shorts. It didn't work. Even as one of the most politically dangerous men in the United States waited outside the Oval Office to see him, Conrad Wilson Taylor kept looking for the dry spot.

"Do you know what day this is, Conrad?"

"Wednesday."

Her green eyes flashed briefly in annoyance, but only briefly. "Today is our sixth anniversary. Six years to the day since we met. Don't worry, Conrad, it's not the kind of thing men remember. Especially married men."

"I'm not good about that kind of stuff, Rosemary," he said, repeating her observation.

"Yes, I know. How is your wife, by the way?" She did not care, but she asked him every day. It added to his guilt and made him more pliable.

"Emily is fine." He didn't look at her. He stared at the fireplace, his shoulders tightened defensively.

"The kids?" The questions, the hateful litany.

"Peter and Joanne are fine, considering they will be celebrating birthdays next month, and Christmas too. Good behavior time."

Joanne Taylor was going to be four years old. Rosemary had been hurt very badly by that. Conrad had insisted he and Emily had stopped having sex. When he told her Emily was pregnant, he'd said it had been a onetime thing. Emily had been crying and upset, and well, one thing led to another, and hell you know how things are, don't you? Rosemary . . . ?

She knew. Like all mistresses know.

"How is she doing as First Lady by now? Has she decided . . . what did she call it?" Rosemary hesitated. She knew what Emily had said. She wanted Conrad to repeat it.

"She said she wanted to 'have an impact,' if I recall." Conrad Taylor did not like this idle talk about his wife.

Rosemary Hawkins pushed again. "Perhaps she'll redecorate, like Jackie, or smile, like Mamie, or go crazy, like Mary Todd Lincoln."

"Goddammit, Rosemary, that's enough!"

She looked across the desk at him, the most powerful man on earth, and gave him a sweet, submissive smile. He could push a thermonuclear button if he chose to, but she, and she alone, knew how to push his. "I'm sorry. I shouldn't tease you like that. Shall we get down to business?" She stuck the pair of glasses the public never saw on the end of her nose, peering at him over the top of the frames.

"Okay. What do you know about Governor Adrian Bennett?'' A presidential question, asked in a presidential tone of voice.

Rosemary pulled a computer sheet from her briefcase, and lit a cigarette. She smoked three packs a day, four when under stress.

''Adrian Bennett, born August 1, 1908. Graduated University of Texas, 1928. Harvard Masters, 1930. Twotime governor. Twotime senator. Semi-retired. One child, Air Force Colonel Jonathan Bennett. Vietnam: 450 missions, Distinguished Service Cross, Medal of Honor. Shot down and captured, 1972. Released, 1975. Currently, commanding officer 354th Tactical Air Wing, Myrtle Beach, South Carolina.'' Rosemary paused, shifted her glasses and continued.

''Adrian Bennett prefers to be called simply 'Governor.' He's a widower. His wife died in 1973, in a nuthouse. A private little $80,000-a-year nuthouse. She spent the last eighteen months of her life there. Her name was Lily. Don't mention her, unless you say simply 'family,' as an all-inclusive. My advice is to stay away from niceties. He was a senator, but he despises the Senate. He wanted to be president, so he hates all presidents. You in particular. The Conservative Caucus of America is a new organization and not very well known. Bennett himself founded it, and it's loaded down with former government officials and retired House and Senate members. The organization is studded with some of the most famous military names in our history. This 'caucus,' or whatever, is flowing strong and deep with the best and bluest blood this country has ever seen. They intend to run candidates all over the country in a few years, from county clerk and dogcatcher all the way up to president. They are extremist in all things fiscal and foreign, and I'm told that Atilla the Hun would be too liberal to make the letterhead. In other words, there can't possibly be anything you and Governor Bennett have in common.''

Conrad Taylor watched her as she folded the report and put it back in her briefcase. His eyes narrowed. ''Where did you get that report?''

"It happens that I have reports like this on almost every citizen in this country who is in a position to politically oppose the treaty you have worked on for the past six months. He's just one, Conrad. There are thousands."

"You didn't answer my question, Rosemary. I want that report, and any like it, destroyed at once! I'll be goddamned if I'll have my National Security Advisor, or anyone else, suggesting that patriotic opposition somehow warrants sneaky tactics like that. Don't you ever pull this again. I want you to concentrate your efforts outside the country, and spreading the word here, with public appearances. You do that stuff so well. Don't be a goddamn Borgia, for Christsakes!" He was very angry, and it was presidential steel she heard in his voice.

Rosemary Hawkins handed the report to the President. "Most of the stuff is just common bio, Mr. President." She was very quiet, very defensive.

"Rosemary, I won't have this shit going on in my presidency. Get rid of it. All of it. Jesus Christ, if a reporter saw that stuff, I couldn't get renominated under any circumstances. Do you understand what I expect of you? After the Thanksgiving holidays, when we come back here, I'm going to give five of the most important speeches any president ever made. I need your help, Rosemary." Conrad Taylor positively glowed with sincerity. "Disarmament. Peace. Yes. But not this White House cloak-and-dagger crap. We'll convince the people, and then we'll convince the Senate." He gripped her hands across the desk. "The General Secretary called me last night. He accepts our proposals, with a few modifications. He's going to invite me to Moscow this spring. I want you to go see him in December. We'll announce it then. At the summit, we'll startle the whole fucking world."

Rosemary was speechless, trembling, her high breasts rising and falling under her blouse. Incredible! The Soviets would go along! She could hardly breathe, as tears filled her eyes, tears of joy so acute she could no longer sit down. She jumped up, ran around the massive desk, and threw herself into Conrad Taylor's arms.

He held her very tightly, his hand in her hair, stroking her, his anger gone, the forbidden reports out of sight and out of mind. Peace! He and his National Security Advisor had secretly and successfully opened a new and frightening door to peace. The *total* elimination of all nuclear weapons by the United States and the Soviet Union. It failed to register on Conrad Taylor or his sensuous companion, that the Soviets were dancing, too . . . or why.

No matter. What they needed now was time, and continued security. The process was involved, and it promised to get more difficult as it went along. Rosemary pulled back in his arms, and looked into his face. He looked very much younger than forty-seven. "I'll stop the political probing, okay?"

"Yes, you do that."

"When do I go to Moscow?"

"December fifth. Officially, you will be attending a NATO meeting with Secretary of State Mitchell. You will slip into Moscow from Brussels, on the sly. Shades of Nixon and China, huh?" Conrad Taylor was very pleased.

"He goes, too?" The National Security Advisor was pouting like a little girl.

"Rosemary, he's the goddamn Secretary of State. Of course he goes! And I'll fill him in on all of my personal consultations with the Soviets, and yours as well, after my speech in New York. You've been a champ, honey, but it's time for everybody to get into the act."

"Starting with the Secretary of State?"

"Yes. Absolutely. He knows most everything anyway. It's the State Department itself I don't like. Too unwieldy. The Soviets go for this hiding in the tall grass stuff."

"So do I, Mr. President."

He patted her buttocks, and pulled her briefly against him. The light on his personal line blinked, and kept blinking. He reached behind him, still holding Rosemary, and punched the button down. "Yes?"

"Governor Bennett, sir."

"Fine, send him right in."

Rosemary pulled away and walked quickly through a

side door, and into her own adjoining office. It was all going to work. She felt she would one day be remembered as one of the most famous women who ever lived. Truth told, that was the single driving force behind everything Rosemary Hawkins did.

MYRTLE BEACH AIR FORCE BASE
MYRTLE BEACH, SOUTH CAROLINA
WEDNESDAY, 1000 HOURS

Colonel Jonathan Bennett, U.S.A.F., walked slowly down the runway, at ease, but ramrod straight. He was six feet tall, and weighed a trim 165 pounds. His nearly white hair was cut as short as possible. His face was deeply lined, like well-worn leather, and tanned to a rich mahogany color, making his flat gray eyes all the more prominent. His overall bearing was that of a soldier, and he carried the weight of the countless generations of Bennetts who had gone to war before him. Jonathan Bennett was the end of the line, the last warrior.

He had never married. His first flight in that open cockpit trainer over thirty years ago had convinced him that nothing in his life could equal or surpass the exultation he felt as the air rushed past his sixteen-year-old face.

His father, the Governor, waited far below, hoping the boy, so frail, so sick all the time, would by God not be afraid this time, would not humiliate the governor of this great western state by throwing up all over the hired pilot.

Jonathan didn't throw up. According to the instructor, he had let the boy put the frail aircraft through a series of looping turns. The pilot had not flown it. The boy had. From that day on, Jonathan Bennett made airplanes and flying them the single most important thing in his life, after his mother. She was important, but she had gone crazy, finally. Now, at forty-nine, he gave himself completely to the perfecting of his skills as a fighter pilot, and the use of those skills in the defense of his country.

* * *

The 354th Tactical Fighter Wing began its orderly pull-out, one by one onto the runways, the heavy A-10A Thunderbolts pushing their noses into the twin tail of the aircraft in front of them, swinging around, bouncing gently in the cool November morning; and then, one by one and section by section, the three squadrons of Colonel Bennett's Tactical Wing pushed into the sky and went about their day's work.

Jonathan had them on their third consecutive day of a total wing exercise, to test them in an emergency situation. As usual, the 354th performed flawlessly, arcing into the cold sky, completing their mission, and returning in two hours and twenty-eight minutes, their ordnance expended on target sleds towed by the Navy. Throughout the exercise, their commander stood on the wind-whipped main runway, hands on his hips, jacket open and flapping in the breeze. An authentic American hero, a Medal of Honor winner, a man brave and patriotic beyond question, a man even the brutal North Vietnamese interrogators had given up on. Better to beat a tree, for the reaction they got. Had they looked deeper into Colonel Bennett's soul, they might have found the key to more than just a blank stare. If they had given him an airplane and an enemy—*any enemy*—Colonel Jonathan Bennett would have been just fine. He remained on the field until the last of his aircraft touched down. Like an old gunfighter, he was only at ease when he knew where all his guns were.

WHITE HOUSE
WEDNESDAY, 10:01 A.M.

For a man over eighty years old, former Governor Adrian Bennett had the walk and the carriage of a much younger man. A very sure, self-confident man, his face tanned from the western sun, his full head of hair wavy and nearly pure white. At six-foot-four, he was an imposing figure. As Conrad Taylor extended his hand and grasped the leather-tough skin of a working rancher, he thanked the fates that the man was too old to run for further political office.

"Governor, please, sit down. It's a pleasure to see you."

"Mr. President." The smile was frosty, but Conrad Taylor expected that.

"We've never met, Governor?"

"No, Mr. President. I was a bit before your time. I do spend time in Washington, of course. Like to keep my hand in, so to speak. It was very gracious of you to see an old war-horse like me."

"Not at all, sir. I understand you are considering starting a third party, is that correct?" The President was drawing a line in the dirt and putting a chip on his shoulder. Adrian Bennett did not rise to the bait.

The Governor laughed heartily, slapping his thigh before settling back into the deep chair. "Nothing quite so extreme, Mr. President. The Conservative Caucus is an idea, not a party. Just some old friends—out of service, you might say, but looking for fresh new blood. God knows this country needs it. The Caucus has some ideas, and we need to express them. We would, of course, support those members of either party who find favor with our views. But a third party? No, Mr. President."

"I assume, Governor, my views are contrary to most of yours?" Conrad Taylor was in his presidential posture, his hand on the side of his face, elbow on the chair arm, a pose many times photographed.

"No, Mr. President. Your views are contrary to *all* of mine. I opposed your election. I oppose you now, weak as that opposition may be during these days of 'peacemaking.' "

"Then, sir, what is it you want of me?" Conrad Taylor was game playing with the wrong man.

"Mr. President, we would like you to rethink your positions. All of them. Peace treaties that are morally bankrupt. The destruction of NATO. Abdication of our responsibilities in the Far East. Scrapping ships and ship contracts. Cutting the defense budget under the guise of cutting waste. Making us naked to our enemies. And, worst of all, in my personal view, abandoning Israel to her many enemies by advocating international treaties guaranteed by the Soviets and the United States. Should I go on, Mr. President?''

"No, Governor, I think your point is made. But you are too late. The tide is turning in my party's favor.''

Arrogance and ignorance, thought the Governor. He could feel the old political heat rise in him. It felt good. "I would remind you, sir, you were elected by less than a one-percent plurality. Hardly a mandate." Adrian Bennett's eyes glowed like hot coals.

"A mandate is what a president decides it is. The past ways didn't work. I'll talk to anybody, anywhere, about anything. I'm giving a speech tonight, in New York. I hope you'll listen. Perhaps your keen political mind will pick up where this administration, and this nation, is heading." The President's blunt sarcasm did not escape Adrian Bennett.

"Mr. President, my organization believes that your National Security Advisor is a lifetime Communist. We intend to begin saying so, unless you let your Secretary of State run the goddamn State Department for a change.''

"Say what you wish, Governor. She's been called worse. Is that why you came to see me? To threaten me with your tiny political group of neanderthal minds? It won't work, you know." There was a touch of righteous indignation in the President's voice. He thought Adrian Bennett was an extinct species.

"No, Mr. President, I came here to take your measure, sir. Nothing else.''

"And, Governor, what have you discovered?''

Adrian Bennett stood up, flicking an imaginary fleck of dust off his gleaming, hand-tooled boots as he did so. "I've discovered, sir, that you, like your policies, ain't worth a bucket of warm spit . . . Good day, Mr. President.''

Mouth agape, flustered, Conrad Taylor could only watch

the tall ex-governor's back as he turned away and walked from the Oval Office. It was as if the heat had been sucked from the room. The President shivered and walked to the roaring fireplace, hands extended. The Conservative Caucus, as represented by Governor Adrian Bennett, was considerably more formidable than he had expected.

Outside the White House, Governor Bennett walked to his car and climbed into the backseat. He intended to stay in Washington for the weekend. He had a suite at the Willard and he wanted to see a lot of people before heading back out west. Spit, that's all. Nothing but warm spit. For just a moment, he'd wanted to strangle the wimpy son-of-a-bitch with his bare hands. The limo pulled away from the White House, a place the Governor revered and held in the highest pantheon of his memories. How many times had he been there, in happier days? He looked out the limo's rear window. The White House looked the same. But now, it was a beautiful nest of pacifists, Communists, and traitors. If he were younger, well . . . reluctantly, he turned his gaze away from the White House.

C.I.A. HEADQUARTERS
WEDNESDAY, 11:00 A.M.

J.R. Kelly studied the terminal screen and frowned. "Those figures can't be right, Nadine, no matter what the computer says." He looked stricken.

Nadine Riley, controller of J.R. Kelly's section, and therefore his paymaster, looked up at him, and smiled benignly.

"Jesus, Nadine, it says I owe the Company money."

"That's true, J.R. It does. And you do. No more draws. Period. But I'll loan you a hundred 'til the first. Buy yourself a turkey next week." She held a crisp hundred over her shoulder, and he snatched it quickly before she changed her mind.

J.R. broke into his usual, lumpy grin, and he kissed her on the top of her head. She waved him off, and went back to her screen. Next week, J.R., Nadine, and the other four members of their section were scheduled for transfer to Pakistan. Fun and games, oh boy . . . how in the hell was he going to keep those long, slim legs and the body that went with them happy on a hundred-dollar bill?

It wasn't that difficult. They didn't call him "J.R." without good reason. In twenty minutes, he had begged, borrowed, and finagled a cool $750.00. That ought to do it, he thought cheerfully. How he would pay it back was something else again.

James Robert Kelly was a free spirit, deeply in debt, but unworried. In a couple of weeks, he'd be running guns in Pakistan, and there was a buck or two to be made there. At lunch time, J.R. headed out to get some cheap booze. He thought again about the lusty blond in his bed, under the New Orleans fan. Well, maybe just this one time, expensive booze.

J.R. Kelly did not look like a spy, Hollywood style. He was a big man, twenty pounds overweight and a hundred dollars in the hole all the time. He had a shock of unruly black hair, including some on the back of his head that stuck straight up in the air, no matter how it was cut. He had a charming smile and a winning personality. He had crooked front teeth. A college football injury had stopped his active participation in sports. He was out of shape, smoked and drank too much, and was ignored by most women with an I.Q. of over 60. When he asked women to dance, they said no.

All these things noted, it was also understood that he was an honors graduate of Michigan State University, and a former L.A. police lieutenant recruited by the C.I.A. for his proven competency. He was a patriot. He took the job in spite of the cut in pay.

THE WHITE HOUSE
WEDNESDAY, 12:01 P.M.

"Tell me, William, what did you think of Rosemary's speech last night?"

William Rodgers, Vice President of the United States, was a team player, and he answered like one: "I thought it was a good speech, Mr. President. The papers were full of it this morning. Lots of calls coming in."

"Pro or con?"

The Vice President hesitated, chewing his steak slowly, staring at Conrad Taylor. A white-jacketed steward appeared, refilled his coffee cup, and stepped back into the woodwork. The homeless camped on America's inner city streets would have been interested to know how their champion took his meals. The White House had never been more formal than it was now. Conrad Taylor, born rich, did not think being elected President should lower his standard of living. "You know, Mr. President. Con, from all my old supporters, before you beat me out of this job. Pro, of course . . . from the majority." It was getting very easy to swallow his pride, what was left of it.

"I'm grateful to you, William. I really am. Your constituency got me the electoral votes I needed. This job will be yours in seven years. I'm going to retire, and write my memoirs."

The Vice President thought that would never happen. He was serving two masters: his conservative followers and the President. That would never do if he were on his own. A vice president, he thought, who never calls the president by his first name, will never follow him in office.

"She really got to them, with that 'erector set' comment. Hell of a speech. But my secretary thinks she shouldn't wear those little slit skirts she wears. What do you think, William?" A little fun, at the expense of the Vice President.

Conrad Taylor knew very well what his Vice President thought. He hated her politics and her power, but the Vice

President was a widower, and Rosemary Hawkins drove him into utter sexual frustration every time she encountered him. She knew it. Everybody knew she knew it. Except the Vice President. Like all vice presidents, he was the least informed "insider" in the White House.

"I would say, Mr. President, your secretary is jealous. She can't dress that way. But she has a valid point. All those Southern preachers! My mail is full of hellfire, and damnation, and Rosemary Hawkins as the devil's helper."

"Really? I didn't know."

William Rodgers pushed his steak away and glanced at his boss. Was the President angry? No. Mocking was a better word. "Oh, hell, Mr. President, I don't pay much attention to the mail. Only the kooks write that way."

"William, I'd like to see the really dirty stuff." The President paused, searching for an adequate reason to read his Vice President's mail. "Rosemary would get a kick out of it. Now, what in particular did you want to see me about? The speech? You got your copy, didn't you?" Conrad Taylor knew his Vice President had no copy. He never sent him an advance copy of anything.

"Ah . . . no, I didn't. I must have missed mine. I just wanted to say . . ." Now. Now, here, in front of the invisible servants, while eating off the gold china and the 1783 silver, tell him! Tell him what you think. Tell him he's crazy. Tell him he's gone too far. Tell him Lenin, for Christ sake, never went this far. Tell him!

"William?" The mocking, hateful, knowing voice. "Something important?"

"No, Mr. President. Nothing. Just to wish you all the very best on the speech. I'll watch it very closely. Is there anything I should know?" A humiliating question, asked without shame.

"Nothing, William. Nothing at all. I'm going upstairs to shower, if you don't mind. You stay, finish your lunch. Enjoy yourself."

"Thank you, Mr. President, I'll do that."

"Okay. See you at the chopper when I leave?" It wasn't a question.

Party loyalty. When you had no self, there was still the party. "Yes, sir, of course," said the Vice President of the United States. When the President went upstairs to his quarters, the Vice President had three stiff drinks and played Let's Pretend in the Oval Office. The stewards showed no preferential treatment. They served everybody exactly the same. The Oval Office fire crackled and popped, and outside, dark clouds formed, and it began to rain.

THE WHITE HOUSE
PRIVATE QUARTERS
WEDNESDAY, 12:30 P.M.

"Connie, I think I should go with you." Emily Taylor called her husband Connie, but only in private. It was her only secret.

"You know I'll be back tonight, Emily. Soon, very soon, I'm going overseas. For a few weeks, probably. You'll go then." Emily rolled over on the bed, naked, her firm body and high breasts completely unnoticed by her husband. The wife of the President of the United States masturbated every day, as often as possible. But she did not cheat on her neglectful husband. She loved him. He was her hero. Sometimes he caught her at her solitary love play, and then he would fall on her, and come in her, and she would pray for another baby and, because she loved him, fail to understand why there were no more babies. She liked to be naked around him. Occasionally, he responded. Sometimes, she could tempt him. He loved oral sex, and *nobody* was better at that than she was. He allowed that. He loved her. She slipped into a housecoat and made herself a drink. A double.

"Emily?"

"It's after noon." Their deal had been not to drink during the day.

"It is twelve forty, Em." He looked sad, not angry.

"Sorry." Her voice was small, timid.

"No more, okay?"

"I'll try, Connie. It would help if you wouldn't pay so little—" She stopped, searching for the right words. "I mean, Jesus, I throw myself at you, and you don't even . . ."

"Emily? Come take a shower with me." Minutes later, looking up at him, sucking him, the shower beating down on her flushed cheeks, she nearly drowned.

THE WHITE HOUSE
WEDNESDAY, 1:30 P.M.

He kissed her on the cheek, and headed downstairs. On the main floor, he was joined by his aides and they headed out to the south lawn. A large crowd of reporters and White House staff closed around him. Beside him, wearing a severe black suit, under which the President knew she was almost nude, stood his National Security Advisor. The Vice President was there. It was going to be a very big speech. He waved, shook hands, waved again.

The rain pelted down. A Marine walked with him, holding an open umbrella. Conrad Taylor stood at the doorway of the chopper, waved once again, and climbed in, followed by his chief aides, two speech writers, and the Secret Service agents. Marine One, the President's helicopter, lifted off the White House grounds, circled once, and headed along the day's selected route to Andrews Air Force Base. At Andrews, the gleaming new 747, called simply, "Spirit 76," waited. The chopper crossed the ellipse, hooked to the north of the Washington Monument, crossed the Tidal Basin, then angled southeast. The Potomac River stretched beneath Marine One. At 1:34:44

two bolts of lightning struck the President's helicopter, lancing savagely out of the dark, rolling skies. Marine One went down at 1:35:00 Eastern Standard Time, destroying itself and most of the Fourteenth Street Bridge.

At 1:47:15 Eastern Standard Time, William Rodgers was surrounded by the Secret Service as he left the White House. He was slightly drunk. They told him he was now the President of the United States. Conrad Wilson Taylor had been found floating faceup in the Potomac River. A federal judge was called. At 2:07:14 Eastern Standard Time William Rodgers took the Presidential Oath of Office and retreated to his regular working quarters in the Executive Office Building.

Rosemary Hawkins was waiting for him when he got there.

THE EXECUTIVE OFFICE BUILDING
WASHINGTON, D.C.
WEDNESDAY, 2:15 P.M.

The newly sworn in President of the United States sat slumped at his desk, the office draperies shut tight, only the tiny green "railroad" lamp on his desk casting any light at all. He looked at his carefully manicured fingers, held his hands out, palms downward, under the green shaded light. They seemed steady enough, he thought. He groped for a cigarette, pulled one from its pack, broke it, reached for another, bent it, and finally, frustrated, he crumpled the pack in his chubby palms, tossing it to the floor. In the darkened corner of his office, a lighter flared briefly, a cigarette glowed, the lighter snapped out.

"Are you all right, William? I mean, Mr. President . . . you are the President now, you know. I'm here to help you, in any way that I can." Rosemary Hawkins, eyes reddened and cheeks streaked from crying, uncrossed her silky legs and walked to the new President's desk, holding the lit cigarette out to him.

William Rodgers took it and she turned away, walked back across the room, resettling into the darkened corner. She crossed her legs and he found that the light from his desk lamp penetrated just far enough across the room to reveal the sleek length of her thigh in the short, tight black suit, her trademark suit, the one that drew all the kooky mail. He puffed on the cigarette, his throat dry. President! Holy shit! He was President of the United States. He had always wanted it, and now he had it. He was panicked and had no idea what to do next.

Rosemary uncrossed and recrossed her legs, her face still in the shadows, only the rustle of silk breaking the silence. Then she began to cry, softly at first, then in huge wracking sobs, and he snuffed out the cigarette and went to her, pulling her from the chair, and she was in his arms, her rich hair in his face, her arms clutching him for support as he held her close to him, gently patting her back, startled by how much of her body he could feel under her suit.

He had an immediate, huge erection, and he withdrew his lower body, but she followed him, sobbing, her shoulders shaking with grief, and she pressed against him, until he was sure his penis was against her pubic bush. He murmured, "There, there," stroking her back, letting her pubis press against him as she shifted, changed position, turning her face away, resting it on his shoulder. Underneath her skirt, he thought he could feel the buckle of a garter belt. Without seeming to, her lower body shifted, letting him sense her, letting him explore her with his hardened cock, without acknowledgment. The new President felt guilty and finally pulled away, leading her to a couch, helping her down, propping the pillow under her head, and covering her with an Indian blanket given him during a long-ago campaign. He went back to his desk, stronger, surer somehow.

He broke open a pack of fresh cigarettes, took one, and lit it with steady hands. He flipped the button on the intercom.

"Yes, Mr. President?"

Mr. President. Jesus. "I don't want us to be disturbed."

"Us, Mr. President?"

"Yes. Ms. . . . *my* National Security Advisor and I. Ms. Hawkins is going over some very matters of the utmost importance to the security of our country." Oh, fuck! He sounded like an idiot. Goddammit. "I don't want to be disturbed in any event."

"Yes, sir." Her voice had changed. Good old Mary. His secretary for a long time. Now she was really going to have a good time.

"Mary?"

"Yes, Mr. President?"

"Don't worry, Mary. I can handle this job."

"Well . . . sir! I knew that, why . . . whatever would make you think tha—" He shut her off, chuckling to himself.

Across the room, Rosemary Hawkins was nearly invisible under the blanket, lying on her side, facing the wall. His eyes traced the full line of her hips and ass. The back of one stockinged foot peeked out of the bottom of the blanket. His hard-on was back, insistent, throbbing, marvelous. Conrad Wilson Taylor was dead. It had taken his death to get William Rodgers and the President's National Security Advisor in the same room together, alone for the first time. Now, if he chose, he and he alone could decide whether she kept her job. A wiser man might have suspected that she had already made that decision for him.

For twenty minutes the new President and the old President's chief advisor and lover remained in their places, two players on the board of an as-yet-unplayed game. But one of the players had decided who should . . . no, who *would* lead the way. Rosemary tossed the blanket back and sat up, sitting on one leg, the other thrust out in front of her, her high heel on the floor. She sat that way, sensual and blatantly sexual for an instant so brief as to be unrecordable. But William Rodgers would remember it for as long as he lived. She had meant him to see that she wore no panties. He wasn't sure what he'd seen.

"I'm terribly sorry, Mr. President. President Tay . . . I mean, Conrad Taylor and I had been working together for a very long time. We had mutual goals, goals I'm sure you understood completely. After all, he could never have been elected without you. Never."

She had moved as she spoke, taking the chair directly opposite him, sitting sideways, knees together as she wiped her eyes clean of makeup, brushed her hair into a long, red, shining net across her shoulders. It was a very intimate thing to do, this woman's repair job from an hour of crying. He'd never seen it done before. He was captivated by how natural all of this seemed, as if they had been old and dear friends. He realized with a start that he had had some kind of goofy, schoolboy crush on this woman since the earliest campaign days sixteen months before. He watched her breasts move under the black silk of her suit, straining for a glimpse of her pale skin as she brushed her hair in a long, straight stroke, her face hidden behind the lush redness before she tossed it back across and down her shoulders for a second time. He now realized she wore no bra. He couldn't be sure, but he thought that somehow, in spite of its severe cut and high vee neck, he'd seen a naked breast. All the time, as he watched and fantasized or really saw what he thought he saw, she had been talking and it finally began to get through to him.

"The Colonel said nothing could have been done. The weather was bad, but Marine One is the safest chopper in the entire defense department inventory. It went down, with twenty thousand witnesses, because it was struck directly by two very heavy bolts of lightning, and it went straight down into the Fourteenth Street Bridge. Remember the 737 that hit that bridge and went into the river? Well, that's where the President's chopper went down. Nose first into the Fourteenth Street Bridge. The Colonel asked me to assure you there will be a complete investigation, but it looks 100 percent like an act of God. Nothing could have prevented it. I told him you understood. I spoke to him four minutes after you became President. He wanted you to know that nobody assassinated Conrad Tay-

lor. They damn sure wanted to. I didn't mention that, of
course.'' The new President had no idea who ''the Colonel'' was. He resisted the temptation to ask.

''Assassinate? Why would anyone want to assassinate
him? He was the most peace-loving man I ever knew.''

''That's why, Mr. President. Some in the good ol'
U. S. of A. would have liked him dead.'' Her green eyes
turned the color of winter grass.

Like me, thought William Rodgers. I wanted him dead.

''Now, of course, his programs are done for. Oh God!
Do you know I haven't even called to see about Emily?
Jesus, what is she going to do?''

The new President studied Rosemary Hawkins, looking
for the slightest trace of insincerity. He detected only real
concern. He punched his intercom.

''Yes, Mr. President?'' The different, more deferential
voice of his secretary made it momentarily hard to identify
her.

''Mary, I want a report, a discreet report, on Mrs. Taylor and the children. I want to do anything I can to help.
You tell her that, will you? Of course, there is no hurry
for me to move into the White House. I'm fine right here.''

''I'll see to it, sir.''

''Thank you, Mary. Remember, any way you can find
to make me useful to her, you let her know it's all right
by me.''

''Yes, sir,'' his secretary gushed, her voice heavy with
approval.

''There. That will help, I'm sure.'' William Rodgers
glanced at Rosemary, seeking her approval.

Rosemary gave him a very intense look, then lowered
her eyes before saying anything.

''What? What is it, Rosemary?''

''Nothing. It's nothing.'' She shifted in her chair, crossing her legs, an inch of creamy skin now visible above her
gartered stockings, the skin stark white against the black
of her skirt. She had hiked her skirt a full two inches at
the waistband, under her suit jacket. You always got a lot
of leg with Rosemary Hawkins. But this was deception

and trickery, and it was effective. Later that day, the new President would see her seated in public in the same suit, with only a couple of inches of skin showing above the knee.

"What did you want to say?"

"I was just remembering presidential history. When President Roosevelt died, Vice President Truman, newly sworn in as President, asked Mrs. Roosevelt what he could do to help her in her time of trial. She took both his hands in hers, looked up into his face, and said, 'Mr. President, it is *your* time of trial. What can *I* do to help *you?*' The quote is often different, but you get the point.''

"Yes, I get the point."

"She was right, you know. Emily needs *family* now. You need help. The nation needs its President. Before I leave tonight, I want you to have one piece of advice. Conduct your business, whenever possible, from the Oval Office. Conrad . . . the President . . . oh, hell, he didn't keep anything of himself in there. It was an office, another political vehicle to ride out the day in. I advised him about that, and most everything else too. My advice is, take the office, if not the house. The country needs a powerful president. Particularly now. The world may just go to hell in a hand basket, and you'd better have a plan to handle it." He stared at her like a trusting child, hanging on her every word. The presidency was a desert, and she was the nearest water.

"After the funeral, and God only knows how Emily will handle that, you will have a short, happy honeymoon with most of the U.S. and the world. Sympathy is a great unifier of thought. Then, the sympathy will dissipate, and the shit will hit the fan." She got up, walked two circles of the room, and sat back down again, lighting a cigarette. She took two puffs and snuffed it out.

"As for me, I'm going to clear out of Washington while the getting is good. Your political friends will have a field day, at my expense. Well, fuck 'em, Mr. President. They can't hang the architect for a house that will never get built. I shall go elsewhere and enrich myself. By the way,

who will you pick as your National Security Advisor?
James Hartwell, I'll bet. Well, he was terrific in the last
treaty go-round. And he won't bow down to the dreaded
commies, like Governor Bennett and his Conservative
Caucus think I, and therefore Conrad, did. Yes, Jim Hartwell will be just fine.'' Rosemary lit another cigarette,
flipping her hair to one side of her neck as she did, her
legs uncrossed and stretched out in front of her. She looked
quite fetching and very businesslike. An alchemist's trick,
and she had mastered it.

''Rosemary?''

''Yes, Mr. President?''

''You will have to stay on. For the sake of the country.
I need you, and you mustn't leave at this time.''

''Oh, I don't mean right away, Mr. President.''

''William.''

''Okay, William. I don't mean right now. But after the
holidays, say, by January fifteenth. That seems a decent
interval. By then, you can have your team in place and
your program can begin.''

''I meant stay, Rosemary. Remain in your job permanently. I need you.''

Rosemary stared at the new President of the United
States. She looked deeply into his eyes and deeper, into
his soul. She liked what she saw there. Her answer was
straightforward and to the point.

''No.'' She gathered up her briefcase and purse, and
headed for the door. The muscles of her buttocks tightened and bunched under the short black silk. Her slim
fingers reached for the door to the outer office.

''Rosemary?''

She stopped, turned around, faced him, her briefcase
and purse clutched in her left hand. She spread her legs
lightly to keep her balance.

''Perhaps you would stay, if I pursue Conrad's foreign
policy initiatives?''

Rosemary laughed, a short, hard, mirthless laugh. ''Mr.
President, do you have any *real* idea what Conrad Taylor
was up to?''

"Not really. But I'm sure I can carry them forward."

"Mr. President, you disagree with everything Conrad Taylor ever said. What has changed?"

"Nothing has changed. Except now, I'm the President and, if I wish, they can be my ideas. Now, will you stay on? I know that if you believe what you and Conrad had in mind was what this country and the world needed, then I should look them over, and if I agree, well . . . we should go forward."

"Mr. President, I'll show you exactly what Conrad Taylor was going to do. If you agree to pursue his ideas as he would, I will stay on. As Secretary of State, after a proper interval."

William Rodgers's mouth dropped open, then snapped shut. "I have a speech to give in an hour, Rosemary. There will be other things I'll need to tend to. Tonight, will you join me here for dinner to discuss this further?"

"I am at your service, Mr. President." Rosemary Hawkins was out the door before the new President had a chance to restate his position. It was no surprise. As a politician, William Rodgers had never had an original position to state, one way or another.

WASHINGTON, D.C.
WEDNESDAY, 4:00 P.M.

In a darkening city, the people of Washington, D.C., flooded like lemmings to the 14th Street Bridge and the President's crumpled helicopter. Marine One had struck the bridge squarely and still clung to its surface, unrecognizable, a charred mass of blackened wreckage that had caught fire immediately and burned to the bridge deck, until it looked like a fried, oversized grasshopper. All eight of its occupants had been killed, probably instantly. The President had somehow been thrown free of the copter, and had been pulled nearly unmarked (except for a neatly severed spinal column) from the frigid Potomac by passersby.

The body had been whisked away in minutes and now rested at a D.C. mortuary, where a curious mortician watched Secret Service agents guard a dead man as he awaited official clearance to prepare the President for burial. He knew it would be a while. A pathologist had determined the time of death and the cause. No problem there. An agent bustled in and handed the mortician a signed death certificate. The cause of death was clearly stated in very technical terms. It said the President's spinal column had been severed at the neck.

The agent had a complete set of the President's clothes. The President's wife had not yet decided whether she wanted an open or closed coffin. They would get back to him. Mildly, with great concern in his voice, the mortician reminded the agent that no one as yet had selected a coffin. The President had been dead less than three hours. Perhaps tomorrow morning would be soon enough? The agents seemed to be in collective shock. His soft-spoken suggestion bailed them out. Yes. Tomorrow. Someone will make those decisions tomorrow.

Meanwhile, a spotless group of young men, one from each branch of the service, was waiting in a side chapel. Again, the soft-voiced suggestion. Perhaps the agents could place the President's body in a temporary coffin? More properly, he felt he should begin his work now. He would prepare and dress the President, and place him in his best burial unit, temporarily, of course.

The family was free to pick any one they might wish. He simply wanted the President prepared, with the least possible trouble to the family. Should he go forward? No one knew. Later, Emily Taylor would call, and say plaintively and in tears, ''Please handle it for me.'' Under the circumstances, for his first presidential burial, he did quite well. By midnight, the President's body was prepared. He left the coffin closed. No matter what he did, Conrad Taylor looked bad in death. Unmarked, but dead, in a way somehow upsetting to view. He'd been an animated, fiery speaker, a charismatic, handsome proponent of world peace. Now, he looked worse than dead. The coffin should remain closed. In the early morning hours, it should be moved to the Capitol Rotunda, draped in an American flag, flanked by scrubbed young men of the military services he had planned to reduce. The coffin would remain there until someone told him when, and how, they were going to bury him.

THE KREMLIN
MOSCOW
WEDNESDAY, 11:00 P.M. (MOSCOW TIME)

"Well, Grenady, what do you think?" The Chief of Staff of the Soviet Armed Forces, at fifty-three the youngest to hold the Marshall's post since World War II, stopped his pacing and stared hard at the Communist Party General Secretary.

"I don't know what to think, but I ordered our forces on maximum alert thirty minutes ago."

"Why, Grenady? Why did you do that?"

"Because I'm not sure what the initial reports mean. President Taylor was killed in an accidental crash of his helicopter. But I know many of my counterparts in the U.S. Defense Department. They are on alert worldwide, at this moment."

"How do you know, Grenady?"

"Our intelligence is very good, sir. You know that."

"His helicopter was hit by lightning, Marshall. Cancel the alert, and the United States will step back and down, if they have not already done so."

"Why? Why would they do that? They have lost a president. An accident, they say. How do we know it wasn't shot down by a portable missile of some kind?"

"We know, Grenady, because 25,000 people saw it happen, and the photo of the actual lightning strike has been published in nearly every newspaper in the world.

As it will be published tomorrow, here, in *Pravda*. Conrad Taylor is dead. It was an accident. And now, Grenady, sit down, and pour us both a stiff vodka, and I will tell you what his death, and the elevation of Vice President Rodgers, will cost us. Unless we are calm and careful. And, most of all, sympathetic. Sit down, Grenady, and I will tell you a tale. But first, cancel all alerts, of any kind. No special activity. Do nothing even remotely aggressive or controversial. You once told me the armed forces of the U.S.S.R. thought as you, in all things. Now is the time to make that pledge true. I want a complete, passive posture. Do you understand, Grenady?" The General Secretary's eyes were very hard. They sought out the Marshall's, demanding obedience.

The handsome young Marshall of the Soviet Union did not reply. But he poured the vodkas, handing one to the General Secretary, before picking up the phone. Two hours later, the Marshall, fully briefed, paid a courtesy call on the U.S. embassy in Moscow. All across the U.S.S.R., the military stood down. In spite of this, the United States remained visibly wary.

THE WHITE HOUSE
WEDNESDAY, 5:00 P.M.

Emily Taylor sat in her dressing room just off the master bedroom in the upstairs living quarters the Conrad family had shared for such a short time. Her husband had been dead for less than four hours. She sat in a love seat wearing a bra and half-slip, staring out the window into a nearly dark capital, a city she'd had no time to put her First Lady's stamp on.

Emily Taylor, seemingly bred for the job of First Lady by her parents, the very rich Kentucky Thompsons, the Thompsons of one hundred years of Thoroughbred horses and cotton and county banks that owned all the farms.

They had bred her, like a Derby horse, to Conrad Taylor, mixing two tradition-rich bloodlines to produce the ultimate winners. And now, like a good Southern child, she must be a good widow. Jackie certainly hadn't been, though she had looked fetching enough at the funeral, with John-John saluting his slain father, surrounded by what seemed to be, and was, dozens of Kennedys.

Of course, Conrad Taylor was another Boston politician. At a party, he used to joke about the mock battle between himself and Emily, to see which accent would finally overwhelm the other. There was no winner, she thought. She sounded Kentucky born, and Conrad sounded more like John F. Kennedy than John F. Kennedy had. Such games, this politics.

She walked back and forth across the room, drinking her fifth unwatered bourbon. Kentucky bourbon, of course. She could hear her mother and father, newly arrived and demanding to see her, arguing with the two Secret Service men outside her door. She had told them to let no one in, except Rosemary Hawkins. Her parents were finally deflected by the agent's suggestion that the grandparents might like to see and comfort their grandchildren. The suggestion worked, and the silence, a thing she could hear, closed back down on her.

Conrad was at the mortuary. She had at least handled that. Well, not handled it. She had simply told the man on the phone to take care of it. What did one do in this situation? Emily knew she couldn't just hide out here, in her dressing room. She was, after all, the nation's First Lady. And a Kentuckian. Examples must be set. Emily Taylor stopped and looked in her dressing room mirror.

Example! Well, shit, there by God was an example! Drink in hand, hair a mess, mascara running down her patrician face, scarring the milky skin that was the envy of every woman in America. What should she be doing? What the fuck did you do when you were the wife of the President of the United State, and his goddamn helicopter was splattered all over the 14th Street Bridge?

That stupid ass William Rodgers had called and let it

be known he was at her service. He reminded her of cigars and back rooms. He was . . . common. And he was also the new President of the United States. He would soon, but not too soon, live in these very quarters. A Texan, for God's sake, though he had a certain un-Texan polish about him when he wanted to. Conrad Taylor, after selecting him as his running mate had once, in the privacy of their bedroom, called him the least inventive mind he had ever encountered. Whom did that speak badly about, she wondered, William Rodgers, for warranting the remark, or her husband, for selecting him anyway?

She sat down, poured herself a fresh bourbon, and began to clean her streaked face with cleanser. Well, aren't I having a terrific jumble of thoughts and observations, she thought, vigorously wiping her pale skin clear and shiny. Too bad I never had one out loud. But that was something else, wasn't it?

Conrad Taylor wanted a First Lady, an impeccable First Lady. Even before he'd won the presidency, he warned her repeatedly and clearly: Don't hurt me publicly. You are an ornament and a bearer of blue-blooded children. In return, I will love you and take you with me to the top. And so he had. As for love, well, there were all kinds of love. She loved him and he, in his detached way, loved her. Her set was replete with marriages just like it. Grand families, joined to rule the little people. Conrad had just done it in a grander way.

The Taylors and the Thompsons, with their own T'n'T Farms just now producing world-class racehorses. Presidential Candidate, their first two-year-old champion, was expected to win the Derby next year. She had envisioned it often, and with great expectations. First Lady of the United States, and finally, and in a special way, First Lady of Kentucky!

Oh, how sweet it would have been, in the winner's circle at Churchill Downs, the brawny colt excited and sweaty after his record-setting Derby run. Oh, it would have . . .

Emily Taylor stopped thinking. None of this would do. She must get dressed. She must get out of this room. She must not be in this shape when Rosemary Hawkins got here and Emily asked her the all-important question "How many years have you been fucking my husband?"

She poured another bourbon, splashing it onto her throat and bra as she drank it down. "C'mon, bitch, let's us have a talk," she said aloud. Her reflection didn't answer.

Somehow, Emily put herself together, and when Rosemary Hawkins arrived shortly before six, she was fully dressed and made up, though not as well or as carefully as usual. She was wearing a severe black knit jersey dress. She looked good in it. She looked like a president's widow. She was also roaring drunk, drunker than she'd ever been in front of anyone other than her husband. But her mind, at least to her, was clear.

In the master bedroom now, cleared of all relatives and Secret Service, she motioned Rosemary Hawkins to a chair, and slumped into one herself. She noted that Rosemary was still wearing the tight black suit she'd worn early today. Great legs, bitch, she thought. She hated Rosemary Hawkins. She had hated her forever.

"How can I help you, Emily?" Rosemary's hands were folded neatly in her lap.

"You can answer a question, for starters." Emily's voice was only slightly affected by the bourbon.

"If I can, of course."

So smooth, so cool. You bitch . . . "Were you fucking my husband? And when did it start? After his election? When you first came to work for him? Did you fuck him, you Georgetown bitch?" Emily was nearly screaming. The Secret Service agents outside the room heard every word.

So did Brian Howell, Major General Brian Howell, waiting outside to see his boss about a speech she had written for the new President to give on prime time, Thursday night. He thought Rosemary had freaked out, and intended to tell her so. Conrad Taylor was dead. William Rodgers would never read a speech prepared by Rosemary Hawkins. As for him, he was going to resign as soon as possible. Rosemary certainly wasn't going to need a deputy in the new administration.

"Did you fuck him, you goddamn whore?" Emily's high voice, etched in drunken rage, came clearly through the door. The agents and Brian Howell shifted their feet nervously, avoiding one another's eyes, wishing they could escape the small anteroom outside the master bedroom.

Behind the door, Rosemary Hawkins abruptly stood up, crossed the plush blue rug to where Emily sat, and slapped her face; not once, but twice. "You're drunk, Emily, and you're hysterical. Unless you want to destroy the memory of your dead husband, at least lower your voice. Remember who and what you are. You are the First Lady of the United States. Act like it!" Rosemary stood over Emily, looking down at her, not angry, feeling sorry for Emily Conrad for the first time ever.

"You fucked him, didn't you? Everybody knows you did." This time, Emily's voice was very low, her head down, fingers twisting her wedding ring around and around on her finger.

"No, everybody doesn't know I did. Rumors. Political talk. Yes, I loved Conrad Taylor. I loved his vision, what he saw, what he wanted to accomplish. Peace. True peace. All the things he worked to achieve. But we were not lovers. Ever. It just never happened."

Emily looked up at Rosemary. "All those trips? All those thousands of hours over the past six years. Never? You never fucked him?"

"You're being crude, Emily. It's unbecoming, and out of place. No, not ever. Yes, if he'd approached me. Gladly. But he didn't. The stories are just that—stories. Political garbage."

Chastised, but still doubtful, Emily said, "You would have, though, right? If he'd said, 'Let's go to bed,' you'd have hopped right in there, I know it."

"I suppose I would have. But he didn't say that, and we didn't do that."

Emily paused. "Well, I guess you could say that about any woman in the United States, couldn't you? Conrad was the President of the United States. He was handsome, and young, and charismatic.''

"Yes, you could say that. But wanting, and getting, aren't the same, Emily. Fidelity, that is what Conrad Taylor believed in. And his job. Most of all, his job. If he . . . neglected you in that way, I'm sorry. But I will repeat: your husband and I were never lovers.''

With that, Emily Taylor collapsed forward in tears, closed protectively, deceitfully, in Rosemary Hawkins's reassuring arms.

Emily Taylor sat across from Rosemary Hawkins on the bed, while Rosemary laid one sheet of paper after another between them.

"Now, here is a list I've prepared for you. Topping the list is the Librarian of Congress. I've taken the liberty of contacting him. Discreetly, of course. He and his staff are busy gathering everything ever written about presidential funerals." Emily stiffened, looked away.

"Emily, you must gather your strength. And please stop drinking.''

"Sorry.'' Emily was timid now, in her "whatever you say, Conrad'' mode. Rosemary Hawkins had the same, overwhelming power about her.

"As I was saying, if you wish, he will come to see you tomorrow morning. You mustn't wait much longer than that. The press is going crazy for details now. As you can see, Rosemary, you have vast resources here to help you through this.''

"You haven't missed anything, have you?'' There was a sense of awe in Emily's voice. "The children. Family. Relatives of all stripe. What to say. What to wear. When to do nearly everything.''

"Suggestions, Emily. I know this is all very presumptuous. I wanted to spare you the detail work by providing you with a list of alternatives. Of course, as a family matter, you and yours may bury Conrad in any way you see fit.''

"He belongs to the country, not my family. And not

me. You've been wonderfully helpful. May I call on you, if I need you?''

"Of course you can, Emily. Together, we can make sure his vision stays alive. I believe William . . . William Rodgers, as the new President, will keep the peace flame alive. He gives a speech tomorrow night.''

"Fat chance! William Rodgers and my husband had very little in common.''

"True. But Emily, I'm writing the speech.''

"Are you?''

"Yes. He's a bit lost. Perhaps I can slip something in. Stranger things have happened.''

"Well, good luck. But his political friends won't let him off easy. They will write his speech.''

"You're probably right. Well, I have gathered all I can think of. Use what helps, discard what doesn't. And call me, at any time, if you need me.'' As Rosemary stood up to leave, Emily stood and walked to her, gave her a quick hug, and, holding Rosemary's hands, said, "Why did you do this?''

"To help you. To take some of the pressure off.''

"And to help my dead husband?''

"Yes, that too.'' Rosemary turned away and headed across the big room to the door, reaching for the angled brass handle.

"Rosemary?''

"Yes?'' Rosemary Hawkins turned back to Emily.

"This morning, in the shower, I sucked Conrad's cock until he shot down my throat. He loved it. He always loved it. He said I was the best cocksucker in the world, and we did it every day.'' Emily, eyes very hard, studied Rosemary's face for the reaction, looking for shock, for hurt, a lover's hurt.

Rosemary Hawkins's face was impassive. "Good for you, Emily,'' Rosemary said as she exited the room.

As the door shut behind her, Emily Taylor stood, trembling, fists clenched, suppressing a scream, knowing everything, and knowing nothing at all.

WASHINGTON, D.C.
THE WILLARD INTER-CONTINENTAL
HOTEL
WEDNESDAY, 5:30 P.M.

Former Governor Adrian Bennett and his colleagues were
not participating in the nation's mourning of the President's death. In fact, the suites and the newly acquired
adjoining but as yet empty rooms at the Willard were
packed with partygoers. The booze was flowing freely,
and the founding members of the Conservative Caucus felt
delivered from evil. Conrad Taylor's programs were surely
as dead as he was. William Rodgers was not exactly a
Caucus member, but his views, the few that he had, were
far to the west of Boston. And therefore, far to the right.

The television networks were beginning to spout an
endless stream of information. The funeral arrangements
and time had not yet been announced, but would be tomorrow. The new President would, or might, make a brief
speech Thursday evening. It was believed, or thought possible, that the heads of most of the world's governments
would be here for the burial service. He would be buried
in Boston, or Concord, or Arlington. The Soviets had expressed deep sadness. Or they had not. The General Secretary would be in Washington, or he would not. The
charred helicopter would be moved in secret, or it would
remain for days, to be examined by the FAA. In the con-
tinuous early-evening broadcasts of every TV and radio
station in the United States, you could hear and believe
almost anything. Conrad Taylor's less than ensconced
newcomers to Washington, and therefore to power, were
sending out vast pages of confused and contrary information.

Apparently, nobody in the White House knew what the
hell to do next. Adrian Bennett was delighted. With no
real news, the networks began a long night of senators',
congressmen's, and all manner of local denizens' com-

ments on the tragedy. Endless tapes of Conrad Taylor rolled on and on. Clearly, the nation, as it did in November of 1963, was going to wallow this November in tears, and tragic, Grecian breast-beating and tearing of hair. It would be a wallow worthy of the technical ability and liberal tendencies of the networks, of that Adrian Bennett was sure.

But that mattered very little. Let the nation cry and cleanse itself. Truly, Conrad Taylor *had* reached them. Right down to the last nigger. When this was over, this half-assed, half-mast tribute to a traitor to the American way, the new government of William Rodgers would step forward. Adrian Bennett chuckled to himself. Okay. Backwards, not forward. In any case, he and his associates, many now very possible future cabinet members, must be ready. In particular, he and the five founders of the Conservative Caucus must be ready to advise the new President. And they must be here in Washington to do it. The old guard, the hard guard.

He sat down at a small phone table and called to Washington the men he most needed to have here, after Conrad Taylor was buried, wherever the hell that might occur.

He called two former senators and one nonpolitical but famous industrialist; one aging but powerful exambassador who had served three presidents; and one exgeneral of the Air Force, forced out of the service because he was a patriot and had wanted to nuke North Vietnam. He also tried to call his son, an Air Force wing commander stationed in Myrtle Beach, South Carolina. He was told his son was flying with his wing, and would not be available for two hours.

Adrian Bennett was not surprised. His son was a warrior. Practicing his skills is what he did. He advised the duty officer at Myrtle Beach he would call again. Events would make it the most important call Adrian Bennett had ever made.

He glanced at the television. Rosemary Hawkins, escorted by General Brian Howell, was shown leaving the White House. The sound was turned down, so he didn't hear what she told the phalanx of reporters jammed around her under the hot glare of Kleig lights.

She had told the reporters two things: she'd visited Emily Taylor; and she was on her way to speak and have dinner with William Rodgers. She had nothing else to say. The White House correspondent from ABC closed his on-air time by saying that Rosemary Hawkins looked "tired, distraught, and dispirited."

WEDNESDAY, 9:00 P.M., EASTERN STANDARD TIME

J.R. Kelly stared at the slowly turning "New Orleans" fan above his bed with one eye, and watched the girl of his dreams pull a long silk stocking up her exquisite leg with the other. The expensive champagne was gone. She'd taken her clothes off to drink it. Now she seemed to be putting them back on. She hooked the stocking to a pink garter and began to work on the other leg. She had the only breasts he'd ever seen that were so firm and perfect they pointed up.

"J.R., I just don't see how you can think about sex at a time like this."

He moved one eye away from the fan, attempting to focus both on her. "I can think of sex anytime. In fact, I think of it all the time, particularly when I'm told to forget whatever I was going to do for the next four days. I'm thinking of sex at this very moment. Here, look for yourself." He pulled the covers off and onto the floor beside the bed. She gave him a sweet, sexy look and reached over and patted him. He jumped under her hand.

"Well, J.R., I'm pleased you feel that way, but there *is* a time for everything. There's a time to live, and a time to die, a time to plant, and a time to reap, a time to—"

"Jesus Christ, Bonnie, don't you see my problem here?" J.R. was getting desperate.

Another sweet smile, as she began to button a pale pink blouse, covering those magnificent breasts.

"Of course I do, and I think it means we might someday have a meaningful relationship. But not tonight. For heavens sakes, the President died today." She said that with a scolding glance at his hard-on.

"I know. What has that got to do with sex?"

"Can't you see? It's just not . . . it's not appropriate."

"My champagne was appropriate. You drank my rent, do you realize that? And what about last night? And this morning?"

"The President was alive then. Now, he's not, and I'm grieving. I don't have sex when I'm grieving."

J.R. Kelly could only watch as she stood up and slipped into the tightest pair of jeans in the entire universe, doing a comical little jump to zip them up.

"You're grieving?"

"Yes. I am. Two years ago, my little dog Agnes got hit by a car, and she died. Well, I didn't have sex then, either. Not for two days! See? It's perfectly clear to me. I can't grieve and have sex at the same time." She slipped into her heels and headed for the door.

J.R. asked, "Did you vote for this guy, or what?"

"Of course not. I don't vote. But I liked his smile. I'll call you, J.R." And she was out the door. Overhead, the fan turned. J.R. stared at it, sure the whirring sound it made was laughter. If it took two days for Agnes the dog, how long did it take for presidents?

At the Willard Inter-Continental, Adrian Bennett, feeling his years, said good-night to his guests. Tomorrow, he thought, would be an interesting day. The party went on.

At the White House, Emily Taylor lay on her bed, wearing Conrad Taylor's bathrobe, staring blankly at the ceiling. For the first time in her life, she felt truly alone.

At Myrtle Beach, South Carolina, Air Force Base, Colonel Jonathan Bennett was up late in his office, doing pro-

ficiency reports on four pilots of his air wing he intended
to get rid of. He ignored the sound of the television coming from the nearby pilot's ready room, occupied as usual
by the six pilots Colonel Bennett demanded be ready every
night of the year to fly, if needed. Outside, in a driving
rain, their aircraft, F-4s, sat fueled and armed. Some of
his younger pilots referred to him as "Winston" behind
his back, and to themselves as "the Few" (referring to
Churchill's famous World War II tribute to British pilots,
"Never has so much been owed by so many, to so few").
To Jonathan Bennett, every day was a possible "Battle of
Britain." He demanded blood and sweat. Tears were for
losers.

Jason Porter Kelly, J.R. Kelly's younger brother, stared
hard at the chessboard. "Harriers" came and went, in
spite of the weather. His gung-ho squadron commander
had the base at Cherry Point, North Carolina, very busy,
practicing night operations. The base had only twelve
night-capable aircraft, but more were on the way. In the
morning, he and four of his fellow pilots were ferrying
five AV-8C "Harriers" out to Yuma. They were going to
reserve units, replaced by brand-new Harrier IIs expected
to arrive at Cherry Point on Monday.

"Check, idiot." Jason studied the board for a way out.
His wingman, a fresh-faced lieutenant on base for only
two months, grinned at him with obvious relish.

"Not my day, I guess," Jason said. "I'm gonna hit the
rack. Ferry flights are long and very, very boring."

"Jason, if you flew as bad as you play chess, you'da
been dead long ago."

"True. But I don't." Neither man had said a word about
the death of the President while they played chess. Pilots
don't care who is president, as long as he sees to it they
have airplanes.

And at the Executive Office Building in Washington,
D.C., a black limo pulled up and a woman in a long gown
exited the rear seat. Rosemary Hawkins, earlier described

as "tired, distraught, and dispirited," looked positively
dazzling for her private dinner with the new President of
the United States. Her demeanor, however, was this time
described as "grim and unsmiling."

EXECUTIVE OFFICE BUILDING
WEDNESDAY, 9:44 P.M.,
EASTERN STANDARD TIME

Whatever political sophistication William Rodgers possessed, and, in truth, he possessed quite a lot for a Texas
oilman, disappeared sitting across the table from Rosemary Hawkins. Their late dinner had overwhelmed him
from the beginning, when she'd casually tossed her mink
over a chair and launched into what could only be described as a vitriolic attack on most of his political allies.
He watched her carefully, waiting, absorbing her politics
while he watched her eat her steak, cooked rare, tiny bites
pushed into her rosebud mouth and chewed with what he
felt must be the precise number of times to maintain the
dazzle of her white, even teeth.

She talked on and on, and the new President wondered
why she was so animated, so lively, so without apparent
grief. *Her* President was dead. Freshly dead. How could
she sit there, in her three-thousand-dollar Galanos dress,
slit to here and fitted like it had been sewn on while she
waited? Had the painfully brief crying she'd done earlier
today while Marine One still burned on the 14th Street
Bridge been it? Was that all this stunning intellectual
chewing her steak needed. And if it was, were all the
things written about her true? Yes. They were most probably true. An opportunistic bitch with too many fancy degrees and too little material in her skirts. That's what
William F. Buckley had called her.

Suddenly, she confronted him. Not verbally, but with

her eyes. They locked on his with the intensity of a heat-seeking missile, and he could not look away.

"Are you listening to me, Mr. President?"

Was he? He couldn't be sure. No. He was *looking* at her. He had no idea what she had said. "Of course I'm listening, Rosemary. You hate everyone that has ever supported me."

"No. Not hate. I don't hate. If I did, I wouldn't be here now. I would be off somewhere, wearing sackcloth and wailing into the night."

"Why aren't you?"

"Because I want you to see this." Rosemary stood up, as usual showing a lot of leg, and walked to where her mink wrap lay. She tossed it on the floor, and from under it produced a small leather case he had not noticed until now. A sheaf of papers, folded loosely into a beige, unmarked file. She walked back to the table, holding the file close to her, as if it were a hand grenade she could not decide to throw at him.

"This is what Conrad Taylor had going. It means peace. I wrote it with him. It is, essentially, his program for the next seven years. If you want me . . . to stay in your administration, you will have to adopt this program. As you will soon recognize, the Soviets have already accepted it in principle." She extended the folder across the table, her eyes hard and very intense. He did not move. He made no gesture to take it, just staring into her eyes, fanatic eyes he'd seen on every peace barricade since the sixties.

"At least read it, William." Her eyes softened, her body leaned, her demeanor changed. William Rodgers gave in immediately, and accepted the folder, gingerly, like he would a rattlesnake.

Rosemary Hawkins walked away from the table, staring out the window, one leg pushed out from the other, her back to him. Galanos would have been proud. Outside, it rained, a cold, appropriate rain for a city about to bury its first citizen.

* * *

The new President was not a fast reader. Conrad Taylor had been famous for digesting anything he read in some kind of speed-reading record. But speed reading would not have played a part in what William Rodgers thought about what he was reading. It was contrary to everything he had ever believed.

It was equally clear that followed to its conclusion, the threat and reality of nuclear war would end. As much as he hated to admit it, it seemed that Conrad Taylor had been on the brink of a possible, incredible breakthrough in relations with the Soviet Union. It was radical. It was dangerous. It might even be revolutionary. But if it worked, it might change the world in a way more profound than the crucifixion of Jesus Christ had. He was reading the possible salvation, or the definite destruction, of the human race.

It was Thursday before he finished. He was a president elevated to his position by disaster. He hated . . . no, he didn't hate the Russians. He *distrusted* them. He always had. How could he change twenty-five years of political thought, political thrust, political orientation and philosophy, espoused at a thousand county fairs and Senate speeches? He glanced at his watch. It was 2:45, Thursday morning. Rosemary Hawkins had stood at the window, moving only slightly, for over four hours.

"I'll let you know, Rosemary."

She turned toward him, her eyes finally tired, her posture not what the press normally photographed. "Downstairs, they are going to think I just fucked you. Whatever you say, they are going to think that."

Startled, William Rodgers, President for only eleven hours, tried to grasp what Rosemary had said. "Why? Why would they think that?"

"Because it's almost 3:00 A.M., and they think I fuck everybody."

"Do you?" William Rodgers, tired and stunned by what he had read, could not believe what he'd asked.

"No. I don't fuck everybody. I fuck presidents." Without further comment, Rosemary Hawkins picked up her mink wrap and walked out the door, to face the same hostile press she had faced since her appointment a year before. Curiously, significantly, the press let her leave without a single question. It was Thursday, and Wednesday had been too much for everyone in Washington to handle.

DAY TWO: THURSDAY

**THE VICE PRESIDENT'S RESIDENCE
NAVAL OBSERVATORY HILL
WASHINGTON, D.C.
THURSDAY, 7:55 A.M.**

William Rodgers didn't look like a man who hadn't slept all night. Three hours sleep, and he looked fresh and eager as a teenager at a prom. He studied his fleshy features in the mirror, the same face he had looked at for all of his life. With one exceptional difference. This Thursday in November, the man in the mirror was the President of the United States. William Rodgers cut himself shaving. It was hard to shave around your lips when you were whistling. He was whistling the theme music from *High Noon*. He had seen the movie thirty-seven times.

**M.C.A.S.
CHERRY POINT, NORTH CAROLINA
THURSDAY, 0800 HOURS**

"Tower?"

"Roger, Shepherd One."

"Shepherd One and four sheep request permission to fly."

"Roger, Shepherd One. Permission granted. Have a good one." These last words were spoken with considerable "have a nice day" emphasis.

"Roger, Tower. Shepherd One and four Cs on our way."

The five Harrier C aircraft rushed down the runway and blasted into the overcast sky after very brief, short takeoff runs. They popped into the clear at 4,500 feet, laden with extra fuel in drop tanks for the long flight west to Yuma, Arizona. Jason Porter Kelly, "Shepherd One," led the formation, his third ferry flight since joining the Harrier squadron. He had more long flight and navigation time than any lieutenant on base. His latest fitness report had been resoundingly positive. Jason Porter Kelly, U.S.M.C., was a comer. The Harriers rushed west, tucked in tight behind "Shepherd One." It was to be a very ordinary, routine flight. His last routine flight.

"Tacka, tacka, tacka . . . tacka, tacka, tacka . . ." The chattering sound exploded in Jason's ears as a formation of six A-10s, painted in a mottled gray-green camouflage scheme, flashed over the slow-flying Harriers in a mock, but frightening attack.

"You die, Marines," a voice squealed in Jason's head phone as the A-10 Warthogs banked left and swung into a high circle above the Marine aircraft. The Harriers slipped wide apart, losing formation.

"Stay tucked, guys. Just those crazy bastards from Myrtle Beach. The Air Farce, as usual." Jason's voice was calm, but the less than military and completely unauthorized game this group of A-10s had played had thoroughly shaken him.

"Sorry if we woke you up, jungle bunnies, but this is 354th TAC airspace."

A wicked looking A-10 rolled up on Jason's wing, only fifty feet away, an ace of spades painted on its nose, over a set of warthog tusks and teeth. Very dramatic, Jason thought. The fucking Air Force! The pilot who had pulled alongside wore a black flight helmet also decorated with an ace of spades. His tail surface had three squadrons' colors painted on it, identifying the pilot as a full wing commander.

"A little too old for this, aren't you, Colonel?" Jason gave the finger to the pilot flying only a few feet off his wing. The A-10 leaped up and banked away. The wing commander had not replied. In minutes, the Harrier flight had the sky to itself.

SUBURBAN MARYLAND
THURSDAY, 8:30 A.M.

Rosemary Hawkins stepped out of the shower and wrapped herself in a large, fluffy towel. Her face, bereft of makeup, was drawn and tired. She had been at work by 7:00 A.M., whatever that work entailed, for over six years. She could not remember the last time, if there was a last time, she had risen from her bed at 8:00 A.M., no matter how late she had been up the night before.

She applied only the barest of makeup, a touch of blush to her pale cheeks, a light touch of lipstick. Very red lipstick to be sure. She pulled on bikini panties and a matching wisp of a bra. Black silk stockings. Black garter belt. Black shoes. Black suit. Semi-short skirt. She wondered if the new President had stopped laughing yet, now that he'd had a night to think about what he'd read. She was very pessimistic.

She needn't have been. Before the day was done, she would be appointed the first female Secretary of State. She would also be the first female to have sex with consecutive Presidents of the United States, on consecutive days. A Guinness record, albeit nonprintable.

THE EXECUTIVE OFFICE BUILDING
WASHINGTON, D.C.
THURSDAY, 9:00 A.M.

"Mr. President?"

William Rodgers, still surprised when he was addressed that way, did not respond at first. He just stared at the intercom and its blinking light.

"Mr. President? Sir?"

"Yes, Mary."

"Former Governor Bennett, sir. He apologizes for showing up this way, without an appointment. He says, under the bizarre circumstances of your newly acquired position, he feels you will understand. He also says he has a branch water thermos, whatever that is."

William Rodgers smiled. "Send him right in, Mary."

For an hour, William Rodgers listened to Adrian Bennett, an old friend, as the veteran politician made suggestions, politely but firmly, about what the new President should do. Could do. *Must* do. As he spoke, the two men emptied the thermos of straight whiskey with a splash of branch water. Whatever else, the new President could hold his liquor.

"Bill, the first thing you need to do is get rid of Rosemary Hawkins. She has no business in your administration. She is—I mean, we, the Conservative Caucus, believe she is—an out-and-out Communist. As for your Secretary of State, well, clearly, Secretary of State Mitchell will have to go. He's a wimp, with only the slightest input on policy. Even Conrad Taylor excluded him. He should go at once, before Rosemary Hawkins. It will make a point that this cuddling up to the third world and the Soviets is going to be re-examined. I hope you will consider this suggestion very carefully, Bill." The new President was not happy at being called just plain "Bill," but he said nothing.

"Let me make it clear. We think the two most impor-

tant changes at this time are the Secretary of State and
your National Security Advisor. I wonder if you would
consider these two names?'' Conrad Taylor would have
rolled over in his casket. The two names were the ''Nuke
'Em'' general, and the seventy-eight-year-old retired ambassador. Both men had supported William Rodgers's vice
presidential nomination, but only after their prime choices
had been rejected. They now represented a dangerous and
unstable fringe element in the party. Red flags to wave at
the party of peace as represented by Conrad Taylor and
Rosemary Hawkins.

William Rodgers did not know what to say to Adrian
Bennett. So he simply shoved Rosemary Hawkins's folder
across his desk and said, ''Read this, Adrian. I'm leaning
toward this as our party's policy. I would appreciate your
comments.''

Adrian Bennett flipped through the thick folder, like a
teenager looking for the centerfold in *Playboy*. The reading took less than twenty minutes.

''This is treason, William.'' Not Bill, but still not ''Mr.
President.''

''Why?''

''Because it overturns our policy. It . . . it is like some
Communist Manifesto. Retreat from Europe. From Asia.
Backing the overthrow of our friends in Central America.
Recognition of Cuba. I haven't read it thoroughly, but I've
seen enough. Surely you can't be thinking about this? Not
with any intent to carry it out. This is Rosemary Hawkins,
pure and simple. You, after all your public service, can't
possibly believe this trash will work?''

''I didn't say I believed it. I just wanted your opinion.
You are an elder statesman. I appreciate whatever you have
to say. And, I agree about Secretary of State Mitchell. At
the appropriate time, I will ask him to resign.''

''Wonderful,'' Adrian Bennett said, with considerable
enthusiasm. ''And will you consider the two names I've
submitted?'' Apparently, he'd quickly forgotten what he'd
just read.

''Of course I will, Adrian. But, as President, you know

I will pick the one person I need with the utmost of care, and only after long and careful consideration. There is no rush.''

"I understand, Mr. President." Better. Much better, thought William Rodgers. "We understand the protocols involved here. We know you are an old pro, and will certainly consider feelings, careers, and all the things you do so well. We would simply like to offer our assistance, in any way we can."

"I'm grateful, Adrian. I intend to give a speech tonight. Perhaps you might listen, if you can find the time."

"Certainly, Mr. President. And thank you so much for your time. Forgive me my presumptuousness, my impertinence. The Caucus simply felt now was the best time to help you."

"Thank you, Adrian." There was a clear note of dismissal in William Rodgers's voice. Adrian Bennett recognized it, and left at once.

Outside, on the White House portico, Adrian Bennett blithely told the press that the Conservative Caucus of America, the long lost and ignored voice of the party, had recommended the replacement of Secretary of State Mitchell, at some time in the future, so the new President would have a free hand in planning American foreign policy.

Forty-seven minutes later, the Secretary of State's resignation was on the new President's desk, effective immediately. The new President, mouse-trapped and embarrassed, accepted the resignation "reluctantly." Adrian Bennett, questioned later in the morning, called it "the right move, at the right time." He then suggested that, as a matter of pure formality, the entire cabinet should resign, freeing the new President to pick his own team. He never mentioned Conrad Taylor.

THE WHITE HOUSE
THURSDAY, 9:30 A.M.

Emily Taylor sat quietly at her desk, dictating to her personal secretary the complete details of what she expected to be the grandest, most perfect funeral her fallen husband could possibly expect, had he planned it himself. Her secretary listened in amazement, her hand flying across the notebook in a frantic attempt to keep up. Who would have thought the President's wife capable of this? She wasn't, but no one would know. She'd adopted Rosemary Hawkins's suggestions 100 percent. She'd met with the Librarian of Congress for over two hours this Thursday before Thanksgiving. Between them, using Rosemary Hawkins's notes, they had laid out a meticulous procession of events, culminating on Monday, shortly before dark, when her husband was to be buried in Arlington National Cemetery, a service to be attended by every world leader capable of climbing and descending an airliner ramp. The world would be here to bury her husband, and the world would watch Emily Conrad. She intended to make Jackie Kennedy look like the airhead she truly was.

THE WORLD
THURSDAY, 9:30 A.M.,
EASTERN STANDARD TIME

The people of the United States had passionate opinions about Conrad Taylor. It was very difficult to be neutral about the charismatic President. Few were. You hated him, or you loved him. The percentages, even now, were very even. Split. Divisive. Conrad Taylor had been born to a royal family, in a country without royalty. A rich man, he had campaigned as a hero to the poor, the homeless, the disenfranchised. He had been elected to the presidency by

a margin so thin it made the 1960 election of the equally
youthful J.F.K. look like a landslide.

Conrad Taylor's death left 50 percent of the citizens of
the United States distraught, and 50 percent of the United
States rejoicing and dancing, however discreetly, in the
streets. The rest of the world was equally divided, with
unequal results.

The Prime Minister of Britain could not sleep. She
hadn't slept properly since Conrad Taylor had been elected.
God, she hated him! Ridiculous, of course, but there it
was, after all. The first time they'd met in private, shortly
after his inauguration, she had measured him. And he
didn't measure up at all.

"Your constituents don't want our air bases on your island. Before the end of my first term, all United States
personnel now serving in Britain will be back here, in the
United States. In the unlikely event you are attacked, we
shall come to your aid. That is my policy."

He'd actually said that. And, in her usual blunt way, she
had said, "You are out of your mind, Mr. President."
He'd given her a slow, intense smile, and poured her tea.

Since that first meeting, Rosemary Hawkins had visited
England three times. The message had remained the same.
The United States intended to pull up its oceans, like blue-
green blankets, and hide from the world. Conrad Taylor
was tired of having the United States, in the guise of its
world policeman role, dying in the line of duty. He intended to change the U.S. role.

Now, he had died in the line of duty. She would go to
his funeral. She would mourn. She might, if the telly was
on her, cry, with considerable but long-suppressed English
gusto. It would serve her, and accentuate the "special relationship" between the United States and Great Britain.
But whatever her public stance, the Prime Minister held
close to one simple truth: the best and only public service
Conrad Taylor had ever done, he'd done by riding his
stricken helicopter headlong into the 14th Street Bridge.

* * *

The rebel commander called his ragtag, ill-equipped battalion together. Battalion . . . well, company, maybe. Was an active count of 150 a company? It was definitely not a battalion. No matter. He would address his men as a battalion.

"Our most dreaded enemy is dead. Very soon, our numbers will double, triple, and multiply beyond mere numbers. We will, I promise you, return to our onetime promise. Offensive operations!"

The troops, filthy and disheveled, stared at him with hopeless, doubting eyes. The government soldiers had pressed them deeper and deeper into the mountains. They had only the weapons they could carry. Offensive operations were out of the question. Central America had been Conrad Taylor's whipping boy. The money was gone. Except for a few lonely voices in Congress and the conservative press, *freedom fighter* was a dirty word. They listened, but they did not react. A U.S. president had died. But nothing would change. The government troops in the Russian helicopters would be hunting them again in a few days. That was all his death meant to them.

The government, in a cynical display of national grief, had called off all operations until after the funeral. The government leaders of all the Central American countries would attend. Their commander finally stopped talking and walked away. They stood in loose formation, not knowing what to do. Freedom fighters. Out of the fight, and out of freedom, running on empty in the jungle.

Europeans for the most part did not trust Conrad Taylor, and they feared his policies would one day leave them vulnerable to Communist expansion. After screaming for decades about American bases, American missiles, American troops, and American interference, Europe had been forced to contemplate the cold fact that what they wanted most was going to happen. "American go home" had changed to "Why are you leaving us to our fates?" His death drew the expected condolences, and the attendance of the heads of state of the European continent was assured.

Behind the condolences, Europe breathed a discreet sigh of relief. Officially, this Thursday in Europe was cast in gloom and sympathy. Headlines across Europe proclaimed Conrad Taylor a man of vision and courage, struck down in the prime of his life, his policies just beginning to take shape. Left unsaid was the expectation that under the new President those policies would die an early death as well.

THE KREMLIN
MOSCOW
THURSDAY, 9:00 P.M. (MOSCOW TIME)

Grenady V. Malitkov, Marshall of the Soviet Union, Commander in Chief of the Red Army, sat in an ornate, opulent room once used by Catherine the Great for romantic liaisons with officers of the Imperial Russian Army. The room was untouched, except for the few modern items required to function in the twentieth century. The walls, brilliant and garish in silken red and black cloth, were a clear reminder of Mother Russia's onetime decadence and excess. Gold-framed mirrors hung everywhere, the most interesting one on the ceiling over Catherine's bed. The bed itself was long since gone, but the space was revered by the Marshall's staff. If only half the stories were true, she'd governed Imperial Russia flat on her back, her royal thighs parted and proclaiming advancement or demotion, if you believed the stories. Grenady believed.

But what did he believe now? The President/General Secretary was apparently engaged in a dialogue with the United States, a far reaching dialogue, to put it mildly. Conrad Taylor had made the Soviet Union a startling offer. The pull-back of United States forces, with the ultimate aim of clearing U.S. troops and bases from Western Europe within three years. The Soviet Union, he had learned during his briefing, intended to remove all Soviet troops from East Germany, Czechoslovakia, and Poland. No Soviet troop concentration larger than needed for defense would be allowed in what the agreement vaguely called "attack areas"; areas to be determined at a later date; with full and intense negotiations planned to begin in Moscow, in secret, on December fifth.

All well and good. Peace was a good thing. Less than six months before, Grenady Malitkov had been given orders to withdraw troops and mechanized equipment from the suggested "attack areas." He had also been directed to replace these garrison troops and old equipment with veteran personnel and the most modern equipment available in three of the nine specified "attack areas."

On this Thursday evening, a very heavy force of new tanks and men, over a million of them veterans of Afghanistan, stood ready, if called, to attack the west on a one-hundred-mile front two days after being ordered to do so. Just exactly what was going on here? If peace were being actively pursued, one might say radically pursued, why were 35,000 modern tanks less than forty-eight hours from the Fulda Gap dividing the two Germanys? The President/General Secretary had ordered him to turn this force around. He had not ordered it to leave its position.

THE WHITE HOUSE
PRIVATE QUARTERS
THURSDAY, 1:00 P.M.

Emily picked at her salad, an enormous creation of multiple greens and multiple meats, garnished with sliced eggs and mushrooms and slathered in a special raid-the-refrigerator dressing she usually ate by the spoonful, straight from the chilled jar. Cook had done her best, but even the "Em" salad that she loved so much was wilting under her indifferent, prodding fork.

Her mother watched her with disapproving mother's eyes, topped by hair blue-white as a Salem cigarette ad, her nose surgically straight over thin lips in perpetual Kentucky pink, edged in cynicism and the down-turned fix of a lifetime of looking askance at everything she didn't understand. Considering she hadn't read a book or a newspaper, aside from and discounting the society pages of the *Louisville Courier* since she was sixteen and virginal, this covered nearly everything in the modern, human world. Looking askance at life was her only "talent." Her idea of a worldly woman was a woman who remembered her banker's private phone number, and used it.

Emily's father, as usual, gave her no look at all. He found it difficult to help his daughter in times of stress. Father–daughter parental stress began at age six, with skinned knees, and went on from there. She hadn't asked her father for help since the second grade. Each time she'd sought it, he'd looked away, rich, powerful, and terrified by the simplest needs of his children. He'd avoided opinions, suggestions, and touching, for over a quarter of a century. Nothing, not even Conrad Taylor's death, would change that. He had thrust and grunted his way to three children. That, in his view, had ended his emotional, as well as physical, involvement. Each of his children had come into a ten-million-dollar trust fund at the age of twenty-one. His conscience was clear, however distant from his offspring. He had paid them off, like fast horses, first to the wire.

"What are you going to do, Emily?"

"Do? What do you mean, Mother? What can I do?"

"I mean . . . after . . . after the funeral."

"I guess I'll take the children back to Boston."

"Boston!" The eyes arched, the mouth never moved.

"Why not Boston? We have a home there. A lovely home. The children will be quite happy there."

"Grow up, Emily! Boston will turn you out! Conrad, when he was president, ruled the world. But his widow must return to Kentucky. She must go home. Emily, you really must. Why . . . those people *hate* Kentucky!"

Emily Taylor turned to her father, her face naked and exposed, once again a nine-year-old, wounded and seeking solace from the world in the arms of her all-knowing father.

"Daddy? Daddy, what do you think?"

"Emily, all this is beyond me." He raised his hands, palms up, the fork in one hand, a crisp, apple-filled sausage bobbing and writhing against the bright sharpness of 180-year-old silver. President Grant, drunk, had once jabbed that very fork into the hand of a dinner guest while attempting to remove a venison chop from a platter. The guest had screamed in agony.

Emily, in far greater agony, turned away from her parents, digging savagely into her "Em" salad. Cook would be very pleased. After lunch, Emily called for a bottle of vodka, but didn't touch it. She wanted desperately to talk again with Rosemary Hawkins, her only real link to Conrad Taylor. She thought she understood Rosemary Hawkins. She would ask Rosemary to advise her. To tell her what to do, if need be. With Connie dead, someone had to . . .

THE WHITE HOUSE
THURSDAY, 1:30 P.M.

Rosemary Hawkins had been completely absorbed in her work since her arrival in her office at the unusual time of 9:00 A.M. She had, by force of habit, stopped by the desk of Conrad Taylor's secretary, asking for a schedule for the day, before realizing that there would be no schedule for the day. Alice, her eyes red from crying, had given her a sympathetic, woman-to-woman look before Rosemary turned away and hurried to her desk, steeling herself for a day of appointments no one would keep.

But they did. Her morning had rolled on smoothly, populated by favor seekers and those who could bestow favors, like any other day. She had gone into the adjoining Oval Office only to get the prized "initiative" folder, the written word on Conrad Taylor's foreign policy. Every word known to her because she had written most of it.

She'd shown it to William Rodgers the night before. At 11:30 A.M. the new President had called her, and suggested she might consider accepting the newly vacant Secretary of State job. In the course of this conversation, she was told Adrian Bennett had suggested to the new President that she was nothing less than a Communist. A preposterous comment, said the President, from an old-time fanatic. He said that he hoped she would write him a suitable speech, which he intended to give tonight. Had she the time? She advised the surprised Chief Executive that she had his speech prepared, and would send it to him immediately. She left the job offer up in the air. If he would give the speech, as written, she would accept the Secretary of State job. If not, if he wanted to change its direction and write his own speech, she would decline the state department nomination. He said he was sure the speech was fine, and that he would use it. She asked him to read it first, and call her back.

Rosemary Hawkins had not always been so assertive. Quite the opposite. The third girl in a family of five girls, she was neither the oldest, nor the youngest. She was the "middle daughter," no trouble, no fuss, no identity. She grew up a solitary child in a house full of children, blending in, spending most of her time reading and painting. She was a gifted artist, and undoubtedly would have made her mark in the art world.

Even her father, a successful builder of homes in large numbers, crammed into small spaces, took time out from his schedule to encourage her clear pathway to the arts. He promised to send her to the finest art school in the country when the time came.

Red-haired, freckled, a tiny yet oddly ungainly young girl, she felt she would be invulnerable, and yet draw attention, if she pursued her artistic calling. This girlish plan worked very well for Rosemary, the awkward, freckled, redheaded girl. And then, in her fourteenth summer, she changed. And so did her plans.

At an aunt's house in Maine, between July and September, while frolicking in the surf and lying on the beach, she tanned, and the freckles disappeared. She lost her angular shape, her hips widening, softening; most miraculous of all, she'd had no breasts in June, but had acquired a full, rich figure by September.

She grew to her final adult height of five feet three inches, height manifested mostly by shapely, long legs, legs with visible muscles that carried her along with a stride that gave a natural roll to her hips; and she matured rapidly and mystically, leaving the child on the beach and walking off the sand a woman. Worse yet, she discovered boys.

All young girls discovered boys. But Rosemary learned very early that *they had discovered her.* And she found a strength she'd never known. She could manipulate boys. Make them do for her. She had three or four boyfriends, all fighting with each other, over her. This went on until she was seventeen, when she selected one, a junior in college, to initiate her into the ways of sex.

She simply let him unbutton her blouse, and her bra, finally impatiently undoing it for him. In his excitement, as she fell back onto the front seat, pulling him over her, her back jammed against the door handle, he came all over her bared stomach, before entering her. Wise beyond her years, she waited, stroking him, her tongue in his mouth, bringing him back, placing him in her, amazed that it didn't hurt, not at all, and she climaxed almost at once. She was twenty-four years old before she believed the woman who had told her in the ladies room that most women didn't climax at all. It was easy for her. She thought it was easy for everybody.

As a result of that first time in the car, Rosemary Hawkins dated only men that were older than she was, and supposedly more experienced, a promise that was rarely true.

She listened to her sorority sisters talk about men, nodded her head, kept her face interested and her eyes wide, believing nothing. Who did these silly, chatty females go

out with? Who did they talk to? Who did they fuck? She
had no idea, and she learned nothing from her sorority
sisters. She decided, in her junior year, to divide her time
between intense study and intense sex. She studied alone.
She had sex with whoever attracted her.

Rosemary Hawkins had an academic record second to
none. When she completed her schooling, she was
launched almost immediately into the international world
of high finance and low but serious diplomacy. A specialist in international law, she quickly surpassed those more
established than she was, a triumph thought impossible by
the old hands of this business. Her liberal, near revolutionary voice began to attract attention, not always for her
political viewpoint. More often for the way she allowed
herself to be viewed. Whatever the prevalent style, in a
calculated act of defiance, Rosemary Hawkins began to
wear short-skirted suits. She wore them everywhere, taking the heat from the feminists, their screech raining down
on her until they began to listen to what she was actually
saying. She was an ardent feminist, with a global platform
to spread her views. Rosemary Hawkins was a revolutionary, with terrific legs. Soon, one characteristic overshad-
owed the other.

Conrad Taylor saw her lecture at the University of
Massachusetts. She was talking about the difference between
West and East Germany. He heard not a word she said.
Sitting behind her, awaiting the question-and-answer period to follow, he locked his eyes on her legs, her buttocks, her slim hips moving as she emphasized a point.
Before he left the hall, he gave her his card. On it he
wrote, "I'm going to be president. Want to come along
for the ride?" Twenty-two months later, after twenty
months with NATO in a legal/military advisory role, she
sent him back the card. It had one word: Yes.

That one-word reply had tied her to a rocket-ride political miracle, the ascendancy of a young, handsome senator to the ultimate political job. She had written his

speeches, sorted his mail, rallied the troops. She had planned his election campaign down to the last vote. He won the presidency by the narrowest margin in history. He named her his National Security Advisor forty-eight hours after he was elected. The party conservatives bayed at the moon in protest. The moon failed to answer.

She had been Conrad Taylor's lover and confidant for six years, thirty-nine days, and eleven hours when he died. His death deprived her of love, but not purpose.

WASHINGTON, D.C.
THURSDAY, 1:40 P.M.

J.R. Kelly had already tried to get into three ultra-crowded restaurants, and now, in the fourth, he intended to stay and eat. The line ahead of him was very long, and he flashed his wallet open, showing his agency I.D. to get to the front of the line. The afternoon maître d' frowned at him, but said nothing.

Toward the back of the restaurant's main seating area, he watched as four men stood up and pulled away from the table designed to seat two. It was near the kitchen, and very noisy. He didn't care. He headed straight toward it, bumping into a large, distinguished-looking man with silver hair.

"Excuse me," J.R. said. The silver hair nodded, the face unsmiling, and the man went out toward the front, pushing through the line and out the door. A very familiar face, but for the moment J.R. couldn't place it. Later, it would come to him.

"Honey, don't be sitting there yet. I haven't cleared the table." A hippy, bleached-out young blond barred his way to the table, moving her hips occasionally to dodge the waitresses scurrying through the swinging doors of the kitchen, laden with trays and bent under the weight of Washingtonian diets gone bad.

J.R. gave her a sympathetic, understanding smile. "I'll take it, and you can clean it up when you get the time. A cold beer would be nice, if you could."

"Oh, what the hell. It's not as if this is a normal goddamn day, is it? I'll be back in a jiff with something cold, and I'll clean the table as soon as I can."

Well, she had that right. This Thursday was for sure not like any other. One president freshly dead, a new one freshly sworn in, and most of the world scheduled to bury the old one on Monday. Yes sir, the times to try men's souls, or whatever. He glanced at his watch. Two hours to waste. A short briefing at the White House, and then he and forty specially picked agents would change jobs for a while. Security of foreign dignitaries, their staffs, and the study and control of foreign agents doing the same thing. Jesus! What a weird four days this promised to be. Idly, he studied the table. They hadn't eaten much, but there were four cocktail glasses. Martinis, by the look of them. Furtively, he plucked the olives from each glass, popped them into his mouth, discarded the toothpicks. What the hell, he was hungry. He began to read the doodles on the paper place mats at his chair, moving a full ashtray out of his way to do it. Three types of cigarettes, two with filters, and one plain Camel. Like every ex-cop, J.R. read cigarettes. The place mat at his chair was a study of not much. Green ink. *A-10* written once on the top corner. The word *Monday* and a very odd line of letters, stacked from the top down.

K

K

K

K

K

K–1

K

K-76

K-218

K-8

K

K

K

K

250,000

150,000

800

???

There were smiling faces at each corner, the kind you see kids draw. It didn't look like much of a power lunch. Ever curious, he checked the other four place mats. Nothing. On one, in red ink this time, someone had drawn a tombstone. Considering all that had occurred in the last twenty-four hours, that certainly made sense.

Five minutes passed, and the hippy, bleachy blond brought J.R. his beer and cleaned off the table. Robbed of his reading material, he began to look around the room. It was packed (a leg man's dream). His gaze settled on a pair of semi-exposed thighs, and he drank his beer. To J.R., the leer was an art form. She noticed, pulled her knees together and her skirt down, frowning. Oh, it was going to be a very grim weekend. He ordered a B.L.T. and another beer. He began to draw a series of exaggerated breasts on his place mat. Some he gave smiles. Some ears. Some wings. All of them had personality.

WASHINGTON, D.C.
THURSDAY, 4:45 P.M.

In the basement of the White House, the agents were given a briefing on what they might expect over the next four days. The nation was burying its controversial young President. The capital would be crawling with foreign dignitaries, not to mention terrorists of all stripes. Rosemary Hawkins, the dead President's National Security Advisor, had requested these extraordinary precautions, and the new President himself had asked for, and obviously received, C.I.A. help, on U.S. soil, regardless of charter. At last count, the estimate of intelligence operatives of all nations expected in the U.S. capital by Friday morning at 0800 hours was a cool, unbelievable 25,000. The forty agents in this room were free-lancers, assigned primarily to the exposure of threats and the exploitation of opportunity. J.R. Kelly was one of four agents asked to report directly to Ms. Rosemary Hawkins. On hearing this, J.R. Kelly grabbed his crotch and began to make obscene noises.

"Now, J.R., goddammit, you behave yourself, okay?" The sixty-two-year-old Assistant Deputy Director of the Records Division, Foreign/Asia Office, looked sternly at J.R. It cracked everybody up.

THE WHITE HOUSE
8:00 P.M., EASTERN STANDARD TIME

"From the White House Oval Office, the President of the United States." The off-camera announcer pointed at William Rodgers, jumped up and down, and pointed again. William Rodgers, unused to the title, finally realized the man was pointing at him. He faced the camera and began to speak. It came more naturally than he would have imagined.

"My fellow Americans. Yesterday, our beloved nation lost its most beloved son. Twenty-four hours ago, Conrad Taylor was vibrantly alive, on his way to New York to deliver the twenty-ninth in-person speech of his young presidency. He was about to face another in a long line of loving, but politically hostile audiences, the American Jewish Congress. Like all of us, they liked his smile, his style, and, grudgingly, his guts. He had no votes there, of course. He would have to brave a few thousand protesters. But by now, he is . . . *[pause]* was very good at that.'' Here, the new President brushed a tear from his eye. *(Two blocks away, in the Willard Inter-Continental Hotel, eight distinguished Americans nodded approvingly, then laughed and applauded "their" new President.)*

"My fellow, grieving Americans, there was much Conrad Wilson Taylor wanted to accomplish. For almost ten months, he and his able staff, particularly his National Security Advisor—''*[here, the new President glances to his right. The camera follows, and falls on Rosemary Hawkins, wearing a severe, black suit. In the hotel suite, the eight distinguished Americans stop laughing . . . frown. The President seems to lose his place, fumbles with his notes, and continues.]*

"I know what must be going through most everyone's mind at this moment, and therefore, I will attempt to answer your worries in a straightforward way. If you believed that I, as President, would change Conrad Wilson Taylor's initiatives, you are wrong. If you believed I would cut back, restudy, evaluate . . . pick your own word . . . you are wrong! *[Silence in the downtown hotel suite, followed by a quick walk to the television set by Governor Bennett. The set is shut off. He addresses each of the seven men in the room with him, eye-to-eye, one-by-one. They all nod approval. They have less than a week to change history.]*

"I want you to know, my fellow citizens, that I, as President, in these saddest of circumstances, intend to push Conrad Wilson Taylor's proposals, not to their limit, but beyond their limit! I ask, now, this day, publicly, that the leaders of all the world's nations . . . and here *[pause, sincere look into the cameras]* I don't want the slightest chance of misinterpretation . . . I ask that the leaders of all nations, and I mean most particularly our present, or future enemies . . .'' *[Once again, the new President appears to lose his place, shuffles his notes. His face glistens in the hot lights.]*

[Pause. Camera to audience. Camera to Rosemary Hawkins.] The President wipes the sweat from his brow. America and the world miss this act. When the camera returns, he looks completely at ease.

"I ask that the leaders of all the world's nations come to our fallen President's interment, to say good-bye, if that is what we are truly doing. But . . . *[long pause. Close-up camera.]* But I ask that the leaders stay here, after the funeral, as guests of our country, to engage in wide-open, anything-goes talks about all the problems that our tiny earth faces. Problems that Conrad Wilson Taylor understood. He cannot state his view, or his hopes, regarding these problems. *I will state them! [Pause]*

"*One.* Disarmament. The United States will go forward. Anything, *and I mean anything,* is negotiable.

"*Two.* Total, one world government. And why not? Do we not all live on the same planet?

"*Three.* Complete . . . that is correct, I said complete, withdrawal of all foreign troops, from wherever they may be, by the nations that put them there. Do I include Israel? . . . I must!" *[Here, the President looks once again at Rosemary Hawkins. She smiles.]* The President, in one sentence, has proclaimed himself in favor of Israeli withdrawal to pre-1967 borders. Within an hour of this speech, the Israeli military begin to plan preemptive warfare against its Arab neighbors. In the Knesset, pandemonium reigns.

"*Four:* In this context, I shall order, on Tuesday, a study of how soon the United States can bring home its troops, from wherever they may be in this frail, vulnerable world we live in. Korea. Japan. Europe. Central America. We will bring them home. Peace is ours. But it will take courage. I, as President of the United States, here, at this dreadfully sad time for us all, officially invite the world's leaders, and thinkers, poets and would-be-poets, to come here, now, to bury our fallen President. And to stay here, in conferences to begin on the Tuesday before Thanksgiving, and to continue until we all have the chance to state our views, and to reshape our world. The United States stands ready to talk to anybody, about anything, and to back it up with action. And now *[pause, lowers his eyes, wipes his brow, a close-up of a sweaty, presidential head]* let us bury our fallen President, who brought me, in the ten months of our shared service to this government, to an understanding of his goals, and the determination to carry them out. Peace, total peace, requires only brave pursuit. May God bless us all. Thank you, and good-night.''

VOICEOVER ABC, NBC, CNN, et. al.

"This has been a live broadcast of the President of the United States, from the White House, in Washington, D.C. We will have a full debate on its contents on Tuesday evening, at 9:00 P.M., Eastern Standard Time."

[Cameras swing to President Taylor's flag-draped coffin, guarded by one member of each of the United States military services.]

THE WHITE HOUSE
THURSDAY, 9:09 P.M.,
EASTERN STANDARD TIME

J.R. Kelly sat in Rosemary Hawkins's office, the three TV monitors droning on, as he waited for his temporary boss to show up. The speech itself had come as quite a surprise. Conrad Taylor couldn't have said it better himself. The instant news analysts were having a terrific time. Tired and depressed by over twenty-four hours of funereal gloom, they latched onto the implications of the speech like hungry sharks on a smelly tuna. All the while, the dead President in his flag-draped coffin hung like a censor over their comments. It was simply not a good time to attack the President or his policies. Either President. The media, as usual, came up empty in the sensitivity department. He crossed the paneled office and shut off the monitors.

Rosemary Hawkins's office had a well-stocked bar in one corner. J.R. poured himself a fresh Cuervo Tequila on the

rocks. It was his third. He never drank on the job. He'd
made his assignment to Rosemary Hawkins the exception
to that rule. He was tired, cranky, and rebellious. In other
words, he was his own sweet self. Normal J.R. Kelly.
Abnormal J.R. was pretty bizarre stuff. Not many people
had seen that, and most of them were dead.

He walked around the room studying the walls, which
seemed to be covered with pictures of Rosemary Hawkins
and Conrad Taylor, with all the world's leaders as fill-ins.
Rosemary in Russia. Rosemary in China. Rosemary in
some unnamed jungle wearing combat fatigues. Rosemary
in Paris. One of the hundreds of pictures drew him to
study it from only inches away. Rosemary Hawkins, in a
tiny bikini, at the beach with her college-aged friends. She
looked young and fresh, and innocently sexy. And yet,
even then, she had that extra something; that something
that seemed to shout, "I will be whatever I want to be."
Boiled down, however, what the picture said to J.R. was
transmitted directly to his groin.

"Do you like that picture, Agent Kelly?"

J.R. spun around, his tequila sloshing in the glass, but
not onto the floor. She had come in behind him, silently,
and she stood against the door, leaning against it, her eyes
locked on his.

"Yes, ma'am, I do like it."

"I was never that young, you know. Never."

"Nobody is." J.R., emboldened by the tequila, and
incredibly aroused just looking at her, figured he'd just
lost this particular assignment.

"True. You are a very astute man. I'm glad to see you
made yourself at home, Agent Kelly. Would you mind
making me a drink? It has been a very long day, and it's
not yet over. I still have to see the President at ten-thirty.
More gossip for the crotch corps."

"The crotch corps?"

"The press, Agent Kelly."

"Call me J.R., if you like. Everybody does."

"J.R. it is. Now, please, that drink. Scotch, with a splash
of water and one ice cube." She had been leaning against

the door the whole time. Now she pushed herself forward, kicking her high heels off as she walked to her desk and slumped into the high-backed chair behind it.

J.R. was startled to see how short she was. She didn't seem to be much more than five-foot-two, in spite of her long and famous legs.

"Tell me, J.R., what is your real name?"

"James Robert. I prefer J.R. It makes me sound like a much more daring and resourceful person than I really am."

"Does it help with the ladies, J.R.?" She was smiling at him. A surprisingly warm smile. A real smile.

"Nothing helps with the ladies, ma'am. I am hopelessly inept with women."

"I doubt that. J.R., we are going to spend considerable time together over the next few days. Could we drop the 'ma'am,' and simply call me 'Ms. Hawkins'? Or, why not 'Rosemary'? I'll call you 'J.R.' You call me 'Rosemary.' We'll be too close for that formal bullshit."

J.R. walked to her and handed her the drink she'd so specifically ordered. Scotch. Splash. *One* ice cube. "Fine, Rosemary. I don't much like Ms. anything."

"Oh, really. Are you antifeminist?"

"No, I'm not. I'm anti-ms."

"I understand perfectly, J.R. So am I. Anti-ms., I mean." Again, the warm smile. She leaned deep into the luxuriously padded chair, crossing her silk-stockinged legs, revealing a sleek stretch of thigh and a slim foot that bobbed ferociously as she rocked back in the chair.

J.R. couldn't keep his eyes off that bouncing foot. How could she have such long legs and be so tiny? Any what the goddamned hell did any of this have to do with national security? And who the shit cared? J.R. gave Rosemary Hawkins the sappiest smile she had ever seen in her life.

In spite of herself, Rosemary laughed, genuinely laughed for the first time since Conrad Taylor's helicopter had roared nose first into the 14th Street Bridge.

"What did you think of President Rodgers's speech?"

"I think it was President Taylor's speech. Or yours."

"Do you? Interesting. I wrote most of it. The shock must still be shaking the halls of this fair city. Faithful minion Rosemary Hawkins, forestalling her grief, switches allegiance to new President. Writes his speech. Takes over, as usual. New President bewitched, bothered, and bewildered. Rosemary Hawkins proclaimed national unfeeling, uncaring bitch of the year. Steps over new coffin into new job. Film at eleven."

"New job?"

"Secretary of State."

"Oh."

"Well, why not? The job is open and I'm qualified. It will assist me in carrying forth Conrad Taylor's ideas."

"What about William Rodgers's ideas?"

"He has none."

"I see."

"You don't. But you will. I shall instruct you."

"Convert me, you mean."

"And why not? Conrad Taylor meant to convert the whole world."

"That will take some doing. Conrad Taylor is dead." J.R.'s voice was very cold.

The foot stopped bouncing and she locked her eyes on his, willing him to look at her. To her surprise, it didn't work. He turned away, to make his fourth drink.

"I will make it happen." She spoke to his back, and he turned to face her.

"When do you intend to run for president, Rosemary?"

Rosemary Hawkins, watching his earnest, sincere face, could think of no legitimate answer. She only extended her empty glass. He walked to her, took the glass back to the bar and refilled it. She came up to him, slipping one hand around his waist to get her drink. She seemed to be able to move about without making a sound.

"Thank you, J.R., for the drink. And for everything else. Now, unless you want to watch me undress, I have to get ready to see the President. Please wait outside. I'd like you to accompany me to his residence, and bring home afterward. Will you do that for me?''

She was removing her suit jacket, switching her drink from one hand to the other as she shrugged the jacket off her shoulder. He caught a fleeting glimpse of full breast barely contained in thin black silk, and then he was out of the office door, slamming it shut behind him. He still carried his fourth Cuervo Tequila rocks. He drank it down in a gulp and set the empty glass down on Rosemary Hawkins's private secretary's desk. His first impulse was to leave. He stayed. In so doing, he launched himself into the heros' hall of fame.

WASHINGTON, D.C.
THURSDAY, 10:30 P.M.

The limo rolled into and around DuPont Circle, heading out Massachusetts Avenue, moving leisurely toward the Vice President's residence on Naval Observatory Hill. Of course, he wasn't the Vice President anymore. It added to the adventure, in J.R.'s mind, and to his anxiety. The limo was unescorted. The Secretary Designate of the State Department was driven through the rain-washed streets of the nation's capital with no apparent concern for her health and safety. J.R. had visions of hand-held missiles, machine guns, bombs and bearded terrorists at every corner, all of them shooting at him because he was riding in a State Department car as if it were a Hertz rental.

"Are you nervous, J.R.?"

"No."

"That's good."

"I'm scared witless. Nervous is for amateur worriers."

"And you're a professional worrier?"

"That's correct. I am."

"I could give you reasons to worry, J.R. Wonderful,

complex reasons to worry. A conspirator behind every bush.''

"Pass.'' The word rolled off his tongue like vomit.

"Pass? Why pass? Don't you want to share my deepest fears? My most secret terrors?'' There was a lilting, laughing tone to her voice. Rosemary Hawkins feared nothing at all. A vain and stupid viewpoint, if you were a spy. J.R. frowned visibly.

"You are not happy, J.R. Why?''

"I was happy. Yesterday I was happy. I had this wonderful blond in my bed. I was leaving the country, to sell guns. At a profit, I might add. Then, without warning, Conrad Taylor died, and I got a new assignment. You. So I am not at all happy.''

"I'm sorry to inconvenience you, J.R. I'm sure if the President had been asked his preference, he would not have flown through that lightning.''

Stillborn, the flippant reply died on J.R.'s lips as he watched Rosemary Hawkins's face dissolve in tears, lines, and tragic loss, a dark portrait for him to see. The limo purred through the rain-swept capital while the most powerful woman in American political history collapsed into the arms of a reluctant CIA operative thrust by circumstance into a role he was perfectly suited for.

The limo sat at the curb, the windshield wipers beating a smooth, rhythmic tattoo against the wind-driven rain, isolating the interior of the car while at the same time embracing the street sounds, from a distance . . . the sound of power, the sound of privilege.

"Do you know Adrian Bennett, J.R.?''

J.R. looked at Rosemary Hawkins's tear-streaked face, trying to listen. Trying to serve. Trying to keep from falling on his ass.

"I know who he is. That's about all.''

"That's enough, I guess. A super patriot, 'old' Adrian. A hero. He has a hero son. Big-time fighter pilot. Medal of honor. A stay at the Hanoi Hilton. An Air Force wing commander, a valiant flyer of A-10s. Protecting this country from . . . from what? Aliens? Commies? Well, fuck him. Adrian Bennett walked into the President's . . . the President's . . .''

"Office?" J.R. was trying to be helpful.

"Yeah, his office. He tells William Rodgers to shit-can his Secretary of State, A.S.A.P., and what happens? William Rodgers, great thinker, says, 'Hey, Adrian, you're right! Soon, we must ask for the Secretary's resignation.' So of course the Secretary hears about this, and resigns. Now, little Rosemary becomes Secretary of State. Well, why not? C'mon, J.R., why not me?" She watched his face, looking deeper than he could shield. She switched on the interior lights, repaired her makeup, and then she slid out the door. She turned and leaned back inside, one hand resting on the limo roof. "You are an asshole, J.R., and you know nothing about politics. I would make a wonderful president. I'll be a lousy Secretary of State."

She walked away, her sleek hips draped in tight slacks, her walk signaling him, and leaving him without signals. J.R. slumped into the deep leather cushions of the limo. He switched on the overhead light and settled in to read the Thursday edition of the *Washington Post*. Twelve minutes later, he sat bolt upright, pulled a flask from his pocket, and took a long, jolting drink of cheap scotch. He studied the state department announcement very carefully.

From the Thursday *Washington Post*

The State Department, with the approval of the White House, this morning issued a partial list of foreign leaders asked specifically to attend President Taylor's interment, scheduled for Monday afternoon, beginning at 2:30 P.M., Eastern Standard Time. Also included in the list, compiled by the *Post* staff, are "expected" members of the administration and other prominent Americans.

President William Rodgers
U.S.S.R. General Secretary
British Prime Minister
French President

Israeli Prime Minister
U.S. Cabinet
   United States Senate
   United States House of Representatives
   United States Supreme Court
      U.S. Joint Chiefs of Staff
      Warsaw Pact Chiefs of Staff
      The Pope
      Prince Charles and Diana

The *Post* believes that approximately 250,000 citizens at a minimum will attend. 150,000 mourners are expected to fill and overflow around the special VIP bleachers erected for the funeral.

Selecting thoughts like color slides from a bad vacation, his mind began to register, and reach for, facts from a restaurant's lunchtime place mats. J.R. had a near photographic memory. He pulled a pen from his jacket pocket, and began to write down what he remembered. It was a slow, laborious process. But J.R. was like a man about to be struck by a train. Unable or unwilling to run away, he stayed on the track. His hands trembling, he began the transfer of random thoughts to the pages of the *Post*.

What emerged, in red ink, turned his heart to stone . . . the slide show in his mind went on in search of a name for the man with the silver hair. Found the name. Matched the name to the face. J.R. emptied the flask, capped it, put it away. The scotch flashed its hot way into his belly, and failed to warm him. What he was thinking was impossible. It was insane. Still, he would look into it.

The distance between the new President of the United States and his guest could be measured in two ways. In real distance, and in power. In real distance, they sat in separate, comfortable chairs approximately six feet apart and close to a roaring fire that warmed them both. In power, as a measuring tool, they were hardly close. He, after all, was the President. She, only the designated Secretary of State, had not yet taken a real job in his administration. So there was little doubt, and no question, who was the more powerful. She was, and William Rodgers knew it.

"How do you think it went, Rosemary?"

"How what went, Mr. President?"

" 'William,' Rosemary. Please call me 'William.' When we are alone, I mean."

"All right. William. And I think the speech went just fine. I thought you were very impressive. Very presidential." She lowered her eyes, and glanced at him. A nice touch. William Rodgers stared into the fire, a slight smile on his face, warmed by her words, flattered, excited, a small man in the big time, loving it and feeling guilty for having it, insecure and powerful and inept.

"I'm not Conrad Taylor, Rosemary. But I think, with your considerable help and insight, I'll be able to carry his programs forward. They will simply become my programs."

"I'm sure you can, Mr. President."

"William." He gave her what he thought was a sexy glance.

"Sorry. William. I'm sure you can bring his . . . our programs forward. There will be considerable resistance, I'm afraid. Primarily from our own party."

William Rodgers turned toward her, his face set in a toughness she had never seen before, a younger man's face, the Texas wildcatter that he once was. "Adrian Bennett gave me a heavy taste of that today. He was at my desk for twenty minutes before he called me 'Mr. President.' " Indignation was spread like melted cheese on the President's face. Rosemary Hawkins couldn't help it. She laughed out loud, stopped, extended her hand toward him, covered her mouth, and then laughed again.

"What? What did I say?" She noticed his nostrils flared when he was upset, like the bad guy chasing after Pauline in a silent movie. She suppressed her laugh, with considerable difficulty.

"I'm sorry, Mr. . . . William. I'm sorry. He called you 'Mr. President' when he got what he wanted, am I right?

He's a very arrogant man.'' She turned in her chair, toward him, crossing her legs.

"I would remind you, Rosemary, that getting what he wanted resulted in your being nominated for Secretary of State less than thirty minutes after the secretary's resignation. That must have driven Adrian Bennett to his fucking liquor cabinet!''

Steel. There was steel in him somewhere, she thought. "I don't know about his liquor cabinet, William. His gun cabinet, perhaps.''

"Let's hope not, Rosemary. He has a lot of guns.''

Rosemary smiled. Without a word, she got up, and walked across the gap between them. "Let's not talk anymore tonight.''

"Slow . . . slow down . . . oh . . . .'' Rosemary watched his face. Conrad Taylor could never wait either.

"I can't hold it. I can't stop . . . I can't.''

"Okay. It's all right. Go on. Let go. It's fine. You go now.'' Rosemary bore down, her slim, fine hips dancing from side to side, pulling him deep into her, clutching him, her tiny body a blur above him as she rocked forward, thrusting her breasts at his open mouth. He went rigid under her, his breath raspy and harsh, his chunky body straining upward, churning out of control, out of himself, pouring into her. She spread her legs wide, moving in tiny, jerky circles, shuddering through a climax, because she always climaxed, one of the lucky few, one of *those* women . . . and she fell across his upper body, tired, sweaty, heartbroken.

William Rodgers lay on his stomach, on the floor, his head propped on his hand, his lower body covered by an Apache blanket given to him during his first run at the U.S. Senate. He had lost that race, to no one's surprise. At no time in his life had he been more surprised than he was now. Sitting less than three feet away from him, naked from the waist down, her sweater still pulled above her taut breasts, her brow flushed and beaded with sweat,

Rosemary Hawkins lit two cigarettes, and extended one toward him, jabbing it in his mouth with practiced ease. She was still wearing high-heeled boots. Her camel hair slacks were tossed aside, one leg still inside out. A pair of champagne-colored panties hung over the top of her right boot. Her hair was wild and disheveled. He had never in his life seen anything more desirable, or more beautiful. She rested her back against a chair, one leg straight out, the other bent at the knee, the very center of her sexuality open to his view. She was completely at ease, sure of herself. She'd been a fantasy and now she was real. She was with him. She was flexing her leg. Open. Shut. Open. Shut. She pulled on her cigarette, her eyes a red blaze to match her hair, a woman so primitive, so sexual, he was afraid to speak, afraid he would wake up and she would vanish.

But she didn't vanish. He rolled toward her, and she shifted down, onto her back, her legs spread wide, pulling his face down, surrounding his head with her thighs, arching toward his tongue, her feet planted, taking in a way he'd never been taken. He wasn't good at this. His dead wife had hated it. He didn't know what to do. But it didn't matter. Her hands moved down, found his mouth, moved it, placed it.

"There. There. Yes. Suck it. Yes. There." And he grabbed her churning hips, trying to stay with her, losing it, capturing it, and finally, doing it right. She dissolved under his tongue, melting away in sleek alabaster skin and scent and sweat, her legs locked over his neck, her hands in the air, scratching at nothing, her mouth open and her eyes registering surprise. He felt like a god.

She'd been in the bathroom only a few moments, but when she came out, he was startled to see how unruffled she looked. Only moments before, she had been a wanton, sweaty and wet and clutching the back of his head as if she were about to die. She looked cool, and competent, and thoroughly like his Secretary of State Designate. He glanced at his watch. Incredibly, she had been with him less than an hour. She crossed the room to his side, giving him a cool kiss on the mouth, pressing her lower body against his for the briefest instant. Brief or not, he could feel the subtle grind, even after she pulled away and sat down. Her eyes were friendly, if not intimate.

"How did that happen, Rosemary? And what does it mean?" William Rodgers was thrilled, and proud and frightened, and mystified. An inexperienced man, reacting like a teenager, who, having seduced the homecoming queen, wonders how to keep her.

"It happened, that's all. I don't know what it means. It made me feel good, for a little while. It blotted out reality. Sex does that for me. Please, William, don't make more of it than it is. And don't be angry with me. I came here to talk politics. To chart a course. To stake a claim. Hell, I don't know! You fucked me! Isn't that enough?"

For the briefest instant, he thought she might strike him. He had no idea what to say. He went toward her, reached for her, but she turned away, stopped, turned back. "I must go, William. This looks bad. It is bad. Don't be angry with me. I took advantage of you. I'm sorry. All of this is crazy. But it felt good. It felt very good. I want you to know that." She swept up her coat, and was gone from the room before he could say anything. He watched from the window as she entered the limo waiting at the curb. As it pulled away, the car's rear window went down, and he saw her pale face looking back at him, her image distorted by the cold rain. Through a glass, darkly . . .

ROSEMARY HAWKINS'S RESIDENCE
SUBURBAN MARYLAND
THURSDAY, 11:50 P.M.

"You live in a weird house, Rosemary."

"Oh? Why do you say that? She handed him a crystal tumbler full of *expensive* scotch. A treat. A real treat. She was standing very close to him, studying his face. In three-inch heels, she was still four inches shorter than he was, a source of continual surprise. He still wondered how she could have such long legs.

"Because there is nothing in this house. It reminds me of a laboratory. Pristine. Sanitary."

"Sterile?" Her eyes were fixed on his, her drink suspended near her mouth.

"Yeah, sterile. Nobody lives here."

"You are very astute, J.R. Good-night. Please pick me up at seven A.M. tomorrow." With that, she turned away, walked down a hallway, and disappeared into what he assumed was her bedroom. He glanced around the room. Bare walls. Chrome furniture. Black and silver. There wasn't a trace of Rosemary Hawkins in the room. Quietly, he went from room to room, passing her silent bedroom, only a sliver of light shining at the base of her door indicating any life at all. All the rooms were alike. Cold. Efficient. Empty. If it was true that there is no place like home, then it was equally true that there was no home like this place. He didn't look back as the State Department's limo pulled away from the curb. What was there to see?

MYRTLE BEACH, SOUTH CAROLINA
THURSDAY, 2457 HOURS

"Colonel?" The controller's voice was diamond clear and professional. The Governor's son heard it without difficulty.

"Roger, Base. This is Eagle One."

"Personal, sir. Your father, when you get down." The disembodied voice sounded nervous.

"Roger, Base. One more run."

"Sorry, Eagle One. He said break in at all costs. Critical, I think he said."

"Roger, Sandy, I read. My father wants me to quit playing airplane. On my way." The controller said no more, only marveling that his commanding officer had known who he was.

The heavily laden A-10 swung wide, and swept in from the sea at 400 knots. As it dropped low over the air base, the invisible timer in Colonel Jonathan Bennett's mind registered his total accumulated flight time in the A-10 "Warthog" at 3,000 hours. In the most recently tabulated year, the 354th Tactical Fighter Wing, flying eighty A-10 aircraft, was officially listed as flying 32,478 hours. One man now had 10 percent of that year's total. He set the fighter bomber down on the runway as gently as a newborn baby.

DAY THREE: FRIDAY

MYRTLE BEACH, SOUTH CAROLINA
FRIDAY, 0800 HOURS

"Heading west today, Colonel?"

Jonathan Bennett glanced up from his coffee and his morning flight "capable" list, fixing a cold stare on his Deputy Commander. The number-two man in the wing looked suddenly very uncomfortable.

"Where did you hear that, Colonel Wolfe?"

"Sergeant Bracken is all over your plane this morning. Wing tanks and all. Just figured you were going west, that's all."

Jonathan Bennett shifted at once into his easygoing mode, the charm beneath the steel. "Pretty good deduction, Colonel. I'm going out to see my dad. He was taken ill in Washington last night, flew home, and called me. I need a training flight to put some hours on that new engine. So, like you said, I'm headed west. Watch the herd, will you?"

"You know I will, Colonel. Any particular orders?"

"No. Might be a good idea to check their pulse, though. I don't think Conrad Taylor had a lot of fans on this base. But except for their flight capabilities, I'm not particularly close to the pilots in this wing. You know that and you know the men. Stand down, if you think they need it. We'll gear up for full routine on Tuesday, after they bury that pacifist son-of-a-bitch."

"Not your kind of president, Colonel?"

"Nope. Not my kind."

"Your old man must have really hated him."

"My father and our late President were . . . political

opposites from the same party. That's what he used to say."

"The President?"

"My father."

"Oh. Right."

"I had no real political feel for Conrad Taylor one way or another. I'm a pilot, not a politician. But I didn't much care for him. Does that answer your question, Colonel? I won't miss Conrad Taylor."

"I didn't mean to pry, Colonel."

"I know that. But let me give you a bit of advice. When I move on, Colonel, you will most likely get the wing. At least, that will be my recommendation."

The colonel's face lit up with pleasure at the rare compliment from his C.O.

Jonathan went on, in a schoolmaster's tone of voice. "Stay out of politics, and stay in the air. Keep your pilots flying, and your aircraft flyable. That is the primary duty of a pilot in the United States Air Force. Nothing else counts."

Jonathan Bennett went back to his morning reports, sipping his coffee. Colonel Wolfe sat there for a moment, and then walked out, his step lighter than usual. Wing commander . . . it had a nice ring to it. He would talk to the men while the colonel was gone. See how they felt about the President's death. Stand down. Yeah . . . lighten up. The next C.O. would profit by being the exact opposite of Colonel Bennett.

Behind him, Jonathan Bennett watched the colonel's measured strides carry him away from wing headquarters, his image distorted through the dirty glass windows of the flight headquarters building. Jonathan set his coffee cup down, pulled his aviator glasses from his pocket, and headed out the door, a distant smile on his face. The colonel was a terrific paper shuffler, and a lousy pilot. He would never command the 354th Tactical Fighter Wing.

"I'm ready to roll, Tower." Inside the cockpit, the engine noise rose, the A-10 a wild thing, straining against a powerful leash, tethered to the ground by Air Force procedures and rules.

"Roger, Colonel Bennett. Wait one."

"Wait one, Tower. And one's enough." The wing commander was not a patient man.

"Roger, Colonel, one's enough, received." Fifty-five seconds later, the voice from the tower said, "Cleared to roll, Colonel. Departure time 0901 hours. Visibility three miles. Winds negligible. Ceiling 4500 feet. Good numbers, Colonel. Have a good flight. We'll look for you. We'll keep the lights on."

"Roger, Tower. On my way." Jonathan kicked the plane loose, moving steadily down the runway, loaded with fuel and carrying extra under his wings in drop tanks. The aircraft hugged the ground, the plane's mottled gray-green camouflage paint job making it look slower than it was. It rumbled down the runway and then leaped into the air, climbing steadily but slowly, until it disappeared into the cloud cover. As usual, when the wing commander was gone, the base breathed a collective sigh of relief. Wherever Colonel Bennett was, tension was high. The opposite was equally true. The 354th looked forward to an easy thirty-six hours.

The A-10 cruised westward at 22,000 feet, eating up the miles at a steady, if unspectacular pace. Jonathan Bennett loved to fly, and flying the A-10 was flying at its best. Flying now at its "droner" speed, as he called it, the A-10 was a mild thing. Attacking ground targets a few feet off the ground was something altogether different. With its formidable weapons system, the A-10 was a ground target's worst nightmare. Attacking troops or vehicles, the A-10 was truly the "Thunderbolt II." Officially, that is. The Air Force name, "Thunderbolt II," named after another legendary strike aircraft from WWII, had not stuck, unofficially. The A-10 was universally called the "Warthog," and the name fit the aircraft and its capabilities and appearance perfectly.

It was, to most people, an ugly airplane. Two huge jet

engines, mounted high over its rear fuselage, made it look ungainly on the ground, more like an airliner than a tactical fighter. It was straight, without curves. Its landing gear and main weapon were off center, which gave it a curious "walk" on taxiing the runway. It was very loud, and slow, and it looked ugly as a warthog. And like the warthog, it was ferocious, and powerful, and nimble beyond belief.

It could sustain massive battle damage and survive. Like all fighters, it had two of every system required to make it fly. But unlike other fighters, the Warthog's systems were separated, on opposite sides of the aircraft. Damage to one side did nothing. Hydraulics, electronics, whatever was needed to stay in the air was built to keep working. The best and surest way to take down a Warthog was to kill its pilot. Not an easy job. He sat in an armored cockpit encased in a bathtub of specially built steel, invulnerable to most air-to-air fire up to and including the Soviets' 23mm cannon. The Warthog had twin tails, but could stay in the air with one shot off. And with its gatling gun–type 30mm cannon, it could deal death with an untrumpable hand.

It could also carry an awesome quantity of bombs and missiles, as well as defend itself in air-to-air combat, even with much faster, "sexier" fighters.

When its pilot referred to it as "the droner" or "my lunch bucket" or "pokey pig," it was a given, having said that, he wouldn't trade it for any other aircraft in the defense department inventory. And if *you* called it a "droner," you'd better smile, because only Jonathan Bennett could call the A-10 the derogative nicknames. And Jonathan Bennett was the toughest man in the Air Force, in his and most anyone else's estimation you might talk to. Jonathan Bennett and the A-10 were cut from the same metal. Both were born to survive.

The F-4 Phantom rolled over and headed into the narrow valley outside of Hanoi, down once more to take out the small bridge the North Vietnamese used so often they put 10,000 workers in there to build it again in two weeks.

Captain Jonathan Bennett hated this particular bridge. He'd hit it three times in the past, and he knew it didn't hurt the slant-eyed little bastards very much. Two weeks. Big deal. And coming out of the valley and climbing, there were all those SAMs to run through, like flying through a cloud of explosive-tipped flying telephone poles, jinking left, jinking right, trying desperately to keep them off your tail. In the rear seat, his weapons officer, his extra eyes, would say, in his ridiculously calm voice, "Missile launched," and Jonathan would press the raptorlike Phantom to its evasive limits. During this phase of the flight his back seat man would talk calmly, but wet his pants. He called it missile piss.

But that was later. Now, on his strike run, he concentrated in his usual, single-purposed way. Kill the bridge. Kill the bridge. Twenty miles away, fifteen F-105s screamed down "Thud Ridge," drawing fire on their way to a diversionary attack on two more bridges. Captain Bennett's Phantom went into its lonely, solitary dive. Sixteen aircraft to get one rebuildable bridge. Who planned this shit, anyway?

The Phantom screamed downward, twisting and turning as it rushed at treetop level through the valley, antiaircraft guns winking below and above him as he flew toward the bridge only a few feet above the twisting, murky river below. The bridge, tiny from 25,000 feet, grew in his eyes to gargantuan proportions as he rushed toward it. In his headphones he heard the backseat man spitting numbers, ranges, heights, fire, rage, terror . . . and he pulled the Phantom skyward as he launched his missiles and released his bombs per the backseat man's instructions. The Phantom hurtled through the first updraft of smoke and fire, clearing the bridge by fifty feet as the bombs struck behind and almost directly below him.

On the bridge, men, women, and children moved supplies steadily to the south. He saw their faces, and forgot them in a rush of exaltation as they blew up and vanished in the fire he had so accurately laid. It was his 150th combat mission over North Vietnam. Like all the rest, it was successful. The Phantom whirled and spun upward, rushing away from the chaos below. This time, thanks to Captain Bennett's fearless attack, the bridge had been totally destroyed. Even the riverbanks were gone. It would take three weeks to repair, instead of two. Whoopee . . . the Phantom clawed to gain altitude, scratching its way into a startling blue, cloudless sky.

"Missile launched."

"Roger."

"Missiles launched."

"Okay."

"Number three."

"Holy shit!" He could see them, arcing skyward, slow but coming harder as they gained altitude. He slipped the first, dipped the second, danced the third, which passed him close enough to read the number 203 in red on its nose. SAMs. Bombs without brains. You showed your tail, they followed. You moved your tail, they went their merry way. Of course, if you didn't pick them up on launch, you were dead meat.

"Bernie?"

"Nothing, Captain. No lock-on. No launch. Let's get out of here."

"Hauling ass, Bernie, hauling ass."

It was at that very moment that the MIG-21, piloted by North Vietnam's first ace, pulled up on Captain Jonathan Bennett, and blasted the Phantom from the sky with an accurate burst of gunfire from less than 500 yards away, killing his backseat man. The MIG's 23mm cannon fire danced across the Phantom's canopy, blew Bernie's head off, and left Captain Bennett in a steep climb, the wind tearing at him through a gaping hole. He pulled the ejection seat release only seconds before the F-4 Phantom exploded and disappeared in an ever-diminishing, ever-slower display of pyrotechnics as it rolled over, fell apart, and dropped back to earth. Jonathan Bennett, unconscious, hung in his parachute harness, falling gently earth-

ward, into the not-so-welcoming arms of the North Vietnamese citizenry.

"Tell me about your childhood, Captain. Was it good? Were you a happy child?"

"Fuck you!"

"You are the son of a famous American, a man of great wealth, a man of power. Was it fun to be his son?"

"Fuck you."

"Aah . . . it was not fun. I understand."

"Fuck you." Jonathan didn't see the rubber hose swing forward. He didn't hear it. But he heard, and felt, his ribs crack.

"Fuck you, Captain Bennett. We'll talk again tomorrow. And every tomorrow. Until the end of time, or your death."

On his stomach, on the ground, doubled over, Jonathan Bennett could only watch the highly polished boots walk by, and away, out of his vision. It was the seventy-third consecutive day of interrogation. It was not over.

"So, Captain, your father taught you to fly, and you came here, to Vietnam, to kill Vietnamese. Is that correct?"

"Fuck you. I didn't say that."

"Oh, but you did. You did say that . . ." The interrogator, a man with no apparent rank, checked his notebook. "You said that in March. This is August. Did you lie?"

"Fuck you. Of course I lied."

"You did not bomb the Vietnamese?"

"Fuck you. No."

"Then how is it you were shot down?"

"Fuck you. I wasn't shot down. No slant-eyed shrimp in a MIG-21 could shoot me down!"

The interrogator smiled. For the first time, in 240 days, Jonathan Bennett was not struck with a rubber hose by a man he never saw.

* * *

"Why do you hate the Air Force?"

"Fuck you."

"Of course. But why?"

"The bridge. The stupid bridge."

"Seventy-six people died on that bridge."

"Fuck you. Fuck them."

"Of course."

"You bet, you bet."

"Of course. Fuck them."

"Right!"

"Why does your father say publicly that he hopes you are dead?" Silence. The captain could not, did not speak.

"He hopes you are dead. He said so. And your mother. She, of course, has been no help at all."

Jonathan lunged forward, was held, thrown back, beaten. His mother. His father. God, end this, end this, end thi . . .

"Are you better now? That was stupid, you know. We take no pleasure beating you. Shooting you down, that was our ultimate beating. This is the four-hundredth day of our talks. We would like you to read this. Sign this. Our talks will cease, if you do." The unranked interrogator extended his hand, a single sheet of typed paper held loosely between two fingers. Jonathan Bennett took it with great dignity, and tore it to pieces.

"Fuck you, General." The rubber hose rained down, cracking his ribs. End this . . . end this . . . end thi . . .

"What would you do, if we let you go? If we let you go home."

"I'd come back, Field Marshall. I'd come back and I'd fly a Phantom right up your ass."

"Sign this. We will send you home. To your mother, who died today. We could send you to her funeral. She died. Think about it."

"Fuck you, Corporal. I never had a mother." When his interrogators left, he sat in the dark hole that had been his home for 800 days. He cried, silently, emaci-

ated, beaten, indomitable . . . and, finally, a little bit insane.

He had hovered, somewhere between life and death, for nine days, racked by one of the hundreds of fevers available to him, a virus, a bug, a phantom illness too weird to describe. And she came to him, every day, wearing flowing white robes, holding him close, protecting him, shielding him from the dark, dominant force that was his father. And her face would dissolve, eyes wide, hair falling out, a taste of madness and decay about her, and he would scream into the tropic night, asking for a plane, a plane to fly away, to strike back, to redeem himself. He did not know, but it was the interrogator that wiped his sweaty brow. On the tenth day, the fever, like everything else in the captain's life, left him for good.

"So, she is dead, and you have survived. Are you ashamed, Captain? The war grinds down, and the United States withdraws. You will go home. A hero, I presume. Back to the Air Force. Or politics. Yes. Politics. That would suit you, and suit you well. Like father, like son."

This time, even the invisible guard with the rubber hose was too late. Jonathan Bennett had the interrogator's throat in his hands before anyone could move. He was denied his adversary's death by a crushing blow to the head, administered by the never-before-used third man in the room.

Seventeen days before his release, Captain Jonathan Bennett, U.S.A.F., signed the paper extended him by his longtime interrogator. By now, almost 900 days after his capture, the captain no longer had any idea who, or what, or why, he was. Up was down. Down was up. He hated everybody. He loved nobody. He had no idea of the international situation. He had no idea he would be free, along with the rest of the POWs in Vietnam. He knew nothing of politics, of trades, or trade-offs. He knew, in fact, only *that he had been through enough and could deal with no more.*

Back in the United States, his father, to quote his son's interrogator, was still repeating his "I hope he's dead" comment to any network that would listen. Not true, but effective. When the prisoners held by the North Vietnamese were finally released, Captain Jonathan Bennett was reunited . . . with war, and combat, and hatred. He went home to the United States, to the Air Force, to public adulation. But he left a vital portion of himself in a dark, dank hole in North Vietnam, where the interrogator brought forth, and embedded forever, a set of demons Jonathan Bennett would never eject from his personal cockpit.

The A-10 with the ace of spades painted under the pilot's cockpit ripped along the brushy draws of northern Texas, crossing into Colorado, headed up the map to Wyoming. Bobbing and weaving as if it were in combat, the heavy wing tanks slowed its progress by over eighty knots. Acknowledging the hindrance, the pilot punched them loose, spending $48,000 in the process. Jonathan Bennett, flying home to Papa, and to fate, could have cared less. The A-10 dropped lower, feeding on its full main tanks, lighter, faster, doomed to its pilot's commitment to whatever decisions were made in the wide open spaces of the west, decisions narrowed by the dark thoughts and ideals of a man that even a half century of public service could not moderate.

THE WHITE HOUSE
WASHINGTON, D.C.
FRIDAY, 8:00 A.M.

"What do you think?" Emily Taylor looked at her husband's longtime lover with bright, chipmunk eyes, in spite of the fact that she had not slept in the past twenty-four hours.

Rosemary Hawkins gave Emily a long, cold look, an appraisal, really. "I think you've done a terrific job, Emily. This is . . . this is really terrific! Conrad . . . I mean, the President would be very proud."

"Would he?" A small, pleading voice, a tiny squawk from a once powerful but now impotent and frightened woman.

"Yes, he would. The amphitheater is perfect. The Tomb of the Unknown Soldier is only a few feet away. Very symbolic. Very impressive."

"Do you really think so?" The pleading voice again.

"Yes. I really think so." The reassuring, lying voice again. Games people play, she thought.

"The superintendent said we—I mean, I . . . I mean . . ." Emily Taylor was suddenly, embarrassingly tongue-tied, and Rosemary cut in immediately.

"He said you could bury your husband anywhere you want, didn't he?"

"Yes. Yes. He . . . he said exactly that." Emily's eyes widened in surprise at her own words. Yes. He'd said that.

"Then do it. The amphitheater is perfect. It seats forty-five hundred in comfort, six thousand in a pinch. Let's figure the six, shall we?" Rosemary Hawkins's eyes were like molten rock, flashing change.

"Yes. Let's figure the six." And then the unspoken thought, Lead me, Rosemary. Lead me. Before I falter. And make a foo . . .

Rosemary interrupted, "Six it is. Well, then. Now, you must guide us, Emily. Conrad should be displayed, somehow. Don't you think?'' Like a good politician, Rosemary arranged Emily Taylor's thoughts in positive ways. She invited Emily to agree with her.

"What did Jackie do?" Emily's pleading voice dropped, shifted, lessened.

"What difference does it make what Jackie Kennedy did! For Christsake, Emily, Jackie sold a presidentially used pussy to a Greek thief! Why does it matter what she did?"

"But . . . but she, and John, Joh . . . ''

"Stop it, goddammit! She wore pillbox hats and expensive gowns by designers nobody ever heard of until she bought their clothes. Who cares? She's a Kennedy. She's a Bouvier. She's an Onassis! Who in the goddamn hell cares? Nobody! Nobody cares. Shape up! If you want to bury Conrad close to the amphitheater, then say so. Call the superintendent of the cemetery. Tell him what you want. He'll do it. Period. End of debate.'' Rosemary turned away, tears rushing down her cheeks, unnoticed, and unaccountable. Fuck it . . . His wife, oh God, his miserable, sad, barren wife . . .

"I want to ship Presidential Candidate out here."

"I beg your pardon?" Rosemary looked perplexed, but she wasn't.

"Our Derby horse. Presidential Candidate . . . I want to bring him here, for the funeral."

"Then you should bring him, of course."

"The asshole at Arlington is not happy about it. He says they must match."

"What? What must match?"

"The horses. The horses pulling the catafalque, and the horse with no rider. They must all be dark colored, or white, or gray. But no mix. It just isn't done." Emily gazed at Rosemary Hawkins, her eyes wide, pleading, seeking rebellion but unable to call the rebels to roll.

"You want Presidential Candidate to lead the catafalque?"

"Yes, I do." She said this with a hint of Kentucky steel.

"Say so, Emily! Tell them what you want. You want your husband's funeral service to be held in the amphitheater. You want him buried near the Tomb of the Unknown's. You want a racehorse in the funeral procession. Tell them you want a racehorse. *Your* racehorse. Let the powers that be deal with whatever you want. No! *Make* them deal with whatever you want."

Emily Taylor looked into Rosemary Hawkins's eyes, saw the truth, and picked up the phone.

The order went out, smooth, plain, in the clear. Air Force One lifted off the runway at 11:55 A.M. on Saturday, headed for Louisville, Kentucky. It returned in nine hours carrying a Kentucky-bred horse, and no less than seven human handler–trainers, and one jockey. He wasn't expected to race the high-strung Thoroughbred. He was expected to keep Presidential Candidate from killing anyone in a fit of temperamental flying hooves.

Emily Taylor and Conrad Taylor's lover pored over hundreds of photographs the superintendent of Arlington National Cemetery had sent to the White House.

"Emily, did you notice the inconsistency here? Or is it a constant?"

Emily, not wanting to appear stupid, arched her eyebrow, her "I understand, but you tell me" look.

"None of these photographs are from the air. I mean, we have no overview of Arlington."

Emily had *not* noticed. But she could damn well cover herself. She reached across the bed, blanketed almost completely by photographs. With an "in charge" voice, she barked into the ears of a downstairs phone operator, a young woman nearly defenseless with grief.

"Get me the cemetery, and ask them a simple, onetime question. Are there overviews of Arlington? And if not, why not?"

Emily glanced at Rosemary Hawkins, sensed approval, and cast her eyes downward. It was the exact physical

sequence she used before taking Conrad Taylor's swollen
cock into her mouth. Rosemary Hawkins had no cock, but
Emily reacted the same. In the face of power, Emily Taylor sank to her knees. She would have stood up tall and
straight, had she known what her demands had wrought
at Arlington National Cemetery. Power is what you think
it is. A voice, any voice, from the White House, has
power.

   "There aren't any. I mean, there just aren't any." The
assistant to the superintendent of Arlington National Cemetery was not looking very well. His pulse was high, his
face shallow and drawn, his health uncertain. As was his
job.
   "What do you mean . . . there aren't any? Do you
mean to tell me we have no overhead photos of Arlington?"
   "No. Of course we do. We just don't have what the
First . . . the former . . . the widow First Lady wants. We
have no photos, I mean, except in boo—"
   "Goddammit, can we give her what she wants?" The
superintendent was nearly apoplectic with anger.
   "No. Fuck no. No way, Chief." The deputy superintendent, satisfied he had given the only answer available
to him, spun on his heels, and walked away. There were
photos, most of them old, most of them *very* old. But there
were no photos that would help the First Lady of the
United States during her trial by sorrow.
   Later, after the funeral, the deputy to the superintendent
of Arlington National Cemetery would make himself
available, if he was needed. At the moment, ignorance
was bliss, or at the least, safe.

BENNETT EMERGENCY AIR STRIP
BENNETT, WYOMING
FRIDAY, 11:00 A.M.

Adrian Bennett sat in the open door of his Bronco II, one booted foot on the seat, the other dangling out the door, gathering snowflakes. He concentrated his gaze toward the southeast, looking intently into the overcast, waiting for the awkward shape of the Warthog to pop free of the gloom and land.

"Palmer, what do you have?" He glanced at the dignified-looking black male sitting next to him in the Bronco's spacious cab.

Palmer Jackson had been Adrian Bennett's "man" for over forty years. He pulled the radio headset off and glanced skyward. "Nothing, sir, since his last message. By my watch, we should be able to see him in five minutes, forty seconds. Mr. Jonathan is never late, Governor."

"Ten dollars?"

"Yes, sir, Mr. Bennett. Ten dollars."

"Bad bet, Palmer."

"Yes, sir. I know that." The two old men, both white-haired observers of the human condition at its best and worst extremes, stared intently into the southeast sky, trying to penetrate the snowy, leaden overcast. Five minutes later, the A-10 settled onto Wyoming soil, taxiing directly to the Bronco. The cockpit canopy split apart and opened, and Jonathan Bennett loosened his harness and stood up, jamming an ugly black cigar between his teeth. The twin engines wound down, and the field was draped in a snowy quiet.

"Who won, Dad?"

"Who do you think?" Adrian Bennett slammed the door shut and waited for his son to climb down and join him for the sixty-mile trip to the ranch house. Next to him his "man" smiled into the wintry gloom. By his reckoning, Adrian Bennett now owed him $57,850. Five more years of winning pretend bets and he could pretend to retire.

The Bennett ranch was tucked away in a rock canyon, its back to a sheer cliff and its single road visible for miles before the house itself was visible. It had only one way in and one way out. The building and its surroundings spoke volumes about the builder. He had built the Bennett ranch home as a statement of his independence and defiance of conventional thought. The house reminded everyone who visited it of a bunker.

BENNETT RANCH
FRIDAY, 1:00 P.M.

Adrian and Jonathan Bennett were in the trophy room of the sprawling ranch house, surrounded by Boone and Crocket record heads of every antlered species hunted by man. Seven varieties of big cat snarled out from wall plaques, and one, a Brazilian leopard, crouched, muscles gathered, poised to leap in a display of taxidermy excess that had cost the senior Bennett $15,000. The room was over seventy feet long. Every major big-game animal was displayed, surrounded by perfect examples of "minor" animals. Adrian Bennett was a world-renowned big-game hunter, a hunter after a new trophy. For this new trophy, he needed a special weapon.

"Tell me, Jonathan, what are your thoughts about our new President?"

"My thoughts don't matter, Dad. I'm just a pilot. I'm happy, as much as I can be happy. What the hell, he's not going to take the 'Ace of Spades' away from me."

"No. No, he's not. He's going to take away your reason to fly, not your method of flight. He's going to give this country, and what it has always stood for, to Rosemary Hawkins! And she will sell us out, totally.''

"I have no thoughts, Dad. Should I?''

"Yes. You should understand what Conrad Taylor's death means to the United States. It means the abdication of world supremacy. The surrender of world leadership. The disappearance of American society as we know it, in a white-hot, nuclear holocaust!''

"You told me the same thing, Dad, when Conrad Taylor was alive. He's dead. End of problem.'' Jonathan Bennett waved his hands dismissively, his face hidden behind a screen of cigarette smoke.

"Rosemary Hawkins is not dead. The leader of the Soviet Union is not dead. The Speaker of the House is not dead. Conrad Taylor is dead, yes. But his goals are very much alive. Rosemary Hawkins has our new president by the cock. She will suck him into whatever she wants.'' Adrian Bennett's eyes glowed like hot coals, glaring, narrowing, boring into his pliant son's soul.

"Well, so what, Dad? So he's fucking his Secretary of State. Sex in the White House is not exactly news. Let's assume that Conrad Taylor, given the chance, would have eventually sold this country down the river. And now he's dead. Dead as can be. Shit, Dad, excuse my impertinence, but you are baying at the moon like a cougar hound without a treed cat. William Rodgers is not Conrad Taylor!''

"He is, as long as Rosemary Hawkins is alive.''

"Really? Christ, it sounds like you would feel safer if she were dead. And William Rodgers too. And what the hell, why not the Soviet President? How about the Joint Chiefs of Staff? How about the . . . '' Jonathan Bennett looked across the granite-floored room, surrounded by dead animals in lifelike poses, and watched Adrian Bennett's eyes close into tiny, slate blue slits. Of course. That was exactly what he wanted.

"It can't happen, Dad. Right or wrong, you can't make it happen. William Rodgers is the President of the United

States. Rosemary Hawkins is the Secretary of State Designate. We're stuck, right?''

"No, we are not stuck. There is a way."

"What? What way are you talking about?"

"You. You are the way. You can fix it, and save our country." Adrian Bennett's gaze turned on his son like a weapon. A cold fist began to gather somewhere deep in Jonathan Bennett's consciousness.

"Fix it? Fix what? With what? I'm an Air Force wing commander. Nothing more." The words left a sour taste in his mouth, a vague, rusty taste. He was aware of the rapid trip-hammer of his heartbeat.

"You are much more, Jonathan. You are my son. And you have suffered. *I read the confession transcript!*" He said this in a tone of a man catching his son masturbating in church. Jonathan could identify the taste now. It was tropic heat, and monsoons, and guilty fear.

For the briefest instant, all the antlered trophy animals seemed to dip and bow toward Jonathan, their horns accusatory and dangerous, aiming at his soul, his past, and outliving his future. He blinked, once, twice, and they returned to their mute stations, currency cashable only among shooters. At that moment, Jonathan Bennett knew exactly what he had to do, and more important, what his father knew. *He had read the transcript.* Adrian Bennett, the master of Jonathan Bennett's life, knew, and had proof, that his son was a coward. A traitor. A man honored by his country and his peers, who had finally betrayed his mission. The facts had not gone public. But Adrian Bennett, his father, had the facts. Jonathan Bennett, unable to resist, slipped back in time, back to his interrogation cell, awaiting his father's command.

"You didn't know I'd seen that confession?"

"No."

"I received it seventy-two hours after you signed it. I was very proud of you."

"Proud . . . ?"

"Yes, proud. You lasted hundreds of days. I knew you would cave in, of course. But you did last, quite a bit longer than I thought you would."

"Last? I lasted quite a bit longer than you thought I would? Well, fuck you, Dad!" Jonathan Bennett propelled himself from his chair, much like he flew the A-10, violently near the edge, but still in tenuous control.

Adrian Bennett watched his son storm around the trophy room, ripping mounted heads from the wall, kicking over stuffed trophies, arranged in dioramas, smashing at the mute symbols of his father's skill with rapid-firing weapons. In a final burst of frustration, Jonathan Bennett tore an eight-point set of antlers (the number-three Boone and Crocket record holder) from the wall, and hurled it overhand at his father. The rack bounced precariously close, but wide of its mark. Jonathan screamed at his father, "God damn you! What do you expect of me?" But he knew. Even as he asked, Jonathan Bennett knew what his father would say.

Adrian Bennett, free of the cuteness of father-to-son subterfuge, answered directly, and truthfully: "I want our new President dead. As a bonus, I want to rid the world of everybody in the international game that he, and particularly Rosemary Hawkins, play. I want them dead. And I expect you, and the 354th, to make it happen. Put at its bluntest, I want you to fly an air strike on Arlington National Cemetery during our fallen President's funeral. I want our new President and all who attend to die."

Jonathan Bennett was very drunk. For over three hours he had chugged vodka from two bottles, until he was virtually unable to talk. He sat on what passed for the front porch of the Bennett ranch, a forty-foot-long, inadequately roofed slice of the house, thrust awkwardly into the November weather, roofed, but without protection from the western winds that roamed the ranch year-round at twenty miles per hour. While he drank, he watched the wind-driven snow pile up against the four six-inch-wide posts that held up the porch roof. It was like watching a twenty-year-old's once slim sexy legs, displayed in their sleek originality, getting suddenly fat calved and thick ankled, losing their sexuality, turning old, and uninteresting, and dead. Dead . . .

Jonathan Bennett wanted, at this moment, to make his father happy. Of course, to accomplish this familiar requirement, he would have to order the 354th Tactical Fighter Wing into combat against the most sacred military cemetery in the world. Well, okay. He knew his father *said* the 354th Tactical Fighter Wing. What he *meant* was Jonathan Bennett and the Ace-of-Spades A-10. One plane. One goal. One horrible, terrible punctuation mark on a family's lifetime of national service. Bomb the funeral. Kill the funeral goers. Change the world! Well, fuck it. He had confessed to worse. And, worse yet, his father knew it.

While Jonathan Bennett drank himself into a stupor on the ancient back porch, his father sat in the trophy room at a large table, cleaning guns that hadn't been fired in years. Adrian Bennett considered guns tools, and like all tools, maintenance was an important factor in their longevity and usefulness. He had not bothered to repair the damage done to the room during his son's violent assault on . . . on what? With Jonathan, you could never be sure. All his life, he had exploded in violent anger, terrifying to watch, but relatively harmless. Of course, he had beaten his mother, but Lily could be a real strain at times. What crazy person wasn't?

Adrian reached for the short brass cleaning rod, its ivory carved handle showing signs of wear after forty years, the snarling wolf's head smooth and less threatening now, its harsh eyes softened and yellowed. He glanced down the Colt's barrel, rammed another unnecessary patch through it, followed by one with a slight coating of oil. In seconds, he put the .45 back together, his slim, long fingers sure as he popped a fully loaded clip into the butt, ramming a round into the chamber. He left it cocked, but slipped the safety to the on position.

In seventy years of shooting, he had never had an accidental firing. The .45 had gone off in the house once. But that had been no accident. No, Lily had definitely wanted to kill him. Behind the paneled wall of his private upstairs study, seven bullets were embedded in the original log wall. He had looked at them—irregular, splintered holes—and decided to leave them there. He'd replaced the paneling, and two days later, he had placed Lily in a very expensive home for the terminally weird and other assorted and certifiable loonies. She had luxurious accommodations and twenty-four-hour psychiatric nursing. It had been costing him forty thousand dollars a year, and then, blessedly, she died in 1973, heavily restrained, tied to her bed, eyes bulging, attempting to kill Adrian Bennett even as her son languished in a Vietnamese prison. She had pulled so hard against her restraints that three nurses in the room, fearing she would break something, had rushed to her bedside. She'd screamed something unintelligible, and then in a clear voice she had said, "You're a son-of-a-bitch, Adrian. God help Jonathan." Then, she simply lay back in bed and died. Her heart just stopped. Adrian, true to his nature, was unmoved. "Send her body to my ranch. Send me your final bill." And that had been that.

Adrian slipped the shiny .45 into its worn holster and pushed it aside, reaching for an already sparkling clean Colt Python with a ten-inch barrel. It was one of his favorite hunting handguns. Scoped, it could easily reach out and take the coyotes that roamed the ranch, from 200 yards away. He liked to shoot them on his trips around the ranch, sitting in the front seat of the Bronco, resting the gun on the Bronco's open window. Adrian Bennett derived considerable pleasure from his weapons. Shooting them. Shooting *things*. Cleaning the weapons. Like now. It cleared his mind. He thought more clearly with a gun in his hand.

Lily had hated guns. He'd swept her off her feet back

east, on a trip to buy horses, because he had the money and he needed the stock. She'd fallen for the rangy, whip-thin westerner the minute she'd met him, defying her family and going with him, totally unprepared for the harshness of life with a western politician.

The women hadn't helped either. Adrian Bennett, most of the time, couldn't "get it up." For all his macho posturing, he needed to go to absurd lengths to complete sex. Lily, virginal and homesick, was led into deeper and deeper flights of sick fantasy, dressing up, acting out, trying anything her husband proposed, until finally, during a particularly disgusting coupling, Jonathan was conceived.

After that, Adrian Bennett sent out for his women and brought them into her home, her bed, even on her living room floor. During Adrian Bennett's search for an answer to a humiliating sexual dysfunction, Lily tried to raise Adrian's child, while avoiding Adrian. His secrets unknown to the public, he rose in politics. In their private life, he abused and debased his wife every day, until, finally, she wanted to kill Adrian. She blamed him for her son's hatred of her, his total rejection of his mother's love.

She was right. Adrian Bennett had taken his son the way he did most things, outside of sex. With power and persuasion, and, in this case at least, love. Adrian Bennett loved his son, insofar as he was capable of the emotion. *Possessed* would have been a better word. Adrian Bennett possessed his son. In the process, he destroyed his wife.

Jonathan's Vietnam experience completed the family's destruction, and Adrian's plans for the funeral at Arlington would simply make it public, and therefore official. For half a century, even in the sparkling glow of a life of public service, the senior Bennett had constructed a life invisible to the public. For fifty years, moving along the corridors of power, he had kept his personal corridors dark. In this endeavor, he had been completely successful.

Sitting on the back porch, drunk, was Adrian's most finely tuned and cared-for weapon. He need only pull his son's trigger, and the amphitheater at Arlington National Cemetery would become a charnel house, incinerating his enemies, and altering the world's power structure forever.

With brisk, clean strokes, Adrian polished the gleaming, satiny blue finish of the Colt Python. He was whistling, not some western ditty, but "Clair de Lune." A cultured, well-read shaper of American ideas and values, Adrian Bennett was a fraud of monumental proportions, yet he was not insane. No panel of psychiatrists would find him so. He was evil. And there is no test for that. He was universally thought of as a national treasure. No national treasury was ever more bankrupt . . . Some said he should be on a national monument, like Mount Rushmore. If his craggy face should ever be carved into a mountain, the only fitting likenesses near him would have to be John Wilkes Booth, Lee Harvey Oswald, and Sirhan Sirhan.

DAY FOUR: SATURDAY

M.C.A.S.
YUMA, ARIZONA
SATURDAY, 0750 HOURS

Jason Kelly opened his eyes and immediately clamped them shut again. A white pain began at the back of his handsome head, turning yellow as it rolled past his ears, finally changing bright red as it settled over his left eye. Hangovers, in the young pilot's method of calculation, were either white (back of the head), yellow (your ears), or red (over his terribly bloodshot eyes). This one, this morning, was a very different red alert. It was different because a full colonel was standing over his bunk in the BOQ (Bachelor Officers Quarters), puffing on a ridiculous, drooping meerschaum pipe, the tiny glow from its rustic curved bowl throbbing with light in the predawn gloom.

"I told them you were the wrong choice." The pipe bowl flared, its tiny fire accelerating like a PBS show on Hawaiian volcanoes.

"Sir?"

"I told them you'd get shitface and fucked up, and you did."

"Sir?" Jason's mind, linked tenuously to his lips, could offer no more.

"Your squadron mates! The young lieutenants we flew out of here last night without you, because you are supposed to be a fire breather and all, and therefore best equipped to fly a factory B Harrier out of here without pranging the son-of-a-bitch." The pipe fire glowed orange. The colonel's voice was perfectly pitched, accented with an English, or Australian, or . . . or what?

117

"Pranging, sir?" The red alert hangover went nuclear, his brain lanced with tequila-revenge lightning bolts. "I'm not sure I understand *pranged*, sir." A new pain trucked around behind his eyes, dribbling down into his teeth.

"Wreck. Crash. Fall out of the sky. I served with the British. Four years. I picked up their slang before you could *spell Harrier!* Bad habit, I know, for a man born in Iowa. *I* know it's an affectation. *You* know it's an affectation. The difference is, of course, *our rank*. I am a colonel, sober and alert, who has had his breakfast. You are a lieutenant. A very junior one, I might add. It seems you threw up your breakfast! *You* had enchaladas and tacos for breakfast, about three hours ago. Most of it went into your shoes. Hit the fucking deck, Kelly! In three hours, you are going to fly that spanking-new, factory-fresh, prime example of Marine Corps aviation 2400 miles! If you prang it, I will personally hunt for your miserable body and beat it to a pulp! Count on it!" The pipe, and the colonel with the British accent, vanished from Jason Porter Kelly's view. His headache went thermonuclear, redder than red . . .

Jason stared into the mirror, marveling that he could still see. Anything. Just fucking anything at all. Face it. Jason Kelly, Irishman, could not drink. Not even a little bit. A dark, pretty face waved at him, disappeared, returned, waved again. Milky white breasts, plunging, oh God, plunging neckline full of . . . of . . . tits! Oh my God, she was, she was . . . what? He couldn't remember. He whipped the Mickey Mouse toothbrush around in his mouth, somehow spattering his hairless chest with fluoride power in red-flecked, yummy-tasting spatters. Oh shit. Oh shit. How had he done this? God! She'd had him by the . . . no. Had she? Oh yes she had. She'd had his fly open, he was throbbing down there, her tongue was in his . . . In his what? Oh, right (brush, brush, spit), her tongue was in his ear, making a kind of slurpy sound, a sucking, a sucking sound that was (brush harder, spit, toss Mickey's smiling black-eared face into the sink). Oh, shit, she'd said. She'd said, "Oh, Jasoon, Jasoon babee, do you know what theese blond-haired Irishman do to me? They make me craazy!'' And then she'd popped it out, and bent over, and he'd . . . he'd . . . thrown up. He'd thrown up on her Mexican peasant blouse, just as she'd . . . oh. Shit. Oh Jesus holy shit. Pranged! Oh yes. He'd pranged all right.

The red glow, darting from eye to eye, stopped. After last night, pain, simple pain, was nothing. Jason Porter Kelly had thrown up on a woman as she was about to prove there were no cultural differences between an Irishman in heat and a Mexican national with breasts larger and more efficient than the thrusters on a Harrier. Her mouth . . . oh my, Jason, you most assuredly did prang yourself. He stood under the shower, letting the cold water beat at his body until the pain went from red, to yellow, to white.

He was stupid. He was young. He was immature. But after his long shower, he was once again the best pilot in his squadron. The factory-fresh Harrier stood on its hardstand, waiting for him. The desert temperature began to climb. The young pilot, skilled and well trained, had suffered a terrible blow to his manhood, to his image—but like many gifted people, he was also lucky. The lady with the "thruster" breasts had no less than three social diseases. Any one of them would have pranged the shit out of him. It is sometimes better to throw up and lose, than never to throw up at all.

WASHINGTON, D.C.
SATURDAY, 9:00 A.M.,
EASTERN STANDARD TIME

J.R. finished his third cup of coffee, waiting for Rosemary Hawkins to end her meeting with the eight senators she knew would oppose her confirmation as Secretary of State. Six of the eight were members of the Senate Foreign Relations Committee—in other words, they held the keys to her State Department kingdom. J.R. figured she had no chance at all, not one. They would listen, but they would not listen. She was not one of the "old boy" network. Rosemary had chosen the Library of Congress for the meeting, a choice J.R. thought was weird, to say the least.

Washington was closed, blanketed in mourning cloth and about to host a hundred or so of the most important leaders in the world. And here she was, in an obscure reading room of the library's basement, trying to turn water into wine. Fat chance. There wasn't a single yea vote in the room with her. The committee would send the nominee to the full Senate with a negative recommendation. The Senate, in its duty to advise and consent, would overwhelmingly vote against her. So J.R. thought. Meanwhile, in the reading room, five of the negative voters were going positive.

J.R. was a terrific spy, and a lousy political observer. No matter. Right now, being a good spy was beginning to seem very important to him. He'd read the list of foreign dignitaries scheduled to begin arriving in Washington. Everybody, it seemed, had loved Conrad Taylor. Topping the list, and arriving the earliest, was the President of the Soviet Union. Sunday afternoon would have been early enough. He was coming tonight. By Sunday night, the city would be a security nightmare. Jesus. All these things worried him.

What worried him the most he had yet to say out loud. But he was convinced he was right. The funeral was going to be attacked, probably by terrorists. But how? He'd sent out a dozen requests for information. Random, hunch-type questions on every known freako in the terrorist world. On the wildest hunch of all, he'd asked for a file on Adrian Bennett, the man with the white hair who liked to doodle on place mats. As an afterthought, he'd asked for a check on Adrian Bennett's son. At this moment, a C.I.A. messenger was entering the library with a bulky package for J.R. Kelly. In it was everything he'd asked for, spit out, copied, faxed, wrapped, and tied by the legion of machines that serve the United States Government intelligence agencies. Included in the package was a picture of

Adrian and Jonathan Bennett, standing near a wicked-looking A-10 fighter, warthog tusks painted on its nose, and above that fierce visage, the Ace of Spades. When he saw that picture, an improbable scenario would harden in J.R.'s mind.

The two men, father and son, looked perfectly natural in the photo. Proud father, hero son, an American family worth twenty pages in the history books. Combined with the phone call he would get from his younger brother later on this Saturday, this package would make J.R. Kelly a candidate for the funny farm. And more. Much, much more . . .

BENNETT EMERGENCY AIRSTRIP
BENNETT, WYOMING
SATURDAY, 9:50 A.M.

The wind sock at the private airstrip serving the Bennett Ranch hung limply in the cold, gray air of the late November morning, fitfully stretching, fluttering, indicating a capricious wind as gusts came from nowhere and no direction, only to disappear. The Ace-of-Spades A-10 shuddered as Jonathan Bennett turned her engines on, invisible behind the dark plate of his helmet's face mask. He watched the relatively simple gauges, but mostly, he "felt" the A-10, knowing when the Warthog was ready to go, when it was unnatural to keep it tethered to the earth, knowing it would shake itself to pieces if he didn't hit the pedals and the throttle and let it fly. He glanced out, to the left of his wingtip, at the dark, brooding (was it? yes, it was brooding) Bronco II, his father's face stark under the brim of his white Stetson, and next to him the dark face of the faithful Palmer, hidden in the gloom behind the Bronco's wheel, old eyes watching the A-10, listening to its pained howl, the voice of a living thing to Palmer, not the howl of a machine. Secretly, he prayed it would crash, and he felt no guilt at all for the thought.

M.C.A.S.
YUMA, ARIZONA
0958 HOURS

"Tower?" The pain in his head throbbed on, but only on the white level.

"Roger, seven one four." The crisp voice from the tower accelerated the pain, raising it to the next color. Jesus, turn down the volume!

"Am I clear to Cherry Point?" Oh, Jasoon, babee . . .

"Roger, seven one four. Don't prang it, now." A sarcastic tower man.

Funny shit. Very funny. Jason punched the Harrier free, calling the tower as he began to roll. "Roger, Tower. Seven one four, out." The crisp, spanking-new AV-8B Harrier II burst down the blisteringly hot runway, leaving the Arizona heat behind, ascending heading to Angels Twenty, his designated altitude. Lieutenant Kelly's wheels lifted off the runway in ninety-four feet, a new textbook (VSTOL) takeoff. He did not prang his kite. Defying his aircraft's stated climbing rate, he leveled off at twenty thousand feet, six minutes faster than it had ever been done before.

BENNETT EMERGENCY AIRSTRIP
BENNETT, WYOMING
SATURDAY, 10:00 A.M.

Adrian Bennett exited the cab of the Bronco II, walking toward the A-10, his eyes fixed on its pilot, his son, his weapon. In the cockpit, the helmeted head of his son turned toward him, rotating slowly, automated, the painted Ace of Spades stark against the black helmet. Adrian could not see beyond the smoked glass of the pilot's visor, but he thought he saw . . . he thought he . . . the head snapped forward, the twin jets howled, hurling the dry layer of

snow on the runway into a thick dirty white cloud as
Adrian Bennett turned away, holding his hat, failing to
keep it on his head, watching as it blew away like a rolling
tire, pushed by the jet's exhaust, bouncing, bounding.
Gone in the milky white fury of snow and black fuel exhaust and wind that tore at him, forcing him to lean into
the wind to keep from falling, his clothes flattened against
his slim, ridiculously tall and bony frame.

Silence. The A-10 was gone, with not even a whisper
as it thrust into the brushy draws, ripping along the rocky
terrain at a suicidal 400 feet, its pilot beyond thought,
beyond fear, beyond caring. It was only Saturday, but the
mission against Arlington National Cemetery, and its
memorial amphitheater, had begun.

Adrian Bennett walked slowly back to the Bronco, suddenly tired, suddenly aware of his eighty years. With considerable effort, he hauled himself into the front passenger
seat, slamming the door behind him, as a wind-driven
blanket of gray snow rose from nowhere and lashed the
Bronco hard enough to set it rocking.

"Well, man, let's get it going." Palmer Jackson looked
at Adrian Bennett for a long time. It was not the look of
a faithful servant. He opened the driver's side door, got
out and walked to the passenger side, yanking the door
open and nearly causing Adrian Bennett to fall out. He
had the stony look of an Easter Island statue.

"Palmer? Palmer Jackson! What the hell has gotten into
you?" Adrian looked into the familiar black face, but he
could see only old eyes, full of heat, coals, fragile and
long-burned, but refusing to go out.

"No bet, then, Palmer. Is that it?"

The eyes glowed, turned brighter, shifted, went out.

"No bet, Adrian. No bet. You drive." A voice from a
tomb . . .

In forty-seven years, Palmer Jackson, Adrian's man, had
never called his employer "Adrian." Without a word,
Adrian Bennett shifted to the driver's seat, and waited for
Palmer Jackson to close the door. He punched the clutch
and headed back to the Bennett ranch. The heater was on,

but it only hummed, factory built warmth. The air was cold, distant, alien.

"You owe me fifty-seven thousand eight hundred and fifty dollars." As he said this, the black face of Palmer Jackson was turned, no . . . pointed, at Adrian Bennett.

"Are you sure of that?"

"As sure as I am of anything."

"I'll write you a check."

"No. No check. Cash." Divorce. Finally. Palmer wanted a divorce.

"Of course. Cash. I have it at the ranch." The blue-light special. Down the hall, behind all the dead animals.

"Yes, I know." The Bronco bounced across the vast acreage of the Bennett Ranch, pulling two old friends to the end of the line.

WASHINGTON, D.C.
SATURDAY, 10:00 A.M.,
EASTERN STANDARD TIME

Rosemary Hawkins had made her pitch, and the senators, convinced and unconvinced, had gone their way. Now, sitting on the edge of a table, her hands clasped around her knees, looking very much like an innocent teenager, she fixed her dark eyes on J.R.

"So, how did it go?" A polite question and a safe one, too. J.R. preferred safe questions.

"It went very well, considering." Her eyes invited further questions.

"Considering what?" His eyes said, *I'll ask the questions, tell me no lies*.

"Considering the total brainpower of the esteemed members of the Senate Committee on Foreign Relations is somewhere near a busted zit, it went the way I'd hoped." She rested her chin on her knee. Very appealing.

"And which way was that? I mean, which way had you

hoped it would go?'' The sarcasm in J.R.'s voice was obvious.

''That is no mystery, is it, J.R.? I'm going to be the
first female Secretary of State. To that end, the meeting
went as I hoped it would.''

''So you changed their minds about you.''

''No, not quite that.''

''Then what?''

''I recruited them to the cause.''

''That is plain, pure bullshit, Rosemary.''

''True. It is. But it's *prime* bullshit. And if you can give
a senator prime bullshit, he will happily get it all over his
shoes.'' In spite of himself, J.R. laughed out loud. Rosemary Hawkins was his kind of politician.

The limo moved away from the library, one of many
moving like milk trucks, from place to place, distributing
wisdom, seeking truth, grasping for power. All this, because a perfectly maintained helicopter had flown through
an act of God and come out less than godly. Oh, how the
machinery turned. How the power shifted. How the grasp-
ers reached for what they could only dream about. Limos,
wandering aimlessly, but dead on aim.

''Whose bright idea was it to have the ceremony for
Conrad Taylor in the fucking amphitheater?''

''You don't approve?'' Rosemary said this without looking at him. She was staring out the window, watching a
cold, empty Washington slide by. Business had stopped,
but no one had gone fishing.

''No. I don't approve. All that brass, in one cupcake
pan. Jesus, it's a security nightmare.'' He gave her a sincere, C.I.A. look.

''I didn't know you cared, J.R.'' Her silken legs
crossed, flew apart and crossed again.

''That shit does not work on me.'' His voice cracked
like Kermit the Frog's.

''What shit, J.R.?''

"That. The crossed-legs shit. It doesn't work."

"Yes, it does." She was right. It did.

"What's the problem, J.R.? Emily Taylor wants her husband celebrated. I agree. He should be celebrated. But for a tragic accident, he would have been the most important president in our history."

"So what you're telling me is, you loved him, right?"

"Right."

"And you are determined to carry on with his programs, is that also correct?"

"Yes. That is correct."

"Then call Emily Taylor, and suggest that the funeral be held in a place less susceptible to attack than the amphitheater."

"No. I can't do that."

"Sure you can."

"All right. What I really mean is, I won't do that." Her face turned toward his. Molten eyes locked on his, her body leaning toward him. Sleek legs mixed with a sleek mind used to getting her own way. She was electric.

J.R. turned away from the heat, from the temptation, from the bright flow of enormous power. For a smart broad, she was missing a very central question. "Will you do me a favor, Rosemary?"

"If I can." The rustle of silken thighs, the skirt riding up, the intense look. It was wasted on J.R. this time. A feeling of unthinkable doom clamped down on him. All kinds of hell was on its way, if he could just identify it.

"Tell Emily Taylor the amphitheater is a mistake. Tell her it is a monumental security risk. Tell her . . . tell her she's a stupid bitch. Tell her whatever you want. But she must change her funeral plans." J.R. Kelly felt like a complete ass. His job was to make sure Rosemary Hawkins was okay. That was it. Who the fuck did he think he was? Rosemary Hawkins surprised him with her reply.

"Okay, J.R. If you think it's important, so do I. I'll speak to the widow if you like."

"Will you? And what will you tell her?"

"I'll tell her my key advisor in foreign affairs, or, for that matter, any affairs, has advised me to stop the official train, before we all run off the track."

J.R. watched her face, looking for the mockingbird. What he saw was an American eagle.

"Thank you."

"My pleasure," she said. But he doubted that.

THE WHITE HOUSE
SATURDAY, 11:00 A.M.

Emily Taylor, for the first time in her sheltered life, firmly believed that she, and she alone, was in control. In control of everything. Her secretary had carried a large box of telegrams and letters into the upstairs private quarters, that were hers for a while, and only hers. Seventy thousand telegrams and letters. It was not possible to walk through her bedroom. His. His bedroom. Had it been hers? No. It had never been hers. It had never been their bedroom, truly told. But who told the truth in Washington, D.C.? Nobody. Not since old Abe, the last, great, true president. Oh, Conrad, you sexy son-of-a-whatever. You didn't know, did you? I can handle this shit! Well, most of this shit. She was, after all, only the First Lady, once removed. (Removed by the 14th Street Bridge, and if she was ever asked, she would dynamite the fucker into outer space.) The *look* on the face of the man from the Library of Congress! Oh, what a precious moment that was. He'd put his hands together, his fingers flexing, the spider on the mirror.

"Surely, Mrs. Taylor, you don't mean to have the burial ceremony in the amphitheater? It . . . it has a *number*, a true *number* of reasons against its selection. It is too close to the Tomb of the Unknown Soldier. It will cause considerable difficulties. Surely, you understand. Now, I have proposed the following schedule, much like the Kennedy funeral, and I think we should—"

"Fuck the Kennedys." Yes. She had said that. Fuck the Kennedys. "This is a *Taylor* funeral. I say he goes into the amphitheater. If you don't like the idea, I'll find some hick from Kentucky to advise me." And thatta had been thatta . . . The Librarian of Congress, the keeper of a nonexistent National Seal, had allowed the wax to melt away.

THE ACE-OF-SPADES A-10
EN ROUTE: BENNETT RANCH/MYRTLE
BEACH, SOUTH CAROLINA
SATURDAY

Three hours into his return flight to the 354th Tactical Fighter Wing, Adrian Bennett's desires, as always for his son, had become a command. Jonathan had visited Washington, D.C., many times in his life. He had lived there on two occasions, both as a child and as an adult. He had done a tour of duty at Andrews Air Force Base. This final decision had been made for him. He would not survive, and he did not want to survive. At the proper time, his father would select and insert into power the men who would lead the country. He'd shown Jonathan the list, the list of men he would place in power. He didn't ask for Jonathan's opinion of the men on the list. He never asked for his son's counsel. He simply told Jonathan what he believed, and his son accepted it. As he had this final, fateful time.

How did you attack Arlington National Cemetery? After a day in the life with his father, it had come down to that single equation. The A-10 had drifted 200 miles south of its flight plan while its pilot went through the real nuts and bolts of planning an air strike. Preliminary, yes. But like a writer, thinking about it was half the battle. The strike itself, he was sure, would go off without a hitch. Afterward, for him, it didn't matter what happened, one way or another. As the jumble of thoughts sorted themselves out in his mind, the A-10 droned on, steady as always.

One thing seemed clear. No one would be able to stop him.

THE HARRIER AV-8B
EN ROUTE: YUMA M.C.A.S./CHERRY
POINT M.C.A.S.
SATURDAY

Jason had flown the hot new Harrier with less than his usual relish for flight time. His head hurt just enough to take the fun out of the whole flight. But it wasn't his headache. It was the thruster tits he would never again see, and had not touched, because he'd puked all over her as she was reaching for the only part of him that wasn't affected by all that tequila. Oh. Oh. Don't think about the tequila. What would they do to him if he threw up in this new B? Christ. Oh, Jasoon, babee, she'd said. Well, all right. Nobody's gonna know, and he wasn't telling anyone. But if he ever again got duty at Yuma, he'd be afraid to go into town. By now, everybody in Yuma must know about ''Jasoon babee.''

As the late afternoon sun shifted farther behind him, he glanced out the Harrier's cockpit. Less than five miles away, a single A-10, flying at about 18,000 feet, caught the sun on its Plexiglas, and winked for attention. Instantly alert, Jason changed the engine nozzles to the down position, ''viffing'' the Harrier, in effect stopping in midair. The AV-8B Harrier II could do that. It was a very weird plane.

The maneuver dropped him behind the A-10 immediately. Rolling into a shallow dive to his left, he closed on the A-10, until he was directly behind, and still above it. Probably headed to Myrtle Beach, he thought. But if he was, he was a bit off line. No. More than a bit. Jason eased the Harrier forward, curious. He pulled close enough to see the A-10 clearly. On the tail was a familiar Wing Commander's insignia. He knew instantly who it was. His headache vanished. *Tacka-tacka-tacka* himself. Well, well . . .

THE ACE-OF-SPADES A-10
EN ROUTE: BENNETT RANCH/MYRTLE
BEACH, SOUTH CAROLINA
SATURDAY

Jonathan wondered if he would have to visit D.C. before Monday. The White House, in the name of the bereaved former First Lady, had announced the funeral would be held in the cemetery's amphitheater, a place she said Conrad Taylor visited when he "made his great decisions." "It gave him peace," quote, unquote. Well, Jonathan had been there, too, on Memorial Day, 1980. Six thousand people were there, with room to burn. But where would they put the 150,000 mourners, the average guy and his family, there to see the show? Jonathan Bennett thought his thoughts, untroubled by what their end result would be. He'd need to make a near perfect first pass, followed by a second, to clean out what was left. Bombs. Yes. Mark 82 all purpose? Cluster? What kind, on the second pass? Cannon fire on the first pass. Pure gunsmanship. He would tear 'em up. Turn the General Electric GUA-8 30mm cannon on, and hold it on. High explosive shells. The angle would have to be just right. It would depend on where, and how, they seated the VIPs. Approach. Should he swing around Washington, and come in from the west? From the north? No. Too far, too many choppers in the air. There would certainly be gunships over D.C. And there were the missile batteries near the White House.

But he could find out quite a lot. He was an Air Force Wing commander. He would know most of the Air Force precautionary security moves around the capital. He would call General Forbes at the Pentagon. Taylor Forbes, his onetime wingman, now deputy to the Secretary of Defense. Yes, he would find the way, though he thought he already knew the way. Straight up the Potomac, turn left at the Vietnam War Memorial, and shoot. Yeah, low level. All the way. A-10 style. Thirty thousand security people would surround those at Arlington to attend the funeral. Nobody would get to the VIPs from the ground. But Washington had no roof . . .

He turned back to flying, reading his gauges and instruments. A little off, here. He would have to conserve his fuel. Stupid. A stupid cadet pilot would have been more careful. He corrected the A-10's drift, and moved the control stick to the correct heading.

It was then he saw the Harrier, less than 200 feet away, slightly behind and above him. The pilot was holding up a sign, in bold black letters. It said, *Bang! Bang!* A kill, stated in marked pen.

The Harrier rolled over on its back and dipped below his sightline, popping up again on his right wingtip. For a moment, the two aircraft flew side by side, the Harrier in the wingman's position to the A-10. Jonathan watched the Harrier pilot, saying nothing, the radio channels open. What was there to say? He was absolutely sure this was the same pilot he'd jumped in a mock attack two days before. It was a different plane, but he was sure it was the same pilot. He waggled the A-10's wings, and banked away, finally locked on a true heading to Myrtle Beach.

Jason flicked one last rigid middle finger at the A-10 with the Ace of Spades painted on its nose, and pushed on toward Cherry Point. He didn't believe in omens. He was very young, and he felt mainly that he'd really nailed the eagle-wearing Air Force son-of-a-bitch. On Monday, he would remember, and wish fervently that he had rammed the A-10 when he had the chance. He would see the Ace of Spades A-10 one more time. The last time . . .

MOSCOW AIRPORT
SATURDAY, 5:00 P.M. (MOSCOW TIME)

The big Ilyushin airliner sat on the tarmac, engines running, awaiting the Soviet President's arrival. He had been scheduled to leave over an hour before. Refueling trucks moved down the runway toward the aircraft, relics from World War II. Russian planes burned fuel at a rate over 50 percent faster than their western competitors. At this very moment, on the Soviet President's desk, was a memo suggesting the Soviet Union buy 120 Boeing 747s. The President, wisely, had read it without taking action of any kind. While the trucks fed the thirsty fuel tanks of the President's plane, he was listening to a last-minute plea from the head of the Soviet Secret Security Service. He was not concerned about wasted aviation fuel.

Finally, after a ninety-seven-minute delay, a limousine rolled out of the Kremlin, bearing the leader of the Communist world to the funeral of the fallen leader of the capitalist world. The advice he received from his security chief was presented with considerable vigor. It was preposterous, but he had listened.

Yuri was an old, trusted comrade, and he deserved the utmost consideration. And so the President had considered the advice, and rejected it. His security chief had suggested that a military aircraft might bomb the President during his stay at the Soviet embassy in Washington. Spies. Well, what could you do with them? The Ilyushin lifted off the runway at Moscow Airport two hours late.

WASHINGTON, D.C.
ROSEMARY HAWKINS'S OFFICE
THE WHITE HOUSE
SATURDAY, 5:25 P.M.

"Yo! Big Brother! How ya doin'?" Jason Kelly's voice was as clear to J.R. as if he'd been in the next room.

"Fine, Little Brother. I'm doing just fine. How was your trip west?"

"Piece o' cake, J.R. No problems." (Oh, Jasoon, Babee.)

"I thought you were supposed to be back at Cherry Point last night, Jace." The "older brother" tone seeped into J.R.'s voice. "You know our deal. You call when you get back."

"Right. That's what I'm doing. I just got back, and it took a couple calls to find you." The "younger brother" voice, accusing the senior sibling of intolerance, or worse.

"Oh?" J.R. kept his voice normal. It would serve no purpose to tell his brother he was temporarily reassigned.

"They wanted me to bring a crispy new B to the point. One more feather for the flyer, right? Anyway, it went okay. Except for the fucking idiot in the A-10. Jesus! So how's it going in the spy business?"

J.R. was instantly alerted. On his desk was a thick folder, as yet unexplored completely. But he had glanced at the file on the white-haired patriot. Gears slipped through his consciousness like a slot machine, lining up the cherries, the apples, the oranges. And then he knew. He finally knew. And his heart dropped like wet concrete in a trough, heavy and sure to harden.

"A-10?"

"Yeah. Some heavy rank from Myrtle Beach. Two days ago, he made a mock attack on the five Cs I was leading to Yuma. Scared the hell out of me, and scattered us all over the sky. We never saw them. If it had been real, we were dead meat."

J.R. was silent for a moment that stretched into two, and beyond. His brother broke into the silence.

"J.R.? You there?"

"Yup. I'm here. I want to ask you a question, Jason."

"Shoot."

"Was the A-10 you saw painted with a warthog's tusks on the nose, and an Ace of Spades below the cockpit?"

"Jesus! Yes, but how did you know?" The phone gave a long-distance squeal, static and noise from the beyond. It figured.

Well, okay. He'd known what the answer would be, but what did he know? Nothing. That's what he knew. As for gut feeling, that was something else entirely.

"Jace, I want you to stay on base until I call you. Can you do that?" J.R.'s voice betrayed none of the turmoil he felt.

"Well, sure, I can do that, but why? The Point's pretty much shut down, with the funeral and all. I don't want to just hang out. I've got a seventy-two-hour pass coming. No flight time."

"Cancel it. Stay there."

Jason Kelly started to say something, and stopped. After a long silence between the two brothers, he said, "Is it something about the A-10?"

"I don't know for sure. Let's just say I may need you to do something for me. Stay on the base. I'll get back to you tomorrow. Stay there, Jason."

"Sure, J.R. Whatever you say."

J.R. hung up, leaving his little brother with countless questions. J.R. pulled the bulky file off his temporary desk and into his lap. He removed the information on the Bennett family, and tossed the rest aside.

WASHINGTON, D.C.
SATURDAY, 8:00 P.M.

J.R. Kelly ran his hands through his hair, staring down at
the photograph of the Bennett men, father and son. What
did he have, really? Not much. The older Bennett was a
very powerful man. Two years ago, he'd been responsible
for a Supreme Court appointment. Half the federal appointments in his home state owed their allegiance, and
their jobs, to him. For a man not active in government,
his hand had an amazingly long reach. Judges, senators,
cabinet members. He went hunting every year with the
current Director of the C.I.A. *That* was pretty interesting!

The son had a spotless record. A wing commander. A
Vietnam vet and prisoner of war, a prisoner, it was said,
that had undergone severe interrogation for over 800 days.

And yet, the senior Bennett had been here, in Washington, doodling on a place mat with as yet unidentified lunch
companions. Only doodles, to be sure, and long since
gone. So what did he have? Nothing. He had nothing. He
reached for the phone and called Rosemary Hawkins.

"Did you speak to Emily Taylor about the amphitheater?"

"You got me out of a hot shower to ask me that?" She
sounded properly indignant, and wet.

"Are you naked, Rosemary?"

"Of course, I'm naked, J.R. Why?"

"Just indulging my fantasies, that's all."

She laughed then, a deep, throaty, sexy laugh. "Is this
phone sex we are having, J.R.? Is that why you called?
Because if it is, I'm going to lie down and get comfortable."

How do you tell her what you think is going to happen?
You don't. Not yet. J.R. pursued his original question.
"Did you talk to Emily Taylor?"

"I did."

"And?"

"She told me to mind my own business, and I said thank you for your time. That's it. The ceremony will be held in the amphitheater. She is moving the body tonight, without fanfare, to the Capitol rotunda. Conr . . . The President will be there all day tomorrow. They will take the body directly from the Capitol to Arlington on Monday, late. The idea is to bury him just before dark, I guess. The burial plot itself is only a few hundred yards from the amphitheater."

J.R. was silent, his thoughts moving ahead to Monday, and thousands of people in one place, at one time, all the leaders of the world in one place. And the Ace-of-Spades A-10 . . .

"Rosemary, who do you trust? Who do you really trust?"

"You, J.R. I trust you." Her voice was a low, kittenish purr.

"No, I mean, who do you trust enough to do whatever you ask, no matter what?"

Rosemary answered without hesitation, her voice steady and official now, recognizing the urgent tone, and obvious need, in J.R.'s.

"Brian Howell."

"The general? Your deputy?"

"Yes. I trust him completely."

"Okay. I need somebody to trust. Something is very wrong in this town."

"What do you expect, J.R.?" Her voice had changed, the voice of a woman with tears in her eyes. "The President is dead. The town's in mourning. I'm in mourning." Click. The line went dead as she hung up.

J.R. punched the phone, his fingers flying. At C.I.A. headquarters in Langley, Nadine Riley, his section chief, answered on the first ring.

"Nadine, baby. How much money do I owe you?"

"J.R.?"

"What do you mean, 'J.R.'? Who else do you lend money to? I'll find the bastard, and terminate him!"

"J.R., are you drunk?"

"Nope. I'm hard at work. And I want to borrow Willy."

"Willy? Willy Corchran? What do you mean, 'borrow' him?"

"I need him, just for the weekend. Tell him to pack up his kit."

"Willy Corchran is an analyst. He sits at a computer terminal eighteen hours a day. He is not field qualified, and you know it."

"I know he's not. That's why I want him."

"J.R. . . . what are you up to?" He could visualize her, tapping her nose with one finger, looking worried.

"My asshole. In alligators. I need him, sweets. It's a national security matter, as we are wont to say."

"J.R., you are a flake, do you know that?"

"Guilty. Yes, I am. Now, do I get Willy or not?" Silence. Silence that stretched on and on.

"Yes. You get Willy. Where do you want him?"

"Here, at Rosemary Hawkins's office."

"When?"

"Right now. Tell him to wear his steel underwear."

"J.R., what in the h—"

He hung up and redialed Rosemary Hawkins's home. The phone rang a long, long time. He slammed the phone down, and sprinted from the office, heading for the ever-present limo. In forty minutes, he was at Rosemary Hawkins's front door.

MYRTLE BEACH, SOUTH CAROLINA
SATURDAY, 2100 HOURS

Jonathan Bennett, alone in his office, studied the maps he had pinned to the cork-covered mission board he used to plan the training activities of the 354th Tactical Fighter Wing which, for the first Saturday since he'd assumed command, was 100 percent on liberty. He'd issued full weekend passes to all his pilots, and all but essential ground staff and maintenance personnel. Myrtle Beach Air Force Base was practically deserted.

Outside, rain swept across the runways, rippling the thin skin of eighty A-10s, silent and lifeless, aircraft engines covered, chucks on the wheels, power down and off. They were neatly lined up, wingtip to wingtip, clumsy in the rain, awkward and oversized, grounded; passive, not war-like at all.

Off to one side, the Ace of Spades A-10 had a yellow umbilical cable attached to it, providing power and life. Tomorrow night, he would bring its guns to life as well. Monday, he would use them.

He was currently engaged in the most crucial part of the mission. The plan. A simple word. Plan. But not simple at all. Time. Distance. Speed. Weaponry. Tactics. No. Not simple. *Critical.*

He studied the maps very carefully. The map he liked best, the map he used the most, was a tourist map published in 1964 by the National Geographic Society. It wasn't very accurate. It did not show the Vietnam War Memorial, which had not yet been needed, or thought of. He liked the map nevertheless. He drew a line in blue ink up the Potomac, around the Washington Monument, hard left to the Vietnam War Memorial (here, he inked in a long, angular V), moving at 300 knots, pull the trigger at the eastern bank of the Potomac River, hold it down, send 1900 rounds of 30mm cannon fire into and through the open, classic columns of the Memorial amphitheater, chipping away at the marble, exploding inside, stone and marble and fire and high explosives dancing among the crowd, crushing and tearing . . . *He could see the bridge in North Vietnam falling into the river, exploding, the peo-ple's faces disappearing in a sheet of flame.*

Now, pull up, and bank hard to the right, come back at 1500 feet, and throw all that ordnance into the amphithe-ater cup, the blast, oh, Lord, the blast would . . . the tomb! The Tomb of the Unknowns. No hits there. He'd have to adjust the strike, shift it a little. Shoot from a different angle.

Nothing. Nothing must damage the sacred Tomb of the Unknowns. Jonathan Bennett went back to his maps, drawing new lines. Protecting a tomb full of the dead. After all, what kind of American could desecrate the Tomb of the Unknowns?

SUBURBAN MARYLAND
SATURDAY, 9:15 P.M.

"You look terrible." He did not say it unkindly.

"Do I? I wasn't expecting visitors." She sat opposite him, holding a white terry-cloth robe closed at the chest, her legs tucked under her, wearing no makeup. Her eyes were red and swollen from crying. She looked like a teenager. He wanted to get up and leave her to her grief. But he couldn't. He decided to plunge right in.

"I need a quick assignment to a U.S. military base for a spy friend of mine. Can you negotiate that for me?"

"I don't know what you mean, J.R. What are you asking?"

"I want to insert a C.I.A. employee into a U.S. military installation, on U.S. soil."

"For what purpose?"

"To monitor the movements of . . . of aircraft."

"To monitor the movements of aircraft," she repeated.

"That's correct." He began to squirm in his chair.

"Where? What aircraft?"

"At Myrtle Beach Air Force Base. That's in South Carolina."

"*Is* it? Is it really?"

"Uh, yes, it is. In South Carolina."

"Fine. Why do you feel the need to insert an employee of the C.I.A., as you so delicately put it, onto a U.S. base, on U.S. soil, on this particular day?"

"Not today. Tomorrow."

"Oh. I see. Tomorrow."

"Right."

"Why, J.R.?"

"I honestly don't know why. Yet. I don't know why, at this time. Call it, call it a hunch."

"A hunch?"

"Premonition doesn't cover it. Nothing really covers it. When I was a vice cop in L.A., a long time ago, we made a fairly routine raid on a gambling operation, with a whorehouse in the basement. I was walking down a brightly lit hall, and nothing felt right, you know? I mean, all the doors were open, the light was fine, but I stopped. It just didn't feel right. I just waited, looking down that long hallway. I waited quite a long time. Finally, I took off my jacket, and threw it, about chest high, down the hallway. As it sailed by the first open doorway, a double-barrelled blast from a twelve-gauge shotgun turned that jacket into dust. I called for the shooter to come out. It was a seventeen-year-old hooker, scared to death. Like I said, it just didn't feel right. Then, or now. I don't want to cross in front of any open doors."

"I see. And who do you think may be behind the open door?"

"Adrian Bennett. And his flyboy son at Myrtle Beach."

"And you think they're behind the door, with a shotgun?"

"No. Not a shotgun. An airplane." He reached inside the folder he carried, and handed her the photograph of Adrian and Jonathan Bennett, with the Ace-of-Spades A-10.

"All I want to do, is put a man on that base to watch Adrian Bennett's kid—and his airplane."

"This is preposterous, J.R., you know that." Pure fact, her tone said. It *was* preposterous.

"Yeah, I guess it is." He reached for the photo, but she continued to stare at it, searching for a shred of whatever J.R. was so paranoid about.

"I did a long security investigation on Adrian and Jonathan Bennett. I gave it to the President on Wednesday. He . . . he scolded me. Told me never to do that kind of thing again. I left out half of what I know about Adrian, and I wish I hadn't. Adrian Bennett hated Conrad Taylor. And he hates me. Me, most of all. He's a political dinosaur, and a crusty revolutionary. He gave William Rodgers a very bizarre list of potential cabinet members, I'll tell you. Fanatics. Even more fanatic, in their own way, than I am. Tell me, J.R., are you suggesting that Adrian Bennett, or his son, or both of them, are going to attack someone, somewhere, with an airplane?'' She'd rolled the photograph into a baton shape, and was tapping it against her shoulder. Tap, tap, tap . . .

Well. There was the question, spelled out very clearly. He had little to go on. The restaurant. The doodles on the place mat. The Ks, and the headstones, and the neatly listed names and figures. The A-10 written in the corner. The son's unscheduled flight out west, and the quick return. The strange interludes, two of them, with Jason Kelly and the pilot of the A-10. And the long report detailing the younger Bennett's terrible interrogations in North Vietnam. Did he believe it? Did he actually believe an air strike on Arlington was possible?

"Yes. I believe they, the Bennetts, intend to attack someone, somewhere, with an airplane.'' He watched her face, waiting for the laughter.

"Can you be more specific?''

"Nothing I have is specific. It's all *Wizard of Oz* stuff.''

"Try, J.R.'' She uncurled her legs, and stood up, walking to him, very short in her bare feet, her face upturned, a young face, a wise face, a face like no other.

"I believe the younger Bennett is going to fly an air strike. On Monday. During the funeral.''

She looked up at him, her eyes roaming his face, looking for the truth, or at least some reason to consider seriously what he'd said. She turned away, and walked to the door, opening it to the chill of the night, the wind rustling and blowing her robe free of her slim legs.

"Go, J.R. Come tomorrow, for breakfast. We'll talk then. Eight o'clock.''

"But—''

"Good-night, J.R." He was dismissed. She'd kept the photograph of the Bennetts, and their shotgun.

SUBURBAN MARYLAND
SATURDAY, 10:00 P.M.

Rosemary Hawkins paced back and forth in front of the fireplace, a double scotch in her hand, trying to grasp what J.R. had told her, trying to understand. She'd propped the photo of the Bennetts on the fireplace mantel, between two slender, tapered candles. Occasionally, she would stop her pacing, and stand near the fire, warmed in front, chilled in back, staring at the Bennetts.

Impossible. J.R. had positively gone over the edge. Spies. All spies see spies behind every bush. Everything is a conspiracy to an intelligence operative. If not, who would need them, and for what? Of course, Adrian Bennett *was* a ruthless man. Some of the stories . . . oh, my. But you could tell stories till hell froze over, and he still couldn't be charged, or even *thought about* as a . . . well, as an assassin. And the son. Jesus. Talk about your spotless record. A Medal of Honor winner. And J.R. thinks he's going to bomb Arlington. Oh sure!

Goddamn, J.R. was way off base with this one. She glanced hard at the photo, and resumed her pacing. She emptied the scotch. Refilled it. Resumed pacing. She stopped at the photo again.

Impossible. She drained the scotch, went to bed, and cried herself to sleep.

ROSEMARY HAWKINS'S OFFICE
THE WHITE HOUSE
SATURDAY, 10:30 P.M.

"Sit down, Willy. What are you drinking?"

"Nothing, Mr. Kelly. Maybe a Coke, if you have one."

"Sure. A Coke it is. And call me J.R., will you?"

"Of course, Mr. Ke—I mean, J.R. Nadine didn't say much about . . . about my field assignment. I mean, it is a field assignment, isn't it?"

J.R. studied Willy Corchran as he handed him a frosty Coke from the well-stocked refrigerator bar. Horn-rimmed glasses. Rumpled suit. Thinning hair. Bad posture. Yup. The perfect spy.

"Yes, you are going into the field. At least I think you are. Do you know anything about airplanes, Willy?"

"Yes, actually, I do. Quite a lot."

J.R.'s eyes widened in surprise. "You do? Well, that could be very helpful. Or it may not help at all. What is it you know about airplanes, exactly?"

"Everything. I'm a modeler. A hobby. I make model airplanes."

"I see. Models. Well."

"I have over one hundred airplane models at home. I mostly just make model airplanes. I used to date, but I don't anymore."

Puzzled, J.R. asked, "Why? Why don't you date anymore?"

"My last date was very, very attractive. She got a little tipsy. No, not tipsy. She was inebriated. She sat on my P-38." Willy Corchran arched one eyebrow to show his indignation.

"Your P-38?"

"Yes. I'd just completed a one-quarter-inch scale model of the P-38 that shot down Admiral Isoroku Yamamoto in World War II. It took me two months to build. Much of it I did by hand. The wing fuel tanks were wrong. Not historically accurate. So I carved them myself. A pretty nice job, I think. She sat on it. And I called a cab for her, and sent her home. I don't date anymore.''

J.R. choked back a laugh. Willy Corchran stared at him, with a completely serious look on his face. Well, to each his own, right? Right.

''Have you ever built an A-10?''

''Yes. Three of them. All different, you know. Paint, weapons, bomb load.''·

''Then you know a good deal about A-10s.''

''Of course. Modelers don't just make them. We study them. Live them. I could, I believe, fly one, if need be.''

J.R. had no idea what to say. He was not sure, but fate seemed to have smiled on him with Willy Corchran. Maybe. Hopefully.

''Willy, I want to insert you onto a stateside Air Force base. An A-10 base. Could you pose as a mechanic, for about thirty-six hours?''

''Of course I could. I could fix an A-10, if it were broken. After all, I've built three of them.''

J.R. could think of no more to say. ''Fine, Willy. Just fine. Listen, you bunk here tonight. Take the couch. Sometime, early tomorrow, you're going to join the Air Force.''

''Okay, Mr. Kelly. Uh, I mean, J.R.''

And Willy Corchran walked to the leather couch, curled into a tiny ball, and went instantly to sleep. Willy Corchran. Model maker. Systems analyst. Spy. J.R. spread Willy's drab, brown raincoat over him. Willy sighed contentedly, but did not wake up. Amazing.

K.G.B. HEADQUARTERS
MOSCOW
SUNDAY, 7:00 A.M. (MOSCOW TIME)

Yuri Popov studied the intelligence data he'd gathered, for the tenth time in two days. Some of what he read was like a fantasy. No. *All* of what he had read was fantasy. The President had listened, but it was a polite gesture. Nothing more. Yuri was seventy years old. The new, younger state leaders didn't think much of what he said. Not anymore. Of course, *they* hadn't been at Stalingrad! *They* hadn't been in Berlin in May of 1945. No! They knew nothing of the Mother Russia he knew. He had freed it from the hated Fascists, foot by foot, yard by yard, mile by mile. And now the President/General Secretary was going to a funeral. And, of course, he *should* go. He and Conrad Taylor were brothers, planning to change the world. For the better? Well, who could say?

He, Yuri Popov, had said, loud and clear, what he thought, and it had gained him nothing. But Yuri *knew*! Yes, he knew the truth. An American pilot, name unknown, was going to bomb the Russian embassy. Today! Sunday, an American officer, a member of a small, elite corps, as yet unidentified, would attempt to kill the leader of the Russian people, to kill him in his bed! Yet he, Yuri Popov, had been dismissed, his intelligence report rejected.

Well, so be it. But he would stir the pot anyway. Yuri Popov, patriot, would send a small portion of what he knew . . . what he knew to be the truth. He would send it in a code he knew the C.I.A. was reading. They would intercept it. They would act. At least, they would do something! They would protect the Soviet embassy, if nothing else. They would not advertise it. But they would do it. Or he was not Yuri Popov!

Caution, of course. This must be done with caution. He went to the Sunday codebook, gathering four key codes,

codes used to identify information sources. He took three numbers from each one, scrambled and mixed them together, creating a nonexistent intelligence source. He then sent the message.

Thirty-seven minutes later, it clattered out in the Soviet embassy in Washington. Unprotected, it was intercepted at once by N.S.A., the National Security Agency, *the* supersecret intelligence gatherer of the United States government. The information was then transferred to "concerned agencies." The Defense Department, the C.I.A., and the White House. All of this happened automatically. The message, decoded and translated, was very brief:

> To: Ambassador, U.S.S.R., Washington, D.C.
>   Expect air assault
>   By helicopter gunship
>   Embassy grounds
>   Sunday.
>   Signed,
>   Scorpio

Nobody at the Soviet embassy, or any U.S. agency of any kind, had the slightest idea who Scorpio was. But at 6:50 A.M., the ambassador called Major General Brian Howell, U.S.A.F., and told him about the message from Scorpio. General Howell thanked the ambassador, reassured him that security in Washington, D.C., was impenetrable, and told him not to worry. Whoever Scorpio was, he'd stirred up a minor hornet's nest. So said Brian Howell to the Soviet ambassador. Yet the nest remained quiet. No precautions of a specific nature were taken. The intelligence information from Scorpio moved slowly, ineffectually along the conveyor belt of a distracted Washington bureaucracy. One copy went to Rosemary Hawkins. She would read it at breakfast, along with the *Washington Post*.

A copy of the Scorpio note was sent to Grenady V. Malitkov, Marshall of the Soviet Union, Commander in Chief of the Red Army. He read it, and ordered a plane to take him west, to the strike point only forty-eight hours from the Fulda Gap. From the west, U.S. reconnaissance identified the troops and numbers of tanks in the three remaining attack areas still pointed westward. The Marshall's trip west from Moscow was also noted. Vigilance, slack for months, picked up, on both sides. No troops were moved, by either side, east or west. But they did *lean toward* one another . . .

DAY FIVE: SUNDAY

ROSEMARY HAWKINS'S OFFICE
THE WHITE HOUSE, WASHINGTON, D.C.
SUNDAY, 7:00 A.M.

"Wake up, Willy. In a couple of hours, if all goes well, you are going to be an Air Force technician. What rank would you like to have?"

Willy Corchran came awake as quickly as he'd fallen asleep. "I don't know, Mr. Kelly, what rank should I be?"

" 'J.R.' Call me 'J.R.' "

"Right. J.R." Willy was not yet comfortable with "J.R."

"How about a line chief?"

"What is that . . . I mean, rank-wise?"

Rank-wise? Jesus. "I think you should be an aircraft mechanic, E-7 rating. How 'bout that?"

"E-7? Well, I'd like that a lot." Willy gave J.R. a boyish, Huck Finn smile.

"E-7 it is. Aircraft mechanic. Able to leap A-10s in a single bound."

Willy Corchran, model maker, gave J.R. a long, serious appraisal. "I can, you know. Leap A-10 aircraft in a single bound."

J.R., grateful for, and to, Willy Corchran, was temporarily at a loss for cute, agency words. Willy deserved more, much more. "I'm counting on you, Willy. What you do on your first assignment to fieldwork may be the single most important job ever. And I mean, ever, as in historically."

"Are you worried about me, J.R.?"

"What do you mean, Willy?"

149

"Do you think a computer plug like me will fuck up this assignment, that I'm a bit weird, and somehow less than what you need?"

J.R. didn't hesitate. Willy needed an answer.

"I think you are the perfect, God-given choice, Willy. I don't think I could have found a better . . . more qualified agent, anywhere in the shop."

Willy Corchran, gave J.R. a smile, a satisfied, trusting smile. J.R. smiled back, masking his doubts. The thought had occurred to him that Willy might possibly get killed dealing with whatever was going on down at Myrtle Beach. You could take it to the bank.

SUBURBAN MARYLAND
SUNDAY, 8:00 A.M.

"Good morning, J.R. Please, come in. What would you like for breakfast?" J.R. pulled his overcoat from his shoulders, handing it to the near-invisible butler, who, like all good butlers, disappeared.

"Scotch would be nice."

"Breakfast, J.R. Not happy hour."

"No scotch, then, right?"

"No scotch."

"Okay. Scramble three, with toast, coffee, and a large milk."

Rosemary turned away, walking down a long hall toward what J.R. assumed was the kitchen. She was wearing a black leather suit, and the skirt was typically (for Rosemary Hawkins) very short. J.R. had an immediate, throbbing erection. Watching the slow, rolling hips, it was difficult for J.R. to think of her as the Secretary of State. A secretary, yes, but not *the* Secretary of State.

"Did you know that nobody eats eggs the way you do?"

She looked up at him, across the table, a forkful of eggs

Benedict suspended only inches from her rosebud mouth. "No. I didn't know that. How, exactly, do I eat my eggs, J.R.?"

"You sort of slide them into your mouth . . . like . . . well, they sort of get sucked into, I mean . . ."

"I know what you mean, J.R. I do it on purpose, suck my eggs. Are you turned on? Do you have visions of . . ."

"Yes. I have exactly those visions."

"I'm very pleased, J.R. It will do you no good, but I am pleased nevertheless. I feel like . . . like . . . ?"

"A widow?"

"Yes. Like a widow. A young, very-much-in-love widow, with slightly round heels."

"Round heels?"

"Oh, yes. They are sometimes very round. I've been known to fall down, defenseless."

"Sure you have." J.R. didn't believe it. And his voice said so.

"I have. Really." Her eyes widened, and one eyebrow arched. She looked very sexy. He crossed his legs, shutting down his hard-on.

"Tell me, when this urge to 'fall down' hits you next, will you?"

"You'll be the first to know, J.R. In the meantime, how do we determine if your theory is correct?"

"My theory? What theory?"

"Your theory that the Bennett family is about to attack a plot of land full of people that are already dead." Rosemary Hawkins asked the question without a trace of sarcasm or doubt. She was telling J.R. that she was at least open to what he had to say. Like Dorothy, she was saying that this sure wasn't Kansas . . .

The breakfast dishes were pushed aside, and J.R. was drawing what he remembered of the doodles on the restaurant place mats. She stood behind him, her hands on his shoulders, her fingers rubbing and probing at his tense muscles, transmitting trust, a hands-on declaration of intent to listen.

"I can't prove any of this, not yet. I have no corroborating information. I don't have a single shred of *real* evidence to back up what I believe."

"I do." She said this in a tone that suggested she knew something he didn't. And she did. "I received an intelligence intercept this morning, from Brian Howell. It doesn't make any sense, and wouldn't have except you tipped me off yesterday, and this information ties in. Not because it fits, but because it exists at all."

She reached over his shoulder, and placed before him the short, enigmatic message from Scorpio, whoever Scorpio was.

"An air attack on the Soviet embassy?"

"So it says."

"Not a chance. A strike on the embassy would have less than a 10 percent chance of success, if that."

"Why?"

"Because we protect the Soviet embassy, very much like we do the White House."

"Missiles?"

"Sure. Hand-held Stingers. The Soviets can tell you all about them. They got run out of Afghanistan by Stingers. No air strikes, no victory. They were losing thirty choppers a week. I was there. I saw them go down."

"So, J.R., you are saying a helicopter assault against the Soviet embassy is impossible?"

"Yes. That's what I'm saying."

"Then why the message, and who is Scorpio?"

"It doesn't matter who Scorpio is. What does matter, is that someone, a powerful someone, thinks an air strike on the Soviet embassy is a likely, if unappreciated, possibility. Scorpio is obliquely confirming what I think will actually happen. An air strike, on the funeral procession, on the amphitheater, on *something*, to kill . . . to kill whatever is available."

"You mean *whoever*, don't you, J.R.?"

"Yeah, I guess I do. *Whoever.*"

"At the funeral, that would include most of the world's leaders, wouldn't it?"

"Yes." J.R. tried to imagine an air strike on the amphitheater. It was a bad dream, too horrific to envision. The death toll. My God. The dead . . . "Yes it would. It would include you, Rosemary. You will be at Conrad Taylor's funeral. And the new President, and the President/General Secretary of the U.S.S.R. And every government official, from every government in the world. Scorpio is telling us something. He's not sure what, but he hopes, *knows* we will dig it up. Tell me, Rosemary, will we dig it up?"

Sitting in Rosemary's library, J.R. was surprised when the butler brought him a decanter of scotch, a bucket of ice, and a glass. He cast a questioning glance toward Rosemary, sitting directly opposite him on a wide, white leather couch. Her black leather skirt made an interesting noise against the white leather as she crossed her legs.

"Breakfast is over, J.R., and that's very good scotch." If this was a test, J.R. failed. He poured himself a stiff drink, splashed over three ice cubes. She expressed neither approval nor disapproval, but she was watching him very intently, green eyes bright and alert. When he'd seen her the night before, her eyes had been dull and lifeless, reddened and puffy from crying. If he was waiting for her to go all to hell and helpless, he'd have quite a long wait.

"How do we discover how much of your theory is fact, and how much is C.I.A. paranoia?"

"I don't have enough time to prove my theory. The day after tomorrow, Conrad Taylor goes into the ground, while every leader, major and minor, watches the descent and plans to take whatever advantage might crop up from the fresh dirt shoveled onto the President's memory."

Rosemary winced visibly. "You certainly have a macabre way with the English language, J.R."

"Truth, Rosemary. Name somebody, anybody at the funeral, who will truly mourn Conrad Taylor."

"I will." Her back stiffened, her legs came together at

the knees, a defensive, prim stance. Her remark was no answer.

"Are you sure? You're going to be the Secretary of State. Power. Real, heavy-duty power, particularly with William Rodgers as President. You may, and I say this conservatively, wield more power, and have more influence, than anyone in this government's history, certainly in this century."

"Power. I see. That's what you think I want. Power, like some money-grubbing CEO after an Iacocca-like stance! Look at me! Whoopee! Rosemary Hawkins, rising to the top over the fried body of her lover. C'mon, J.R., surely you don't believe me capable of that kind of ambition? Hey. My main squeeze, who just happened to be President of the U. S. of A., my main clit licker, my main dick, died, and my goodness, I just better move on in the new government, to carry on the torch . . . let's push Connie Taylor, because he had a vision, and I'm the carrier. Like AIDS? He gave it to me, I should pass it on to the country? You're an asshole, J.R., you know that?" She folded her arms across her chest, her eyes flashing hot anger.

"Yeah, I know that. But who else is going to tell you, Ms. Hawkins? Who else is going to open your beautiful green eyes to what is happening here? My job is to keep you company, to keep you alive, and to ferret out the bad guys. Well, being a ferret means never having to say I'm sorry. So I won't say it. You want me to clarify my theory, to make you understand?

"Okay. Conrad Taylor had no friends. He had no acolytes. He had many undeclared disciples. That's all he had. Fence sitters. Now, he is dead, and I'm convinced that all the non-acolytes are lined up to rain on his funeral parade. I'm convinced that the Bennett family intends to bomb Conrad Taylor's ideas even as they are buried with him, on the fanciful idea that new ideas will somehow take root after he's gone. The funeral is going up in smoke, to create hundreds, maybe thousands of funerals! Think about that, goddammit, while you think up more cute State Department words to cover paranoia! The amphitheater at Arlington will be a big cup of fool's gold, bad, shiny shit that passes for world leadership. The Bennetts are going to tip that cup over. Unless we . . . you and I . . . stop them.''

Rosemary Hawkins, full lips set in a petulant, *Cosmo* magazine pout, leaned back in her white leather decorator's statement, crossed her legs under her black leather skirt, and stared at J.R. Her green eyes flashed conflicting signs of anger, sexuality, fright, and finally, exasperated acceptance. Her bouncing foot bounced even more feverishly, her spike heel flying off and onto the white carpet, as she too visualized her worst nightmare, an A-10 rushing up the Potomac, guns blazing. It couldn't happen. But, if it did . . .

Rosemary looked up from the three-page résumé of one Willy Corchran, government employee, model-maker supreme, and would-be, should-be spy.

"An untestable I.Q.?"

"Yeah. The numbers don't go high enough. Wee Willy is a certifiable, but untestable genius."

"Let me get this straight, J.R. Willy Corchran, government employee and hobbyist, is going to be inserted onto a U.S. air base, as an A-10 mechanic, and he's just sort of going to . . . to hang around? To hang around and watch the Ace-of-Spades, and tell you if it flies, or sits, or blows up? And he's going to do this without detection as a fraudulent mecho, who couldn't fix an A-10 unless he could glue it together on his workbench, with Testors glue?"

"Willy Corchran can leap A-10s in a single bound. He told me so."

"Oh. He told you so. I see."

"Yes. He told me so."

"Well. I guess that qualifies him, doesn't it?"

"Yes. Yes, he is definitely qualified."

"And Brian should make sure there are no hitches, is that right?"

"Well, he *is* the general, isn't he?"

"Yes."

"Well, then tell him to do what general officers have always done."

"And what have general officers always done, J.R., in your view?"

"Rules. They make 'em . . . they break 'em."

Rosemary Hawkins called Major General Brian Howell, who was pacing impatiently outside her study, into the room. He could tell from the expression on her face that considerable excrement was about to hit the rotating bladed cooler.

"I can provide . . . what wa . . . ?"

"Willy Corchran."

"Yes. Willy Corchran. I can provide Mr. Corchran with proper I.D. and a complete military record, although it is highly unlikely anyone will read it, or pay attention to it, if they do. You intend to use him only until noon on Monday, is that correct?"

"Correct, General. If nothing goes awry, by then, we— I mean I—have wasted government funds and my career opportunities. If Willy sees no evil, I will resign."

"Very noble, Mr. Kelly."

"J.R. Everybody calls me J.R."

"I am not everybody, Agent Kelly. I will call you 'Mr.' or 'Agent,' or anything but 'J.R.' I think you are a glory-seeking, but totally unbalanced, paranoid, and possibly psychotic individual. I work for Rosemary Hawkins." Here, General Brian Howell nodded in the direction of his boss's feverishly bouncing foot, while avoiding her eyes.

"Brian, you're a pompous ass, do you know that? Come down off those two stars, and help Mr. Kelly make a fool of himself. Do what he asks, without comment. Get Willy accredited, and onto the flight line at Myrtle Beach. He's small; he's skinny. He wears thick glasses. The perfect spy, right, J.R.?" She bent over, retrieved her wayward shoe, and slipped it on. Black leather skirt rustled against white leather cushions once again. She gave him a dazzling smile.

"Right, Rosemary. He's the perfect myopic, underweight, undertrained C.I.A. employee. But he will know if the younger Bennett climbs into the Ace-of-Spades anytime Monday morning. And if he knows, we will know.''

"Brian?'' Rosemary Hawkins fixed her steady, stately gaze on her deputy. Brian Howell, born in Villa Rica, Georgia, had come a long way for the son of a black sharecropper. And he wanted to go further. Rosemary Hawkins was the ticket he needed to ride.

"I agree. Mr. Kelly, Willy will have his Air Force documents in the morning.''

"No. Today. This morning. Willy needs to be on station by thirteen hundred hours today.''

"Impossible.'' Brian Howell puffed and huffed, his smooth mahogany cheeks pouching out like chocolate-colored balloons.

"Brian?'' Again. The power question that wasn't a question at all. The chocolate balloons deflated.

"Thirteen hundred hours, Mr. Kelly?''

"Call me 'J.R.' '' Not likely, but Brian Howell reached for the red phone on Rosemary Hawkins's desk, linking him directly to the Pentagon. The order creating Air Force Mechanic and Plane Captain, E-7 Rating, for Willy Corchran, superspy, went out at 0915 hours, Sunday. He was on station at 1345 hours the same day. The A-10s were real, but Willy Corchran gave them the same loving attention he gave his precious scale models. He had less than twenty-four hours to live.

BENNETT RANCH
SUNDAY, 9:00 A.M.

"Roger? Adrian. How are you?''

"I'm fine, Ad, how are you. Have you heard from Jonathan?''

"Yes, I have. He says he's going to be in Washington

on Monday. He says he might participate. What is your feeling on that, Roger?"

"On participation?"

"Yes, on participation. Jonathan is convinced—I mean to say, I've discussed his participation. He has agreed that he should, for the family's sake. How do you feel about that?"

"I think he should participate, Adrian."

"Thank you, Roger. We'll talk later."

"Yes. Later." Roger Carlyle, two-time ambassador, hung up, a broad smile spreading across his face.

"Robert? Adrian here."

"Adrian! How the hell are you?"

"I'm more than fine, Robert. Jonathan is fine, we're all fine."

"Is he? He's well, then?"

"Yes. He's well. Active, you might say. Rarin' to go."

"Perfect, Adrian. Well, as you know, you can count on me."

"Thank you, Robert. I'll be in touch." Click. It was the first time in nine years that the industrial tycoon had been cut off in a telephone conversation. He didn't mind.

"Darien Talmage, please."

"I'm sorry, sir, but Mr. Talmage is in conference all day today. May I have your number, and get back to you?"

"No, you silly little cunt! You tell him Adrian Bennett is on the fucking phone, and if he doesn't get on it in less than thirty seconds, I'll hang up. Permanently!"

"Yes, sir!" The famous southern voice was on the line in seconds.

"This is Darien Talmage."

"Dar, this is Ad."

"Ad? Well, how are you?"

"I'm fine, Ad. Going to Washington to pay my respects."

"Are you? Well, Ad, is Jonathan going with you?"

"Yes, he's going with me."

"Well, like I said the other day, have a good flight."

"We will, Dar, we most surely will."

"Barney?"

"Adrian? How are you?"

"I'm fine. Terrific, actually."

"Well, I'm glad to hear that."

"Yes. Well, Jonathan and I are going to D.C. on Monday."

"Are you?"

"Yes. Jonathan intends to be there right on time."

"Well. That's very interesting, Adrian. But I don't think I can make it."

Adrian Bennett was silent for a very long time. The tape ran for over forty seconds before he responded. "I'm sorry to hear that, Barney. We, Jonathan and I, were hoping you would be in Washington with us on Monday."

"I understand that, Adrian. I just feel I can't make it."

"I'm sorry to hear that, Barney. I hope it doesn't hurt you in the future." Click . . . Barney Bernard, two-time governor and four times appointed ambassador, stared at the silent phone until it began to wail in its twentieth-century, technological tone, an annoying sound that spoke in a tongue he associated with the mad man on the phone. He slammed the phone down into its cradle, a seventy-year-old revolutionary with no ramparts to storm. Barney walked to his fax machine and sent a note, in the clear, to Garrison Bernard, his son, the oldest, in-grade captain in the United States Air Force. It was a simple, pure message: WATCH YOUR ASS, GAR!

"Frederick, how are you?" Stung by Barney Bernard's reply, Adrian's voice was tinged with an unnatural, forced eagerness. A supplicant's voice.

"Adrian, you old hoss thief. How are you? Have you stolen any horses lately?"

"No, Frederick. Not lately. How are you? How's the family?"

"We are tip-top, Adrian. We have an invitation to the festivities this Monday. Are you going?"

"Yes. We are going. I suggest you pass on the invitation."

"Do you?"

"Yes. Washington is going to be very crowded. It's going to be very difficult to get home from Washington after the funeral."

"Is it?"

"Yes, so I'm told. I wouldn't go if I were you. You might get stuck there."

"I understand, Adrian. I'll keep the family home. Hell, if you've been to one burial, you been to them all, right?"

Adrian, in spite of himself, chuckled. "Well, not this time. No. This time is a bit different. Crowded, you know."

"Paul?"

"Mr. Wolfe is not here at the moment. May I help you?"

"Who is this?"

"Michelle. Michelle Hadley. I am Mr. Wolfe's secretary."

"Are you now? Shit, Paul Wolfe hasn't had a secretary in thirty years."

"That may be true, sir. But he has one now."

"How old are you?"

"Twenty-four, sir."

"Tell Mr. Wolfe Adrian Bennett called. Then tell him to forget it!"

"Yes, sir, I'll tell him."

"Jesus, you know, the fucking world is going to hell in a hand basket, do you know that?"

"I'll tell him, sir, as soon as he gets home."

"Thanks, cunt." Adrian Bennett hung up the phone. Two hours later, a transcript of six and a half minutes of monitored calls was on J.R. Kelly's desk, in complete and total violation of the C.I.A. charter against spying on Americans on American soil. The agents sitting in a motel less than forty miles from the Bennett Ranch listened to the tapes, and forwarded them without comment. It all seemed very innocent to them.

And it should have. They were Army Reservists from the 200th ASA Detachment, Fort Lawton, Washington. Intercepting messages from tanks on maneuvers, they had picked up something more than "tracks," as ordered by Brian Howell, less than nine minutes before Adrian Bennett, feeling confident and safe at his ranch, had called the men he knew best.

C.I.A. HEADQUARTERS
LANGLEY, VIRGINIA
SUNDAY, 10:45 A.M.

The printout of information draped across J.R. Kelly's desk and onto the floor read like a public relations professional had written it personally. The men identified from Adrian Bennett's early morning phone calls were pillars of American society. Their biographies, when printed, would be jammed with patriotism, success, and family values. They had, for the most part, been good public servants when called to serve, and good capitalists when serving themselves.

The first intercepted call had gone to Roger Carlyle, a socialite multimillionaire, Connecticut-born, blue-blooded, twice a European ambassador during the Eisenhower, as well as the Kennedy, administration. There didn't seem to be a single thing about him to call to question. On the surface, he and Adrian Bennett were the most unlikely of·friends.

"Robert," the second call intercepted, had no last name. But the intercept line supplied it. Robert Perry, corporate raider, buyer and destroyer of companies. He'd busted more unions that any industrialist in American history, and he'd done it while providing nothing but incompetent management to the companies he acquired. Bad management equaled sell-offs, much to the credit of his multibillion-dollar bank account.

Darien Talmage, a famous man unrelated to the even more historically famous senators and pillars of southern history that shared his name—industrialist, maker of munitions, champion of Israel, even though he was Baptist through and through. He had a booming voice, and was a regular on Sunday morning current-events programs. He owned television stations, radio stations, and five independent but influential southern newspapers that spoke with a predominantly southern conservative voice. He and Adrian Bennett seemed a better political fit to J.R. than the first two men on his list.

Barney Bernard. Two-time western governor. Four-time ambassador. A calm, quiet voice in politics since the end of the Second World War. Seventy-seven years old, with a thirty-seven-year-old wife, and two small children, ages five and six. He also had a son in the Air Force. A computer specialist and onetime Korean war ace, he had simply quit flying, gone back to school, and was now a very old captain designing tactics in a small room at the Pentagon. Barney Bernard, at least, had said no, much to Adrian Bennett's displeasure. But no to what?

"Frederick," the man asked to stay away from Washington on Monday, turned out to be Frederick Mc-Causland, Adrian Bennett's first cousin, and outside of Jonathan Bennett, his only remaining family. He owned a great deal of Idaho and Wyoming, a gentleman rancher and failed candidate for both the House and the Senate. He seemed to have no particular political views, right or left, and had tended to his business interests for the past twenty years. Like Adrian, he was a hunter and gun collector, yet active in numerous conservationist groups. He had a pleasant wife, and three pleasant sons to help him run his growing western ranching and mining interests. That was it. A successful relative.

The last name, Paul Wolfe, the man with the twenty-four-year-old "secretary." Not much here at all. He'd been Adrian's partner in a venture or two, and managed his last successful political campaign. That had been a long time ago. For the last eighteen years, Paul Wolfe had only a blank slate, interrupted by his appointment to the occasional prestigious board of directors of a major U.S. firm. He was rich, but the sources of his income were vague.

J.R. dialed Paul Wolfe's number. It rang three times, and a sleepy young woman's voice answered.

"Paul Wolfe, please." J.R. attempted to sound like a friend.

"He's not up yet. May I have him call you?"

"No. Thank you very much, Miss . . . ?"

"Hadley. Michelle Hadley. I'm Mr. Wolfe's personal secretary."

J. R. hung up. Personal. Well, she seemed to be that, all right.

So what did he have here that was worth a flying fuck? Adrian Bennett had made six phone calls, lasting a total of six minutes. He'd received what appeared to be four positive replies, and one very definite negative. One call had not been completed. What did these six men have in common. Wealth? Yes, they had that. Politics? No. They had political views, but they didn't seem to have the same political views. They were conservative, for the most part, which seemed to be their most grievous sin. He checked deeper on Paul Wolfe. He'd been in politics after all. Quiet politics. An arms negotiator in Vienna, and later Geneva, Switzerland. He'd been "removed" for refusing to budge from his anti-Soviet and hard-line view on nuclear weapons. He'd not headed either team, but had ranked third on one and fourth on the other. One other fact. After leaving the army after Korea, he had remained in the Reserves He was a major general in the Maryland National Guard. He was scheduled to retire in eighteen months. Interesting man. They all were, to one degree or another. But why did Adrian Bennett call them specifically? What tied them together, at this particular time? And did it make any difference one way or another?

* * *

Long before he'd become an intelligence agent, J.R. had been a cop. One thing you didn't see on the TV cop shows was how much time they spent on the telephone, checking this list or that list, trying to tie a stolen Winnebago to a car thief in debt to his pusher. Or a runaway fourteen-year-old prostitute her father had sent J.R. the picture of, to the corpse that now lay in the morgue, and whom he would now have to call out to L.A. from Prairie View, Texas. Well, he could still use the phone like a cop. The difference was, his phone could be serviced by man's biggest prostitute. The computer. You jammed the data you had into its gaping circuits, stroked it, and waited. Whatever you asked for, you got, if it was in there. The computer, irreverently named "the bitch," began to print, and print, and print. J.R. made phone calls, took information, fed "the bitch," made more phone calls, and finally, he began to find the one thing that tied them together. They had all been in Washington, D.C., on Thursday. They had all been at the Willard Hotel on Thursday night. And so had Adrian Bennett.

From there, it was easy. Airline reservations confirmed that all were gone early Friday morning. Adrian Bennett left Washington in a chartered plane Thursday night. The aircraft, a sleek twin jet, belonged to Bob Perry, phone call number two. J.R. knew the men were here, in the capital, on Thursday. If so, were they also doodling on place mats at lunch that day? "The bitch" had given him all he'd asked for, which, regrettably, still proved absolutely nothing, except to J.R. Kelly. J.R. was not absolutely certain that Jonathan Bennett was going to fly an air strike against the presidential funeral. He couldn't prove it. Not with what he had. He grabbed his coat, and headed out the door, piling once again into the ever-present limo provided by Rosemary Hawkins. He was at her White House office in forty minutes. Time, it seemed to him, moved much faster than ever before.

ROSEMARY HAWKINS'S OFFICE
THE WHITE HOUSE
SUNDAY, 11:55 A.M.

"This is not much, J.R." She dropped his brief report and looked up at him as he hovered over her desk.

"They were all here on Thursday."

"True. And so were hundreds of others just like them. Down to the capital to see the show."

"They all left the next day."

"All but Adrian. He left Thursday night."

"Sure, Rosemary, but he left because he was expecting to see his son out west on Friday."

"And did he?"

"As far as we know, yes."

"Okay. You still have nothing here but a bunch of men, old friends, in the same place at the same time. Maybe they had lunch. Maybe they stayed at the same hotel. Simple pleasures they have doubtless indulged in before, many times over the years. Adrian had been in Washington for days, seeing old friends. He saw Conrad Taylor only a couple of hours before Marine One hit the bridge."

"And then he visited William Rodgers on Thursday morning?"

"That's correct."

"Why?"

"He wanted to get in quick, I suppose, and influence the new President. He made suggestions for the cabinet that appeal to his rather peculiar political philosophy. The President did the polite thing. He listened, nodded his head a lot, and then came to me for advice. You heard the speech. Adrian came away empty, so he went home. According to his Washington friends, he took sick. No other reason. The same reason that covers Colonel Bennett's rush flight to the Bennett Ranch. Not conspiracy, and if it is, it sure can't be proved, or even suggested. If you have more, I'll listen. But at the moment, you have a few old friends meeting for lunch, listening to a speech they didn't much like, and saying to hell with it.''

"I know I'm right about this.''

"Well, J.R., you're the only one who does. Brian Howell thinks you should be locked up before you hurt yourself. And he's the one who got you the information you have so far, with the Army intercepts from the ASA Unit. Surely, J.R., you realize how pathetic this is beginning to look?''

"Are you ordering me to drop my inquiries? Do you want me to see no evil?''

"No. I want you to do your job, as you see it. But I'm convinced you're wasting your time, and I won't allow you to waste more of mine. My God, J.R., the funeral procession is less than twenty-four hours away! Now, please go about your business. Please come by my home tonight, about ten o'clock. We'll discuss our timetable for tomorrow. Meanwhile, I have a busy day. The new President is bewildered, and the old President's widow is trying to drink herself to death. Be where I can reach you, J.R., and that could be just about anytime. In any event, come by the house tonight.''

J.R. stood in front of her desk, looking down on the top of her head as she went back to her papers, her red hair glistening in a brief ray of sunshine suddenly lancing through the glooming Washington skies and bathing the room in its warmth.

She looked up at him. "Well, J.R.? More to say?''

"No, Rosemary. No more to say. I'll be around.'' He looked for the report "the bitch" had punched out, but couldn't find it. Well, fuck it, maybe Rosemary Hawkins wasn't as bright as he thought. He turned, and left the room, more determined than ever that he was right. Like a scene from a comic movie, J.R. spun on his heel and walked back into Rosemary's office.

"J.R.?" He felt like a child about to ask a parent for a new bike, expecting a no, desperate for a yes.

"I need a plane and a pilot, a fast plane, with no markings, and your permission to fly down to Cherry Point. Can you get me one?''

"Cherry Point? Why?"

"You told me to go about my business. At the moment, visiting my brother at M.C.A.S. Cherry Point is what going about my business requires."

She watched his face for a long time, her eyes serious, measuring him. "Fine, J.R. You go visit your brother. Perhaps the time spent will be worthwhile. But I want you back tonight, as I said. Go on out to Andrews. I'll arrange for a fast little government truck for you."

The "government truck" turned out to be a State Department Lear jet. He was alone on the plane when the pilot put a heavy foot to the "truck" and cleared the runway at 2:30 P.M., Washington time.

Jason Kelly had not seemed very surprised when he'd been asked by telephone to meet J.R. when the plane landed at Cherry Point. Both men seemed to feel the meeting would be decisive, one because he thought he knew the answers, and one because he thought he knew the questions.

M.C.A.S.
CHERRY POINT, NORTH CAROLINA
SUNDAY, 1640 HOURS

The two brothers stood outside the Cherry Point Officers Club "Ready Room," drinking a Sunday afternoon bloody mary. The O Club overlooked the Cherry Point Golf Course and the Neuse River. The view was spectacular.

"Nice course," commented J.R. By remaining outside the club itself, whatever he had to say would not be overheard.

"Six-thousand four-hundred forty-one yards. Par seventy-two."

"You shoot par golf?"

"Scratch. Seventy-two on this course, for an eagle eye

like me, is expected. Got time to play a round?'' This was Jason Kelly's way of asking how important this day was.

"Nope. Not today. I'm going right back to Washington."

"Pretty hot limo you flew down here in. How did you arrange that?"

"Rosemary Hawkins."

"Rosemary Hawkins? Conrad Taylor's N.S.C. advisor? What the hell are you doing in that rarefied atmosphere? Course, she'll be out of a job soon, won't she? God, she's a sexy woman. One of my squadron mates has a picture of her taped on his locker door. He cut it out of *People* magazine, with the wind blowing a long, slit skirt open up to here." Jason Kelly held his hand over his head waving his drink for emphasis.

"That high, huh?" J.R.'s face broke into a crooked grin.

"Well, Jesus, she does have the longest legs in all creation."

"Nope. She's about five-foot-one, maybe. But most of it is legs, all right. And brains. Plenty of brains. She's going to be the next Secretary of State."

"What? She'll make a sexy one, won't she? Goddamn. I gotta read more than just the *Windsock.* "

"What the hell is the *Windsock?* "

"Our base paper. A pretty good one, too. A very pretty sergeant who works on the paper took some pictures of me on carrier ops last summer. She kind of likes me, I guess."

"I thought officers didn't date N.C.O.s."

"We don't, officially. She's going to do a feature on me, next week, after the President's funeral. I'm being promoted. First Lieutenant Jason Porter Kelly, U.S.M.C. Has a nice ring to it. A flight commendation from the base commander goes with it."

Jason looked at J.R., a shy smile on his handsome young face, a face so open and honest that a sudden feeling of fear gripped J.R.'s heart.

"That's wonderful, Jace, it really is. I'm very happy for you. Proud too."

"Just trying to keep up with you, big brother." Jason lit a cigarette, the Zippo flaring and snapping shut.

"I'm a pretty goddamn poor role model, Jace. I'm just older than you, that's all."

" A lot older, J.R." Jason went into the club, returning with two more paper-cupped bloody marys, a wide grin on his face.

"Yup. A lot older." J.R. stared out over the course, watching the golfers playing a Sunday round. There seemed to be a lot of them. The Neuse River flowed by, brown and sluggish.

"Why don't you tell me why you're down here, J.R.? This isn't the usual J.R. social call, because you haven't asked me to find you an easy lay for a pudgy guy, and you haven't tried to borrow any money."

"I'm that shallow, am I?"

"Not shallow, J.R.—charming, but not shallow. You're my idol, but you're also a poverty-stricken, sexually deviant secret agent. So why are you down here?" Jason Kelly's voice had hardened. The tacky jokes that began every meeting between these totally different brothers were over, and his facial expression matched the tone of his voice.

"Recognize this guy?" J.R. slid the picture of the Bennetts and the Ace-of-Spades A-10 from his briefcase, and handed it to his brother.

"The plane, yeah. And the pilot. He had his visor down the first time, but not yesterday. Wing C.O. markings on the tail. I don't recognize the older man."

"The Bennetts, Adrian the elder, Jonathan the younger, and, of course, the pilot of the plane, as you said. He's a wing commander at Myrtle Beach. Medal of Honor winner, a national hero. The North Vietnamese interrogated him nonstop for over eight hundred days. Some, no most, say he didn't break. I say he did, only worse. I say he went crazy, in a way a flight surgeon would never see. His father would see it, would know it. He's a very manipulative man.''

"Some kind of politician, wasn't he?''

"Some kind, yeah. Senator. Governor. He's semi-retired now. Eighty years old. But he pulls a lot of strings. All over the country. He lives out west, in Wyoming.''

"Is that where the A-10 was coming from when I saw him?''

"Yes.''

"He was way off course, for Myrtle Beach. I'm surprised he made it back. No wing tanks.''

"Would he need them for a flight like that?'' J.R. Kelly knew nothing about military aircraft. Unless they were being hijacked by the C.I.A.

"Sure. One way, at least. He must have taken them off before he came back.''

"And just how would he do that?''

"Stop at an airbase. Leave them. Refuel. The A-10 can fly one long way on internal fuel. But not round-trip to Wyoming.''

"He probably refueled at the Bennett Ranch. His father has a twenty-four-hundred-foot airstrip out in the fucker-brush.''

"Maybe. But I'll bet when he left Myrtle Beach, he had wing tanks. And they should have been there when I saw him.''

"Okay. Then he just dropped them off somewhere.'' Because he didn't give a shit, thought J.R., because it didn't matter anymore. Nothing mattered to Jonathan Bennett. Not after Monday afternoon. J.R. felt Jonathan Bennett was being chased by demons he couldn't escape.

"That's crazy, J.R.! Even a wing C.O. can't just 'drop' his wing tanks. Hell, when they find out he did that, if he did that, he will have to face a quiet little board of inquiry. He is the base C.O. So they will call in some interested outsiders. But they will investigate. They won't like it, but that's a lot of money to dump in the desert somewhere.''

"Jonathan Bennett is not worried about an Air Force inquiry into missing drop tanks.'' J.R. lit a cigarette, to mask his nervousness. Jason was not fooled and offered his older brother a warm smile.

"I'll bite, J.R. Why isn't Jonathan Bennett worried about an inquiry? I'd probably be court-martialed and dropped from flying if I dumped tanks. You figure he's a colonel, and he'll just get out of it, right?" In the distance a slim woman in a bright day-glo pink skirt completed a swing at a golf ball, clearly missed it, and hurled her club down the fairway. It arced through the steamy southern heat, tumbling end over end. Back at the tee, she'd placed both hands over her mouth, obviously embarrassed. Her playing partners were doubled over in laughter. A peaceful Sunday, like any other, except the nation was supposedly in mourning. 'Twas the night before doomsday . . . J.R. felt like a radar operator at Pearl Harbor on December 7, 1941, calling his superiors, telling them about the planes, being told to "check your equipment."

"Jonathan Bennett is not worried about a flight regulations inquiry, or a court-martial, or anything else that takes place after the President's burial late tomorrow. Because he expects to be dead. He knows he will be dead. And I know he will be dead." J.R. fixed his gaze on his younger brother's face. What Jason saw, when he looked back, J.R. could only wonder. The older brother, the protector, now come to sacrifice his younger brother on the altar of the absurd. J.R. wanted to get up, to run away, to "hop the fast truck" back to D.C. But he knew he couldn't do that. Even for Jason.

"How do you know Jonathan Bennett will be dead tomorrow night, J.R.?"

"Because I believe he will be in the air over Arlington tomorrow. And if he is, you will shoot him down, and kill him for me. I think it will come down to a gun fight between you and the Ace-of-Spades A-10, piloted by Jonathan Bennett."

"I don't understand any of this, J.R." Jason's face remained calm, but his posture changed, stiffened. "Why is he going to be in the air over D.C.? There will be a ceremonial flyby of aircraft, including Air Force One. Is that what you mean?''

''I didn't know about that. No, he will be there on his own. No ceremonial flyby here. I'm convinced he intends to fly an air strike against the funeral itself. If I'm right, I want to be sure you'll help me kill him if I can't prove what I know, or what I think I know. And as of this moment, I can't prove anything I believe. Not even to you. I flew down to ask you to kill an assassin for me if I'm right, and to ruin your career if I'm wrong. Oh, hell, it will probably ruin your career either way. Not exactly like asking you to go to the store for me, is it, Jace?'' Unsteadily, J.R. walked a few feet away, sitting down on the flawlessly maintained emerald grass, afraid to look his little brother in the eye.

They sat side by side, without talking, sipping again from heavy-hitting bloody marys produced from somewhere inside the Officers Club, poured innocently into huge plastic milkshake cups, by an employee of the club Jason had once done what must have been a considerable favor for. Jason, usually drunk after three mild drinks, had ingested approximately six ounces of liquor, with no apparent effect on his faculties. J.R. attributed this aberrational result to the fact that his brother was in at least a mild state of shock. The adrenaline must really be pumping by this time, he thought.

''C'mon, J.R., let's walk.'' Jason stood up, ''milkshake'' in one hand as he pulled J.R. to his feet with the other. J.R. was surprised at how rough his brother's hands were. Flying a Harrier must be harder work than he realized.

They walked briskly, too briskly for J.R., out of shape and mentally drained.

''Look at 'em, J.R.''

''Look at what?''

''The streets. The roads. The boulevards. Names. Arthur Drive. Polk Place. Taft Court. Truman's Road. Roosevelt Boulevard. And we have Tyler and McKinley and

Hoover and Grant and Coolidge. Ol' Silent Cal has a court, yes he does. Harding and Johnson have places. Yes, sir, places. All these presidents with streets and courts and boulevards. What do you suppose Conrad Taylor will get, J.R.?''

''A drive, I think. It has a nice ring to it. Conrad Taylor Drive.'' They sat down on a quiet street, kids playing, bikes going by, a rumpled, bearlike C.I.A. agent and his taller, more handsome blond-haired younger brother, in his dress uniform a walking poster for the acquisition and training of a ''Few Good Men.''

''Can I see whatever else you have in that briefcase, J.R.?''

J.R. pulled the short synopsis of what he knew, or thought he knew, about what would happen on Monday. It covered only eight single-spaced pages. J.R. just sat and smoked, one cigarette after another, while Jason read the report. Finally, Jason handed it back to J.R., and finished off his bloody mary. He was completely sober. On less than a quarter as much alcohol, only a day before, he'd missed out on the sexual experience of his young life. Today, Sunday, ''Jasoon Babee'' felt a hundred years old, and wiser than he wanted to be.

''You really believe this, don't you, J.R.'' It wasn't a question, and J.R. didn't answer it as if it were.

''If he goes after D.C. during the funeral, could you get him? Could you shoot him down?''

''I don't own the Shamrock, J.R. I can't just fly a Harrier into Washington, D.C., because I need the flight time. I presume, basically, that you want me to steal one.''

''Not exactly steal one. I will make the arrangements to get you a plane, if it finally comes to that. And it may not. But if it does, I'll get you a plane. What the fuck is the Shamrock?''

''My AV-8B. Mine, because I fly it all the time. It has a big green, a *Kelly green,* shamrock painted on it.''

''You and the Ace-of-Spades. I never could understand all the stuff you guys paint on U.S. government property.''

''Brothers in arms, that's us. Hot-dog pilots, blow'n

smoke with crew chiefs and plane captains handy with paint and stencils.''

"Is the Shamrock night capable, Jace?''

"One of only twenty on base. Yes, she's night capable. Fully night capable. As for me, I have damn little flight time clocked in at night.''

"You didn't answer my question, little brother. If it comes down to it, if . . .''

"If you ask me?'' Ask me, J.R., he was saying. Ask me.

"Yes. Bottom line, if *I* ask you to, can you shoot this guy down?''

"Technically, or morally?'' A hard look blanketed Jason Kelly's handsome face. J.R. thought of himself as a tough guy, a fighter, the experienced agent used to things hard, things shitty, things unthinkable, but done anyway. Looking at his brother, he realized they were very, very much alike. If anything, considering the problem, Jason was the tougher of the two, age and experience the only barometer separating them.

"Both. Technically, can you defeat this guy if he shows up over the amphitheater at Arlington, intent on killing . . . Jesus, I guess intent on killing *everybody* there. If he shows up at all. And morally. The harder question, I suppose. Can you kill a man, an American pilot, a bandi-flucking hero with impeccable credentials who has proved repeatedly that he is a patriot? A man who believes, if I'm right, that flying against Arlington is his patriotic duty, because his father and a few thousand North Vietnamese ghosts tell him so.''

"It would be a lot easier, J.R., wouldn't it, if my seventeen-year-old lazy older brother were asking little Jace to go to the store with a phoney note for cigarettes?''

"You remember all that, Jace? Sure you do. Good times. I got the cigs, and you liked to go down to the store for me. But now, I can buy my own cigs, and you can fly to the store. Answer the question, Jason. We don't have much time. Rosemary Hawkins expects me back in Washington by ten o'clock tonight.''

"Hell, J.R., that little racer you flew down here in can get you back to D.C. in eighty minutes. But I'll answer your questions now, anyway, because the answers are very important if you're right, aren't they?"

"The most, Jason. The most important in the history of the world. Our world, anyway."

"Okay. Technically, yes, I can defeat him in aerial combat. The book says so. But this guy, this . . . "

"Bennett. Colonel Jonathan Bennett."

"Right. This guy has more hours in the air than I have in the whole of my Marine career, ground or air. The A-10 is a very tough bird. The air-farce brags a lot on competitions between services and war birds that we hold out in the desert each year. F-15, F-16, F-14—you name it, they all try to kill this bird. They fail 90, 95 percent of the time. It looks easy, awkward, slow. And it is. But it can turn on a wingtip, fly stable while it cuts the grass, and that cannon, oh, Jesus, that GAU-8, 30mm cannon. If I knew in advance where he would be, I could just hover off to the side, and launch missiles at him from up close. Even then, the plane might not go down. It can survive all kinds of battle damage. I would, given the *technical* question, try to kill the pilot, not the plane, up close and personal with 25mm fire into the cockpit. But I can tell you this for sure. He's experienced. He will, if you are correct, fly without worry about the next day. Combine that with my zero combat time, and the more likely scenario is that Colonel Bennett would shoot me down."

"He's better equipped, then."

"No. The Harrier can hang in the air, it's fast, it's well gunned. He's better equipped because of who he is. The Harrier can defeat the A-10. I just doubt very much that will make much difference against Colonel Bennett. Christ, J.R., he's Superman compared to me!"

"Well, you're at least Mighty Mouse, aren't you? If he goes, and I know he will, I'll know exactly when and where he is. I'll put you on him, and he won't know it."

"Okay. Then I'll shoot him out of the sky. After which, of course, I'll be arrested, locked up, and charged with first-degree murder by airplane, a new and unusual weapon. Should be a very exciting court case.''

"No. Not murder. Jonathan Bennett, if he flies tomorrow, will be guilty of *attempted* murder. Mass murder. I estimate, if he gets through, twenty thousand people will be casualties to one degree or another." Those numbers seemed to stun Jason Kelly.

"Okay, J.R. I believe you. Then why don't you just arrest this guy, round up the usual suspects, and ride off into the sunset like Humphrey Bogart? If you know all this, why not just turn it over to the FBI or the Secret Service or somebody, and bust him?''

"I'm going to try to do that, Jace. But in this great democracy of ours, the rules of evidence still apply. The Bennetts have done nothing wrong. Already, the people I need most are ready to throw a net over me and drop me in a deep, dark hole. Rosemary Hawkins believes *I* believe all this, so she is giving me the opportunity to make a complete fool of myself. Brian Howell, Major General, United States Army and deputy to the National Security Agency and senior staff, is assisting, in a limited, grudging way. You are the one facet of all this nightmare I don't intend to share outside the family, so to speak. And since we are our only family, I'm saying that my asking you to shoot down a man that might not be guilty, or show up, or might just possibly be a total paranoid expression of my personal inability is . . . well, he's . . . ''

"I'm your backup, J.R. If nobody will listen, you can get the Shamrock shook loose from the base and armed, somehow, and you want to know, aside from technically, if I'll do whatever you ask, simply because you ask it. Is that right?''

"I couldn't have put it better myself, Jace. Will you kill this guy for me, if I ask?" Jason Porter Kelly looked at J.R. for a long time, the hard look gone as his face softened, regressed, went back in time, breaking J.R.'s toughness with its unstudied, pure innocence, blinding him with its virtue. Little brother, big brother. Times change, but some things never change, time be damned.

"Tell me, J.R., do you want me to pick up some milk while I get your cigarettes?"

And there, on the manicured streets of M.C.A.S. Cherry Point, the chubby, unkempt agent crushed the picture perfect Marine in an embrace so fierce and loving he thought his heart would burst.

MYRTLE BEACH AIR FORCE BASE
SUNDAY, 1455 HOURS

Willy Corchran, spy, sat in his assigned quarters (visiting airmen quarters, a maintenance and stress-inspection specialist temporarily assigned to spot-check each and every A-10 at Myrtle Beach air station). He was studying the last fiscal year base report, with considerable envy. The C.I.A. had *never* been this thorough, though when he returned from field duty, he *would* make some changes.

Willy, being Willy, studied the numbers from the number chewer's viewpoint. Take the Myrtle Beach A.F.B. Credit Union, for instance. It had more members than ever in its history. It had loaned more money than ever in its history. Its assets were higher than ever in its history. So naturally its dividends dropped when compared to the three previous fiscal years. More members. More loans. Less income. The American way, and pretty well managed, in Willy's view.

The average number of school years of the enlisted personnel was stated at 12.98 years. For officers, 16.28 years. Overall average, all personnel, 13.3 years of school, a very swift bunch. Civil industry should do so well. But they didn't. The base library lost money, like all good ones do. They took in $18,000 plus, expensed $60,000 plus, for a net income of $40,000 minus. Good books, provided free, at a loss. Typical, well-run libraries could do no more. He was astonished that Myrtle Beach offered its "tenants" bowling, golf, artcrafts, auto rebuild, youth activities, chaplain programs, family services, veterinary services, child care, outdoor recreation. Of the seventeen recreational services offered, only seven lost money. The base's gross payroll (military) was 70 million!

The personnel data, for Willy Corchran, was the most fascinating. Colonel Jonathan Bennett commanded a force of 290 officers, 2,791 enlisted men, for a total of 3,081. Add 410 civilian employees and the 354th Tactical Fighter Wing employed 3,491 humans to keep 82 A-10 aircraft in the air. The base hospital admitted 428, had 4,616 inpatient visits, and 92,707 outpatient visits. Since Myrtle Beach AFB shared its runways with commercial aircraft, it also supervised 8,864 controlled landings involving aircraft from 8 accredited airlines. It had 42 operational and training buildings, 68 maintenance and production buildings, 31 supply buildings, 7 hospital and medical buildings and 21 administration buildings. It had 816 on-base housing units, and 1 mobile home park with 65 lots. The runways comprised 158,340 square yards, "other" airfield pavements held 649,500 square yards, and airfield "pads" totalled 90,384 square yards. The 354th Tactical Fighter Wing itself comprised the

    353rd TAC Fighter Squadron
    355th TAC Fighter Squadron
    356th TAC Fighter Squadron.

All had their supply squadron, transportation squadron (3,095 service orders a fiscal year, downtime for parts only 1.9 percent). Component repair squadron, equipment maintenance squadron, aircraft generation squadron, and finally, the 354th Medical Group (USAF Hospital and MASH copycat).

Then, of course, there were the tenant units, much to Willy's surprise, and deepest admiration. As a model maker, these were beyond his scope, but critical to the planes, and those that flew them. How the fuck could he, Willy Corchran, know so little about what kept our, the U. S. of A.'s, skies so free? Tenant units, meant, well, tenants. Renters. Hangers on to the hangars . . .

They included the 73rd Tactical Control Flight, the 2066

communications squadron U.S.A.F. Judiciary Defense
Council (lawyers!), Detachment 12, 4400th Management
Engineers (big-time modelers!), Detachment 3, 3rd
Weather Squadron, Defense Logistic Agency, and off base,
the 701st Radar Squadron, Det. 1, 0/2./B 1913 CS
(AFCC), whatever the hell that meant! What all the figures
and numbers of the economic resource and impact statement of the 354th Tactical Fighter Wing, Myrtle Beach
Air Force Base, South Carolina, meant to Willy Corchran,
superspy, was this: Jonathan Bennett ran it all, and, if he
moved the Ace-of-Spades A-10 anytime tomorrow, Willy
was to call J.R. and say one word: *Testors*. As in Testors
glue.

Willy's arrival had been routine, compounded by the
fact that Myrtle Beach AFB was nearly deserted. He'd reported at the Consolidated Base Personnel Office (CBPO)
on the ground floor of Building 106 on Avenue A. Since
it was a Sunday, he followed instructions and called the
billeting office, phone extension 7691, Building 12, also
on Avenue A. That had brought to him what appeared to
be the only working airman on base, handling everybody
new, used, or unusual. He thought Willy looked pretty
unusual, but assigned him a billet anyway, advising him
that *someone* would see his orders, or whatever, at 0715
hours Tuesday morning. Willy, speaking very calmly for
his first field job, asked what would be required to get him
access to the aircraft lined up wingtip to wingtip on the
rain-swept airfield. His was a temporary assignment, to
check for stress cracks on gun pods and fairings. He didn't
intend to wait until Tuesday, unless so ordered. He handed
the airman a yellow flashed I.D. card, that he hoped would
gain him access to the mass of dormant A-10s on the base.
What better time to work, he asked?

The young airman hesitated, pulled a series of rubber
stamps from under a desk, and listlessly began to stamp a
series of papers.

Here, Willy Corchran became a true spy. He actually
snarled. "Hey, fuck this . . . I'm going to work the flight
line, starting today! With a little luck, I can complete my

work and be *gone* by Tuesday. Okay? Jesus, I'm just going to check for stress fractures on eighty-two aircraft, and only on two key fuselage joints at that. Who's the ranking officer on this base for the next three days?''

"The Boss. Colonel Bennett. He's here. He let almost everybody else go on a seventy-two. Never did that before, in my memory, and I've been here twelve years."

"Good. Call him for me. Tell him why I'm here. I'm temporary, that's all. This is perfect. I can check his aircraft while the weekend goes to hell with inactivity."

"Call him! Call the C.O.? You're a fuck'n nut." He said this with real conviction, and a true bureaucrat's voice.

"Well, you just assign me a rack at the Visiting Airman Quarters, and I'll work on my own. If, in the unlikely event I should run into the Wing Commander out on the line, I'll tell him who I am, and why I'm there. Otherwise, you call him, right now, and set it straight." Willy Corchran gave him the "J.R. look."

Small, rumpled, wearing thick eyeglasses, Willy Corchran was turned loose on eighty-two A-10s, and one Wing Commander. In his pocket, for luck, he carried a tube of Testors glue. The welcoming clerk went back to bed. He hadn't expected any new personnel on base. There wouldn't be any more, he was sure.

FAMILY QUARTERS
THE WHITE HOUSE
SUNDAY, 3:00 P.M.

"Rosemary, how many people have seen him?"

"Emily, I have no idea. Many, many thousands, I would guess. It was very dramatic, moving him . . . moving the President to the rotunda late last night."

"Dramatic? Do you really think so?"

"Of course I think so. You did, after all, establish a new presidential burial sequence. People have waited for hours to view the coffin. Some have simply not left, just sort of . . . well, they just stay there, on the Capitol steps.''

"I've ordered the security people not to bother them. They told the TV news people they were going to join in the funeral procession from the Capitol to the amphitheater tomorrow. These people really loved Conrad. You know how committed he was to ending the problem of the homeless in this country.''

"Of course, I do, Emily. No president in history gave that problem more thought. He hated the homeless—I mean, what they were going through.''

"He did, didn't he,'' Emily said, her eyes dulled by vodka and orange juice, and the nearness of the end of her life. Emily intended to join her husband, as soon as possible, after his interment. She intended to, but she knew, deep inside, that it would take more courage to kill herself, than it would to live richly ever after.

"You know, Rosemary, I shouldn't say this, but I've never received so much attention in my life. When Connie was alive I just stayed in the background, coming out to look pretty at this or that ceremonial occasion. Now, I'm receiving seven hundred thousand pieces of mail a day. And the switchboards! I declare, they never shut down.''

"The people love you, Emily. I've told you that, and now you know it's true.''

"Yes. They seem to. Rabble, most of them. But I appreciate it anyway.'' Emily Taylor poured herself another glass of ''orange juice.''

"Rabble, Emily? Surely you don't mean that!''

"Oh? Why, of course I do. The great unwashed, all the poor little people doing the things they need to do to keep their poor little lives together. Rabble? Yes, it fits. Conrad called the citizens of this great republic 'stupid, docile sheep'!''

"I don't believe you, Emily. Conrad Taylor loved this country, and particularly its people.''

"He had you fooled too, huh? Well, it's the truth. In the bedroom, after sex, he would rave on and on about what he was going to accomplish as President. It had precious little to do with what the people wanted, I can assure you. He was a great man, and great men have no time for small minds. He told me so, in those exact words."

Rosemary had listened to the drunken monologue for an hour, watching Emily Taylor drink one glass of vodka and orange juice after another. She'd had enough of Emily Taylor. More than enough.

"Well, Emily, you seem to have not much to do but wait until tomorrow, and the funeral. I know how hard it will be on you, so I'd like to suggest that you . . . that you taper off on drinking between now and then. Your children and your family will need you."

"Oh, I have a lot to do. I've asked my secretary to invite the Russian Premier and the British Prime Mini—"

Rosemary leaped from her chair. "What! You've done what, you stupid, drunken cow? You've invited visiting heads of state to come here, to the White House, before the funeral ceremony?" Filled with sudden, ugly rage, Rosemary knocked the drink from Emily Taylor's hand, and then slapped her face as hard as she could, sending her sprawling onto her lacy bed, legs akimbo, her robe open.

"You withdraw those requests, and you do it at once! Conrad Taylor was talking about *you* when he said he had no time for small minds. Protocol, bitch! Protocol! You're not the queen of the United States, you're the widow of a dead President. A widow, unemployed and without power, and you just don't invite heads of state to drop by for tea while you flash your barren body at them through a fog of alcohol. Now, I'm going to give specific orders to your staff, and believe me, they will obey them! Stop drinking. Take a bath. Button your lip, period, or I'll see to it you don't even show up to bury your husband. You're a disgrace to Conrad's memory, and to yourself, and to your country. And I'm going to see to it you either shape up, or ship out. You will not disgrace this country! Do you hear me, bitch? Are you listening? Do you understand me?'' Rosemary's hands were clenched in tiny fists at her side.

Emily, sitting up on the bed, oblivious to her nakedness, her disheveled, wanton appearance, could only nod her head in agreement.

Shaking, Rosemary strode from the private bedroom, through the second-floor trappings of flowers and cards and condolences from all over the world. She called a meeting of Emily's personal staff, and told them what she wanted, no, demanded, that they accomplish. Stay with Emily Taylor. Clean her up. Never leave her for a second. Make her ready for her last and greatest appearance on the national stage. She wanted, and expected, to see a widow the Virgin Mary herself would weep for. From that moment, Emily Taylor was a virtual prisoner in the family quarters, to be let out only after she looked the part of presidential widow.

The staff scurried away, and Rosemary Hawkins went to her office, and into her private study, locking the door behind her. She threw herself down on the couch, and burst into tears. But she had little time to cry. Emily Taylor would see no world leaders. But the new President would, and she had to pave the way. She sat up, wiped away her tears, and began to write down what she felt William Rodgers needed to know about the approximately 150 national leaders from all over the world he would meet. Beginning Tuesday morning. The Tuesday before Thanksgiving. Turkey and dressing at the White House? Why not. A select few. Twenty, twenty-five. That would be a very interesting Thanksgiving dinner. East meets West, over a stuffed, steroided, flightless bird. It would require French wine, Russian vodka, British ale, and German/Polish sausage stuffing. She would wear red, of course.

She'd forgotten J.R's flight to see his brother. But she did remember she'd asked him to come by her home tonight at ten o'clock. What she hadn't yet admitted to herself was why she wanted to see him. Why, indeed . . . ?

MYRTLE BEACH A.F.B.
SUNDAY, 1550 HOURS

Willy Corchran, dressed in Air Force fatigues, walked down the center of the aircraft parking apron, a short thirty minutes from his assigned quarters. On each side of him as he walked, the A-10s were lined up neatly, engine covers on, the four-colored strips on the covers identifying them as 354th Tactical Fighter Wing aircraft. To his right as he walked, across a 9500-foot runway, he could see the busy Sunday commerce of commercial airline traffic as it moved in and out of the Myrtle Beach civilian jetport facility; and behind that, the golf course. Tactical fighters and commercial airliners. A curious mix, but thrilling to Willy Corchran, who'd built all of them, to scale, at one time or another.

The base was nearly deserted. No one had challenged him, but then, why should they? There didn't appear to be more than a dozen airmen on the whole field, an occasional power line run to an aircraft, hooked but not supplying power. He walked on, across the west-east axis taxiway, hunting for the Ace-of-Spades A-10. He was not surprised when he found it. Like he'd been told, it was off by itself, parked near the calibration hardstand. A sign said WARNING FIXED CANON FIRE TEST AREA. STAY WITHIN MINIMUM SAFETY ZONE DURING TEST. The Ace-of-Spades looked passive enough. But bright yellow and black umbilical cables were attached to it on both sides. Power to the aircraft was constant. A panel was open on the left side, exposing avionics equipment. A few yards away, the ALS (Ammunition Loading System), especially built to arm the aircraft with 30mm cannon shells, stood partially covered by a tarp. He could see the feeder, jammed with shells ready to load the onboard ammunition drum. The fully loaded drum held 1350 rounds. There were no crewmen about, and no activity, but he knew the loading process was nearly automatic. One man could do it. The process took thirteen minutes.

He turned away, and headed back toward the parked A-10s. He selected one nearest the calibration hardstand, and began to remove its engine cover, then its cowling. He was looking for microscopic stress cracks and he expected to find some. He said a fervent prayer that no microscopic stress cracks would appear in him. He hauled a large blue tool service box over to A-10 #655. All he needed was there in the box, including a stick-on stencil which he applied at once. It said *S/SRGNT William Corchran, Fixer of Cracks*. He'd made the stencil himself, at Langley. Soon, he was engrossed in his work, and filling out a work order to replace cracked and stressed rivets on 655's left engine cowling. He felt perfectly at home.

"What the hell are you doing, Mac?"

Bent over the engine cowling, high up on an access ladder, Willy answered without turning around. "I'm working, asshole! What does it look like I'm doing?"

"Airman. You get your ass down here right now!" Command. A command voice. Willy tried to remain calm, but eccentric, befitting his job title of "Fixer of Cracks." He turned around, looked below him, and into the hard face of Colonel Jonathan Bennett, his eyes covered by reflector-type aviator glasses.

"Yes, sir, Colonel. Sorry I cussed at you, sir, but I didn't know who you were. Tell you the truth, I didn't know anybody was here."

"Stay up there, son. I'm Colonel Bennett. I command this wing. I know most of the men in this lash-up. But I don't know you. Why is that?"

Willy thought that whatever he said had better be good. "I just got here, Colonel, and I'm only scheduled to be here a week. The duty man wanted me to wait until Tuesday to start my inspections, but hell, Colonel, this is perfect. Stand-down time, no flights, nobody asking me why I look at two-inch squares of metal with a machine nobody else understands, just to find stress cracks nobody cares about. Well, shit, sir, begging your pardon, but *I* care about the two-inch cracks, and if I find 'em, I fix 'em.

And when I fix 'em, I give that aircraft an extra two hundred hours for each inch I fix, and it won't come apart on you while you try to shoot up a T-72 on its way into West Berlin. So I'm working, sir. Don't much care for the politics of it, sir, but I've been in the Air Force eighteen years, and I'm not likely to go much higher in grade. But aircraft I look at with this little scoper of mine fly long, fly hard, and stay in the air. I can get half your wing checked by 0600 Tuesday, sir, if you'll allow me.''

''You got orders?''

''Yes, sir, of course I do. They're on my bunk. I know I'm not to start work until Tuesday. I asked the man in receiving to call you and let you know I'd be out here. But he said that would be a cold day in hell. So, I just sort'a went to work on my own. I'd like to continue, sir, with the Colonel's permission. I don't drink, don't smoke, and don't carouse with women. I have eighty-five percent of the money I ever made in the Air Force, and after my thirty years is up, I'm going to build a design of my own that will outfly, outshoot, and outlast anything the Air Force ever built. And it won't *ever* have stress cracks.''

Jonathan Bennett, on a mission, and near the end of his planning, could find nothing wrong with Willy Corchran, U.S.A.F. He seemed a man with a single purpose in life. Find those stress failures. Fix those stress failures.

''Carry on, Sergeant, carry on. But keep your mitts off the A-10 near the hardstand. That belongs to me, and I prefer to fix it myself, it it's broke. All pilots are relieved of duty until after the funeral tomorrow. There will be no military flights this weekend prior to 0600 Tuesday. I may do some engine testing, but that's about it.''

''Will you need my assistance, sir?''

''I will not.''

''Fine, sir. May I return to my duties?''

''Carry on, Sergeant.''

''Sir, I'll present my orders to you on Tuesday, sir, when scheduled.'' A slow, dry, terrible smile spread across the colonel's face, and he removed his mirrored glasses, staring up at Willy, still perched on top of the tall access

ladder. The colonel's eyes were very blue, like glacial ice.
They were completely empty of human emotion of any
kind. The colonel ran a blue handkerchief across the lens
and replaced the glasses, hiding the emptiness behind reflected life.

"I'm sure you will be there, Sergeant. If I'm not, please
give them to my deputy. Carry on." He threw a lazy salute
toward Willy, and walked back between the long lines of
parked A-10s, toward the headquarters building.

Willy Corchran, heart pounding, went back to #82,
hunting for stress with clammy hands and a dry mouth.

ANDREWS AIR FORCE BASE,
WASHINGTON, D.C.
SUNDAY, 1630 HOURS

The State Department's Lear jet touched down as pre-
dicted by his little brother, eighty minutes after it pulled
into the stark blue skies above Cherry Point. As it rolled
onto a taxiway, J.R. looked out the porthole-shaped
window, startled by the number of foreign-owned, state
aircraft. They seemed to be everywhere.

The Ilyushin of the Soviet delegation, led by the Presi-
dent/General Secretary, was parked in an area usually re-
served for Air Force One, which had been flown to a base
in Maryland to prepare for its participation in tomorrow's
flyby. The larger reason was security. The threat from
Scorpio, whoever or whatever Scorpio was, necessitated
placing the Ilyushin in the safest possible place. Air Force
One's hangar seemed to fit the bill, at least psychologi-
cally. No particularly special moves had been made to
protect the Soviets. They were just one delegation, among
over a hundred, half of which had been, or were about to
be, at war with the other.

THE PENTAGON
OFFICE OF THE DEPUTY TO THE
SECRETARY OF THE AIR FORCE
SUNDAY, 1600 HOURS

"General Forbes?"

"Yes, Captain."

"Colonel Jonathan Bennett calling. He said not to bother you if you're busy."

"Did he now. Well, goddammit, you just put him on. Captain Leary, do you know who Colonel Bennett is?"

"Of course, sir. He's the C.O. at Myrtle Beach."

"You don't know where he came from, do you?"

"Sir?"

"From my wing, dammit. I was his wingman before you got your first toy airplane, *if* you ever had a toy airplane. Put him on." The general pulled a large black cigar from between his teeth and picked up the receiver.

"Jonathan! Goddamn, boy, it's good to hear from you!"

"How are you, General?"

"General, is it?"

"I'm sorry, Taylor. Air Force, you know. I talk to generals the way majors talk to me."

"Understood. Now, what can I do for you, Jon? And how is your father?"

"Dad's just fine, Taylor. Tough as nails. Older, of course, but still plenty tough. He asked about you recently. Wondered if you'd be interested in the early pronghorn hunt next year. The ranch is crawling with 'em. There are record heads up Wadums Canyon. He just thought you'd enjoy it. You haven't hunted the Bennett Ranch in five years."

Major General Taylor Forbes, growing paunchy and out of shape, gave an audible sign, remembering the harsh beauty of the Bennett Ranch, snow topping the ridge as he and Jonathan rode along it, and the big muley had jumped up, dead run away, and Jonathan had let Taylor

Forbes take him, the mule deer scored as the second largest trophy ever killed, mounted now over his fireplace in Georgetown. Oh, God, he'd been a long time away from a horse's back . . .

"You tell your dad I'll be there, with bells on! You'll be there, too, won't you, Jon?"

There was a slight hesitation, but only slight. "Hell, yes, Taylor. Somebody has to find them for you."

General Forbes chuckled at that, the first real laugh he'd had since Marine One had taken the President down. Not that he cared. He hated Conrad Taylor's policies. Most of the Pentagon did. Discreetly, of course. "Jonathan, you made my day. No, pass on that, you made my year, what's left of it."

"Are they giving you a hard time, Taylor, since the man with your first name as his last discovered Marines can't fly helicopters worth shit?"

"Yes, they are, but don't remind me about the name shit."

"Pretty bad in the Department of Defense, huh? I'll bet you wish you were down here with me, flying every day."

"True, I do wish that. But then, I wouldn't be a two star, would I? No offense, Jon."

"None taken. Hell, I *command* this base. Good enough for a retired gunfighter."

"You deserve more, Jonathan. You should be a brigadier, out at test flight. I know it. Everybody knows it."

"Political strokes. I'm not good at that. Hell, who knows that better than you? And by the way, just between you and me and the trophy heads, what the hell is going on for old 'Connie,' anything special?"

"Well, it's classified, Jon, you know that."

"Well, sure, I guess it would be. Forget I asked, Taylor."

"I don't believe I said that, Jon, that security shit! Christ, this has been a bad week. Who has higher Air Force security than you do?"

"General Taylor Forbes, for one." Again, Jonathan

provided Taylor with a genuine laugh. Two, in one day. Oh, boy.

"Well, let me tell you, Jon. We are going to flyby 80 aircraft, at what you might call the climax, if you'll excuse the expression. Just before they haul him out of the amphitheater, we are going to fuck up every radar screen and satellite scanner on earth. Eighty planes, lining up, sort of offstage, so we can overfly at about, no, exactly eight minutes before dark, where the engines will show off whistles and bells and jet exhausts. Spectacular, I would guess. And the cherry on the topping, that big fucking Air Force One, will dip its wings at the exact time they hand the widow the flag. By then, it should be dark. If it rains, of course, it will *look* dark, whether it is or not. Personally, I don't think any of this will come off on time. So I have made it my responsibility to get those eighty aircraft in the area early enough to be on time. I'll have the squawk box. When I say flyby, everybody goes. Two stars gets you that, Jonathan."

"You can have it, thank you very much. But I have one more question. Who of our illustrious corps of fearless flyers is involved?"

"All guard units. Hell, who gets more flight time? Maryland and Virginia air gnats. Some Navy. Marines from Yuma."

"Yuma! Jesus, that's a long way."

"Yeah, well, they'll be here anyway. A flight of six C-130 tankers. How's that for dramatic?"

"I don't know about dramatic. Loud, yes. But not dramatic."

"You're right. Actually, I had to scrape airplanes from every base on the east coast."

"I notice you didn't scrape up any A-10s from M.B."

"Your men are full-time professionals. I thought you would be insulted. To tell you the truth, I figured you'd punch me in the nose if I asked. Hell, we have plenty of AFRES units. You know the reservists. They'll fly anytime."

"Yeah, I know. Taylor, it looks like the sky over D.C.

is going to need a traffic cop.'' Jonathan knew Taylor Forbes very well. What the general said next finalized Jonathan's strike plan.

"Correct. No security here, just try to keep them from running into each other, that's the main thing. The whole pass is scheduled to take less than eight minutes. After that, they can start to shovel the dirt on the bastard.''

"I gave the 354th seventy-two off. This base is deserted. If you need refuge after the funeral, fly on down. You need the air time. Take it light, Taylor, and take it wherever you can.''

"I will, Jonathan. And thanks for the call. You made my task considerably easier.''

"I'm glad, Taylor. You made my task easier too, such as it is.''

"Oh? And what task is that?''

"Trying to stay out of your way, Taylor. Just trying to stay out of your way. Then again, I just might join the parade, if I'm bored enough. If you see one lone A-10 in your parade, just make a little hole. I promise to stay in line.''

Once again, for the third and last time this day, or any other day, Jonathan Bennett provided Major General Taylor Forbes a hearty laugh.

CIA HEADQUARTERS
LANGLEY, VIRGINIA
SUNDAY, 6:00 P.M.

"What do we have on Scorpio, Nadine?''

"We have nothing, J.R. Personally, I don't think Scorpio exists. The codes don't match anything we have, and yet they were sent clear, like they wanted to be sure we picked them up. We did, and that seems to be the extent of worry. The Soviets claim they are not concerned about a helicopter assault on their embassy. The Soviet President was said to be anxious to visit the rotunda tonight, to see his 'comrade,' President Deducted Taylor.''

"Not nice, Nadine. Funny, but not nice.''

"Yeah, that's me. Not nice. The upshot is, he's wandering all over D.C. tonight, including a visit to the Nam wall. I say fuck it. Everybody loves this guy. It's not like he was walking the streets of Moscow. *There* he might get shot. Security in this town means agents from one hundred countries are tripping over each other. Speaking of agents, how is Willy?''

"Willy is doing his duty, above and beyond the call.''

"Where?''

"He joined the Air Force.''

"Right.'' She gave him her pained mother look.

"Well, you asked.''

"Forget I asked. And call this number, will you? The honey voice on the other end sounds like somebody sure to get you charged with communicating with minors, and I do mean minors for immoral, illegal, and otherwise unlawful reasons.''

"Who is she?'' J.R. thought Nadine was the funniest woman he'd ever met. Ugly, but funny.

"Don't know. She didn't leave her name. All I could get out of her that made some kind of sense was that she hadn't voted for Conrad Taylor, and she was sorry if she drank your rent. Or something like that. She told me her morning period was over. I congratulated her on not being pregnant, and told her you would get back to her sometime before World War III.''

"It's the blond! The five-hundred-dollar blond!''

"I'm happy for you, J.R., but all the news is not so good. Rosemary Hawkins sent a personal messenger over here. I'm a spy, but I didn't open it.'' Nadine handed J.R. a small envelope, pink, with his initials on the front in purple ink. He tore it open. The message was brief, and to the point: *My home. 10:00 P.M., without fail—R.*

Okay. Ten o'clock. Four hours. He knew who was attached to the phone number. Bonnie, who had once grieved for her little dog Agnes, deceased, for two days,

abstaining from sex for "the whole time." His question
was answered. She grieved for presidents, particularly
presidents she hadn't voted for, for three days. He called
her. Much to his surprise, she agreed to meet him at his
apartment, in thirty minutes.

He decided the nation could survive for an hour without
him. This time, he passed on buying champagne. He
climbed into the limo, and told the driver to take him
home. Bonnie showed up, thirty minutes later, right on
time.

J.R. was bent at some absurd angle, Bonnie above him,
one of her legs hooked behind his head, the other spread
out wide, her hips moving against him, holding him tight
inside her, her breasts hot and glistening with sweat, as
she asked him to move, first slowly, then faster, and she
seemed to draw him into her and swallow him up, her
breasts pushed into his face, her hands gripping them and
thrusting her nipples, both of them jammed into his mouth
at the same time, and then he climaxed, a climax so huge
and wrenching he thought he would die, and she screamed
her pleasure, one cowboy boot locked across his neck,
impossibly swirling around him, her body long and lithe
and floating as she screamed again, this time in Russian.
Russian? Then she fell away, onto her shoulders, her an-
kles locked behind his head, sighing, calling him "lieb-
chin." German. German? Oh, Jesus H. Christ in a
handtruck, what did he have on his hands now? As for her
hands, they were thrust down between their sweating bodies, one stroking him, one deep inside her vagina, until
they both screamed once more, this time in English. It
was the greatest sex he'd ever had in his life. And that
included the Valley Girl from the Treasury Department
steno pool who played nude chess. With no hands.

"That was pretty terrific sex, J.R. A ten on a scale of
ten. I missed you."

"Did you know you fuck in three languages?"

"Not always. I speak six. I only fuck in foreign languages when the sex is good. With you, it's more than good.'' She was *Vanity Fair* beautiful, all golden and sleek. She was lying with her stomach next to him, propped on her elbows, her breasts, those wonderful breasts he'd figured he would never see again, swinging just above the surface of the sheet, the nipples hardening when they touched. She was doing it deliberately, watching his face.

"Do you like my tits, J.R.? I want you to like my tits.'' She moved over him, brushing across his chest, her breasts against his chest as she nuzzled his ear, her hair falling across his face, her leg swinging over him, pulling him into her, incredibly, then sitting up, not moving, her hands on his chest. Warning lights went on in his head. This didn't happen to him. Not like this. Bonnie was movie star beautiful. She was young. And most important of all, she was fucking him again, her hips moving in long, slow circles, and even as he gushed into her and she screamed out her own climax, he knew this was not at all what it seemed to be.

"My name is Bonnie Parker. You know, like Bonnie and Clyde.''

"His last name was Barrow.''

"Yeah. Well, anyway, I'm an interpreter for the State Department. And you, J.R., work for the C.I.A. I sort of hunted you down, actually. My best friend went to high school with your brother. She dated him. She was in love with him, I guess. When he went to Annapolis, and then into the Marines, she saw him a few times. She's a law clerk at the State Department now. We share an apartment in Georgetown. She has pictures of Jason, still, even after all this time. He writes her once in a while. He sent a picture of himself, taken last summer, during final flight school. You were in the picture.

"He told her to find you a nice 'bad' girl. I volunteered. And here I am, falling in love with an overweight spy twenty years older than I am. I called your brother in October. He told me a few things about you. I tracked you down, and the last time, our first time together, you were drunk, and I just sort of picked you up. No. Not sort of. I did pick you up. Then, afterward, and all the next day, I panicked, and pulled my little 'hick' routine on you, and ran away. All of this is the truth, J.R. I like you. I more than like you. If you're interested, I could see as much of you as you like. If not, well, I'll just go back to my roomie, and forget the whole thing.''

"You must be looking for a father, Bonnie. I'm a rusting old degenerate, broke most of the time, and gone all the time. You're the kind of fantasy I pay five hundred dollars a night for in Hong Kong or Milan, or East Berlin.''

"Okay, J.R. Do you have five bucks?''

"I think so.''

"Well, get it.''

J.R. got up from the bed, aware of his growing paunch, wishing he were still a halfback at Michigan State, wishing he were still twenty.

"Got it?''

"Yeah. I got it.''

"Give it to me.'' J.R. handed Bonnie the five-dollar bill.

"Okay. I'm paid for, now come back to bed and let me earn it.'' She rolled on her back, raised her knees, and placed her feet wide apart. None of this could be happening. Not to him. She placed her hands between her thighs. "C'mon, J.R., taste me, and see if I'm real.''

Over her head, she waved the crisp five-dollar bill. She raised her hips high off the bed, crooning to him in what he presumed was Russian. This time, at least, he spoke the language. During the worst nightmare of his life, God, or some higher being of some kind, had sent him a savior of his sanity, a soft, effective medicine to calm a man walking the dark edge of terror and violence too horrible to deal with and stay sane. In a world of the unknown and the unreal, she brought him back to the human race. Like Willy Corchran, she was exactly what he needed. And like Willy Corchran, she would be dead in twenty-four hours.

THE VICE PRESIDENT'S RESIDENCE
NAVAL OBSERVATORY HILL
OCCUPANT, WILLIAM RODGERS,
PRESIDENT OF THE UNITED STATES
SUNDAY, 7:00 P.M.

"Did you enjoy dinner, Rosemary?"

"It was exquisite, Mr. President. You will bring a new style, not to mention a new menu to the White House. Tastier and, I suspect, a whole lot less pretentious."

"Well, I like the basics, done well. Fish and game, light sauces, American food created with respect. Of course, I'm known for downing large quantities of chili, and beef to excess."

"Conrad and Mrs. Taylor were aware, should I say, that the White House is a rather formal place."

"Stuffy, you mean."

"Sometimes. Some guests of the White House need and expect stuffiness. You could serve them Nike tennis shoes, if you did it with servants in the proper livery."

"And you know them all, don't you."

"Is that a question, Mr. President?"

"No."

"Yes, I know them all."

"That sheaf of papers you brought me tonight. Is it important that I read them before Tuesday?"

"Not important. Absolutely imperative!"

"My, my."

"You may tut-tut all you wish, Mr. President. Your guests in Washington have come to bury *you*, not Conrad Taylor. But to bury you, they must first take your measurements. I know, from personal experience, your measurements are quite formidable."

William Rodgers placed his large hand over Rosemary Hawkins's small one. She let his hand rest on hers briefly, then pulled away.

"I will just have to wait to check those measurements

again, personally, William. Right now, I'm more concerned with your opponents and potential opponents.''

"Was the other night a mistake, Rosemary?"

"Yes. From a timing standpoint. What, if anything, develops between us in the future is not something to think about or discuss at this time. But I do remember, William. With gusto, I might add. But now, you must concentrate on the synopsis I have prepared for you. The Chief of Protocol will be here in one hour, to completely brief you on what exactly will take place tomorrow, when it will take place, and where you are to be from 6:00 A.M. until 6:00 P.M. Monday. At 6:01 P.M., you must become the President of the United States in deed, as well as fact. I've come up with a small idea for your consideration. Thanksgiving dinner. Here, or at the White House. I think the White House should be the choice. Emily will be gone Tuesday morning. You must move right in. Our country's future depends on it.''

"Thanksgiving dinner?"

"Why not? You have given a public speech, inviting a wide-open series of talks between nations, at every level. I will serve, just this one time, as your official hostess. Of course, after the guests leave, I shall have to stay and discuss how it all went. I will probably have to remain quite late. If you don't mind.''

"A dinner. A Thanksgiving dinner. What a wonderful idea, Rosemary. Please, invite whom you think you should. You have my full backing.''

"I will, of course, withhold information on this dinner until after Conrad Taylor's interment.''

"Of course, Rosemary. That is as it should be. Now, let me see those character sketches. Let's start with the Soviets, shall we?''

"As you wish, Mr. President." Triumph. Rosemary Hawkins, if she played her cards right, believed William Rodgers would do anything she asked him to do. If it was a sweet triumph, why did it leave such a sour taste in her mouth? As she watched William Rodgers read her skillfully drawn reports on foreign leaders, she thought about

J.R., and just what he might be doing. And the Bennetts.
What were they doing? She was in the woods to Grand-
ma's house, and the wolves were everywhere . . .

WASHINGTON, D.C.
SUNDAY, 6:00 P.M.

The city was now jammed with foreign visitors. Dulles
International Airport was crowded with international
flights. The Concorde was parked, and would remain
parked, the French delegation having determined they
would need a ride home. The French President, the head
of a shaky coalition, had brought along with him most of
his enemies. The talk with the new President of the United
States would solidify his power, and he wanted his opponents to see, and be impressed. He had considered himself
a personal friend of Conrad Taylor. They both had horses,
and pretty young wives. Conrad Taylor had been a French-
man at heart.

At nearby National Airport, extra aircraft had been
added to handle the expected surge in travel to Washington. Unlike Dulles, National handled only domestic flights.
Cab fares into downtown, normally about eight dollars,
were up to thirteen. From Dulles, the fare averaged fifty
dollars, up from the normal thirty-five.

Baltimore-Washington International had become the
landing pad of choice for the ''lesser'' nations and their
delegations. Splashily painted aircraft from poverty-
stricken countries of Africa and Asia, countries that nevertheless had one full and technically equal vote in the
United Nations. Taxi fare from B.W.I., thirty-five to forty
dollars, jumped to over one hundred.

Dulles held the Sunday record for big-timers. The British and the rest of the members of NATO were spotted
and placed at one safe area of Dulles, while lower-rung

officials looked on as their aircraft went on their way, still flying international commerce.

In short, on this Sunday night before the President's funeral, aircraft were parked, dispersed, hidden, or flown away, in a direct pecking order, noticeable to those who cared. Cab and limo service was grossly inflated, if you could find one. The State Department limos moved the "biggies" of the international scene. The small fry had to fight it out among themselves to acquire the "exclusive" services of the city's many limo companies. The smart few used Washington's excellent, clean public transportation systems. Hotels, of course, were packed. There was no room at the inn. The suburban hotel and motel chains jacked their prices sky high, and had no trouble filling up.

Add to all this the murderous businesses of drugs and the crime that went with them in the "real" Washington, D.C., where the populace was once again on a record pace of killing one another to support the smiling drug kingpins of the Far East and the vicious warriors of distribution from Colombia and Central America. Shake well, and mix, and a cocktail of surrealist dimensions could be prepared. All in Washington drank of it, but nobody noticed.

Hookers did a thriving business, whether they were thousand-dollar call girls servicing diplomats or twenty-dollar street walkers lowering their prices and their mouths just behind the Greyhound bus depot at First and L Street. Of the nine thousand taxidrivers in the city, it was said only one didn't know where to find you a hooker, or drugs, but he'd only started at 5:55 P.M., and it was his first day on the job. By 9:00 P.M. he'd met at least four hookers and four drug dealers personally. Up close. The average cabbie made upwards of eighty dollars per hour between 6:00 P.M. Sunday and 8:00 A.M. Monday. After that, things got somber, and the cabbies did too.

Maryland, Virginia, the District of Columbia. Full of the most powerful people in the world, served by the greedy, the sick, and the powerless. The tourists were there, and they did some of the things tourists do. But for the most part, Washington was a cold, wet place. Populated by ambulance chasers, hoping for a glance at the wreck, and an even closer look at the people who would need to clear away the wreckage, and get the world's train back on its peaceful track.

The embassies were jammed with their regular staff, doubling and tripling up to make room for the Savile Row suits, the French gowns, the colorful African and the somber but expensively dressed Asians, wearing perfect copies of Savile Row. Languages, a maddening number of them, danced across and strained the phone wires of the world. Most of the talk was simple gossip. Who would see whom? Who would talk privately with the new President?

Much talk, of course, centered on Rosemary Hawkins. America's Dragon Lady, said the Chinese. America's Bhutto, said the Pakistanis. America's problem, and good riddance, said nearly everyone she'd encountered on her world travel for Conrad Taylor. In essence, good old-fashioned gossip.

A world wake, with everyone checking rival countries, to see who had gained or lost weight, bought a new army, or sold an old one. Treaties old, treaties new, treaties in work, treaties broken. A wonderful mini-series, with the whole world watching by satellite. And in the Capitol rotunda, the man whose death brought this carnival and its players together lay in a flag-draped, closed coffin, while thousands of people passed quietly by, surrounded in the strange atmosphere of peace when near the dead. If there was a cheap ticket this Sunday, paying your respects to Conrad Taylor was it.

But the *chief tickets, and who had them,* was the number-one talk among the rich and infamous, and those who followed them. Journalists, at 6:00 P.M. that Sunday night, were given a detailed list of those invited to attend the formal service for Conrad Taylor. All were invited, of course. But 5,488 people had been delivered gilt-edged invitations to attend the service *inside* the amphitheater. A special section was set aside for the most important. The list was, then, a world pecking order. The special section, with additional and extensive seats, would hold less than three hundred people. In the seats surrounding this elite group, would be the entire government of the United States and its three branches, as determined by the Constitution. Senators. Congressmen. Judges. Governors. The amphitheater would have, in one place and at one time, the most intensive gathering of world and national power in known history.

Outside the amphitheater, it was expected that one hundred thousand people would walk through or sit in the special sections being marked out in a furious race against time by every available member of the cemetery staff itself, assisted by 250 National Park Service personnel, and watched over by a security force too large, too complex to even estimate.

Emily Taylor, through Rosemary Hawkins, was staging the grandest funeral the world had ever seen. No one, not even the press, could come up with a figure even close to its actual cost. The liberal press, whose champion lay in state, said that whatever the cost, it was not enough.

Conrad Taylor was thought to have been on the verge of bringing the world to the peace table, and his death must keep the momentum going. An odd way to look at it, said the conservative press, who believed the funeral was vulgar excess, to match his peace plans. So nothing much changed. A new president, a new administration to be named early next week, and a long series of the very kind of talks Conrad Taylor had hoped to conduct.

Washington, and the rest of the world, would pay their last respects, and get on with the business of business. Where you sat at the funeral of Conrad Taylor took up the front pages of newspapers from the Baltic to Brooklyn, from the Caribbean to Cairo. The amphitheater, at Arlington National Cemetery. The place to be, if you were a player. Only a few men knew enough not to be there, not to play in this game at all . . .

THE VIETNAM MEMORIAL
THE WALL
SUNDAY, 6:00 P.M.

The three men stood very close to the wall, people moving silently around them, some touching the wall, crying, making imprints by "tracing" the indented inscriptions, pencils flashing across paper to leave the impression. A game. A thing children had learned centuries ago, using cliff chalk and leaves.

"Mr. President. Mr. General Secretary! Sir, this is insane!" The Soviet ambassador to the United States, wearing a heavy coat, his hat pulled low over his eyes, looked about him, eyes darting, searching every face he could see. His thick glasses were dotted with a fine mist that had just begun to fall and, in fact, he was now for all practical purposes, blinded.

"I had no idea, Nikky. It's overwhelming."

"Sir, what if we are recognized?"

"I'm wearing a . . . what is it called, Joseph?"

"A Washington Redskins jacket, sir. Very popular here. They are a football team."

"Ah. Soccer. I like soccer."

"No, sir. American football. Until the accident Wednesday, they were scheduled to play a home game today at RFK Stadium against the Dallas Cowboys."

If the President knew what the RFK stood for, he didn't mention it. "Ah, Cowboys and Indians. The United States. What a country!"

"Yes, sir."

"We must go back, Mr. President. Our security agents have no idea where we are."

"Of course not, Nikky. I snuck out, as Joseph so aptly put it. Am I, or am I not, the President/General Secretary of the Soviet Union?"

"Of course you are, sir."

"Then if I choose to go for a walk, I will go for a walk. I wanted to see this Wall. I needed to see this Wall."

"Yes, sir."

"Good. Then let's go on, shall we?"

The stark, black wall, with its thousands of names, had moved the Soviet President in a very unexpected way. He had been near tears, for the young men represented on this rain-swept, downward flowing slab of marble might just as well have been Russian. He'd come to see the Wall for himself, because a delegation of young veterans, soldiers of the eighties, had come to see him in Moscow.

Thirty young men, Afghanistan veterans, and they had spoken, and written, to American veterans of the war in Vietnam. A long war, like Afghanistan. A costly war, just as the Soviets had lost in Afghanistan. Fifty-two thousand Russian dead, a figure that only a few highly placed people in the Soviet government knew to be the true extent of the toll in human lives.

The war had been very much like Vietnam. But here, this Wall, this plot of land separated the two countries in ways he had never acknowledged to himself before.

He was the most popular leader in Soviet history. He was *Time* magazine's "Man of the Year." He was the acknowledged leader of a worldwide thrust for peace. All of this was good, of course. Peace was a good thing, if it furthered Communist goals. And now, temporarily, it was a survival tactic. The Soviet Union needed some time. Twenty years, at the minimum. Its far-flung adventures had very nearly destroyed the Motherland. Another popular revolution was inevitable. He understood that, and, to stop it, decided to lead it himself. And it was working, at least on the surface.

Underneath the surface, well, Russia was Russia, now as it had always been. When required, Russia would expand. West. East. Wherever. Then Conrad Taylor had won election to the Presidency, and, with the able assistance of his ravishingly beautiful National Security Advisor, the two countries had begun to plan, and were near implementation, of the most comprehensive drive for peace, a "one world peace," that the world had ever seen. It was a plan ideally suited to the Soviet Union. Implemented, it would one day be a disaster for the United States.

Now Conrad Taylor was dead, and Rosemary Hawkins would be William Rodgers's Secretary of State. All was not lost. Perhaps it was just beginning. Peace. A peace Russia could live with, until it chose not to. William Rodgers had said he intended to follow Conrad Taylor's ideals. Like his enemies in Russia, the new President would have to deal with his political rivals, as well as his friends. Politics. A wonderful life!

"The American people come here by the thousands, each day of the year. It is quite impressive."

"I can see, Joseph, why they come here. And I can see why Conrad Taylor was planning his own peaceful initiatives. Each name is a young man, most barely twenty-one. We have monuments all over the Soviet Union celebrating the dead from the Great Popular War. I understand this movement very well."

"That is crap, Your Excellency," said the Ambassador. "This is not a war monument! Twenty million dead in the Great Patriotic War! This is nothing." He waved his arms dismissively toward the Wall, knocking his misted glasses askew.

"Nikky, listen to me. At this very moment, two American submarines are lying quietly off our coast. The two submarines can kill one hundred million Russians in less than thirty minutes. Study this wall, Nikky. We are going to put up a wall very much like it, in Red Square, celebrating the dead from the 'small' patriotic war in Afghanistan. If we do, I believe one, and perhaps two, of those Trident submarines will go away."

"I don't understand, Mr. President."

"I know you don't, Nikky. But you, Joseph, you are twenty-eight. You served in Afghanistan, did you not?"

"Yes, Mr. President. For two years."

"Do you, then, understand?"

"Yes, sir, I do."

"Fine. Good. Very good. I will need you by my side,

until I leave. I have not yet decided what day that will be. I may stay until Thursday. You, Nikky? Is that agreeable to you? I know how you hate all this formal ceremonial duty. You run the embassy, as usual. Joseph speaks perfect English and French, and he is very handsome. Rosemary Hawkins, she will find him very interesting. The stories one hears, eh, Nikky? Are they true? I'm told she . . .''

Here, the President/General Secretary of the Communist Party threw his arms, bearlike, over the shoulders of the two men, and led them through the drizzle toward the Soviet embassy. Nobody noticed them, but Joseph smiled when someone shouted ''Go Skins,'' as they left the Vietnam Memorial grounds.

ARLINGTON NATIONAL CEMETERY
SUNDAY, 6:00 P.M.

A small army of regular Arlington Cemetery personnel accompanied by electricians, carpenters, and specialized construction workers descended on the amphitheater and the entire cemetery grounds, closed for the day. Network television executives had haggled, bargained, and finally begged for position to broadcast the President's funeral. CBS, famous for its golf coverage, wanted to put a man and a camera atop the mast of the Maine Memorial. The White House, with the superintendent's urging, found a spot for all near the service area of the amphitheater, and one, ABC, would have access inside the amphitheater itself, providing the feed for all three major networks. CNN, pugnacious and effective, would broadcast from a special booth near the Tomb of the Unknowns only a few yards away from the amphitheater entrance.

Very little work would be necessary inside the amphitheater. Bulletproof glass was installed in some quantity around the selected VIP sections. The Secret Service supervised this installation, which took all night to complete. Removable colored tape was laid down throughout the amphitheater, directing the participants from one place to another. It would take approximately three people for every one in the amphitheater just to get them squeezed into the correct spots. It was a security nightmare, and agents from all over the world toured the cemetery, literally looking under rocks.

The burial site itself was near the amphitheater, and accompanied by the sounds of news helicopters overhead, the plot was surveyed. The area was roped off, and finally a canvas canopy went up over the gravesite. Conrad Taylor's grave was dug under a plywood-and-canvas circuslike tent attempting to hide the process from the news media. The sides of the grave were finished with a long-handled shovel. It was to be marked with a simple white cross. A humble touch, a warm, people touch. So reported the media. It had been Rosemary Hawkins's idea, eagerly accepted by Emily as her own.

At the Capitol rotunda, thousands of people streamed past the President's casket, paying their final respects. They would continue to do so until dawn. The team designated to carry the President's casket the next day practiced, out of the public eye, with a weighted casket exactly like the one that now held Conrad Taylor at rest under the flag-draped catafalque that had borne the bodies of both Lincoln and Kennedy in the past. Getting the casket onto the horse-drawn caisson for the trip to Arlington posed no particular problem. Getting it into the amphitheater, and to the spot designated for the service, was another matter entirely. Stairs in, stairs down, stairs up, stairs out. The body and casket were particularly heavy. There would also be a stop at St. Matthews Church, for a Catholic mass, although Conrad Taylor could hardly have cared. From the rotunda, to the caisson, then on to St. Matthews, up the church stairs, out and back down the stairs to the caisson, and then, worst of all, in and out of the amphitheater. The lieutenant leading the casket team worked them very hard until past midnight, until he was sure they could handle their duties without dropping the deceased President at some point along the way. The slightest error would be forever documented, and at worst could disrupt the solemnity of the funeral. The casket team would perform its job admirably.

For all the fuss and bother attendant to the burial of a president, he was no more special on Monday than anyone else eligible to be buried at Arlington National Cemetery. Twenty-four burials were scheduled for Monday, and cemetery employees would conduct them all with dignity and the appropriate military honors before the 4:00 P.M. state funeral was scheduled to begin.

At Fort Meyer where the dead President's Kentucky Derby hopeful, Presidential Candidate, was being stabled, considerable hell had broken out. The Thoroughbred was no Black Jack, the horse that trailed the caisson bearing Kennedy in 1963. He was not calm. He was not trained. He was not disciplined, except to run fast. He was a racehorse and expected to be treated like one. Three veterinarians, two of his regular jockeys, and a host of lesser Fort Meyer personnel were doing their best to keep him from killing himself, or anyone near him. His trainer was nearly hysterical. Presidential Candidate was a potential fifty-million-dollar syndicated stud. Win the Derby. The Triple Crown. Horse of the Year. Bingo. Big-time dollars. He could only bury his face in his hands as the horse lashed out at his stable door. One tendon. One anything. Oh, it was her horse all right, and she could do what she wanted with it. But the trainer thought Emily Taylor was the stupidest woman in the world. Finally, he ordered one of the vets to tranquilize the Thoroughbred. He didn't like the idea, but he liked even less the thought of losing a potential fifty million dollars, and his 20 percent cut.

In minutes, Presidential Candidate was down, eyes open, respiration normal. He was going to be a weird-looking horse, trailing that caisson, drugged out of his equine mind.

It was at about this time that another "Thoroughbred" began to kick out at her stall. Emily Taylor, less than twenty-four hours before she was to preside over her husband's funeral, went alcoholic crazy and began to throw things. Little things, like chairs and tables, and bottle after bottle of booze and exquisite, expensive perfumes. Her private study, bath, and bedroom began to resemble a sweet-and-sour-smelling Beirut. The scotch went crashing against the walls, ruining thirty thousand dollars worth of wallpaper. The perfume bottles were directed at the doorways, intercepting and occasionally hitting a brave soul attempting to get in and put a stop to the carnage.

In a final act of exorcizing her demons, she stood before a full-length, triple-view mirror, completely nude, holding a seventeenth-century chair worth $100,000 over her head. Screaming "bitch, bitch, bitch" over and over, she hurled the chair with all her might into the mirror, destroying the image she could no longer stand to look at. She was then quiet, and went docilely with two female staff members into Conrad Taylor's bath, allowing herself to be bathed and her hair washed. She did not touch another drop of liquor for the rest of her life. Meaning she would remain temperate for twenty-three hours.

Not a word of the rampage got out. But the smell, not quite identifiable as booze or perfume, hung over the private quarters of the White House, in spite of a ten-person cleanup team. The 17th century chair was a shattered mess, and so was Emily Taylor.

MYRTLE BEACH A.F.B.
SUNDAY, 1900 HOURS

Willy Corchran was sitting on the wing of an A-10, eating an apple when he saw a jeep drive along the access road, headed toward the Ace-of-Spades A-10. He watched intently as Colonel Bennett pulled up to the aircraft, got out, and did a slow walk around it, actually kicking a tire. After his inspection, he jumped back into the jeep, and headed back the way he'd come. Willy thought spying was easy. It was also pretty boring.

Hungry, Willy jumped down from #82's wing and ambled back toward his assigned quarters. He knew roughly where the dining hall was. As a transit airman for the week, he could get a meal at odd hours. The Ace-of-Spades would just have to do without him for an hour or so.

MYRTLE BEACH A.F.B.
SUNDAY, 1920 HOURS

While Willy Corchran ate a stale sandwich, the Ace-of-Spades GAU-8 30mm cannon was also being fed. Two armorers, technicians of high quality and training, rolled the ammunition loading system dolly up to the aircraft, and under the watchful eyes of Colonel Bennett, they fed 1350 rounds of high explosive incendiary (HEI) cannon shells into the A-10's onboard drum. The previous best time for this operation was twelve minutes fifty-one seconds. It took them nearly fifteen minutes to complete the job. But Colonel Bennett did not reprimand them. He simply ordered them to button up, and tow the ALS back to the hardstands. They didn't ask why he wanted his aircraft gunned up. They were twenty-year-old airmen. He was the base commander.

When Willy Corchran returned to the line at 8:00 P.M., everything looked completely normal, but the ALS dolly and its belted machinery were nowhere to be seen. Two hundred and fifty yards from where he stood was a pay phone, beacon bright, and empty. The plane hadn't left, but the ALS system was gone, and the open loading panels were shut tight on the Ace-of-Spades. He deemed this information too valuable to ignore. He called the special number given to him by J.R. A voice he didn't recognize answered. He hung up, dialed the number again. This time, Nadine answered. He asked her to get the message to J.R. that the flight he was interested in was "over-loaded." He hung up without telling Nadine where he was.

He then walked back to the plane next to the much-climbed-about #82, and pulled himself up onto its access ladder. He was out of shape, nearsighted, tired, and scared witless. But he was still on post. This time on A-10 #177, only 150 yards from the object of his by-now-more-than-vivid appreciation for and about aircraft. The Ace-of-Spades looked positively malevolent, unlike the silent line he was working on. He was absolutely sure the colonel's plane was going to fly. Not tonight, maybe. But it was going to fly. He hoped his cryptic message to J.R. expressed exactly that.

WASHINGTON, D.C.
SUNDAY, 8:24 P.M.

J.R. reached for the phone, while Bonnie rustled around somewhere under the covers, hunting, trapping, enveloping him in sensations so exquisite he could not think straight. Her mouth was hot on him, her thighs curled warmly around his waist, and somewhere, from another world, Nadine gave him Willy Corchran's message about "overloaded aircraft, some goddamn place," and he sat bolt upright, and only Bonnie's quick reflexes saved him from being castrated.

She nearly fell off the bed, her cheeks flushed, her hair wild and damp, her mouth slack with what he had discovered was a near insatiable desire for any variety of sex. Her eyes met his, and changed, aware. He was troubled, or in trouble, or worse. She pulled away and sat up, crossing her legs, watching him talk, or as seemed to be the case, listen. He rolled over and hung up the phone, over-weight, overwrought, and more desirable to her than all the young studs that hounded her day after day in the world's capital of young, available, and abundant women.

"What is it, J.R.?"

"I have to leave, Bonnie. I don't know when I'll be able to see you again. Soon, I hope. I just don't know."

He bolted toward the bathroom, and she could hear the water beating against the glass shower walls. Last Wednesday, he'd sung in the shower. But not tonight. She got up from the bed, slipping into her bra and panties, wanting the scent of him on her, and in her, and to hell with the shower. She pulled a soft cashmere sweater over her head, snapped the tight wraparound leather skirt to her lush hips, and stepped into her high heels. She tossed her pantyhose into her purse, and grabbed a hairbrush, all in one motion. When J.R. emerged from the shower, she'd fetched them each a cold beer, made up his bed, and was sitting quietly on the couch, head back, watching the slowly twirling New Orleans fan that served no discernible purpose whatsoever, because the air in J.R.'s apartment never circulated, no matter the season.

J.R. had changed somehow. He'd shaved, and he was wearing a very sharply pressed dark blue suit, a white shirt, and an expensive pearl-gray Italian tie. But the change was not limited to his clothes. He looked like a younger, harder man, a very dangerous man. J.R. Kelly pulled a Browning 9mm pistol from his dresser drawer, and slipped it into a shoulder holster. She extended her hand to him, the beer she held glistening with dewlike drops in the heat of the room. She'd drawn a smile on its delicately steamy, slick glass surface. He took it from her without thanks, but bent to her, kissing her softly on her throat, the smell of Aramis cologne lingering when he pulled away and sat down on the bed opposite her.

"This is all very serious, isn't it, J.R.?"

"Us? Yeah, it probably is."

"No. I don't mean us. I mean whatever has turned you from the man in my bed to what you are now. A few minutes ago, I had total, complete control of you. Now, I hardly know who you are. I've never seen you working. You're working now, aren't you?''

"Yes. I'm working now. I wish it didn't have to be this way. But it does."

"Can I help? Is there some little way I can make this easier for you?"

J.R. hesitated. "No. No. But I want you to promise me something." He gave her his best sincere look.

"Blind promises? C'mon, J.R., I love you, I think. But you could be in Tasmania tomorrow. Marry me. Then ask for blind promises." Marry me, she thought. Had she actually said that?

"Stay away from the funeral tomorrow. That's what I want you to promise. Just that."

"Why? I'm a government employee of the State Department. My bosses expect me to go."

"Just do as I ask. Promise me you won't go."

"Nope. No promise. I don't know what the hell you're worried about, but if I can't help you except by making my bosses mad at me, then I'll have to pass." Bonnie sat up, reaching for her purse, digging for a cigarette.

"Okay. Then help me. Take a package down to Cherry Point, and give it to the guard at the main gate. I'll have the package for you in about two hours. You'll be flown down, but you will have to drive back. I'll arrange for an agency friend of mine to have a cab waiting for you at the civilian airport. Drive to the base, deliver the package, and drive back to Washington. To here. To this apartment. Stay here, until I come for you. And ask me no questions."

"Do you love me, J.R.?"

"I don't know, to tell you the truth. I was married, a long time ago. It didn't work out. I do know you make me happy."

"Good enough, for now. Is the package important?"

"Too important to give to just anyone. It's for Jason. And he must have it."

"Is it ready?"

"No. But I'll have it ready by 9:45. You will have to

be here in this apartment at that time. It will be delivered by a cabbie. He will just come to the door, and give it to you. Tell him you want to go to Andrews Air Force Base. But he will take you to National, because that's where your plane will be. Get on, and you will fly down to Cherry Point, arriving at New Bern's Simmons-Nott Airport. A taxi will take you from the New Bern Airport to the air station's main gate. Give the package, and a big smile, to the sentry at the gate. Tell him to deliver it to the O.O.D., and get back in the cab. Ask him to drive you back to Simmons-Nott Airport. A rental car will be there, in your name. Drive back to D.C. and wait here, for me. That way, or no way. I could have someone else do it, but I don't trust very many people at this moment. Probably, I trust some I shouldn't. So, you wanted to help? That's the only help I need, and it's the most important.''

Bonnie slid out of her reclining position, and walked to where J.R. sat, pulling him to his feet.

"Big deal, huh?''

"The biggest.''

"Tell me about it, when it's over?''

"Yes. When it's over.''

"And about your wife? And marriage. And good, long, slow fucking that makes beautiful babies?''

"Bonnie, for Christ sake, I'm too old, and in the wrong job for babies.''

"Maybe. But will you talk about it?'' She'd moved closer to him, her hands around his neck, her face even younger than he'd noticed before. Like his brother, he had no choice here either. Use them up, J.R., right? That's your fucking job.

"Yes. We'll talk about all that domestic bliss shit.''

She kissed him, a long, slow, deep kiss, and lay down on the bed. "I'll do it, J.R. Go on. Fix your package. I'll take a nap. It looks like I'll need one. Will I see Jason?''

"No. Not this time. But you'll see us both, later.'' He didn't sound like he believed that.

"When is later?'' A seeker of truth, under a fan, on his bed, looking at him with wide open faith.

" 'Later' is when it is." Unable to look into her trust-ing eyes for another moment, J.R. turned away, and softly closed the door behind him.

C.I.A. HEADQUARTERS
LANGLEY, VIRGINIA
SUNDAY, 9:18 P.M.

J.R. studied the packages. Not much, but all he could do on his own. It would probably not be necessary. Sure-ly, the powers that be would listen to him. Surely they would . . .

J.R. had a great number of friends, for a spy. Some of them were not exactly friends, but people that he'd done favors for, like Marlon Brando in *The Godfather*. Marlon, playing the Mafia leader, Don Corleone, had said some-thing like, "There may come a time when I will ask a favor of you in return for this small thing I do," like dumping a headless or bodyless horse in a recalcitrant Si-cilian's bed. And like that.

J.R. had done his share of favors, and now, this cold, dismal night before an even colder dawn, he called them in. The nonfield agents dealing in Soviet fighter tactics supplied him with a strike profile flown by an American pilot on Moscow, and then obligingly reversed the sce-nario, using D.C. as a target. A Marine colonel from Cherry Point, on temporary duty, interceded for J.R. with Jason's commander. Ostensibly, the Shamrock would be the lone aircraft in the flyby from Cherry Point. The Ma-rine colonel was a former participant in the Vietnam "Phoenix Program," a certifiably psycho shooter of what-ever he was pointed at. He would "gun-up" the Harrier during a stop at Patuxent River N.A.S. Guns and missiles, compliments of a Marine colonel who believed J.R., be-cause he *knew* J.R. What finally emerged was a way to get Jason Kelly and his beloved Shamrock Harrier IIB in place, near Washington, D.C., *if* Colonel Bennett showed up for the shootout over the D.C. corral. If not, Jason would join in the flyby, legitimately. However you looked at it, J.R. Kelly was calling in his favors, making up codes and code names, to "steal" his brother's fighter, piloted by his brother, with a considerable amount of information hand-delivered for his brother by Bonnie. In other words, J.R. Kelly was sacrificing the lives and careers of a score of people, simply because they believed in him, and, therefore, in his boogeymen.

"I can't stay married to you, J.R., not as long as you stay a cop. I can't worry about you anymore. I mean, do you ever think about Bobbie and me? Ever? When you stalk those goddamn streets, in your fancy clothes and your fancy cars and your fancy women, all in the goddamn line of duty? How much shit do you have to roll in, before you get it all over us? Bobbie is nine years old, and he tells his school friends his daddy's a cop who deals drugs and drives a Mercedes! Yesterday, he got beat up by two little niggers who really do push dope. They're ten! Ten years old! How much slime do you think you can walk around in? Quit! Quit! I mean right now! Or, so help me God, I'll take Bobbie back to Michigan, I'll go back to teaching, and . . . and I'll divorce you." Her heart broke, saying it.

J.R. Kelly, L.A. Police Department detective sergeant, had been chasing, and getting next to, the biggest pair of drug dealers in Los Angeles. *"Another year. Give me another year,"* he pleaded, his voice a near whine. When he was like this, J.R. made her sick.

"No! Now! Quit now, or we are gone."

"You wouldn't do that. You wouldn't just walk away from me. Cheerleaders never leave Michigan State, all-American football players." The boyish smile, hidden in the carefully cut beard. The smile that always cut to her heart, melted her resolve, and ultimately defeated her.

The next day, Laura Metcalf Kelly, and her son Robert John Kelly, packed up the small, neat house in Westwood, and went back to Michigan.

Because of his job, J.R. was unaware his family had left until five days after the fact.

ROSEMARY HAWKINS'S HOME
SUNDAY, 10:00 P.M.

"Ms. Hawkins is waiting for you in her study, Mr. Kelly. May I take your coat?" Well. The butler could speak, and politely, too. J.R. shrugged the heavy gray coat from his shoulders. It was an old coat, dating back to his L.A. undercover jobs. It had cost $7,000, if you counted the $5,000 worth of coke sewn into the lining. As usual, like a good butler, he disappeared after leading J.R. down a softly lit hallway to a room he'd not yet seen in his previous visits.

If most of Rosemary Hawkins's home seemed sterile and unlived in, with its stark blacks and whites and chromes, this room looked as if it had been transported from another century, intact. Bookshelves lined the walls, thousands of books. A fire snapped and roared in the huge stone fireplace, bathing the rich mahogany wall trim and the creamy green walls in a comfortable glow. The furniture was rich-looking, old and expensive, but used, not just displayed. And the warmth was augmented by the most eclectic selection of lights and lamps he'd ever seen, the stuff you see in trendy, out-of-the-way antique stores. Railroad lamps. Banker's lamps. Tiffany lamps. Behind her desk was a multiple pole lamp right out of the sixties. The carpet was a rich, soft shag. On one wall was a glass case holding what looked like hundreds of thimbles. This room, in spite of its maps and official papers, was where Rosemary Hawkins showed more of herself than he'd seen before. The room made him feel comfortable.

Rosemary Hawkins, wearing gym shorts and a sweatshirt with a picture of the Beatles on it, was pumping furiously on an exercycle at 10:00 P.M., after an eighteen-hour day. She acknowledged him with a glance, but continued her workout until a timer at her feet began to ring. It was a white, old-fashioned ceramic timer for stove tops, made by Sears in the fifties. She jumped off her cycle, grabbed a towel, and shut the timer off. A lock of red hair was stuck to her forehead and sweat dripped from the tip of her nose. "Back in ten minutes, J.R. I'm sorry to ask you to wait." She turned away and skipped across the room and through a door apparently leading to her bedroom. The gray sweatshirt, soaked in sweat, clung to her back like a soggy, second skin.

J.R. walked about the room, more amazed with each tick of the clock. Most of the beautifully bound books on the shelves had the worn look of being read by the owner, many times. There were classics, histories, biographies, and a section of erotica, over fifty volumes, many of them nineteenth-century classics. There was a photography section, how-to books as well as coffee table types. Two shelves contained children's books. One three-foot-wide shelf, stretching upward to the ceiling, held a complete, bound section of books entitled simply, "Treaties, U.S. Government, 1788, 1988." They had clearly been used over and over. Erotic works, government treaties, Dickens and Chaucer and Arthur Conan Doyle. And, in a small alcove in each corner of the room, psychedelic lava lamps, in four shades of blue.

Rosemary Hawkins and this room, and what it told him about her, far outstripped anything he might have previously believed. It also explained the provocative, short skirts. In her own mind, what could she possibly have cared about whatever people thought about how she dressed? It had nothing to do with her at all. She was what she was, and you either dealt with that or you didn't. Her body was an asset, like the jammed bookshelves. His respect for her, and his interest in her, soared. She was the most complex human being he'd ever encountered.

* * *

"My goodness, J.R.! You look wonderful. Where have you been hiding that wardrobe? You look almost civilized."

"Don't let it fool you, Rosemary. I'm not in the least bit civilized."

She'd changed into a black silk jumpsuit, tightened at her tiny waist by a wide, silver belt. She was barefoot, her hair brushed straight down her back, and she smelled of soap, a flower he couldn't identify, and then he did. She smelled like orchids. Or frangipani. Or something hot and sweet and far removed from the late November chill of the capital. There was a hell of a lot about Rosemary Hawkins he liked. But she scared the hell out of him, and could make him feel like a kid with a single, superior arch of her eyebrow. He tried to imagine what it would be like to be around that powerful personality every day. It would be exciting, and then you'd go up in flames, mastered by her intellect and her sensuality. Or so he thought.

"I spoke to the President. He's invited a number of prominent leaders to have Thanksgiving dinner with him at the White House next week. What do you think of the idea?" She was sitting on the floor near the fireplace painting her toenails a bright, Chinese red, as if she were alone in the room.

"I think it's a fine idea, but nobody will show up."

"Oh? Why not?"

"Because there is a very good chance, in my view, that they will all be dead by then."

She glanced at him, eyebrow arched, and went back to her toenails, the brush moving across her foot in delicate, even strokes.

"You have something new then, J.R.?"

"A little."

"What?"

"Jonathan Bennett gunned up the Ace-of-Spades tonight."

"Gunned up?"

"He armed it. That 30mm cannon is now loaded with enough firepower to knock the amphitheater into Tennessee."

"You know this for sure?"

"Willy didn't see it loaded. But the loader is gone, and the panels are all secured. That would indicate, in this particular situation, that the A-10 is definitely loaded and ready to shoot."

"Fine. Let's assume for the moment that what you say is correct. The A-10 . . . *The wing commander's* A-10, has been armed. So what?"

"Well, it means . . ."

"J.R., you know it means nothing! Brian Howell tells me the entire wing is scheduled to begin a simulated combat operation on Tuesday. Two squadrons of the wing are going to fly out west and the third squadron is scheduled to conduct joint operations with Marine strike aircraft from fleet Marine Corps, Atlantic, on Wednesday."

"Brian Howell said that?" J.R. tried, but failed, to hide his incredulity.

"Yes. Major General Brian Howell. My deputy. My trusted friend, as well."

"So a gunfighter with loaded guns, under the circumstances, is no big deal."

"Well, J.R., is it? Does it sound all that odd to you?" She had switched feet, one leg extended, while she bent her leg at the knee to begin to paint the toes of her left foot. She had a way of moving her body, like a ballet dancer at the practice bar. It bothered him, and it made him angry.

"Yes. It sounds all that odd. Operations begun on Wednesday will last through a four-day Thanksgiving. That doesn't happen in this country. Ever. Those four days are holidays."

"I didn't say over the holidays. I said Tuesday and Wednesday. And I saw the orders." The brush continued its even, rich march across her toes. She did not look up at him.

"General Howell showed you the orders?"

"He did. Operations end Wednesday at 1600 hours. All units are released until the following Monday at 0800 hours. It's a surprise operation, to test readiness. Planned for months, I might add.''

"How do I verify that, Rosemary?"

"You don't, J.R. I just did. That should be enough, don't you think?'' It was not a challenge.

"Yes, of course, that should be enough. I mean that is enough.''

"Well, just to assuage your fear, I, believe me, I knew they would need to be assuaged . . . is that a word you like, J.R.?''

"Yes. Assuaged fears. Love it.'' Sarcasm now, and he didn't give a shit.

"There. On my desk. Brian Howell's full report on Operation Paladin. Planned over six months ago.''

"I don't have to read it.''

"Yes you do. Read it.'' A command this time. J.R. picked up the report, threw his jacket over a chair, and rushed through what appeared to be a very complex, detailed, surprise test of readiness. It was genuine, without doubt. It was also impossible. The flyby scheduled for Conrad Taylor's funeral would render this defense test null and void. And Brian Howell had given this fantasy to Rosemary Hawkins. As fact. As reality. And why had he done that? J.R. was faced with a moment of truth. For a spy, these moments did not apply.

"Well, I guess you're right. Apparently, I'm full of shit as a Christmas goose.''

And then she was standing very near him, behind him, her hand tapping gently against his holstered 9mm. "I've never seen you wear a gun, J.R. Have you always worn it?''

"Only on dark nights, or in dark alleys, or when I expected the lady's husband to show up and beat me to a pulp.''

"This is not a dark alley. And I have no husband. Also, I'm no lady.'' He could feel her body against his, could sense her nudity under the jumpsuit as she pressed against him, her arms encircling his waist, one hand, then the other, hooked into his belt.

"I'm afraid, J.R. I'm afraid of everything, especially the dark. Stay with me tonight. Sleep with me. Hold me." For the briefest instant he gave himself over to what she said, and how she felt, pressed tightly against him.

"Can't do it, Rosemary. Not tonight. Somebody has got to keep the country safe from the Communist menace." He stared into the blazing fireplace, hoping she would not move her slim fingers lower. She held herself even tighter against him than before, pushing her breasts against his back.

"I'm the Communist menace, is that it, J.R.? Well, if I am, take me to bed, and the world will be safe."

He turned inside the circle of her arms, displaying more grace than his shambling bear physique seemed to possess. He gave her a warm look, a kind look, and then he turned shitty. "No. Not tonight. We need to go over all the details of tomorrow's . . . festivities."

She stiffened in his arms, released him and turned away, walking behind her desk. She punched a button and a small hotel room-sized refrigerator door popped open. Rosemary had her fridge, he had his New Orleans fan. "Well . . . if you won't sleep with me, will you at least share a beer with me?"

At that moment, as Rosemary stood with one hand on the refrigerator door, the other poised to reach for the neatly stacked bottles of beer in the refrigerator, J.R. was absolutely, irrevocably convinced that Rosemary Hawkins was the most desirable woman alive. And because he was a really good spy, this time it meant only a cold beer.

"Yes. I'd like a beer very much. Three, actually, because I'm a very big man."

"Three. After three beers, J.R., do you get silly? Or will you still be able to protect us from the multiple variety of Commie, Pinko, Fascist, designer-specialties conspiracy. Or conspiracies. Which is it?"

"Conspiracy. As in one."

"Good. I trust you to deal with one conspiracy. I'll tell Brian you are on the job, converted, and that he need not throw a large net over you at this time, while calling for measurements that put white coats on backwards, thus re-straining forward movements as well as masturbatory in-stincts.''

She opened three long-necked Budweisers, set them on her desk, and plopped heavily into a fuzzy, eighty-dollar flea-market chair. The refrigerator door remained open. But dark.

''You need a new light bulb, Rosemary.''

''Hard to find, J.R. The fridge is forty years old, and takes a six-inch light bulb.''

''Not to worry. The vast resources of the C.I.A. will find you one.''

''You'd do that for me, J.R.?''

''I would.'' He was chugging the second beer and reaching for the third.

''You're a prince, J.R. A true prince.''

''Yes. I am a true prince. Now, let's go over what needs to be done tomorrow, shall we? I have to be out of here by midnight, at the latest.''

''Hot date, J.R.?''

''That doesn't even deserve an answer.''

''True.''

''Show me tomorrow, Rosemary.''

''Right.'' Folders began to fly across the desk. J.R. caught most of them.

The funeral planned for Conrad Taylor, as shown in the clean, white pages of the schedule for Monday, even to J.R.'s experienced, jaded eyes, seemed to be without flaw. The clean ride from the Capitol rotunda, following the Kennedy route. The stop at St. Matthews for a Catholic mass, the continued procession to and across Memorial Bridge, the ceremony at the amphitheater, the gravesite, the final, last shovel of dirt. It all looked so perfect, so darkly clean, so appropriate. He read on, marking the schedule with a red pen, where he was to be, and where Rosemary Hawkins was to be. Wherever she was, he was scheduled to accompany her, a presence, if not an important one. He read it very carefully, this fantasy of what Monday would bring.

One hundred thirty-two of the world's leaders/dictators/rapists/smugglers, with official sanction to operate. In one place, together, preaching brotherhood over the grave of a fallen brother. Jesus. Conrad Taylor, sellout artist, still selling even after his store closed down, its proprietor gone . . . a closeout sale on closed-out ideas, attended by world-class rummage-sale experts. J.R. could deal with the political realities. Shit happens. Deal with the shit.

But he knew none of what he was reading had anything at all to do with reality. It had to do with plans, executed by faceless men in small rooms all over this swampy capital, doing the bidding of bigger men, on the scale of payrate, directing the world to disaster. He knew it. And, among the few he had identified that knew what Monday, Monday, meant, he mentally, critically, and fatally added the name of Major General Brian Howell, the short, leggy redhead's most trusted advisor. It was near midnight, and, like the hour itself, time, for this day, was gone.

Jason would have to fly, Willy would have to stay awake, and Brian Howell would have to somehow be circumvented. Bonnie was safe, off delivering sausage. Rosemary Hawkins was in acute peril. Desperate peril. And J.R. Kelly, from this moment, would be branded forever a traitor, a patriot, or worse, a caricature from every bad spy movie or book ever produced.

"Well, J.R.?"

"Looks just fine, Rosemary."

"Do you mean that, J.R.?"

"No."

"Why not?"

"Because they pay me not to believe anything that makes sense. Any kind of sense. Tomorrow, you do exactly as I say. Period. Or relieve me of my duties, as of this minute."

"I can't agree to that, J.R. I run my life. My way."

"Fine, but I'm not talking about *your* life. I'm talking about the life of this country. Of this world. Of this shitty, tiny planet we like to think is properly managed. Tomorrow, the grossest case of planetary mismanagement in the history of the known universe is going to manifest itself in the clearest of terms. I believe what I'm saying. Because I believe what I'm saying, and because I can still feel you against my back, I want you to agree to do what I ask, when I ask, or fire me."

"Fair enough, J.R. You're fired." He should have known.

J.R. drank the third beer, tipped it toward Rosemary Hawkins, and left her by herself. He'd been hopeful it might be easier, that somewhere in the government, particularly here, as represented by Rosemary Hawkins, the facts, however vague, would open a dialogue of distrust, suspicion, and, in the end, the acceptance of the truth. Jonathan Bennett was going to kill the government leaders of every nation in the world, and if he did, anarchy would rule by Tuesday, worldwide. Iran–Iraq. Any nation in Southeast Asia. Central America. Israel and anybody. The Soviet Union, headless, but with 42,000 frontline tanks. And in the U.S., the grim possibility that the highest ranking member of the surviving government might possibly be the postmaster of Iowa Falls, Iowa . . . shit happens, multiplied . . .

Sunday ended, in Washington, D.C., quietly, and without fuss. J.R. had been fired, and that action had put him in the *normal* position of liar, thief, cheater, and basic abuser of human, economic, or military rights. He was now free to fuck up, without official sanction. Worse, for J.R., he was truly alone. Normally, a situation like this would have been his ultimate heaven. But this Sunday before Thanksgiving, this Sunday before mourning in America, was not in the least to his liking. He had dispatched his terrifyingly young lover southward, carrying what she thought was a package of great national importance. And, in its fragrant way, it would result in a nationally important decision.

Jason Kelly would receive an even more important

package. A directional message that might kill him, and, at best, get him thrown from the service he served with such devotion. Jason Kelly was a United States Marine. Today, tomorrow, he might be branded a traitor, a nut, or worse yet, a corpse.

The world, this Sunday, had no idea what J.R. Kelly saw in the future. The world, without exception, would surely have locked him up. The world was at peace. Treaties were in the works, all over the world. Europe was about to become a "community," with like-minded tariffs, trade laws—even the marriage laws were to be standardized.

Yes, Conrad Taylor's dream of the United States joining the "One-World Community" as he and Rosemary Hawkins so often spoke of, was to be a reality, in spite of his death. The new United States President, ascendant by accident, had said so, on worldwide television. Oh, there were those small, vocal minorities. Particularly in the United States and the Soviet Union. China, being China, remained inscrutable, in the Oriental way.

The unpaid debts of the sixty-seven "underdeveloped" nations, was, by all sensible equations, a potential worldwide disaster. The airwaves, meaning any network with enough clout and millionaire anchormen with smiling faces and empty brains, were saying, in all seriousness, not to worry. Of course, if the worldwide debt structure collapsed, which all knew could never happen, every poor man in the western world would attack, physically, his/her nearest neighbor. So on this Sunday, the Sunday before Thanksgiving, the world was full of "down the road" potential hurt.

But the international community would bury the by-now-proclaimed "visionary" U.S. President ("visionary" for only three days of a 100 percent bullshit media blitz), and embrace his one world, "all at peace, with those at war" theories. Talks. Private. Public. Televised. The world would lean to the left, the direction, the true direction, of peace.

But J.R. Kelly, alone except for those he loved, inspired, or could coerce, knew positively what would happen in the future. The Ace-of-Spades A-10, piloted, directed, and triggered by Adrian Bennett, would fly up the Potomac and butcher the traders in the most sacred temple on United States soil. If he was right. If. Big word. By 12:09 A.M., Monday, J.R. Kelly had created codes, words, addresses, and a persona designed, in his view, to save the world as he knew it.

EN ROUTE, CHERRY POINT, NORTH CAROLINA
SUNDAY, 10:57 P.M.,
EASTERN STANDARD TIME

The cabbie had knocked at the door to J.R.'s apartment, as J.R. had said he would. He'd handed her a package, wrapped in white butcher paper, and asked where she would like to go. She'd pulled on a short, black leather jacket over her cashmere sweater, and shut off all but a single light, near the bed. And, of course, she'd left the New Orleans fan going its meaningless rounds. She wrote a short, to-the-point note, and stuck it to his pillow, with a pin from her hair: *J.R. To wherever it ends. B.* She'd told the cabbie to take her to Edwards Air Force Base. He'd nodded, opened the back door of the cab, and taken her to Washington National Airport. Now, she was dropping out of a dark sky, the Atlantic somewhere off to her left, and settling onto a runway. She wasn't sure exactly where she was until the lone steward, since she was the lone passenger, said, "Miss? This is Simmons-Nott Airport, New Bern, North Carolina. You get off here."

The plane, a DC-9 with American Airlines markings, rolled to a stop. She was escorted from the plane by what appeared to be, and was, another cabdriver. At 11:47, she smiled at the guard at the gate of Cherry Point, and thrust her breasts out as far as possible, which was a considerable thing to see. He saw it, took the package, and in less than six minutes, the officer of the day began to bother the C.O. of Cherry Point, North Carolina.

The package Bonnie delivered contained everything required to free up the Shamrock at 0100 hours. Meanwhile, north of Cherry Point, at Patuxent River N.A.S., another beautifully endowed blond, this one the wife of a Marine colonel of some distinction, delivered an identical package, containing a more important set of instructions to the Shamrock's pilot. It was all very intricate, and designed to free Bonnie from suspicion of any kind if J.R. Kelly turned out to be a nut. Bonnie's package contained the best, the very best, sliced Polish sausage attainable in the United States.

Jason Kelly's C.O., an old friend of J.R. from Michigan State, could hardly deny J.R.'s little brother night-flight training time, following so soon on the heels of his own commander's commendation, and Jason's promotion to first lieutenant. If J.R. wanted to make his little brother the youngest flying captain in the Marines, well, why not? Fuck a bunch of funerals. Jason Kelly, eager beaver, would fly tonight. His C.O. would toss down a few, and slowly, slice by slice, savor the best sausage ever made.

And so it was that Bonnie delivered a gift. And up north, at Pax River, another package, the real "package," was delivered. Unofficially, deceitfully, and perhaps treasonously, it arrived and made its way through the bureaucracy that is the United States military. In the end, Jason would arrive on time at Pax River, the package would arm the Shamrock Harrier, and put him and his aircraft where he should be.

Bonnie, thrilled that she had helped her lover, put the hammer down on the quick little Mazda RX-7, turbo, red, and very, very fast. Just outside of Washington—Washington, North Carolina—on North Carolina Interstate Highway 13, Bonnie Parker met head-on with a pickup truck driven by a drunken fifteen-year-old farmer's son on his first date. Firemen, using mechanical crow bars, separators, and torches, needed two hours to discover that three people, hardly recognized as human, had been in the two vehicles.

Bonnie Parker had left J.R. Kelly a note, *to wherever it ends*. She had left the note, full of love. It ended 1.2 miles from Washington, North Carolina. The wrong Washington. J.R.'s best hope for real, long-lasting love, was dead. He'd sent her with sausage, to keep her safe. As usual, he'd underestimated the grit and determination of the women in his life.

Jason Kelly flew over the site of the accident. He didn't notice it, and neither would J.R. By the time the body was identified, the government of the United States would be attempting to identify V.I.P. bodies of a number unprecedented in the United States or world history. Bonnie, lovely, sexy, sweet Bonnie, was, in the scheme of things to come, the least of anyone's worries.

DAY SIX: MONDAY

ROSEMARY HAWKINS'S OFFICE
MONDAY, 12:14 A.M.

J.R. Kelly, fired by Rosemary Hawkins, continued to use her office, and the White House staff communications office. He fired off messages to Cherry Point, and then to Patuxent River, the critical stop in Jason Kelly's flight north. Pax River asked for confirmation, and J.R. provided it. From the White House. "Flash Point: Desert Flower." Heavy duty stuff. Phoney, but heavy duty. Jason's Shamrock was cleared from Cherry Point to Pax River. More coded messages would send Jace to the deserted racetrack eight minutes from Arlington. Ten hours before it would be needed, the Harrier would be bedded down for a long day ahead, guided earthward by two willing drivers from the C.I.A. motor pool. Willing drivers. That meant they had accepted $500 each to ruin their plans for the night.

CHERRY POINT, NORTH CAROLINA
MONDAY, 0100 HOURS

"Permission to fly, Tower."

"Wait one, Six-Five-Three."

"Six-Five-Three, roger, Tower. Wait one." Jason tried to keep his voice level and professional, as if this 1:00 A.M. flight into a rainy night in a newly acquired, fully night-capable Harrier AV-8B were something he did often. His brother had been a busy man. Cherry Point's tower usually stayed open only until 2300 hours. Jason wondered what the hell J.R. had told his commanding officer to get this flight approved.

"Six-Five-Three?"

"Roger, Tower."

"You're clear to Patuxent River N.A.S. They are shut down for the night. Do you want the lights on?"

"Negative, Tower. I'll turn them on from the air."

"Received, Six-Five-Three. You are cleared for takeoff. Take it easy, Six-Five-Three. Nasty weather all the way."

"Will do, Tower. Six-Five-Three on my way." The Harrier leaped forward and rushed down the rain-swept runway. Jason vectored the engine nozzles and true to its nickname, the Harrier jumped into the dark and headed toward Patuxent River Naval Air Station. There, if all went well, he would receive additional fuel. And, of course, weapons to shoot down the A-10 his brother had stated flatly would hit the presidential funeral at exactly 3:45 P.M. this day.

Jason felt he was flying into a certain court-martial at the least, and perhaps death. The alternative, if he was to believe his C.I.A. brother, was the wanton slaughter of the leaders of the government of the United States and many other governments as well. It was so savagely bizarre, so terrible in its plan, so violent in its possible execution of thousands of innocent victims, he was sure it was true. Somehow, he would have to shoot down the Ace-of-Spades colonel, Wing Commander Jonathan Bennett. He turned the Harrier's nose to the sky, and at 11,000 feet he eased through the cloud cover and into the clear above the inclement weather, caught in moonlight and starlight and peace. He leveled off and headed up the coast. He had no idea what to expect when he got to Pax River. If his brother hadn't made the arrangements, though it seemed impossible to Jason, he would be stranded. But J.R. would come through. Because J.R. . . . because J.R. was J.R. . . . and he always came through.

"Sir? Sir?" The young ensign at Patuxent River N.A.S. did not like waking the base commander at 0250 hours, but the coded message he held from C.I.A. headquarters in Langley, Virginia, needed more attention than the lowly opinion of a very junior officer of the day only months out of the Naval Academy.

"Sir?" The ensign finally shook his superior awake. "Captain, I have something here that I feel needs your approval."

The base commander rolled over in his bed, eyes blinking in the glare of the young officer's flashlight. "Unless someone has bombed this base, mister, I believe your naval career is going to be very short." He struggled up in his bed, snapping his bed light on, glaring under fierce bushy eyebrows at the shaken duty officer.

"It's a Flashpoint message, sir."

"Flashpoint? What the hell is Flashpoint?"

"On today's code list, sir, Flashpoint is the White House."

"Holy shit! Well, let me see it." The duty officer handed it to him, shining the flashlight on it, even though the table lamp was turned on. The captain glared at him.

"Ensign, why in the hell did you decide to join the Navy?"

"My father and grandfather were both admirals, sir. I guess I had no choice."

The captain smiled, briefly, and read the order. It was cryptic, but to the point.

At 0300 hours, this date, a single Harrier AV-8B from Cherry Point M.C.A.S. will arrive Patuxent. Its pilot, Lieutenant Jason Porter Kelly, will land and taxi his aircraft to ordnance area for refueling and arming. Sealed package will be delivered to the OOD by 0400 hours this date. It is to be given to Lieutenant Kelly. It is considered top secret, and is to be delivered unopened. Confirm receipt and execute order. Lieutenant Kelly is to take off Patuxent N.A.S. by 0425 hours. Without fail. Repeat. Without fail.
J.R. Kelly
Flashpoint

"Bullshit! What kind of garbage is this?"

"I don't know, sir. But we do have a single aircraft on approach, sir. Tower is closed, so he just unbuttoned the lights and seems to be right on time."

"Well, why don't we just see about this. Get me a confirmation, Ensign."

"Yes, sir. Sir, Flashpoint messages today are bound to be a little strange, all things considered."

"You're right. But I want confirmation anyway. Meanwhile, rustle up a ground crew for that Harrier, just in case."

"Yes, sir!" The ensign vanished, leaving the base commander perplexed and pissed off.

By the time the captain got dressed and left his quarters, he'd already heard the growl of the Harrier as it swept over the station and, just as the coded message had said, headed directly toward the ordnance station. The ensign met him as he stormed toward his car to meet the taxiing jet.

"Sir! Confirmation on the message."

"Read it!" snapped the captain.

"0302 Hours Monday. Orders confirmed. Execute at once. Signed: Desert Flower. Flashpoint."

"Desert Flower? Who the fuck is that?"

"According to my codes, sir, this message is from Rosemary Hawkins, newly designated Secretary of State, and the White House itself. Orders, sir?"

"Orders? You bet. Comply, Ensign. Get that Harrier whatever it asks for. Do you understand? Whatever!"

The ensign extended a heavy envelope toward the captain. "Yes, sir. And a civilian delivered this to the main gate at about 0230. The guard said it was the most beautiful woman he'd ever seen. Blond, with big—"

"Ensign!"

"Sir!"

"Carry out the orders, and deliver that little package to the lieutenant in the Harrier. What was his name?"

"Porter. Uh, no. Kelly, sir. Jason Porter Kelly."

"Kelly. The same name on the Flashpoint message?"

"Yes, sir."

"Well, I'll do it, but by God, I'm going to find out what it's all about if it's the last thing I ever do. Now, I'm going to bed. You get the fucking jarhead back in the air, and on time, do you hear? And send Desert Flower or Flashpoint or the goddamn Pentagon a message of order compliance."

"Yes, Captain."

"You bet your young ass, mister." The captain stormed away toward his quarters. But he didn't go there. Lighting his pipe, he cut a few corners and put himself within watching distance of the AV-8B from Cherry Point. It looked brand-new. Its outboard wingtips carried two bright red avionics pods. Night capable. Top of the line Harrier, the paint hardly dry. Under the lights at the ordnance station, the large green shamrock painted under the cockpit stood out clearly in spite of the dark camo paint. Sure. Kelly. From the looks of all this, Lieutenant Kelly was going to need a fistful of shamrocks.

The captain had been in this man's Navy for twenty-nine years. In eight months, he would be a civilian, sucking lime rickeys in the tropics. He watched the clean Harrier "dirtied up" as its GAU-12 25mm cannon was loaded and four AIM-9L air-to-air missiles slung under its wings, all the while getting his fuel topped. Guns and missiles. Air-to-air. Well, fine. This captain was going to bed. He didn't understand why, but he felt a very powerful sense of urgency and daring-do surrounding this plane and its pilot. He figured that whether this pilot failed or succeeded, his retirement was in jeopardy. This pilot had come here this miserable morning to fuck up the captain's career. He walked back to his quarters. But he didn't sleep.

Jason slipped the cockpit lever and the canopy swung back and up. It was not raining at Pax River, but the early morning air was crisp and cold. A Naval lieutenant scram-

bled up the access ladder and Jason handed him a typed
sheet.

"This is what you want, Lieutenant?"

Jason only nodded, still wearing his flight helmet, the
smoky-colored visor down.

Looking at him, the Naval ensign could see the glow of
the cockpit lights reflected in the visor. He could only
sense the eyes, but knew they were fixed on him. "I'll
need to confirm your I.D., sir." The ensign sounded very
nervous.

Jason pulled his helmet off and handed the Navy man
his I.D. With only a cursory check, it was immediately
handed back. "This was delivered here for you, Lieutenant. I was instructed to give it to you personally." The
ensign tossed it into the cockpit, and scrambled down the
access ladder.

Jason tore the envelope open. It was a short note, and
included a sectional aeronautical chart. The note, in J.R.'s
sprawling handwriting, read, *Be at the Big Red X by 0545,
Little Brother. Love ya, Big Brother. (We'll leave the lights
on.) J.R.*

The Big Red X marked a spot not far from Washington,
D.C. He'd seen the area once or twice before. A drag strip
just off the Patuxent River, between Robinson and lower
Marlboro. It was less than five miles outside the Washington, D.C., VFR terminal area. There were stacks and tow-
ers and all manner of trauma-inducing danger all over the
site his brother had chosen to conceal the Harrier until the
Ace-of-Spades tried to trump the world's deck. Now all
he had to do was find the strip, in the dark, and set the
Harrier down, without bending the equipment. Terrific.
Just fucking terrific.

The Harrier AV-8B boomed up the Patuxent River at a
very good clip, following the river's natural course. As
Jason read the massive avionic picture available to him in
the cockpit, the visual terrain mapping system moving as
he did kept him from harm's way, and in less than thirty
minutes, he was circling a dark patch of ground, identified

on his target system as his dragstrip. He circled the heavy craft at very slow speeds, wondering how many lights would go on below, and whether they would be house lights, or farms, or some unnamed conspirators' search-lights. The answer, when it came, was simple. Two cars, directly beneath him and less than one hundred yards apart, abruptly switched on their lights.

With a dexterity far beyond his flight time in an AV-8B Harrier II, he jockeyed the plane over the Red X, vectored the engine nozzles downward and set the heavily laden jet down, a stamp of approval on the Harrier flight manual. As he touched down, the car lights went out and a pair of hand-held lights began to direct him just off the drag strip and into a clump of trees, forming a leafless but heavy layer of twisted branches over the Harrier. He was parked less than ten minutes flying time from the White House and he was invisible.

It was 6:00 A.M. Monday. The Harrier now had to sit, with its anxious pilot, until 3:00 P.M. The two cars drove off, leaving the Harrier and its hot engine to crackle and snap in the cool morning air. Jason had no idea who had driven the two cars. As dawn came, pulling the night away on its cold, damp string, he realized he and his aircraft were truly hidden, unless somebody decided that on this funeral day for the nation's fallen President, a drag race was a hell of a good idea. About then, it began to rain again, turning the early morning into a dark, gothic imitation of a new day.

THE BENNETT RANCH
BENNETT, WYOMING
MONDAY, 12:30 A.M.,
MOUNTAIN STANDARD TIME

Adrian Bennett paced the rough-hewn floor of his study, a man committed to, but uninfluenced by, the pending but certain death of his only son. He knew that Jonathan would execute the attack with his usual, thorough professionalism. He was equally, no, *acutely,* aware that Jonathan would also attack the target more than once, thus ensuring his own death. The normal father–son feelings did not apply in the Bennett family, so this sure, tragic, shameful death of a national hero, his only son, caused the elder Bennett no particular sense of loss. Triumph, yes. But not loss.

All had gone very well, considering how little time there had been to set this up. Of course, the North Vietnamese interrogator had provided the father with the key to the weapon, meaning his son. For as long as he'd been alive, Adrian Bennett had dominated Jonathan Bennett, using a twisted, psychological verbal abuse that had notched together like a finely built, split-log cabin when Jonathan had been shot down and captured.

The rest of the group had fallen into line, knowing what was to take place, and coveting what they would gain in power afterwards. All but Barney Bernard, and God only knew what had changed his mind! But no matter. He'd finally reached Paul Wolfe. The major general of the Maryland National Guard had decided, reluctantly, to defend his country from enemies, whoever they might be, if Monday turned out the way Adrian Bennett suggested it might. He'd gone so far as to give his "secretary" four days off. Yes. They would need soldiers, and Paul Wolfe's guard was less than three hours, wearing full battle gear, from the Vietnam Memorial in Washington, D.C. All things considered, Adrian Bennett was a happy man. His son was going to die in a matter of hours, taking with him virtually the entire sitting government officials of the United States and the world. Chaos, anarchy, revolution! Music to an old man's ears. The wolves would eat the rabbits, and the eagles would outwit the bears.

THE COMMUNICATION CENTER
N.S.A SAFE HOUSE
GALLOWS ROAD, VIRGINIA
MONDAY, 3:30 A.M.

Major General Brian Howell, Deputy Director of the National Security Council, and senior military officer of the supersecret National Security Agency, had been immobile for two hours. Asleep at his desk, oblivious to the chatter, the beeps, the winks and blips of the sophisticated equipment that spread throughout the 180-year-old farmhouse nestled in the trees just off Gallows Road. An appropriate name for the secret business handled, or, as most of the present Congress said, loudly and often, "mishandled, if we could see their books." Of course, the good men of the United States Senate Committee on Covert Action, overt action, and dirty fucking tricks department, said these things only in private, and off the record.

Before Brian Howell had fallen asleep, he'd given the faceless young men in the white shirts a very simple order. "If you intercept anything involving the men on this list, wake me up." He'd given the list to the senior N.S.A. analyst, who must have been all of twenty-four years old. It was this fuzzy-cheeked nonentity that shook Brian Howell awake, interrupting a delicious dream of Rosemary Hawkins's mouth, descending on his . . .

"Sir? General Howell?" Blue eyes. Earnest blue eyes. Brian Howell hated blue eyes.

"What is it?" The general had the practiced, but effective knack of coming out of a sound sleep without lashing out at whoever, or whatever, had awakened him.

"Sir, we are intercepting considerable traffic between Flashpoint, Desert Flower, and M.C.A.S., Cherry Point, and N.A.S. Patuxent River."

"Yes? What about it?"

"Sir, Flashpoint is the White House, as of 0001 hours

this A.M. Desert Flower is, from that same hour, Ms. Rosemary Hawkins. But the sender is on your list, sir.''

"Who?''

"J.R. Kelly, sir. C.I.A.''

"No problem there, mister. He's authorized.''

"Yes, sir, I know. But he's using Desert Flower code as well as Flashpoint. The messages concern, or seem to concern, his younger brother, Jason Kelly.''

"And why is he doing that?''

"We don't know, General Howell. Jason Porter Kelly is a Marine pilot at Cherry Point. One message indicated clearance for J.R. Kelly to Patuxent River N.A.S.''

"When?''

"Now, sir. Lieutenant Kelly's AV-8B Harrier is on the ground at Patuxent River N.A.S. He seems to be . . . to be ready to fly again, sir.''

"Is he? And where is the intrepid young Kelly headed?''

"Forgive me, General, but we have no idea.''

"Well, then, why don't we just contact J.R. Kelly, and ask him?''

"Yes, sir, we'll try. But he seems to have left his office, without . . .''

"Telling anyone?''

"Yes, sir.''

"He's a spy, asshole! Who would he tell? Send a message to Patuxent, requesting, *politely*, why the younger Kelly is there, and where he might be heading.''

"Yes, sir. Right away.'' The white shirt with fuzzy blue eyes left Brian Howell's office as fast as his chubby legs would carry him.

"Sir, we have that information on Jason Kelly, direct from the officer of the day at Pax River. Lieutenant Kelly's aircraft lifted off Pax River at 0437 hours. Its destination and flight plan are unrecorded. The O.O.D. adds that Lieutenant Kelly is, as he put it, a 'comer.' Cherry Point advises Lieutenant Kelly is on a training exercise to Yuma Marine Base, Arizona. He is flying a fully armed and fueled aircraft. Guns and missiles.''

"And where did you get that piece of information?"

"Radar intercept, sir, twelve miles out of Pax River."

"And?"

"Hot image, sir. We are attempting satellite confirmation."

"Forget it."

"Sir? A hot aircraft, without a recorded flight plan?"

"Forget it. I see nothing here except an older brother, temporarily in the White House office of the future Secretary of State, using a code or two to further his little brother's flight time, and his career, in a night-capable aircraft. Disregard all further contact with Lieutenant Kelly's aircraft."

"Yes, sir. That's pretty much what we thought too, sir. But you wanted to know, and we ran it down."

"Well done . . . what is your rank, mister?"

"Major, sir. Major Edward Tallon."

"Major? How old are you?"

"Twenty-six, General."

"I was thirty-four years old before I became a major. Did you know that?"

"Yes, sir, I did."

"Well, don't take much from that, Major. Because now I'm forty-four, and you'll be a hundred before you wear two stars."

"No doubt, sir. May I be dismissed?"

"Beat it, Major. But keep listening. To everything. You may be a colonel by tomorrow night. Stay on it!"

"Yes, sir!"

Better, much better, thought Brian Howell, as he reached for the secure phone to call Adrian Bennett, way out west in Wyoming.

THE BENNETT RANCH
MONDAY, 2:30 A.M.,
MOUNTAIN STANDARD TIME

"Governor Bennett? Major General Howell here."

"This had better be very important, Brian. I expect a busy day tomorrow."

"It may be important. It may not. Rosemary Hawkins has been assigned a special agent, a veteran C.I.A. man."

"So?"

"His brother, his younger brother, flies AV-8B Harrier jets out of Cherry Point. He's on the loose tonight, supposedly headed west, to Yuma, for night-flight training. He's flown to Yuma four times, including leader of a flight only three days ago."

"And, in your view, what does this all mean?"

"Nothing, Governor. I just felt the information might be helpful. I'm told he's a very good pilot, flying a very good aircraft, and his older brother is on special assignment with Rosemary Hawkins. At this moment, we have no idea where the younger brother and his Harrier are, but we know it is fully armed and combat ready."

"Why? Why would it be in a combat status?"

"Forgive me, Governor, but I haven't any idea. I'm simply relaying the information. I assume you will handle it however you see fit."

"Thank you, Brian. Thank you for all you've done for your country. It will be remembered."

Adrian Bennett hung up, and immediately dialed Myrtle Beach Air Force Base, a number tied directly to his son's quarters. Unlike most calls to U.S. bases, no operator would ask politely "Is this a collect call?" before putting it through. Adrian Bennett would talk to his son one more time before he died. This was the time. It would change nothing. By this late date, the Night Strike was a thing with a life of its own.

MYRTLE BEACH A.F.B.
MONDAY, 0500 HOURS

Jonathan Bennett let the phone ring, studying his maps, trying to outlast the caller. But the phone continued to ring. He studied the maps, lit a fresh cigar, and walked to his desk, removing the receiver from its connection, placing it on the chair next to his desk, returning to his maps and flight charts. Fifty-five minutes. From takeoff to Arlington. Just fifty-five minutes.

He hung the phone up, and went back to his strike preparations. Insistent, the phone began to ring again. Exasperated, he answered it.

"Colonel Bennett here." He used his gruff C.O. voice.

"Jonathan?"

"Hello, Dad. What can I do for you?"

"Are you all right, Jonathan? Are you still on track?"

"I have no problems here, if that's what you mean. The base is quiet, as you might expect. I feel there is very little doubt I will attend the funeral tomorrow."

"I have been advised that the lady in question has a very discreet escort."

"I understand, Dad. But I see no problems there, do you?"

"The escort, I'm told, while he himself is discreet, has a younger brother. A flyer, I'm told. It's said he is on the loose, in a combat mode, on his way to Yuma, Arizona. Does that concern you at all?"

"No, Dad. It doesn't. The jungle bunnies fly out to Yuma all the time. I see nothing unusual here."

"What about his discreet brother?"

"If you are worried about whether or not I can attend the festivities, don't be. I'll be there. With bells on. If discretion is the better part of valor, we have little or nothing to worry about. The service will go off on time."

"Fine, Jonathan. I just felt you should know, and consider, what possible delay you may encounter."

"I'll make revisions, if required. Take care, Dad. I

probably won't talk to you again, at least not before Tuesday.''

"Yes, Jonathan. We'll talk again on Tuesday. Have a good trip.''

"It will be like the bridge, Dad. A very good trip. Give my love to Palmer.''

"I will, Jonathan. I surely will. And remember, we are all very proud of you.'' The line went dead, as lines do . . . Jonathan Bennett went back to his maps.

THE BENNETT RANCH
BENNETT, WYOMING
MONDAY, 3:00 A.M.,
MOUNTAIN STANDARD TIME

"So you're going to let him go through with it?'' Palmer, sitting across from Adrian Bennett, had listened to the phone conversation between the senior Bennett and his son, a boy that Palmer Jackson loved very much. Jonathan Bennett had been the son that Palmer's lifetime of devoted service to Adrian Bennett had made impossible.

"Let him go through with what, Palmer? I'm not sure I understand.''

"Oh, you understand all right! And so do I. Do you actually think I could spend the better part of my adult life in this house, in this atmosphere, and not understand? You are an arrogant, sick old fool, Adrian! But even by your standards, this . . . surpasses all.''

"All of what, Palmer? What does 'this' surpass?''

"I've watched you abuse everyone that ever cared for you. Everyone that ever placed their faith, and their love, and their hope in you. You might just as well have murdered Lily! All that trash you brought into this house. All those sluts, trying to get it up for you, trying to make you the man you never could be, never, in the best years of your life! And so Lily died, yes, murdered, I believe, because you messed with her mind until she had no mind. And now Jonathan. Down there at Myrtle Beach, with no mind at all, with no will of his own, fucked up beyond belief by the North Vietnamese, and now you use *him*, like you've used them all. Like you've used me, and your country, and now, I know exactly what you intend to do, and I won't let you do it.''

''What is it you think I intend to do?''

''I've listened in on all your phone conversations. I have for over thirty years. You've taken that poor child, and pointed him in the direction you want him to go. By this time tomorrow, that child, like his mad, sad mother, will be dead. Dead, in my view, at your hand! What is that called, Adrian? The killing of one's children?'' Adrian's hand moved toward the comforting steel tucked into his waistband. ''Yes. It's a 'cide' of some kind. Like genocide, or fratricide, or . . .'' Palmer's mind went blank.

''I agree, but only to a point. I'm not, nor have I ever, committed a 'cide' of any kind.'' The gun Adrian always wore moved forward.

''And you won't now, either.'' Suddenly, Palmer Jackson had his black eighty-year-old hand filled with a sleek, chrome-plated .357 Magnum. He pulled the trigger a fraction of a second before his employer could center the glisteningly clean, 1911 Colt .45, the same gun that his wife had used to try to kill Adrian so long ago. Fractions. Fractions of seconds. The 125-grain hollow point from the .357 Magnum hit Adrian Bennett in the shoulder, throwing his arm wide, and his shot, and his aim, off. The .45 caliber round-nosed 200-grain lead slug hit Palmer Jackson in the upper thigh, traveled along a direct path to his hip, broke and shattered the bone, and spun him off the couch, and onto the floor.

Never a combatant, always a passive observer, Palmer turned tiger. Two men, in their eighties, veterans of all conceivable chicanery, murder, malevolent distrust, family terror, and injustice for all. Two old men, one with a forty-year-old accumulated debt of $57,800 due to the other, shooting it out in the employer's trophy room . . .

Palmer Jackson rolled over on the polished wooden

floor, polished nearly every other day for over forty years. Polished by his labor, and his alone. The .357 went up, his arm extended, his hip a screaming, soul-killing, shattering pain, pain that clouded his vision, but not his memory. He pulled the trigger, and the .357 roared its displeasure, its rigid, vindictive violence, and Conrad Taylor's nemesis took a hit in the jaw, ripping it loose from the fixed upper teeth, silencing the political rhetoric, and knocking Adrian onto his back, hit twice now, and dying, as was Palmer Jackson.

The two old men, both down on the slave-polished floor, rose up, facing one another for one last time, the only time ever as true equals. Firearms made them equal, accompanied by hate. The .357 roared. The Colt .45 thumped, recoiled, fell to the floor, clattering as it bounced and slid six feet beyond Adrian Bennett's grasp.

Palmer Jackson, crawling on his one good leg, slithered through their mutual blood spill, placed the .357 Magnum against Adrian Bennett's pleading face, and pulled the trigger one final time. The top of Adrian Bennett's head splattered upward, and stuck to the rough-hewn hundred-year-old trees that made up the roof of the Bennett Ranch. Only then, bleeding profusely, did Palmer Jackson make his last major effort to save his country. With a bullet in his chest, the result of Adrian's last, wild shot, Palmer crawled through the garbage that was left of his slave's life, sliding in blood again, mixed with the remnants of his former employer. He reached the phone, picked it up, and just before he died, realized, to his horror, that a shot, his or Adrian Bennett's, had torn the phone to pieces.

THE WHITE HOUSE
PRIVATE QUARTERS
MONDAY, 5:30 A.M.

Emily Taylor stood in front of the window, the curtains drawn shut but for a two-inch space down the center. Outside the White House, the city was dark, dark with the deepened absence of light before dawn in the wintertime. She was completely nude except for an ankle bracelet, a gold ankle bracelet she hadn't worn since she was sixteen years old, when she thought it was very sexy indeed. She had good legs. Better than most. Better than the Hawkins bitch. What had gone wrong? Why was her husband dead, and why had he never really loved her?

For years and years she had listened to him, to his protestations of love and devotion, knowing all along that he fucked everything he could get to stand still long enough. A proud woman, without pride. She had stayed with him because, in fact and truth, where was she to go? Kentucky women stayed married, particularly if you were married to a Bostonian from the Taylor line. Breeding. Oh, Lord, he'd certainly had that. The sly smile, the dimples, the shallow, sick view of what real people, ordinary people, thought about him. Exploitive. He had been that. And she had been, in her own passive way, an enormous help to him.

She turned away from the window, and walked to the bed, raising her leg, setting her foot in the soft comforter, looking, critically, at her leg. It really *was* a good leg. The ankle bracelet made her slim ankle ever slimmer. Should she wear it to the funeral? No. Probably not.

Conrad had loved that ankle bracelet. Oh, not on her ankle . . . but when she circled his erect penis with it, lowering her rosebud lips down on him, feeling the cold, gold ropes constricted against his heat, feeling him buck under her . . .

Well, she'd had him, then, and always, when he was in

her mouth. Helpless, a mewing, whimpering male, strained upward, saying over and over, "Baby, baby, baby!"

And that had been basically it. When she sucked his cock, she was important. A hard thing to realize, after two campaigns and two children and a presidential election. Emily Taylor was Conrad Taylor's prime cocksucker. Other than that, she had no idea what he actually thought of her.

And later today, she would have to play the grieving widow, veiled and blanketed in expensive black silk, hidden from prying eyes, holding her two perfect children by the hand, bravely walking the full distance from the Capitol rotunda to the cemetery, with a one-hour break at St. Matthews. Emily lay down, raising her legs, spreading them wide, planting her feet, her fingers moving across her thighs, slowly, like she wished he had.

Church. That was a laugh. Oh, sure, he had been *born* Catholic. They had been married by a cardinal, for Christ sake.

But he wasn't a Catholic. Not by any measuring stick you wanted to use. He did, on political occasions, attend mass, eyes cast downward, the weight of the world on his shoulders. He looked positively beatific. He would lean toward her, whispering sex talk in her ear, touching her thighs, all the time the picture of the churchgoing Catholic husband and father. He thought it was hilarious. Pious sex, he called it. She often had to listen, far into the night, while he ripped into the Catholic Church and its hierarchy, its basic beliefs, its very foundations. He was a violent, public opponent of abortion, yet he had forced her to abort their third child.

Her fingers dipped lower between her thighs, pressing, probing, seeking, and as usual finding. Emily loves Emily. Emily fucks Emily. Conrad Taylor had sung that little ditty to himself while he shaved, loud enough for her to hear, loud enough for her to do it again, waiting to catch her, falling on her, telling her to leave her fingers inside, pushing in, coming almost at once, sending her scrambling across the bed after her husband, humiliated, needing to suck him dry, to claim . . . to claim *something* of her marriage to this cold, charismatic, lying champion of the oppressed.

The oppressed! Holy shit, she could tell them about the fucking oppressed. *She,* by God, was oppressed. Her slim fingers reached down to her ankle, unsnapped the catch, stretched the finely spun gold into a stiff line, moving it rapidly across her clitoris, screaming out her release in pain and anguish and self-hatred, a naked widow, whose very silken, blond skin was sackcloth of the most permanent kind.

How, goddammit, did he dare die in an accident? While he was President! She, she, Emily Taylor, should have at least had the pleasure, the supreme pleasure, of killing him. There was that time, not too long ago, with the vision of Rosemary Hawkins leaning over Conrad Taylor's shoulder, telling him some delicious secret. That vision, while she had his cock in her throat. Then. She'd thought of it. One, just one, really terrific bite from her Kentucky-bred teeth, and Conrad Taylor would have been a eunuch . . .

The story of her life. Opportunity unexploited is opportunity lost. Tears streaming down her face, she continued her solitary love play, waiting for the French maid to knock on her door. It was planting day in Washington, and, as a Kentuckian, she would, could, plant with the best of them.

ROSEMARY HAWKINS'S RESIDENCE MONDAY, 5:30 A.M.

Rosemary had not slept. She had flirted with the possibility of two or three Seconal tablets, disregarding the idea as unworkable and foolish, two negative counts. They would put her to sleep, and make her drowsy and lethargic for the rest of the day. She could hardly be that.

Function. That was what Rosemary Hawkins was most concerned about this early, cold Monday morning. Function, and J.R. Kelly. Particularly J.R. Kelly, so sure the nuts were unthreaded and the bolts were doomed. So sure. His quiet confidence that his preposterous scenario was a sure thing had shaken her to the core. He was not a man to dismiss as some looney-tunes paranoid from the C.I.A. He was not a man to dismiss under any circumstances. But she had dismissed him. She had fired him. Terrific, Rosemary. Now how do you get him back in your corner?

With a man like J.R. Kelly, you basically go to your knees and beg. For Rosemary Hawkins, that was an entirely unacceptable scenario. For J.R., too, she was sure. No matter. She would try anyway. It was going to be a long, difficult day, and J.R. Kelly would make it more . . . more . . . J.R. Kelly would make it possible to survive the day without making a complete and absolute fool of herself. None of what she was thinking approached what she feared most. That J.R. Kelly was right, and a lunatic was going to torch the funeral, at the sinister direction of his more lunatic father, supported by a cadre of American patriotic icons. Holy, jumping Jesus Christ!

Brian Howell had checked even the most farfetched ideas that J.R. had presented as fact. He had gone way out on a limb, potentially damaging a career that to date had been meteoric in its rise. Brian Howell could become the first black American to serve as Chief of Staff and Commander of the U.S. Army. He had provided Willy Corchran with the wherewithal to become a spy in Air Force fatigues. He had intercepted, and recorded, phone messages from J.R.'s "conspirators." He had, in short, done everything she'd asked of him. The results, as he'd said they would, made J.R. Kelly look like a candidate for a very funny, funny farm.

Rosemary Hawkins believed in facts. It was her job, and her destiny, to take facts and create foreign policy. What J.R. had to say had very little to do with facts. The truth was something hidden in a "bodyguard of lies." Winston

Churchill had said that, and Rosemary Hawkins was an
ardent admirer of the famous British statesman. Occasionally, she allowed herself to compare what she was trying
to accomplish with his many and varied, but sometime
vilified, career decisions. Like Winston Churchill, Rosemary knew she was controversial. His cigars. His booze.
His outlandish rhetoric. He was, nevertheless, a kindred
spirit, bucking the trends, defying the system, occasionally fucking up, but in the end the "definer" of the "Iron
Curtain" as it was in 1948. Rosemary Hawkins had turned
his phrase to her advantage, with a slight change.

She had called it the "Black Curtain," the "Broken
Curtain," the "Shuttered Window," screeching to the
world at large, in behalf of Conrad Taylor, that whatever
you called it, the curtain had to come down.

When the chopper, that meticulously maintained chopper, took its two lightning hits and went down, she had
done exactly what she should have done. She'd gathered
her programs, Conrad Taylor's programs, and gone directly to the new President. She'd spread the word and,
shamefully, she'd spread her legs. Now the programs would
go forward.

But would they? The President said they would, and,
for the moment, she believed him. He had, after all, publicly named her Secretary of State Designate. The Congress would fuss, she knew that. But she had claimed the
Senate Foreign Relations Committee in her impromptu
meeting at the Library of Congress. The Senate would
follow. She intended to be America's Disraeli, changing
the times, the thoughts, the passions of the American people. If. If J.R. Kelly was as out of step with reality as she
thought. Believed . . . was . . . was what? She believed
him. It was all twisted up in loss, and grief, and desire,
and God knew what else. No. No, she didn't believe him.

It was not yet daylight, and Rosemary Hawkins, the
most powerful female in American political history, had
not the slightest idea of what she believed. She only knew
that she must talk to, if not recapture, C.I.A. Agent J.R.
Kelly.

ROSEMARY HAWKINS'S RESIDENCE
MONDAY, 10:30 A.M.

"Please, J.R., sit down."

"If you like, Ms. Hawkins."

"I like, Mr. Kelly."

"Okay. Got any booze?"

"You've been here before. Of course I have booze, as you so delicately put it."

"Delicate I'm not. I'm just trying to stay drunk, so when the fucking world blows up, I won't give a sheet."

"That's shit."

"Right. Give a shit."

"Better. Much better. I expect advisors to be able to say 'shit.' Not spell it, perhaps, but say it."

"I did say it. Give a sheet."

"J.R., are you sober?"

"Of course I'm soober. How could you pout it?"

"Doubt it?"

"Yeah. Whad I say?"

"You said 'pout' it."

"Yeah. Exactly what I mean. Do you know where my little brother is at this moment?"

"If he's your little brother, I assume he's in bed with a fast lady."

"He is. That is exactly where he is. In bed with a fast lady. Probably not fast enough, but fast, up-and-down fast."

"Up-and-down fast. Kelly speed, right?"

J.R. exploded upward, knocking the carefully set breakfast table upside down. Rosemary Hawkins hardly changed expression.

"Well, well, macho ape strikes again."

"Right. Macho ape. I'm macho ape senior. Jason is macho ape junior. He's going to go down hard because you live in a fat Georgetown house and fuck presidents."

"Fucking presidents has nothing to do with where I live. Tell me something. Prove to me that airborne shit, in the shape of a plane piloted by a national hero, is going to blow up Conrad Taylor's funeral.''

J.R. stood up, suddenly, inexplicably sober. ''Listen to me, Rosemary Hawkins. I can't prove a thing. Zero. Nada. But I have sent the best fuck in the United States to a place where she will be safe. And to make matters worse, I have put in harm's way my brother, two close friends, a helicopter pilot who's only been sober for two days, and I've added to this parade the cashing-in of every chip I've earned in thirty years of service to my country. Now, you sleek, unreal dreamlike bitch, what do you make of that?''

''Stupidity, J.R.''

''Fuck you, Rosemary.'' The next time J.R. saw Rosemary Hawkins, she would be half naked, and nearly on fire.

WASHINGTON, D.C.
MONDAY, 1:45 P.M.

The funeral parade, procession, walk, or whatever, went off without visible flaws. It began, with much ceremony, at the Capitol rotunda, where the well-drilled (some would later call them slavish) pallbearers made not a mistake, moving Conrad Taylor, and his ideas, smoothly down the Capitol steps to the street, where the catafalque of Lincoln and Kennedy waited, as it had in the past, for a dead man's last ride.

Emily Taylor and her children had chosen to walk. To walk the whole distance which, if you were dead, was no distance at all, since you were not walking. But being pulled, carried, pushed, photographed, and basically adored. Had Conrad Taylor been alive, he would have waved, smiled his Conrad Taylor smile, and pinched a nearby cropped top or silky bottom. Staring upward with dead eyes, into a lead-lined box, he behaved himself, the first, only, and last time of his political life. Well, life, such as it was.

WASHINGTON, D.C.

The mass, the long, interminable mass, allowed Emily Taylor to rest her tired feet, and to console her tired, less than understanding children. Seventy-two hours before, they had been the most desirable playmates in Washington, or Los Angeles. Or Paris. Bright children, said all the newspapers. In almost all the languages. French. Spanish. Russian, for Christ sake.

Of course, Russian children, Philadelphia children, San Franciscan children, needed no little time to discover that the presidential offspring were pretty damn stupid. They were, incredibly, totally socially unaware. Ghettos were where you went to buy things that all children could buy. Couldn't they? Of course they could.

And so the day, its pageantry, its solemn promise to the dead, wore on. Even the high-strung Presidential Candidate, thought to be at least disruptive, pranced, Kentucky born, as the procession moved across Washington, passing 400,000 or 800,000, depending on the network you listened to. The procession passed across Memorial Bridge, and only here, after 2.5 miles of good behavior, did Presidential Candidate bolt and run. Mildly, he bolted and ran. He tried to jump the bridge, missed, and smashed his forelegs before crashing into the Potomac. A handler, among thousands of what could only be called worshipers, shot the fastest racehorse in the United States in the head.

The horse, dead but unsubmerged, floated under Memorial Bridge, lodged there, and was not removed for three days.

* * *

By 3:20 that afternoon, all the players of the world political scene, plus a few thousand hangers-on, were in
place, listening to the platitudinous praising of Conrad
Taylor, delivered by selected priests that knew him not at
all. Those in the amphitheater, in a state of quiet, tired
acceptance, waited anxiously to bury the old, and get on
with the new. The new, when it appeared, would be flying
at 350 knots. Whatever else it did, the Ace-of-Spades A-
10 ended the monotonous boredom of sitting in one place,
to bury one man.

MYRTLE BEACH A.F.B.
MONDAY, 1500 HOURS

Willy Corchran popped another little black pill into his mouth
and tugged the thermos of coffee from his tool kit. The black
pills had been guaranteed to keep him awake, and as he
washed them down for what he hoped would be the last time,
he resumed his inspection of A-10 #865, the word *Hammer-
head* inscribed on its side. It was a 365th Squadron plane,
one of the Green Devils. The pills worked—that was the only
fact he had gathered in his day at Myrtle Beach. That and
the impressive shape of the 354th Tactical Fighter Wing. As
far as he could tell, they were kept in magnificent condition.
Called into action, he felt confident the wing would go off
with ease, 100 percent.

He looked down the long line of aircraft, neatly parked,
quiet, efficient machines at rest, but only temporarily. Tomorrow, Tuesday, he knew the flight line would burst into
life, and get back to the serious business of defending the
United States. He felt sad knowing he would have to go
back to his machines, his blinking lights, his inputs and
outputs and printouts. What a thrill it would be, just to be
here tomorrow, when all these machines, real, hands-on
machines, roared and coughed to life and followed each
other into the wild blue yonder of Willy Corchran's imag-

ination. He closed his eyes, rocking back and forth on the wing, trying to sense it, to really feel the shake and thunder of fighter aircraft, the wondrously destructive Warthogs, on the move. Not models. Not dreams held together by Testors glue and the unique building and carving talents of a lonely, introspective man with little or no human contact in his life.

One hundred yards away, there was a sort of bark, a hiccup, and then a TF34-GE-100A turbofan engine whined its way to a screaming, roaring life, followed almost immediately by the same cough and whine to full power as the second high-bypass turbofan joined the first, forming a constant, quieter, unified sound. The Ace-of-Spades, canopy open, Jonathan Bennett in the cockpit, had come to life.

And, to Willy's horror, it now looked exactly like one of his models. Slung under each wing, in firing pods, were three air-to-surface AGM-65 maverick missiles. Somehow, in his daydreaming state, the colonel's aircraft had been set up in its most dangerous, destructive attack mode. Cannon fire and six guided missiles.

Willy reacted very quickly. The Green Devils A-10 he was sitting on was parked only twenty yards from the phone booth he had used to alert J.R. that the Ace-of-Spades carried a full drum of 30mm cannon ammunition. Now, he must say just one word. Clearly. He scrambled down the high access ladder, and raced to the phone. Surprisingly, his hand was completely steady. The operator was quick, the connection clear. The number rang only once. "Testors. Testors. Do you read that, goddamn it?"

"Willy?" It was Nadine. Thank God.

"Tell J.R., 'Testors.' Just that! Testors at"—Willy Corchran looked at his watch—"at 1520 hours! Twenty after three Eastern Standard Time! Testors! Do you have that?" Willy didn't know it, but he was screaming at the top of his voice.

"For Christ sake, Willy, of course I heard it. Testors. Whatever the hell that means! I'll get him the message."

"Now! Get it to him now!"

"Oh, shit, Wil—"

But Willy Corchran had hung up. His job was done. Whatever J.R. needed, he, Willy Corchran, systems analyst for the C.I.A., had provided—a job well done. But sadly, not over for Willy. He did not walk away. Instead, resolutely, and with a sure stride, he walked straight down the taxiway, right in front of the Ace-of-Spades A-10; and its pilot, visor down, was undoubtedly looking right at him. Somewhere, behind the Darth Vadar mask, was a madman. Yet Willy Corchran, model maker, walked on. The A-10's cannon looked at him with its multiple eyes.

The A-10 is not a sophisticated aircraft. In the late twentieth century of the B-2, with its Stealth technology, the F-15, F-16, F-14, and any number of equally exotic planes, it was very much a Model T, or at best a gun with wings. Therefore, the man behind the flight helmet, and its smoke glass cover, did not have a lot to do to prepare to get the Ace-of-Spades into the air. No fancy computers to guide him. In fact, the A-10 had *no* automatic flight systems whatsoever. You warmed it up, like a good car you care about, on a cold day, checked your fuel, buttoned your seat belt. It would have been much better for Willy Corchran if Jonathan Bennett had been flying another, more sophisticated aircraft. If he had, he might have been occupied with a lot of preparation to fly. But he wasn't, so he had seen Willy spring to the phone booth and now, with the Ace-of-Spade's high-mounted engines purring docilely, he was watching Willy Corchran, the A-10's canopy still tipped back and open.

Willy walked to the base of the front wheel well, standing directly beneath Jonathan Bennett, peering up at him like some small, angry landlord, with a tenant about to flee without paying the rent. Willy was not quite tall enough to have to crouch to walk *under* the A-10. Fully upright, his head would very slightly brush the squared bottom of the fuselage, directly inside of which Willy Corchran knew was a fearful, killer cannon, the plane's only reason for existence. He had no idea why the code word

Testors was so important. But deep inside, he knew that
behind the mask was a breaker, a squasher of models.
"Can I help you in any way, Colonel?"

The engines, running at low power, were fairly quiet,
high mounted and to the rear of the aircraft. But not that
quiet. Jonathan Bennett pushed a button, and the retract-
able boarding ladder from the cockpit came silently, hy-
draulically down. The masked face said nothing, but the
hand gesture invited Willy Corchran up the ladder.

Willy, foolishly, heroically, scrambled up the ladder,
and stared at the reflection of his own face, mirrored in
the smoky visor. Brown. The visor was brown. Damn! On
all his models, on all the delicately carved, intricately
painted tiny pilots he had inserted so carefully into the
models' cockpits, the visor had been blue plastic. Not
brown. The guy was a colonel. Didn't he know that? The
visor was supposed to be blue!

The gloved hands came away from the A-10's control
stick, pulling the helmet off. The eyes! They were blue.
Empty. Just blue, like a crayon. "Well, Sergeant, what
can I do for you?"

Willy, standing on the access ladder, felt the A-10 shud-
der, moving like a woman, but better, much better. "Well,
Colonel, I thought I might . . . uh . . . assist you in your
takeoff, sir. You know. Like a plane captain." Willy said
this with a bright, hopeful smile on his thin face.

"The Air Force has no plane captains, Sergeant. Perhaps you meant the Navy. Or, more likely, the Marines."
The Colonel stared at him, his eyes a blue, cold grotto.

Willy watched the dark, satiny Baretta Model 92 9mm
rise toward him for what seemed to be a very long time.
The hole in the barrel appeared to be ridiculously small,
for such a big gun. And then, with his model maker's eye
for details, he watched as the copper-colored hollow point
slowly traveled down the length of the barrel, moving
across the scant two feet of space between himself and the
empty blue eyes. He was quite sure he saw that, and the
second one too, as he fell violently off the access ladder,
slapped by a painful fist twice to his chest, a pain so in-

tense his shoes came off in the short fall of seventeen feet to the ground. He couldn't be absolutely sure he saw the second, copper-colored, slow-motion bullet. In his last moment, one thing was very clear to him. As Colonel Bennett leaned out the left side of the cockpit, Willy knew for sure he was too far away to see the three more, copper-colored objects that the pale, dead, blue eyes sent one behind the other, dancing across his chest. Testors. Not even Testors would fix this model. The latest, and only, spy version of Willy Corchran was busted for good.

Silently, the access ladder retracted. With a tiny *whoosh*, the canopy moved over Jonathan's head, slapped into place. The visor, brown, not blue, slipped down over Jonathan's face. Smoothly, effortlessly, death moved down the taxiway. The control tower called to him. He requested takeoff clearance. Willy, splashed on the taxiway, was out of sight. The wing commander was routinely granted clearance for engine test.

Carrying 1350 rounds of cannon ammunition, and six Maverick missiles, the takeoff weight of the Ace-of-Spades was approximately 42,000 pounds. He estimated a fifty-five-minute flight to the Washington Monument. He had also provided himself with enough fuel to ''loiter'' for forty minutes over the target, if necessary, and ten minutes combat time. His flight plan would take him directly over Tabor City and Elizabeth Town, flying up Highway 701, to Selma, crossing the line there into North Carolina, over Roanoke Rapids, Lawrenceville, crossing Interstate 85 at Dinwiddie. Into Virginia, splitting Interstate 295, 64 and 360 north of Richmond. On, then directly over Bowling Green and Fort A.P. Hill. Across the lower Potomac near Fredericksburg, blistering Highway 301, over Piscataway Park, Fort Washington, Mount Vernon, to Alexandria, and down on the water, finally skimming the Potomac, around the Capitol dome, down the throat to the Washington Monument. The strike. The strike plan. Simple. Turn left at the Lincoln Memorial. Straight forward, and on his way at 1530 hours, E.S.T.

ROBINSON/LOWER MARLBORO
DRAGSTRIP
THE SHAMROCK
MONDAY, 4:18 P.M.

Jonathan Bennett boomed over Dinwiddie, Virginia, at 400 feet altitude and 485 MPH. At precisely that moment, Jason Porter Kelly was notified by radio, a message broadcast by Nadine, who still understood nothing, but trusted that J.R. did. "Testor" would "come unglued" in eighteen minutes. Eighteen minutes! J.R. had promised him more. But it would have to do. If Jonathan Bennett was eighteen minutes away, Jason had to find him, and shoot him down, in seventeen minutes.

It took nine-year-old Jason Kelly thirty minutes to walk the nine blocks from St. Marys Grade School to his house on a normal, after-school walk with his friends from the fourth grade. Usually, this walk was a last, leisurely time spent in the company of schoolmates before doing the small chores at home assigned to him by his mother; chores that gave him the princely sum of two dollars a week, to do anything he wanted with.

But for three weeks, the pleasant character of the walk had changed, and the time it took to get home had expanded to one hour, as he ducked through back alleys and across fields, always wary, always one mistake away from confronting ten-year-old George Adams, the class bully who had recently taken Jason as his personal whipping boy. Starting with shoving him to the ground at recess whenever the watchful nuns had failed to watch, it had progressed to intercepting him on the route home, mocking him, grabbing his hat and throwing it into the street, occasionally punching Jason in the stomach, all the while calling him a sissy and a mamma's boy as a growing number of his classmates watched with the cruel fascination of the uninvolved, the unthreatened.

Oh, some days, George Adams had better things to do, and Jason would hurry home on a regular route, alone, the companionship and horseplay of his classmates forgotten in his effort to avoid the humiliating confrontations. Then, one week ago, George Adams had caught him attempting the regular route home, and while a circle of his classmates watched, among them the much-loved but unattainable Beverly Willhelm, Jason had been beaten up without resisting, and a laughing George Adams had stripped Jason's week-old birthday gift from his wrist, waving the watch over his head gleefully before stretching its fine band to fit it on his own thick wrist.

While blood from his nose trickled down into his mouth, Jason had lain on the wet grass and cried, making no effort to get his fine new watch back, tearfully hoping that George Adams would be satisfied for the day and let him go home . . . to Mamma. The sneer on George Adams's face amplified Jason's fear, but the sad look on Beverly Willhelm's face broke his heart, and he wept long and hard as he watched the bully strut away from his fallen victim without a backward glance, surrounded by admiring children, expressing the offhand but savage cruelty children are capable of when formed in a pack with a leader to follow and emulate.

That had been a Friday, and on this, the following Monday, Jason stood, gripped with fear, and stared down the street along his regular route home, blocked once again by George Adams. Hatless, Jason stood at the opposite end of the block, a fine rain plastering his curly hair to his forehead, his escape route a simple right turn and through a field behind the school. George Adams was much bigger than Jason, but Jason knew he could run like the wind, that George could never catch him.

Jason's older brother had watched him all weekend, with that curious but knowing look he had, the "you have no secrets from me" look; but he had refrained from questioning him, and either had not seen or had not noticed his naked, accusing, empty wrist. Jason had wanted to

*confide in his teenage brother. He'd wanted to ask him to
beat up George Adams. But he didn't.*

*Jason Kelly looked off across the field, its tall, wet grass
an inviting green trail to freedom for another day; freedom
from the fear rising in his throat and coursing through his
body, making him shiver with youthful apprehension. But
home was on the other side of that escape route, and he
was not too sure that was a better place to be than where
he stood right now. In a few hours, his mother would be
home. What would he tell her? What could he tell her?
He could not lie to his mother, although he had tried often.
She saw right through him; he would flush red and stumble
with his words, and that would be the end of that. He had
long since given up lying as a bad business. He would
catch it, all right. And J.R. would know he was a coward,
unable to take care of himself.*

*He didn't have his watch; George Adams did. It did not
belong to George Adams; it belonged to Jason. It was his
first watch, a fine watch, and it was his . . . choking back
his fear, Jason Kelly squared his thin shoulders, and ig-
noring the easy right turn, he headed down the street,
keeping his eyes on the other end of the block, on the
huge, grinning George Adams, conqueror of the fourth
grade, and the wearer of a birthday gift that was not his
to wear. As Jason neared the end of the block, George
Adams began to grow before his eyes into gargantuan proportions, standing with his legs spread wide, his jacket
open over a wet shirt front, oblivious to the rain, invin-
cible.*

*Jason's resolve faded as the distance lessened, until he
could see the faces of his classmates, the shiny eyes ready
to applaud the bully and discard the victim with the con-
tempt due him. Jason began to cry as he walked shakily
along the wintry street, the tears hot on his cheeks, turning
to warm salt as they mixed with the rain.*

*And then he was opposite George Adams, still crying,
still frightened, but he didn't stop, didn't speak, just reared
back and buried his skinny fist in the pit of George Adams's
stomach, following that with a vicious kick to the knee of*

*the larger boy as he bent over with a woof of expelled air,
surprise on his face, unable to get his breath even to
scream in pain as the knee buckled under him. Crying and
sobbing, his thin face set in tight-lipped ferocity, Jason
waded into George Adams and followed him to the ground,
his clenched fists windmilling and raining blows on the
shocked class bully, whose only reaction was a futile attempt to cover his face and get to his feet.*

*Jason pressed on, amazed, as he watched the mighty,
indestructible George Adams hiding behind his arms and
backing away, screaming loudly at Jason to leave him
alone. But Jason didn't leave him alone, only redoubling
his efforts, smashing at the boy's exposed stomach and
lashing at his head when the arms came down, the tears
magically transferred to his opponent as quickly as they
left Jason.*

*He was possessed of enormous fighting skills, never be-
fore known to him, as he moved relentlessly against George
Adams, the thief who had stolen his pride as well as his
watch. He was Joe Louis, he was Bat Man, he was Superman . . . His cause was righteous, and he pummeled
the bigger, stronger boy until he noticed that George Adams was curled in a ball at Jason's feet, crying and asking
Jason to stop, to please leave him alone . . . and Jason
Porter Superman was arm-weary and tired, and just a
little taken aback at his unexpected triumph, standing over
the first obstacle to his becoming a man, tasting the sweet
taste of self-esteem, of fear, although sickeningly present,
overcome for at least a little while, long enough to do the
job required of him.*

*Breathing heavily, Jason bent down and grabbed
George's wrist, pulling the watch free and slipping his own
hand through the fine, expandable band, feeling its solid
heaviness as it snugged his wrist, back where it belonged.
His . . . his watch. Someone had taken it from him, and
he had taken it back. With a look of utter disdain on his
face, he awarded the quiet, respectful spectators a long,
slow gaze, sweeping around the tight circle, the newly
crowned king of this particular October Monday. He*

stepped over the former champion and walked away, alone,
before the mask of bravery slipped for all to see. A large
victory, for a very small boy . . .

Remembering that long-ago day, tight-lipped and appre-
hensive, Jason Porter Kelly fitted his flight helmet to his
head and pulled on his gloves. It was time, once again, to
face the bully.

The Harrier's Pegasus engine roared to life, unfettered,
finally. He began to flick switches, pull knobs, shove han-
dles. Like some prehistoric, ungainly, but predatory insect, the Shamrock moved from cover, its exhaust nozzles
vectored downward, and rose from the gloomy, dusky
murk he had hidden in all day. The Harrier burst free
vertically, outriggers hanging down, retracting, the wheels
going up, the aircraft getting sleek and mean, translating
smoothly into normal flight. Jason Kelly's green machine
finally moved toward Washington, toward the Colonel, toward vindication of J.R. Kelly, who knew things nobody
knew, who'd said things nobody believed. But his little
brother believed.

Slowly, Jason moved west, and a little south, looking
for the *tacka, tacka, tacka* colonel, this time, with real,
stick-it-to-you tacks. Jason Porter Kelly, U.S. Marine pilot
was, to his amazement, unafraid, and calm . . . he began
to think he was as crazy as Jonathan Bennett.

WASHINGTON, D.C., AIRSPACE
MONDAY, 4:30 P.M.

The skies over Washington, or more precisely, around
Washington, were full of aircraft of every shape and size,
gathering, in spite of the traffic, to fly over the ceremony
nearing its completion at the Arlington Memorial amphitheater. Radar operators had them all pretty well pegged.

They all seemed to be in the right place. Eighty aircraft, eight minutes away from a slow, eight-minute pass over Conrad Taylors's wake. All eighty were there. All over, their screens blipped green. Orderly but cluttered green. Far to the north, loitering, was the brand-new 747 Air Force One, the most elegant caboose any sky-train ever pulled.

THE PENTAGON
MONDAY, 16:31:37 HOURS

"They look pretty good, General."

"They do, don't they." Taylor Forbes was very, very worried, but you don't *look* worried when a Lieutenant Colonel suggests you have nothing to worry about. Eighty fucking planes. Blanketing the radar screens, flight commanders talking softly, but authoritatively to their respective groups, "training up," the verbage personally coined by General Taylor Forbes to describe this nightmare he was responsible for. Jonathan Bennett was right. When this day was over, he was going to take the younger Bennett's suggestion to heart. Fly down to Myrtle Beach. Get some flight time. Get shit-faced. Get laid.

"They really do look good, General."

"Colonel?"

"Sir."

"You're full of shit, do you know that?"

"I do sir, if you say so."

"Well, I say so."

"Yes, sir. Seven minutes, sir."

"Right. In seven minutes, we'll see if we can keep the 'train' from running into the goddamn Washington Monument."

THE POTOMAC RIVER
ABOARD THE ACE-OF-SPADES
MONDAY, 1634 HOURS

Jonathan Bennett hooked up the Potomac, angling right, crossing the tip of the East Park public golf course, skipping like a mottled green stone above the Washington Channel, pulling harder right, clinging briefly to the Anacostia River, over the corner of the Frederick Douglass Memorial Bridge. He topped the old Navy yard by forty feet, pulled wide right, then left, lining himself up on the United States Capitol Building. He crossed its dome by less than six feet, at 180 knots. Flying down the mall, intent now. Beneath him, people hurled themselves to the ground. He was flying, according to his altimeter, at zero height. He rushed at the Washington Monument, banking to the right.

Strike Plan. Simple. Turn left at the Washington Monument, left again at Lincoln, and shoot. Overhead, eighty aircraft were nearing perfection in the train to overfly the amphitheater. And one aircraft, hovering drunkenly over McMillan Reservoir, launched two AIM 9L air-to-air missiles at the Ace-of-Spades, and applied full power to his aircraft. The Shamrock responded beautifully. But Jason Porter Kelly had found Jonathan Bennett too late, with too little.

OVER THE WASHINGTON MONUMENT
MONDAY, 4:34:37 P.M.

The network helicopter had been around the circle for over two hours. Up close, and personal. They had flown over St. Matthews, peeked into the White House, scouted the amphitheater. What the nation saw, live, was a sober, carefully orchestrated broadcast of a somber, gray day.

What they *didn't* see was the flow of booze and grass that went on in the back of the chopper. By White House correspondents' standards, not much. But concerned citizens for cemetery decency would have been outraged.

Jason had done everything but park the Harrier, hunting for the bulky, mottled A-10, the Ace-of-Spades, and its determined, demented pilot. He had been challenged once, by a ground controller from Andrews. But his cover as the lone Harrier participant from Cherry Point had gone smoothly. With a slight admonition to "get in line, Cherry Point," he'd been mostly ignored. He had no idea what he should look for, or where. The minutes ticked away, and he spun, a turntable airplane, hanging in the sky, smoothly, slowly, gunned up and ready to shoot. But he didn't see anything to shoot. The Ace-of-Spades was invisible, or he was not here. And then he was. Jason Kelly had *never* seen flying like the Ace-of-Spades was attempting . . . no, not attempting. He was *doing* it. As the husky A-10 rushed up the Potomac, Jason lined up on him, locked on, and then . . . the A-10 shifted, fucked up his shot solution, hung a hard right, over the Navy yard, all the time causing the waters of the Potomac and the cold, bleak earth to rise and fall in his wake.

Jason controlled the turntable motion, kicked the rudder pedals, applied power, and, in the seven seconds these attack preparations took, the Ace-of-Spades had cut in, out, and then began an attack run, less than forty feet off the ground, in a rush toward the Washington Monument.

Jason had no choice. Computer off, he launched two missiles, and vectored forward, hurtling at the A-10, trying to quell his admiration for the pilot, trying to justify killing a fellow American airman, yet sure that the flat, ugly menace of the A-10, with its DC-9 radar image, its clumsy gait, its nearly invisible profile, had to be killed. Now. With these two sophisticated missiles. A pipe dream for a man too young to smoke one without being laughed at. The Harrier rushed forward, chasing its own missiles, trying to kill the A-10.

* * *

The AIM-9L bears its name because of its aim. This time, the two missiles lived up to their billing perfectly. Perfect hits. On the wrong targets.

OVER THE WASHINGTON MONUMENT
MONDAY, 4:34:39

The missile that hit the network helicopter cut it in half. It fell in two neat pieces, its hot engine, the beacon for the first missile, landing, by itself, in the tidal basin. The helicopter's blade, still rotating, whirled its way across the mall, and into the Smithsonian Institute, through the roof. A ready-made display unit, torn, bent, and embedded in the ornate roof. Roof ticket sales guaranteed. In mid-intercourse, serious if not very effective fucking, the two most photographed superstars of network television news tumbled end-over-end into the tidal basin. The two other reporters on board were simply never found.

4:34:40

Jonathan Bennett saw the Harrier, recognized the Harrier, and changed his flight profile. Not much, but enough. He hit the button on the one defensive system he trusted on the A-10. The chaff from the pod tumbled out into the gloomy Washington skies. The missile, momentarily stupid, followed the splintered, torn, and technically correct aluminum garbage. It exploded, harmlessly, in the air. If you consider taking off the top third of the Washington Monument harmless. It took eighty years to build the Washington Monument. It was refurbished in 1934. There

is a line, a "watermark" on the monument, clearly showing the work. It tipped over, right there, and slowly, very
slowly, fell down. Not all of it. Just the top third, crum-
bling from neglect, from overuse, from less than the attention that should have been paid to one of the most
recognizable monuments in the world. Eighty-four people
died. Twelve were children, nine were foreigners, legal,
and two were illegal immigrants. Jason Kelly had fired
true, but had been thwarted by a cheap-shot helicopter,
and aluminum foil, the kind the American citizen had
learned to recycle as a matter of course.

Recycle. Yes, Jason Porter Kelly's shot had certainly
done that. He didn't know it. And he pressed forward,
arming his 25mm GAU12, the junior version of Jonathan
Bennett's 30mm.

The Ace-of-Spades A-10, freed for a split second, cut
about four inches of grass from the already trimmed emerald green grass surrounding the monument, and Jonathan lined up the A-10; a straight line, whipping up the
waters of the reflecting pool. Memorial Bridge, an arrow
to Arlington, lay just ahead, and looked like a long, as-
phalt bowling alley crammed with people. Thousands of
people. He began a sharp, left-hand turn as he crossed
over the Lincoln Memorial, and pressed the trigger on the
GAU-8 cannon. Behind the masked face, eyes without soul
watched the full-auto, three-second burst arch downward,
splashing near the bridge, chipping away the concrete,
walking its deadly way through the pack of humanity.

From that moment on, people began to die in earnest
in Washington, D.C. The three-second burst destroyed one
of the A-10's seven barrels. It also sent 315 rounds of
30mm cannon fire directly onto the bridge leading to Arlington National Cemetery. Jonathan Bennett did not wait
for the "book's" one-minute delay to save his weapon.
Fifteen hundred yards from the amphitheater, eighty feet
off the ground, he fired eight hundred more rounds into,
against, and between the elegant columns of the Arlington
amphitheater. He swept over the gravesite at four hundred
knots, stood the A-10 on its tail, rolled over, and started

run number two, nearly stalling the aircraft, using the Maine Memorial, as planned, for his aim point. A 1.5-second burst totaled his gun, and sent the last of his 1350 rounds of 30mm cannon fire into what had become a charnel house . . . he banked left, swung across the Potomac, banked right, and began his third run. This time, he intended to launch six Maverick missiles into the "cup." Six.

As the A-10 completed its sweep northward, a stately, ascetically beautiful flight of United States military aircraft, all unarmed, began to parade across the funeral site, a little early, but called in by General Taylor Forbes, because he was worried they would be late. Better early than late. The parade began, and still not one of them had seen the black, churlish, bloody smoke beginning to rise above the capital of the United States. There were 3,800 people dead in the amphitheater. And the A-10, standing off, but closing, needed only four to eight seconds to place all six of his Maverick air-to-ground missiles into the mess he had already created.

On the ground in Washington, D.C., the world, and its beliefs, were going up in smoke.

WASHINGTON, D.C.
MONDAY, 4:35 P.M.

On the statue in the Lincoln Memorial, its exterior Colorado marble, its interior floors Tennessee marble, its walls Indiana limestone, are carved the words: *To bind up the nation's wounds,* and *To care for him who shall have borne the battle.* At 4:35 P.M., there were more wounds to bind than anyone had ever seen.

Overhead, at 1500 feet, the eighty aircraft that were part of the funeral ceremony began to fly through smoke, while below them, Jonathan Bennett maneuvered to strike again. This time, he would not be unopposed. Jason Kelly opened fire on the Ace-of-Spades A-10 a split second before the six Maverick missiles were locked on their target. His 25mm GAU-12 began to chew up the A-10's armored fuselage, and the missiles were launched without aim, sparing the amphitheater more damage, and more death. Of course, they would come down somewhere, wouldn't they?

There were 28,000 people on the Arlington Memorial Bridge that hour, most on the Virginia side, packed close to the cemetery, lining the bridge its full length to one degree or another. The bridge itself was virtually indestructible. The bridge piers are thirty-two to forty-one feet thick, and they rest on rock thirty-five feet beneath the water. The high-explosive incendiary 30mm cannon shells did chew up a lot of masonry, and the repairs would be long and extensive. Repairing the packed humanity near the cemetery end of the bridge would be a more difficult chore. *Impossible* was a better word.

When Jonathan Bennett attacked his bridge in Vietnam, and was shot down, he was told he had killed seventy-six Vietnamese. An accurate count such as that would be impossible. Thirteen weeks later, it would be officially set at 6,200 killed, 13,000 injured, and 200 missing and presumed dead. Of the 13,000 injured, 2,400 would die of their wounds and 4,757 of the injured would suffer amputations. None of those on the bridge were government officials. To Jonathan Bennett, it was the same bridge, the very same bridge he had attacked before. He was a captive of his demons, once again, and incapable of remorse, or any other rational thought. But he was still a flyer. He banked away quickly when Jason Porter Kelly began to shoot up the Ace-of-Spades.

THE ARLINGTON NATIONAL CEMETERY AMPHITHEATER MONDAY, 4:35 P.M.

Rosemary Hawkins had seen him. She had seen him shoot, over the rim of the amphitheater. At least she thought she had seen him. She wasn't sure. She would never be sure. But she knew he would be there, because J.R. had told her and she hadn't listened. The A-10, framed against a dusty sky, had seemed monstrously big when it arced over the amphitheater. She didn't know it then, but it had already shot up the bridge, packed at one end by Conrad Taylor's most ardent admirers, barricaders, marchers for peace, the whales, the environment, the womb . . .

Her first unconscious thought was, Why had Emily allowed firecrackers to be strung between the classic Roman arched pillars of the amphitheater? They were inappropriate, to say the least. Noisy, flashing arcs, an obscene display of pyrotechnics. The amphitheater lit up like a Broadway stage, and then all the lights flashed at the same time, and she was flat on her back, camera flashbulbs going off all around her, but the lights weren't camera flashbulbs, and why didn't she have one stocking on? And for God's sake, where was the bottom of her dress? And what the hell was a man's arm doing on her chest? A man's arm. In a suit. Without a body. Rosemary Hawkins hurled it away, stood up, and screamed in total, mind-stopping terror. She was not aware of that. The screaming.

Four days later, when she could bear to look at them, she saw the still photos of a television tape, a tape they ran throughout the attack. In the center of it all, Rosemary Hawkins, mouth open, wearing the top half of a dress, one stocking, one shoe, one pair of panties. Much of the tape . . . *most* of the tape, would never be shown. But she would see it. It would turn her heart to stone.

She had recovered almost immediately, the shrieking scream releasing her to take action, any kind of action. It seemed her scream had lasted quite a long time, because when she began to look around her, the plane was back. This time from the north, and the pyrotechnic display began all over again.

It was as if someone, some ungodly, terrible someone, were hurling monstrous light bulbs at the columns of the amphitheater. That was the more correct sight-and-sounds description. *I mean, you must remember this, Rosemary, you, of all people, will be asked, "hey, bitch, where's your dress?" And you must be able to tell them the facts, the real facts, that the arm tore your dress, so you threw the arm away, the bastard, who does he think he is, for Christ sake? . . .*

Joseph was sitting very near the Soviet President. Very near. Near enough to see him vanish before his eyes. He hadn't vanished, of course. He was still in the amphitheater. Or some of him was. Joseph was, for some unknown reason, completely unscathed. The seventeen-man Soviet delegation, in the special seats, the seats of honor, near the casket itself, had all been killed in one, massive blast. But Joseph had not. He'd not been killed in Afghanistan, either. He was not surprised then. This time, he was surprised. Why? Why had they attacked the Soviet President here? Why not the embassy, as Scorpio had said? Joseph, unscathed, walked out of the amphitheater. He walked all the way back to the Soviet embassy. Who was Scorpio, and how did one find him?

Not a single shell hit the bulletproof glass protecting the United States President. No, not one. But a chainsaw of marble chips had knocked it inward, a million, tiny shards of glass rummaging in the section, killing some, sparing others. The Secret Service detail, 250 strong, could do nothing. The twenty agents nearest the President could do nothing, although those who were not killed drew their Uzi submachine guns from the specially built holsters they all wore. Some pressed their radio earplugs closer to their heads, to hear directional commands, to know who to shoot at. Others had their radio plugs blown off. Some had them blown in. Most were down. All would die by the time Jonathan Bennett made his second pass. The attack that would kill one president and rekill another.

William Rodgers had not been President very long, but he had the place of honor, nearest his former chief, behind the 100-foot bulletproof glass partition constructed for the favored few, those closest to the President. Family. Conrad Taylor's family. His children. His wife. His closest advisors. Rosemary Hawkins had been far away, relatively speaking, sitting opposite the coffin, directly across from William Rodgers. That was as close as Emily Taylor would allow. With the State Department's ground pounders. Well, fuck it. He'd nominated her as his Secretary of State, and she would *be* his Secretary of State. *Now* you bury your old boss, and *then* you get on with the task of throwing the whiney little drunk out of the White House private quarters!

But then the bulletproof glass had bathed him in a blinding, white-hot shower of metal and glass and suits and one cuff link, which embedded itself in his cheek. He stumbled down, away from the privileged few, falling, getting up, pulling the gold cuff link from his cheek, the letter *P* on it. Who was *P?* He'd staggered to the President's coffin, and he leaned back against it, his arms thrown wide, protectively, and he'd felt safe, because he was protecting Conrad Taylor, or . . . or was Conrad Taylor protecting him? And then ten rounds of 30mm cannon fire had walked down the circular stairs surrounding the casket, and number ten had passed through William Rodgers and exploded against the heavy steel coffin, and nobody ever found a trace of either man again. The gold cuff link with the *P* was hocked two days later, taken to a D.C. pawnshop by a forty-five-year-old man who claimed to have found it on his doorstep. Seven miles from the amphitheater. It was pure gold, and weighed 1.2 ounces. He got seventeen dollars for it. He was happy.

* * *

The United States Supreme Court had not met since the President's death on Wednesday, which was only proper. They were together, however, when they were decimated by granite, bleacher seat wood, glass, and nearly a ton of marble schrapnel. They were killed, without being asked their opinion. There had been no dissenting opinion.

Only thirteen members of the United States Congress had not been present. One senator was ill, having suffered an asthma attack the night before, an attack that would kill him anyway. The senators had been on one side of the coffin, nearer the President, befitting their "Advise and Consent" image. The House of Representatives had been seated, in a close pack, directly opposite the Senate. Which, as pecking orders go, seemed fair. And it was. The Senate died in the first attack, the House of Representatives, less twelve abstaining, in the second. The lawmakers of the United States were all dead in the amphitheater. The judges of the Supreme Court were all dead, the President was dead. One supposed he was dead. He was not found.

The governments of fifty-two nations, large and small, mostly small, were killed outright, or wounded, in the second attack, the attack that had really done the most damage, if you were a commentator for the networks. Any network. The promotion ladder was jerked crazily off its hinges by the Ace-of-Spades A-10. All major network personnel, with the exception of those in helicopters or the Goodyear blimp, were killed. For seventeen days, the four major United States television networks would scramble to find anchormen and —women from their respective major cities' stations. But *they* had been there too. On Tuesday night, a famous, but more important alive, talk show host would anchor the news on ABC. On NBC, the co-anchor of the New York affiliate, just signed, would do only the second national broadcast of her career. CBS news was handled by four satellite stations across the country. It had no live broadcasters left to do a national program. In a

rage of pained grief and black humor, the head of CBS
news said to be sure to watch "20 Minutes" on Sunday,
and "30 Hours" on Wednesday.

The entire Joint Chiefs of Staff, their aides, their syc-
ophants, their families, were at the President's funeral. So
were the forty-eight most powerful and highly ranked officers of the four military services. From this group, the
highest ranking survivor was a Lieutenant Colonel of the
Logistics Department, working directly for the Chief of
Staff of the Army. He lost both legs in the attack. Again,
the moves upward on the promotion ladder would be fast
and impressive. No. Not impressive. The military jugular
vein had been cut. It would bleed for a very long time.

Emily Taylor, her two children, her in-laws, her parents, her entire family, were killed. Instantly, the broadcasts said. Not true. Emily Taylor, poor Emily Taylor, had
lived long enough to see two things. Rosemary Hawkins,
dress torn nearly off her body, her legs as sleek as ever,
maybe more so, with one stocking. And she had seen the
new President and her husband's coffin vanish in the final
explosion that killed her on its gruesome way around the
cup of the amphitheater.

OVER AND ABOVE WASHINGTON, D.C.
MONDAY, 14:35:45

Jason Kelly could see all too clearly what damage had
been done, but he could do nothing about it now. His
attack with the missiles had come too late, and he had not
executed it very well. He felt personally responsible for
the smoke and flames curling up into the gray-black skies
over Washington. He turned the Harrier after the A-10, as
it skimmed along the ground. A thin line of white smoke
flowed back and up toward him. The A-10 was hurt, but

it suddenly pulled up and climbed into the flow of aircraft still flying over the burial site. Jason followed it up, triggered the 25mm again, watched the hits light up the right wing and tail surfaces of the A-10, with no apparent effect on his flight capabilities. The A-10 split the stream of aircraft, and Jason quit firing, but followed the A-10 through the same open airspace. His aim had not been wild. He'd put all the rounds into the A-10. But the steady, in-line train of aircraft began to understand that something was very wrong. To emphasize it, an F-15 from the Maryland Air Force Reserve pulled up to allow the A-10, followed immediately by the Harrier, to flow up and through the formation. In doing so, he rammed into the F-15 in front of him, which then ran into one of the C-130 tankers from Yuma, M.C.A.S. The three planes tumbled from the sky like the missiles misfired in Jonathan's last attack on the funeral site. They too had to come down, somewhere.

Jason Kelly clung to the Ace-of-Spades's tail, even while they both climbed, tearing at the thick sky, pulling themselves up and through the assembled aircraft, into the mottled clouds until the A-10 vanished in thick cloud cover. But he hadn't vanished. Jason could "see" him. The night-capable Harrier could do a lot of things. Avionics on the Harrier. None on the A-10. Jason Kelly was very frightened, but he read the dials, punched the numbers, and pulled the trigger. He missed.

The A-10 staggered around in the cloud cover, badly hit. Smoke filled the cockpit. The urge to eject was strong in Jonathan Bennett. But his enemies, his *country's* enemies, were still not taken out. The bridge! The goddamn bridge! It was still standing. Who planned this shit anyway? He checked his weapons. None. He had none. Expended. Like him. Expendable. He pulled the A-10 over, on its back, and dived toward the ground, from 28,000 feet. Flanking him, riding down with him, Jason Kelly read the readable, and discarded what he *felt* might be. The readable was correct. The Ace-of-Spades A-10 was in a powered dive, out of munitions, its pilot long ago out of his mind.

Below the diving aircraft, pigeons were coming home to roost. The first aircraft to hit the ground, the Maryland (AFRES) F-15, plowed into the west face tower of the Cathedral of St. Peter and Paul, known as the Washington Cathedral. The hit demolished the aircraft, killing its pilot. The Cathedral tower, still not finished after 100 years of work, suffered $21 million in damaged stone work, and the loss of two of the central tower's fifty-three bells when the F-15's engine went through and out of the tower. The cathedral has no membership of its own. By the 1893 Charter to the Episcopal Church from Congress, it is a house of prayer for all people. The church was nearly full this funeral day. Mercifully, incredibly, only the pilot died in this episode of Jonathan Bennett's flight over Washington, D.C. On this ever more grim Monday . . .

AIRBORNE, THE SHAMROCK
OVER WASHINGTON, D.C.
MONDAY, 4:37 P.M.

As the A-10 began its power dive, Jason Kelly shifted the nozzles on his Pegasus engine, "viffing" the Harrier, nearly stopping in midair, then he dropped straight down, rolled on his back, and pulled directly behind the A-10, which clearly intended to dive straight into the hell it had created in the capital and beyond. His heart beating wildly, his fear gone in a rush of clear and total hatred for the Ace-of-Spades and its demented pilot, he pushed the Harrier to its maximum and began to shoot the A-10 to pieces. He understood, now, that the A-10 was without offensive weapons. But it still contained hundreds of gallons of aviation fuel. And it still had its pilot. The pilot was the A-10's last, and most effective weapon.

AIRBORNE, THE ACE-OF-SPADES
OVER WASHINGTON, D.C.
MONDAY, 4:37:17

Jonathan Bennett could not yet see the ground clearly, as he dived through intermittent cloud cover, full power from 28,000 feet. The cloud cover ended at 7,000 feet, high for this time of year. High, and advantageous. From 7,000 feet, he would have enough time to fly the A-10 right into the amphitheater. If not, the bridge. Yes. The bridge. Better the bridge. Kill it, Jonathan. Kill the bridge. The A-10 was suddenly staggered by gunfire, bits of the wing being chewed off to his right side. The Ace-of-Spades shuddered under the impact, slowed, slewing violently onto its side, out of control. The hammering went on, as the Harrier's gunfire walked the tail surfaces in short bursts.

Staggered, Jonathan fought to regain control, slowed to less than 300 mph, righted the aircraft, continued downward, the wing on the starboard side burning along its leading edge. He began to laugh wildly, the first sounds Jason Kelly had heard from the A-10's pilot.

ABOARD THE SHAMROCK
MONDAY, 4:37:20

It was very obvious to Jason Kelly, his guns banging away at the A-10, that the Ace-of-Spades had to blow up. If it was so obvious, why didn't it happen? Grimly, his jaw set, his whole body attuned to the little Harrier's every motion, he clung to the A-10, pouring fire into it, wishing it down, willing it to blow up, to explode, here, in the sky, before it reached the ground. He had to stop it. He had to.

THE ACE-OF-SPADES
4:37:22

The A-10 shuddered and stumbled through the sky like a
drunken sailor on a slippery street, dipping its wings,
righting itself, straightening out, stringlike, back on target. *The fucking gook in the MIG-21! How had he gotten
on his tail? Where's the wingman? What a fuck-up all this
is. Who plans this shit?*

THE SHAMROCK
4:37:23

Jason closed on the A-10, until he was close enough, even
in the cloudy skies, to see its bulky shape with perfect
clarity. At that moment, the A-10 broke through the cloud
cover, and burst into the clear at 7,000 feet. Almost directly below was Arlington Memorial Bridge, still packed
with humanity, humans in total shock, milling about,
without direction or purpose, except to run, to get off the
bridge, slippery with blood and bathed in terror. Jason
closed with a rush, the Harrier bent at an absurd angle.
The perfect deflection shot presenting itself if he could just
master it one time. He powered up, held the gun button
down, the Harrier vibrating with full auto-recoil and
G stress far beyond the design specifications. From fifty
yards, Jason sent the 25mm shells dancing the length of
the Ace-of-Spades, lighting tiny fires across the tail section, down the rear of the air-frame, over the top, to the
canopy . . .

THE ACE-OF-SPADES
4:37:23

Jonathan Bennett, eyes fixed on the bridge, could feel the
hits against the A-10, as if they were hits on his own body.
Still, he stayed on course. Controlling the by-now-slow
dive of his aircraft, his blue eyes bright with death. He
felt the hits, sensed them moving along the A-10's skin,
as if it were his own skin. Then the canopy blew off, and
the instrument panel blew apart in front of him, glass and
steel and aluminum flashing like a fire storm around the
cockpit, mortally wounding him, blinding him, killing him
with a not swift, but sure, certainty. He could see nothing,
his face raw meat, his chest open, his right leg gone out
through a hole in the weapons bay under his seat. He was,
for all intents and purposes, a dead man. Perversely, the
cockpit exploded in fire, clawing, licking flames moving
up his one leg, consuming him in molten metal and burning straps. The agony was beyond description, death at its
worst, the most terrifying death a pilot can imagine. To
burn up, inside the cockpit.

   Jonathan Bennett may have been dead, or he may not
have been dead. The Ace-of-Spades carried on, still held,
still pointed down, still in the air.

THE SHAMROCK
4:37:25

Jason Kelly could not believe his eyes. The A-10 was a
shambling wreck, but it still flew on, burning from one
end to the other. Its pilot burning, but somehow still upright, the black flight helmet clear in the flames, the Ace-
of-Spades in sharp relief against the black. The sky was
dark, terribly dark; night, and flames, and death had come
out of the sky, and more was on its way. It was more than

Jason Kelly would allow. Deliberately, he aimed the Harrier at the burning wreck in front of him, and accelerated, full power, directly at a space just in front of the A-10's nose. A split second before the Harrier collided, Jason Kelly punched the "stencil type" 10B ejection seat used in the Harrier AV-8B. It blew him out and up, away from the Harrier. Then the two aircraft came together in a cataclysmic explosion that vaporized both aircraft, the blast knocking Jason Kelly, strapped into his ejection seat, an additional 1500 feet up into the dark sky, breaking his left arm, and singeing the hair off the left side of his body, from his hairline to his feet. At 4,700 feet, the seat blew itself away from Jason, and the chute, that blessed, bulbous chute, opened above him. Slowly, dangling under the yellow chute, he drifted earthward. Badly injured, but alive. The two aircraft, the objects of so much plotting and planning, and counterplotting and -planning, had disappeared in a fireball of aviation fuel.

THE RETURN TO EARTH
JASON KELLY'S RIDE DOWN
A VIEW FROM ABOVE WASHINGTON
MONDAY, 4:38:50

For the rest of his life, Jason Kelly would remember. Not his dogfight with a madman. Not his killing of the A-10's pilot. Not even the tiniest of details would ever sort themselves out for him about the last five minutes in the air over Washington, D.C., and its environs. What he *would* remember, vividly, was his slow, silent ride back to earth, looking between his swaying legs, in the grip of terrible, fiery pain. While he dropped earthward from 4,600 feet, he catalogued a series of flashback images that would plague his dreams for the rest of his life.

To Jason Kelly, it looked like all of the capital was on fire, or in danger of catching fire. Through a fog of pain and shock, he tried to figure out how the A-10 had done so much damage. The Goodyear blimp drifted by him, its startled pilot jerking the nose up a little, its little engine humming merrily, as the TV crew on board focused its cameras on the inferno the Ace-of-Spades A-10 had wrought. For the briefest moment, they centered the mini-cam on the falling Jason Kelly. But he was no news. Down below was news. Jason scanned the city, a human recorder for later playback nightmares . . .

The yellow-cream walls of the amphitheater, so classic and beautiful only five minutes before, were seared black and shattered the full circle of the cup. The cannon fire directed into the amphitheater had created a hellish, whirling dervish of flying objects, rolling like a "wave" cheer around a football stadium. The blue roof of the Tomb of the Unknowns was scorched, but otherwise undamaged. The amphitheater columns had not fallen over. They had shredded. Around the amphitheater, roads were clogged by burning buses, limousines, cabs. Nearby, the Maine Memorial stood sentry while the grass around it burned to the dirt, and its revered dead from the Spanish American War roasted under a domino ground of destroyed tombstones and markers. The road near the amphitheater seemed alive with fire from the air, a saucer circling the amphitheater's cup. The whole scene as the sky turned dark was surreal to Jason, a painting by a Spaniard, perhaps, or an Italian from the Dark Ages. Off to his left, the top left corner of the Washington Cathedral burned furiously. Red and blue emergency lights flashed throughout the city as they tried to deal with a disaster far beyond the training manual. There seemed to be a half dozen or more major fires burning. Jason drifted in and out of consciousness, trying to focus on the chaos below him, wondering where J.R. was, and if he was all right.

There were eight fires, in fact. Six missiles fired, six missiles hit, all over Washington. The biggest fire was at the War College, at Fort McNair, at Greenleaf Point. A serene and peaceful place, in spite of its mission in life. Housed here was the largest collection of military books in the United States, stretching back to revolutionary days. The perpetrators of Lincoln's assassination were hanged here, at the confluence of the Potomac and Anacostia Rivers. Only Britain's Military Library collection is larger than the War College Collection, and only because Great Britain has been around much longer to put the collection together. It was here, on this lush green carpet, surrounding one of the most beautiful sets of buildings representing martial America, that three of the air-to-ground missiles came to rest.

In the center of the complex lies a small, brick building. The ropes used to hang the conspirators are said to be still in the building used to dispatch them. One Maverick missile demolished this building, without loss of life. One struck just above the circular southeast colonnade, entered the roof line there, and exploded. The fire would burn furiously until dawn, a conflagration so savage it could not be approached. Fire boats, used later in the evening, could not get close enough to reach the fire. Three custodians died, and one officer, a major, who was using the occasion to brush up on battalion tactics. The third and final Maverick overshot the brick buildings, and skipped like a rock across a parking lot, into a swarm of barracks just north of the marina, where over sixty yachts were berthed. The fire that ensued went unchecked, until, by 2:00 A.M., it was finally knocked down, having torched three-quarters of the facilities at the fort. All of the boats would burn to the waterline. Ninety-eight men, twelve women, and one child died at the complex. The library was completely, irrevocably destroyed. Some would see this as poetic justice.

The strikes of the AGM-65 Maverick missiles would later be categorized as "perverse," or "fated." The Maverick air-to-ground missile would gain a crude, cruel nickname among the builders of weapons around the world. "The Manual Missile" or "All Gone Made" for AGM. The three missiles launched from the outboard wing had come to earth within 100 yards of each other at Fort

McNair. The three from the inboard launch pylon did too, in a fashion. They were spread apart over 100 yards, 300-plus yards hit-to-hit, point-to-point. They struck, in order, the Supreme Court Building, the Library of Congress, and its Annex, the Folger Shakespeare Library. The AGM-65 was a destroyer of human knowledge, as well as human lives.

The hit on the Supreme Court Building was reminiscent of the damage inflicted on its members. The rocket slammed straight into the middle of the eight columns fronting the court steps, sending marble fragments careening around the courthouse steps, killing eighty-six people outright, and injuring thirty-one others. All of the dead were government employees, holding a separate prayer gathering on the court's wide, sweeping steps. The damage to the courthouse itself was extensive. It would cost eighty million dollars to repair. The court, without judges, would be far down the list of priority repair work.

The second and third AGM-65 Mavericks hit their un-planned targets almost simultaneously, leading most people in the area, and there were very few, to believe it had been one massive explosion. It was two, fractions of a second apart. The Folger Shakespeare Library was struck first, though it was, by scant yards, the more distant landing place. The Folger Library is a stolid, blue-gray, not particularly attractive building. Again, the rocket was seen to skip, hitting the ground and bouncing before it ripped a forty-foot hole in the library wall, plowed through five reading rooms, and exploded, turning the room it landed in into a raging furnace, and triggering the automatic sprinkler system, which, efficiently enough, put out the fire. Then it went amok, as every sprinkler in the building went on, and stayed on. Less than 50 percent of the library's contents would be salvageable. The loss, in dollars, was incalculable. In lives, kind. No deaths, one superficial wound to a cop driving at breakneck speed through the streets, heading for the trouble, when all around him, he had trouble to spare. The police cruiser was totaled.

The third and last rocket hit in the "Capital East Area,"
as it is called, and struck the magnificent, sculptured blue
dome of the Library of Congress, angled straight down,
and immediately blew up, sending its fiery blast into the
bowels of the library. The center of the library was gutted,
and six people, all working at cleaning chores, in spite of
the occasion, were killed. The fire, for inexplicable reasons, never really got started, and for whatever the technical reasons, snuffed itself out, thus sparing the world
from a literary disaster to rival the burning of Alexandria
in ancient times. Less than 2 percent of the library's contents were lost. A miracle, and a gift, on a day to rival
that of any day in recorded history for its consequences.

The last F-15, after its brush with the C-130, immediately flashed fire warning lights, and the cockpit filled with
smoke. The pilot, a young National Guard flyer from the
State of Washington, panicked, and punched the eject button. He sailed upward, free of the F-15, only to strike the
leading edge of a second C-130 tanker's wing, crushing
him instantly, and ripping the wingtip off the C-130. It flew
on, bent, but not broken. And so did the F-15, which was
not on fire at all. A tire had exploded in the wheel well,
sending black smoke up and into the cockpit. No fire. Just
smoke, but enough to send the red fire warning lights
blinking and the aircraft alarm ringing. It remained steady,
flying on without benefit of a pilot, but its auto pilot not
engaged. And its nose was directed earthward. It came to
rest in the poorest, most crime-ridden section of the
"murder capital" of the U.S.A. It rolled up the street,
bounced high into the air, stood on its tail, and fell straight
back down. The death toll here would be out of all pro-
portion to the rest of the night. Six square blocks of tightly
packed, wall-to-wall apartments and homes, in the poorest
section of the northeast neighborhoods of Washington,
D.C., went up in smoke. Eight hundred seventeen men,
women and children died. The heaviest toll, naturally, was
the children. Six hundred seventy of the victims were less

than ten years old. Only seventeen of the victims were adult males.

The C-130 is a very big airplane. It is a workhorse for the Marine Corps, a reliable horse, hauling troops and fuel and food day in and day out, without complaint. When the first F-15 fighter reared up like a skittish horse, to avoid the onrushing Ace-of-Spades the pilot had flown directly under the C-130, brushing it from formation, tearing open its belly, but not exploding. The F-15 had then plummeted into the Washington Cathedral, killing its pilot, but no one else. The C-130, clawing for a hold in the sky, pulled northward, into Virginia, struggling to remain airborne, its pilot and copilot manhandling an aircraft without a "floor." Two of its crew had fallen through the hole to their deaths. The C-130 pilot, unfamiliar with the D.C. area, searched frantically for somewhere to put his aircraft down safely, his ears filled now with the disjointed communications of a ceremonial duty gone terribly awry. Below the C-130, the pilot could see a cluster of lights, and, in the growing darkness, a ribbon of reflected light. A river. He didn't know what river, or where, in any direction, he was headed. But where there were lights, he could set the plane down where there was darkness, and therefore, no people to die. The pilot, heroically, intended to try to ditch his aircraft on a darkened river, away from the nearest lights. He nearly succeeded.

The C-130 swept toward the earth, under the nominal control of its pilot. He was fifteen miles downriver from the capital. The cluster of light he used to guide himself away from lights was Mount Vernon, the home of George Washington. Built in 1743, it became Washington's in 1759. Acting as his own architect, he added an upper story, and two wings, chirping about the "money saved by my time invested." Or so it was quoted. Most historians doubted it very much. He was a plantation owner, and a very successful one at that. He owned slaves, and kept indentured English criminals, to work off their sentences. The Father of Our Country was not a beast. It was the times; and for him, Mount Vernon was the best of times.

He once recorded that the pleasures of his estate were so great, and varied, that his family "did not sit to dinner in twenty years." Any ship of the U.S. Navy passing the estate on the Potomac, dips its flag to half mast, tolls its ship's bell, and the crew comes to attention. On this grim November night, a "ship," flown by members of the Marine Corps, the Navy's infantry, visited Mount Vernon. The big aircraft settled onto the Mount Vernon estate, taking out a barn and 1500 feet of manicured estate before coming to rest, upside down in the river, less than 500 yards from George's house.

None aboard the C-130 survived. Aside from gardening and landscaping costs, with a bit of money for a new "reconstructed" barn, Mount Vernon was untouched.

Shortly before dark, on a late November day, if you were a pilot crossing the *T* of the Capitol dome with the Washington Monument, what you would see, on a normal November day, is quite beautiful. Below the darkening sky, the Capitol dome glows, but not too brightly, the lights strategically placed, almost, but not quite, inconspicuous. The pool reflects trees, bushes, the essence of Washington. Broad vistas move out at right angles, to the left, if that is possible, and to the right. Stretched out, laid out, in a straight line, the mall corridor reaches to the Washington Monument, with its glowing orange tower.

Beyond, if you were a pilot, is the Lincoln Memorial, all pastels and light and courage, done to commemorate the birth, and near death, of a nation. Angling to the left, you would fly down the length of Arlington Memorial Bridge, crossing without trouble into Virginia. You would then fly the river, dissecting it at Mount Vernon. And so he had done, Jonathan Bennett. He had flown this spectacular, colorful, quintessentially American view of things grand, things marble, things important. That is the view you would see, if you had flown it a split second before the Ace-of-Spades A-10. Failing that, you would fly the same route, five minutes behind the Ace-of-Spades.

The capital is aflame. Fire covers what seems to be the

entire city. The Washington Monument has no cheerful, lighted top. It has no top at all. The Supreme Court is a skyrocket of blazing, chipped columns. The Library of Congress is dark, ominously dark, its power, and prestige, knocked out. The Shakespeare Library is a sheet of flame, shooting eighty feet into the air. The arrow of Arlington Memorial Bridge is lighted, from end to end, with fire. One end, the Arlington end, burns with a red, bloody glow, an unnatural fire of unnatural proportions. And not too far beyond the bridge, the amphitheater of Arlington National Cemetery glows in the dark, splashing its violence out of the amphitheater cup, drenching the dead in a living, fiery flame that torches everything in its path. Off to the right, children burn in the dark, as a packed, inner city ghetto flashes bright, and falls to the ground, trampling its children. A bright firefly glow rises from down river, while Fort McNair flares and falls to the ground, torching all it sought to teach. To the left, Washington Cathedral's tower collapses on itself, a fitting symbol for the night, as Washington, D.C., and Maryland, and Virginia, U.S.A., flicker their souls into a black sky.

Jonathan Bennett, in five violent moments, had destroyed the capital, many of its inhabitants, and most critically its institutions. And he had assassinated the governments of fifty-two nations, in one awesome strike. A "night strike," in the truest sense of the words.

ARLINGTON NATIONAL CEMETERY MONDAY, 4:45 P.M.

Rosemary Hawkins did not know how J.R. Kelly had appeared in the center of the amphitheater, sweeping her up in his powerful arms, carrying her through and out of the twisted, charred remains of the amphitheater. He carried her like a small child, stepping over the dead, around the dying, slipping on bloody debris, her head buried against his neck, her eyes averted. She was crying, a soft, helpless cry, overwhelmed and suddenly, hopelessly afraid.

The amphitheater was a glowing circle of fire, arcing over the rim, flickering between the classic arches, blackened now, chipped and torn. People walked aimlessly inside the amphitheater, many horribly burned, blistered, most with their clothing gone. Very few people were uninjured. J.R., his face set and grim, walked on, and out of the amphitheater, across the dirt road and through a ring of flaming grass circling the amphitheater and stretching back all the way to the Maine Memorial. He could hear sirens wailing in the distance.

Across the Potomac, the arrow of Memorial Bridge seemed to be a solid sheet of flame. The bridge wasn't on fire. The people on the bridge were on fire. The roads and access areas to the amphitheater and the rest of the cemetery grounds were strewn with burning vehicles of all kinds. Wherever there was open space, the lightly injured tended to the needs of the more seriously injured. The dead, for the moment, were left where they lay. Everywhere, there were the dead, crumpled in grotesque positions, many of them blown right over or through the open walls of the amphitheater.

J.R. walked clear of the worst of the devastation, gently placing Rosemary on a clear patch of ground. He had carried her over 600 yards. She sat there, her dress torn from her body, her face blackened, a small cut on her ankle the only visible wound. He pushed her down, gently, his hands probing, checking for serious injury. She'd stopped crying, and was staring up at him, her eyes comically wide against her smoke-blackened face. He stripped off her remaining stocking, unsnapped her garter belt, and threw them into a nearby spot fire. Except for the small cut on her foot, she seemed to be uninjured. He unzipped the front top of her dress, checked for blood, found none, closed it back up.

"Taco to Taco Two. I have Desert Flower, two clicks or so north of amphitheater. Get in here and pick us up." J.R. was speaking hurriedly but clearly into a hand-held radio. Rosemary, still lying down, stared into his face, a look of wonder and surprise, and something else in her green eyes.

"Taco, this is Taco Two. How do I find you? From up here, it's just a sea of fire."

"Taco Two, we are on the dirt knoll, due north of amphitheater. This is probably the only place here that's *not* on fire. Get in here, dammit! One pass. Down, and right out again. Nobody else gets on, no matter how badly they are injured. Do you read that?"

Rosemary said, "But J.R., we need to help anyb—" He silenced her with a look so cold, so stern, she broke eye contact.

"Read you, Taco. But I have room for more."

"Negative, Taco Two. If I'm right, Rosemary Hawkins is the new President of the United States. Get down here. Right now!"

"Roger, Taco, on my way. Destination?"

"The White House lawn."

"Roger, Taco. The White House lawn." The chopper pilot, a C.I.A. veteran of Cambodia and Central America, came in very fast and low, finding Rosemary Hawkins, once again held in the strong arms of J.R. Kelly. The chopper hovered over the knoll, whipping up the burning grass, causing a wave of flame to rush away into the blackness, lighting the way to the Potomac River.

J.R. didn't wait for it to land. When the helicopter was a few feet off the ground, he deposited Rosemary on the chopper deck, and pulled himself inside. Immediately, the chopper lifted off, banking toward the river. Nobody tried to board it. In all likelihood, nobody even saw it.

"What do you hear from Jason?"

"Nothing, J.R. Not yet. Somebody reported a yellow chute coming down near the Lincoln Memorial. Nadine's working on it, but she can't get to it. The roads are a mess."

"Okay, listen. You drop us off, then check, will you? It could be him."

"Sure, J.R. I'll check. But reports are coming in from

all over. There are fires all over town. Planes down, missiles, bombs, nobody knows. That chute could belong to anybody.''

''I know that. Just find out, one way or another. Information is going to be hard to come by. We need whatever we can get. The world, as we've known it, is changed, as of this day.''

''Shit happens,'' said Taco Two, as the unmarked helicopter settled on the south lawn of the White House. Once again, J.R. Kelly picked up Rosemary Hawkins and strode across the deserted White House lawn. Only two Secret Service agents rushed out to meet them, guns drawn.

''Put them away, assholes. This is Rosemary Hawkins. I'm J.R. Kelly, C.I.A. The President is dead, and I think everybody in the fucking government is dead too. Rosemary Hawkins is the new President of the United States. Call and get us a federal judge, if you can find a live one. And bring in all the troops from the Marine barracks. The White House has to be sealed off, and right now! Band members, whatever! Get them here, armed. Do you understand?''

''Miss Hawkins? Is that what you want?''

She turned to them, still in J.R.'s arms, her head on his shoulder. ''Do what he says. We all have to pull together now. Our country . . . no, the whole world is in danger of going up in . . . in, I don't know what. Just do what he says. And contact my deputy, as soon as possible. General Brian Howell.''

The guns disappeared into the tailored suits of the Secret Service agents. But it would be many hours before any of J.R.'s or Rosemary Hawkins's orders were carried out. Emergency communications were operable. But who did you communicate with, and where did you find them? The world was leaderless, full of order takers, with no orders to take.

J.R. carried Rosemary into the silent White House, straight to her office, where he placed her gently on the couch.

He walked to the bar, picked up a bottle of tequila and

two glasses. Tucking a bottle of scotch under one arm, he walked slowly across the room to where she lay, one hand held over her eyes, the fingers slowly rubbing her eyebrows. He slumped down next to her, his back against the couch, pouring two glasses brim full, tequila for him, scotch for her.

"Here, Madam President. Or Ms. President. Or, whatever. Drink this down. You're gonna need it in the next few hours."

Wordlessly, she took the glass, sipping at it, short, tiny sips, until it was half gone. Then she tipped the amber liquid in its Waterford crystal tumbler, and drained it in one gulp. "You were right all along, J.R."

Outside the White House, Washington seemed to be on fire everywhere. An orange glow lit the sky, flickering its light across the darkened inner office walls. Her smoke-blackened face was nearly invisible. Her eyes were white spots against the black, her bare legs long and aflame in the eerie, orange glow from outside.

"Yeah. I was right. And so what?" His voice was flat, empty of emotion. Jason. Where was his heroic little brother?

"I'll do anything you say now."

"It's too late, Rosemary. Much too late."

"You saved my life, J.R." Her hand rested lightly on his shoulder, her fingers on his neck.

"No, I didn't. I didn't save anything at all." Bitterly, he drank his tequila straight down, and refilled his glass. The wail of emergency sirens filled the night air. Rosemary Hawkins got up from behind him and went into her private bathroom. J.R. didn't even notice she was gone.

THE WHITE HOUSE
ROSEMARY HAWKINS'S OFFICE
MONDAY, 5:45 P.M.

Rosemary Hawkins emerged from her bathroom freshly scrubbed and with only a trace of lipstick to highlight her pale face. She wore a pair of tap pants, under a white terry-cloth robe, hanging her trademark black suit on the doorknob as she passed. She bent over behind her desk, and reached for a pair of black kidskin boots, calf high.

"Tell me, J.R., what do you wear to the end of the world?" It wasn't a question she wanted answered, but he felt relieved to hear it. She sounded in control, and caustic, as usual. At least she was trying to carry on. He'd not been very sure she would be able to deal with what might come next. Excrement. Lots of it, all about to hit the fan.

"The robe and boots would be nice. Hell, you're the next President of the United States. Wear what you want."

"Maybe I'm not, J.R. The next President, I mean. How do you know that?"

"Because I carried you out of the amphitheater. You're next in line. Believe it. I know."

"Okay. I believe it. Do you suppose your uh . . . friends could locate the Librarian of Congress, or a Supreme Court Judge, and get him or her over here?"

"I don't know about the Librarian of Congress. A Supreme Court Judge is out."

"Why?"

"Because they are all dead."

"Oh." Her voice was small, almost timid. "Are you going to tell me about it?"

"I told you about it before it happened." It was his morgue voice, the cold "there's the body" voice, the one he used to hide what he felt.

"It was the colonel, from Myrtle Beach, with his A-10, right?" She looked at him with wide eyes, her voice calm.

"It was him, all right, with bells on."

"I saw him, you know. After his first pass, he banked away, almost straight over the amphitheater and he just rolled over, and he was back, just like that. I saw the Ace-of-Spades very clearly under his cockpit, on the nose. He had on a black helmet. He couldn't have been more than fifty feet off the ground. There were missiles under his wing. Six, I think. And much higher, all these airplanes, like they were on parade, just flying along. They were very beautiful. I remember, just before he came back again, that they looked very beautiful.

"A man knocked me down, and tore my dress off. I remember wondering why he did that, and how in the world he could think of sex at a time like this, with the flashbulbs going off and all, and who the hell was he?" She gestured with her slim fingers, a child, explaining show-and-tell day.

"But it wasn't a man at all. Just a man's arm, with the shirt and suit sleeve still on. He had a class ring on his finger. Red, I think. I threw his arm away. I shouldn't have done that. I saw Emily, for a second. She looked right at me, and Lord, how she hated me. Then, she just sort of vanished. No, I mean, that whole half of the amphitheater just turned white and all those people, all of those people were gone. Where did they go, J.R.? I mean, they must be flying around somewhere . . ."

J.R. slapped Rosemary Hawkins's face, not very hard, but twice, and she fell into his arms, clutching him tightly, sobs shaking her sleek body like a dog with a rag doll, from end to end. He held her very tightly, and slowly, gradually, the sobs turned to tears, and the tears dried up. She would not cry again, for as long as he knew her.

"Why do you want to see the Librarian of Congress?"

"Because I'm not sure I'm the President. I've been *nominated* by the President. The Senate has to approve me as Secretary of State. I have to go before a formal congressional, senatorial panel."

"There are no senators. They were sitting right next to the President, opposite you. There are no congressmen.

There are no Supreme Court Justices. The will of the President was to see you confirmed as his Secretary of State. He said so, publicly, on every major network.''

"Still, I must see the Librarian of Congress. I must know if I am the constitutionally correct President of the United States.''

"No.''

"No?''

"First, you take the Oath of Office. Then you issue orders as the President of the United States. The United States could be run by a well-organized motorcycle gang by tomorrow night at this time. You will take the oath, and in taking the oath, you will *take the job of President.* Otherwise, the United States could very well cease to exist.''

"Why? How? J.R., what are you saying?''

J.R., grief-stricken over what he was sure was the loss of his younger brother, would stand for no more political niceties. He strode to where she sat, jerking her to her feet, her terry robe flashing open, her body smell assailing his senses even while he lost all sense of propriety and place.

"You listen, you just listen! Let me tell you what the Ace-of-Spades colonel did.'' The words drifting in now, loud and clear. "The Soviets. All of them, right next to Conrad Taylor's successor, behind all that wonderful safety glass. All dead, I'm sure. The British, the fucking French, the Sudanese, the Japanese, the Chinese. Dead. *All of them.* And if not, the survivors will scramble for power. All over the world, through the magic of satellite television, over one billion people watched that air strike. Russia. Think about the Russians. Scorpio. Remember him, Rosemary? He said we were going to kill the Soviet President by bombing the embassy. Well, he was a little off, but the President of the Soviet Union is almost certainly dead!

"In a couple of days, maybe a week, maybe even a couple of months, if we're lucky, all the little colonels are going to be generals, and some hard-line son-of-a-bitch in every country in the world is going to decide that now, right now, is the opportunity of a lifetime to kick the shit out of his neighbor. Or worse. It could get much worse. Holy War. Jihad in the Middle East. Look at the guest list! Look at it, and see who almost certainly was killed in that holocaust in the amphitheater. Then ask your National Security Advisors to get you a list of who *wasn't* in Washington. Who stayed home, while the bosses came to praise Caesar?'' He pulled her even closer to him, their faces only inches apart.

"Because when you read that list, you will also find a few names here, in the good ol' U. S. of A., that stayed home. But they will be here. Soon. And you'd better be ready to deal with them. By tomorrow morning, skirmishes between Israeli and Arab aircraft will begin. In a week, Syria will invade the Golan Heights. Iraq will assist. China will move into positions in Siberia within two months. And the young, newly appointed Commanding Officer and Chief of Staff of the Soviet Armed Forces will move his forces west, reluctantly, pushed by every hardliner left behind. You *are* the President. You *will* take the oath. You *will* give the orders. I believe if you don't begin, right now, on this bloody, terrible fucking night, that within a year's time, a nuclear world war is inevitable. Get a judge in here. Take the oath. Argue its constitutionality later. Really, Rosemary, what choice do you have?''

J.R. stepped away, releasing her abruptly. She toppled back down onto the couch, her robe open, naked except for champagne-colored tap pants. She looked at him in horror, not because she was sprawled like a hooker on a leather couch, but because she was sure everything he said was the absolute, terrifying truth.

THE WHITE HOUSE
ROSEMARY HAWKINS'S OFFICE
MONDAY, 6:00 P.M.

"I am not a constitutional specialist, Ms. Hawkins."

"I accept that you are not. But I want your educated guess."

"I'm sorry, Ms. Hawkins. I'm not a very adept guesser."

"Assuming all ahead of me, in line for the presidency, are dead. Assuming the majority of the American people know I was named, nominated, designated Secretary of State, to fill a position publicly resigned by my predecessor, the resignation accepted by the President, do you have an *opinion?*"

"I do."

"Well, in God's name, and for the sake of your country, would you please voice it?"

"It is my belief, Ms. Hawkins, that once sworn in, you are the rightful, constitutional President of the United States. If asked, I would say so, publicly, if that will help."

Rosemary Hawkins breathed a sigh of relief, and cast a sheepish glance at J.R. as he sat at her desk, drinking her booze, his face a hard gray mask. Outside the windows, the fires were reaching their peak. The White House looked like Tara in *Gone With the Wind,* surrounded by the dead and the about-to-die, but still standing.

"Thank you, sir. Will you please remain? A federal judge has been flown by helicopter to the White House lawn. From Virginia. Leila Hamilton. Do you know her?"

"Very well. A fine American from a fine American family. I am most pleased. You could not have selected a more suitable judge for this most auspicious, if regrettable, ceremony. No offense, Ms. Hawkins."

"None taken, sir. I didn't select her. She just happened to be the only federal judge we could locate. I will expect you to assure her on the constitutional matters, as you've stated.''

"Ms. Hawkins, I can hardly assure her of anything. She is an acknowledged expert on constitutional law. The next Supreme Court vacancy would have been hers.''

"No problem, pal," chirped J.R., drunk, but still in control. "All of the Supreme Court is vacant. Rosemary in the terry robe will, someday, appoint a new one. A completely new one. Boggles the mind. Boggles it.''

J.R. went back to his drink, and a small, fiery-eyed white-haired woman was ushered into the inner office by a fierce-looking Marine, carrying an M16, with four grenades strapped to his flak jacket. J.R.'s original order to the Secret Service agents had been carried out, protocol and chain of command notwithstanding.

"My name is Hamilton, Ms. Hawkins. I am here, at the request of two disreputable-looking characters that set a damn helicopter smack into my garden, to issue to you the Presidential Oath of Office. I don't like you much, Ms. Hawkins. You're too pretty, and you don't have enough material in your skirts. But I do know one thing. I am told you are the last surviving senior member of the United States Government. I understand what that means today. And what it could mean tomorrow. I am prepared to swear you in as President of the United States. Madam President, I suppose, although two centuries of Hamiltons must be turning over in their graves. Are you prepared to take on this job, Rosemary Hawkins?''

"I hope so, Judge. It is my duty, nevertheless. I accept the responsibility, if that's what you mean.''

"Precisely. Young man?" She turned to the Marine, who, in spite of his size and ferocious military bearing, looked all of his eighteen years at the moment.

"Yes, ma'am. Your honor, I mean . . . ah, judge.''

"Are there members of the press available? Here at the White House?''

"Yes, ma'am. Not many, but some. A lot were uh . . .''

"Killed?''

"Yes, ma'am."

"Well, get what you can rounded up. I saw a CNN crew at the front entrance. Get them in here."

"Yes, ma'am!" The Marine sprinted from the room, equipment laden, a military tin man from the Land of Oz, U.S.A.

The room, spacious as it was, seemed crowded with servants, butlers, four newspapermen, four Marines, and eight Secret Service agents. In the center of all this, in a small circle, stood U.S. Federal Judge Hamilton, of the State of Virginia, and Rosemary Hawkins, dressed now in a short black suit, black boots, and no stockings. J.R. still sat at Rosemary's desk, ignored and unnoticed, the executive chair tipped so far back it looked like it would fall over at any moment. He was outside the circle, and could not see Rosemary or the judge. A sound man clambered up on the desk, holding a boom mike over the crowd, joined at once by a young woman in a skirt so short that J.R. could clearly see she shaved her pubic area. The young woman held a long bank of lights, and flicked them on, a cable wrapped around her waist and disappearing, snakelike, into the crowd.

"Hi, she said, looking down at J.R. "Pretty exciting shit, ain't it!"

J.R. looked up her skirt, and tipped his drink toward her blond airhead. "Exciting doesn't cover it, kiddo."

"Yeah! Right!" She turned back to the ceremony, spreading her legs to keep her balance. J.R. paid absolutely no attention to what normally would have sent him into a mouth-slobbering state of sexual jerkdom.

The room grew quiet and, in spite of the continued wailing of sirens, an occasional explosion and the audible sounds of a capital city under the worst conditions imaginable, J.R. heard Rosemary Hawkins, slender hand placed on a two-hundred-year-old Hamilton family Bible, recite the Oath of Office, and, in so doing, become the first female President of the United States of America. When the applause, the incongruous applause in this quiet island amid the dead and the dying, slowed and stopped, Judge Hamilton said, and everyone heard her say, "God bless you, child, and may your presidency save us all from ourselves."

Rosemary Hawkins became President of the United States at precisely 7:01 P.M. She would fight the presidential challenges later. And there would be plenty to fight.

THE WHITE HOUSE
MONDAY, 7:02 P.M.

"What do I do now, J.R.?"

"Act presidential. Issue orders. Stop the chaos. Make the coffee. Take off your clothes. How the hell do I know. You're the fuckin' President."

"Are you drunk, J.R.?"

"Possibly. No. Probably. Yes. I'm drunk. It seems like a terrific day to get drunk."

The phone rang, and since he was sitting nearly on top of it, J.R. picked it up. "Hello. This is the White House. How may we be of service?"

"Who is this?" Brian Howell was not accustomed to cavalier answers or attitudes when he called Rosemary Hawkins's office.

"This is J.R. Kelly, late of this country's supersecret, crack intelligence agency. Who the fuck is this?"

There was a short silence, punctuated by a cough. "This is General Howell. May I speak to Ms. Hawkins."

"No. But you may speak to President Hawkins."

"Kelly?"

"Yeah?"

"I was wrong."

"No you weren't. You were involved. You're a dead man, General." Before the general could respond, J.R. hung up.

"Who was that, J.R.?" Rosemary was chewing at a fingernail, something she'd never done in her life.

"Your faithful servant."

"I beg your pardon?"

"Brian Howell. I seem to have hung up on him. Call him back. He will tell you that I threatened to kill him. He will also tell you that he has called in the Maryland National Guard, under the command of Major General at large Paul Wolfe. They will see to it that order is kept, here in the capital. He will have a number of suggestions to make. Nadine . . . oh, you don't know Nadine, but she has been trying to reach Adrian Bennett at his ranch. The phone seems to be out of order. Pretty fucking convenient, don't you think?"

"J.R., what are you talking about? Brian Howell is my most trusted subordinate."

"No, he's not. I am. I'm going to kill him for you. Not yet. But someday."

"You're drunk, J.R."

"Yes, I suppose I am. The capital is on fire, the world's leaders are dead, and my little brother is dead. So you are right. I'm drunk. But I'm still the only son-of-a-bitch in this town you can trust. You shoulda listened, lady. You really shoulda listened."

Rosemary walked to the desk, gently extracting the full glass of tequila from J.R.'s hand. She sat on the edge of her desk, holding the glass, the black skirt of her suit riding up to her slim thighs. Even as President, you would always get a lot of leg with Rosemary Hawkins. "J.R., what do you mean, your little brother is dead?"

"Simple. Conspiracy. I conspired to get my little brother, and his Harrier jet, in place, near Washington, early this morning. I told him what to do. I also told him it was probably treason. But he loves me. Oh, yeah, he loves his big brother. Loves his country too. So, when Ol' Colonel Bennett shows up with superplane, my kid brother tries to shoot him down. Shot the motherfucker to pieces, too. I watched. Oh, yeah, down here on the ground, discredited and dishonest. I watched him chew that A-10 to little burning pieces. And it was still coming, like it would live forever, burning from wingtip to wingtip. Old Taco was up there, trying to help, but he couldn't get in there, what with Taylor's fucking ceremonial parade all over the sky. So, my little brother, Jason Porter Kelly, U.S.M.C., the best flyer ever produced by Marine aviation, he just sort of rammed into that A-10. Blew them both to shit. If we ever get a Congress, or anything else, he deserves a medal. A very big medal.''

Rosemary Hawkins looked at J.R. with a woman's eyes, and a woman's heart. Terrible forces were gathering around the world, and she was the only, if not precisely constitutionally, sworn President of the United States. But it was the woman that stepped forward, closing in her embrace the grief-stricken hulk of a man bigger and better in all ways than any man in her long experience.

THE LINCOLN MEMORIAL
MONDAY, 7:15 P.M.

Jason Kelly opened his eyes, trying to focus on what seemed to be a scene from Dante's *Inferno*. A pain rocketed through and down his arm as he tried to move. And trying to move had made him drop a full eighteen inches from where he hung in his parachute harness, fifty feet off the ground, his chute caught on the corner of the Lincoln Memorial facing directly across the burning arrow of the Arlington Memorial Bridge. Directly opposite him, less than fifty feet away, an unmarked helicopter hovered, occasionally darting away when its prop wash caused the seriously injured pilot to sway precariously in his harness. He'd seen that chopper before, just below him when he'd made his last, desperate move against the Ace-of-Spades. J.R. J.R. would know. J.R. would be here soon. Jason Kelly, hanging by one burned chute strap and less than ten yards of parachute silk from a twelve-nch cornice of the Lincoln Memorial smiled, screamed in pain, and passed out cold.

J.R. sat in Rosemary Hawkins's chair, watching the capital burn, unconcerned and defeated. Whatever happened now, it meant damn little. He was out of gas. He'd shot his bolt, and missed. Only his little blond was safe, driving back to D.C., out of all this. One good thing. But only one, and not much.

"J.R.? J.R.?"

"Yes, Madam President?"

She chose not to respond to his sarcasm.

"A man named 'Taco Two' is on the radio. Your radio, over by the couch. I don't know how to make it work. And whatever you might think, I'm busy as hell right now. Will you please handle it?"

Taco Two. Taco. Taco Two. J.R. leaped from the chair, banging his hip on the corner of Rosemary Hawkins's desk as he snatched up the radio. "Taco Two. This is Taco! What have you got?"

"I got your little brother, J.R. He's hanging from the Lincoln Memorial, by the skin of his chutey, chute, chute. There's no help available. J.R., I'm going to come get you, and we'll think of something on the way. Get outside, and bring whatever muscle you can find. E.T.A. two minutes. Do you read?"

"Loud and clear. Two minutes."

Rosemary Hawkins looked up from a stack of reports she was reading, a phone tucked into the crook of her neck. Her brow shot up in a silent question.

"Jason's alive. Hanging by his nuts from the Lincoln Memorial. I'm gonna go fetch him. Get me a surgeon. Here, in the White House. I'll put him upstairs in Conrad Taylor's bed."

"But—"

"You're the President of the United States, Rosemary. Call a doctor for my brother, who just happened to save your shapely ass!'' And then J.R. Kelly was off to the south lawn, dragging four husky Marines with him.

THE LINCOLN MEMORIAL
MONDAY, 7:30 P.M.

"Jesus. How are we going to get him down from there?'' The C.I.A. helicopter was flying a slow circle around the monument, staying far enough away to keep the prop wash from blowing Jason Kelly from his precarious perch. He seemed to be unconscious. On the ground below him, thousands of people still lay where they had fallen on the bridge. The city's fire and police units, and all those from surrounding Maryland and Virginia, were overwhelmed. Fires burned unchecked, while heroic men and women, using individual initiative, did their best wherever possible.

J.R. didn't answer Taco Two's question. He gestured toward the Memorial roof, indicating that the chopper should land there. The helicopter swung around to the opposite side, and settled onto the roof, its rotors still turning.

"What's on this thing, Taco?''

"Plenty of ropes, J.R., in the back. But if we touch that kid before we're ready, he's going down. He's hanging there by one strand of his chute. That's it.''

"Okay. Gotcha.'' J.R. had to scream to overcome the chopper's engine noise, coupled with the cacophony of sound from all over the capital. He glanced around at the four young Marines gathered near the doorway, looking apprehensively at J.R.

"Listen to me. That guy on the end of the chute is a Marine pilot from Cherry Point. He's also my brother. The kid shot down the nut in the A-10, by ramming him on his final pass. Like I said, he's a Marine, just like you. We have to go over the side, and take him down.

And we have to go together. I can't think of any other way. We'll tie two ropes to the chopper skids. Real tight. Then, I'll go over, tie them to my brother, and the chopper can lift off and carry us to the White House lawn. I'll need two of you on top of the wall, to secure what's left of the chute, and two of you to ride down the rope, and back to the White House. It will mean swinging in midair for about five minutes. You could get killed. We could all get killed. But I'm going over the side. Who's with me?"

J.R. jumped from the helicopter's open side door, and stared into the group of Marines, their faces framed in black and bathed in the orange glow of the still-burning fires from the amphitheater. They hesitated, and then they exited the chopper, dragging one-inch-thick rope with them.

"Leave your weapons in the chopper. Take off everything that will hinder your movement. Coats, everything. Just dump them into the chopper."

Wordlessly, the four Marines followed J.R.'s instructions, stripping down to fatigue pants and T-shirts. The chopper rose slightly, and moved closer to where Jason Kelly's parachute was hooked on the corner of the memorial roof. Nobody talked. Blessedly for Washington, D.C., it began to rain, a downpour that would go on throughout the night, extinguishing fires that no fireman could possibly have gotten to. But it made the rescue of Jason Kelly a very difficult, dangerous proposition. J.R. Kelly and his Marines secured two ropes to the chopper skids, and began to go over the monument's steep wall, J.R. leading two Marines, while two remained on the roof, watching the chute strap, frayed beyond belief, but afraid to touch it.

THE WHITE HOUSE
THE OVAL OFFICE
MONDAY, 7:40 P.M.

The press officer said to the small group of print reporters, and the ever-present camera crew from CNN, "Ladies and gentlemen, the President of the United States." From a side door, from her old National Security Office, Rosemary Hawkins entered the Oval Office. She knew how important what she said would be. How she handled this first encounter with the press, less than three hours after the Ace-of-Spades exploded in the sky over the mall, might very well set the stage for further catastrophe. She carried a small clipboard, with a narrow sheaf of papers on it. She sat behind her . . . yes, her desk, crossed her famous legs, and brushed a stray hair from across her forehead. To her startled surprise, the crowded room erupted in warm applause, a tattered-looking group of American public-opinion makers who either loved her or, more likely, hated her at 4:29 today. But that was then, and this was now. The world had watched or heard her take the Oath of Office. And the world was frightened of tomorrow. Of all the coming tomorrows. They hoped, the men and women around her desk, that she would somehow have some mystical way to sort all their fears out, to brush them aside, to stop the terror they had all witnessed, and breathlessly reported, for three hours. For these reasons, their applause was hopeful, fearful, and sincere.

"Thank you all, very much. I have no statement to make, but I will answer whatever questions you may have. As you know, I myself was at the amphitheater only three hours ago. I was advised to wait to speak to you. But I'm new at this job, and I don't take advice very well anyway. I'm afraid I don't recognize any of you, and I fear I know why. So please, just introduce yourselves. We'll just have to make do. Although I will say that I intend to make a speech to the nation as soon as possible, probably in the morning. So, for tonight, you are my best conduit to the American people. So please, fire away. Oh. Bad choice of words." She gave them a perfectly charming smile. The CNN camera crew set the lens on her face, and left it there.

"Mr. Presi—I mean . . ." The questioner, a young blond woman, looked flustered.

"Madam President. Or President Hawkins. That sounds best. Let's go with that."

"My name is Sarah Compton. I'm with AP. I was the only one available to send when you asked for this press conference. A lot of our people are . . ."

"I know, Sarah. Please, go on."

"Who did this?"

"Colonel Jonathan Bennett, U.S.A.F., flying a fully loaded A-10 directly from Myrtle Beach, South Carolina. He is a famous war hero, Medal of Honor winner. He was held captive during the Vietnam War, in a small room, for 845 days. His father is Governor Adrian Bennett."

An audible gasp swept the room, a gasp of disbelief.

"You mean it was an *American?*"

"Yes. Colonel Jonathan Bennett."

"Why?"

"We don't yet know why. We are doing our best to find out. General Howell has ordered a military intelligence team to go to the elder Bennett's ranch. Our initial belief is that Colonel Bennett was deranged, possibly from his Vietnam experiences."

"You're saying he was crazy?"

"I'm saying that is our initial belief. Of course, in the interests of national security, no possibilities will be overlooked."

"Foreign involvement?"

"Who are you, sir?"

"Bob Klepner, ma'am. The *London Times.*"

"I'm saying that at this time, no possibilities will be overlooked." There was a very hard, presidential edge to her voice.

"Can you tell us about casualties, Ms. Hawkins?"

"You've all been outside. In fact, you look much like casualties yourselves." A murmur of laughter, as the assembled reporters glanced at one another's smokey faces and filthy clothes. They *did* look like casualties.

"I can tell you, they are very, very heavy. They change, upward, almost minute to minute. I have ordered the Pentagon to dig up every available doctor and nurse in the Armed Forces outside the District of Columbia, and fly them here as soon as possible. The Maryland National Guard will arrive within hours. I have declared the District, Maryland, and Virginia, disaster areas. I have also declared martial law, which the Guard will enforce. I have issued 'shoot to kill' orders for looting and other serious crimes.

"Anarchy is possible, but I will not allow it. I ask the people of this nation to remain calm, and assist the thousands of injured that still lie untended on the streets of the capital. Civilian doctors and nurses, I ask, right now, to come to Washington and offer your services. The National Guard will construct canvas medical facilities, right here in the capital. Flights from all over the United States will begin tomorrow morning. I hope to have thousands of doctors and nurses here and working by tomorrow night. Andrews Air Force Base has been cleared to handle only incoming and outgoing medical flights, to handle the emergency. And, as you can see, God has taken a hand in this too." Outside, the heavens had opened up, and sheets of heavy, cold rain rushed earthward, in desperate combat with fires that threatened to level the entire city.

"Can you tell us who you know survived?"

"I don't understand the question, Sarah."

"Government officials, for instance."

"Not very accurately, Sarah. Not yet. You have undoubtedly seen the list of dignitaries present in the amphitheater during the attack. So far we have less than fifty emergency people working at the amphitheater itself. Arlington Memorial Bridge is completely blocked. As I said, you have the list. I can only say that I was there. It was very bad."

"Can you tell us how you got out, President Hawkins?"

"I was rescued by a C.I.A. agent assigned to me during the past four days."

"We have some film of you, Ms. Hawkins. We will make it available, if you wish."

"It's a free country, Mr. . . . ?"

"Baker, Charles Baker, CNN."

"I suppose it shows me with my dress blown off."

"It does, ma'am. But it also shows you trying to pull people from the fires. You had an arm on you, ma'am."

"Yes. The arm. I remember that. Well, there will be horror stories enough for all, I'm afraid."

"Yes, ma'am. But could we get back to who we *know* are dead?"

"I can only say this. There were nearly 6,000 people in the amphitheater. There were over 50,000 people on Memorial Bridge, which suffered a brutal cannon attack on the Virginia side. Northeastern Washington, D.C., is in flames over a twelve-square-block area. The Library of Congress was struck, as was the Supreme Court Building, and the Folger Shakespeare Library. We believe these hits were not intended, but random unaimed missile strikes from the A-10 after it was attacked."

"Attacked! The A-10 was attacked?"

"It was. Attacked and rammed by a Harrier AV-8B from Cherry Point, here to take part in the overfly during the funeral. It was armed, I believe, because it was scheduled for a long test flight to the Yuma Marine Corps Air Station for additional combat training. The pilot's name is Kelly. A Marine. And a very brave one."

"Is he alive?"

"We don't know yet. A rescue attempt is being made as we speak. We do know he was badly injured when he rammed the A-10."

"Where is the rescue attempt? Where is he?"

"Near the Lincoln Memorial. That's all I can say. The roads are impassable. I have ordered that if the rescue is successful, he's to be brought here, to the White House. A top Naval surgeon is waiting to tend him. This pilot is a national hero, who undoubtedly saved hundreds, perhaps thousands of lives.''

''Preferential treatment, President Hawkins?'' It was the man from the *London Times*.

''Yes, if you wish to call it that. He's shot to pieces, hanging from the Lincoln Memorial by a shred of parachute harness. You may call it preferential treatment. But I would like to say this. If Prince Charles were hanging from the goddamn monument by a piece of string, and he had just saved thousands of his fellow human beings' lives, we'd go give *him* 'preferential treatment' as well.''

''But madam, Prince Charles was in the amphitheater.''

''Yes. So he was. And Diana. And the Senate. The House of Representatives. The President of the United States. The Soviet President and a seventeen-man delegation. Yes, dammit, I know who was in the amphitheater! You want casualties? Read the guest list! Very few will get out of that charnel house alive. And fewer yet, if alive, will be uninjured. It's a catastrophe, ladies and gentlemen, and we are doing all we can to end it. If that is the word.'' Rosemary Hawkins looked away.

''Thank you, Mr. . . . Madam President,'' said Sarah, of the Associated Press, in the time-honored way of ending press conferences. As they filed out of the Oval Office, Rosemary Hawkins walked back into her old National Security Office, poured herself a drink and sat down, certain she had done more harm than good. In fact, her straightforward, heartfelt answers, even her anger and defiance, would lift American spirits during the darkest hours the world had faced in fifty years. Outside, the rain, the blessed rain, lashed at Washington, D.C.

THE LINCOLN MEMORIAL
7:55 P.M.

J.R. hung from the rope, rappeling down the sheer side of the memorial, swinging out and down, like an experienced rock climber, which, in fact, he was. In his college days, it had been one of his passions. Dropping down above him, on each side, were two very young but very brave Marines, trying to save one of their own. It seemed to take an eternity, but, rain lashing at him, the wind rocking Jason in his harness straps, J.R. finally reached his brother's side.

"Jason! Hey, kid, can you hear me?"

Jason Kelly, head slumped to his chest, did not respond. J.R. noticed that the entire left side of his brother's flight suit was gone, burned off somehow, his skin blistered and charred. Fighting back tears of gratitude and rage at what he saw, he motioned the two Marines to drop below and to both sides of his brother. It was a slow, dangerous trip for both men, but they made it, the rain lashing at them, Jason's white helmet glistening in the flickering light from the fires, and slick from the water, the painted green shamrock blistered, with one petal scorched off.

"I brought my med kit, sir." The Marine to Jason's left pointed at his belt, at the Marine green packet with the red cross on it.

"Yeah, what's in it?" J.R. was shouting to be heard. The rain whipping the walls of the memorial sounded like a rushing river as it battered the rescuers as well as the injured pilot.

"Morphine."

"Good. Let's wrap him up now, and be careful! I'm gonna cut that last harness when we got him. Then the four of us are going to fly away. Make sure the ropes are crossed under your shoulders. Then, lash me to him, under our armpits. I'll carry him all the way."

"You can't, sir. That's too far! What if you drop him?"

"I won't drop him. Like the song says, 'He ain't heavy, he's my brother.' Now, do it!"

The two Marines secured themselves first, as J.R. had ordered, then moved to Jason, one crawling over J.R. to get there. J.R. swung the knife out of his belt sheath, the little sticker he always carried. As the two Marines touched Jason, his head snapped up, and he screamed in pain, his eyes bulging.

"It's his arm, sir. It's all busted up!"

"Give him the morphine. Put it in there." Swinging from the rope around his chest, the Marine stiffened his legs against the wall, "walking" toward Jason Kelly. As gently as possible, he tore the wrapper from the ready-made syringe, popped it expertly into Jason's arm, reached for another, and repeated the process.

"That's too much!" shouted J.R.

"No, sir. I did more in Beirut. Two's what he needs. Now, if you're ready, I've had all the history of Lincoln I need tonight."

The two Marines moved to Jason Kelly again, pulling him gently along the wall, the muscles on their arms bulging, straining with his deadweight 220 pounds, which seemed like 400 pounds. This time, with the morphine taking effect, he did not protest. They pulled him to J.R., locking a rope around J.R.'s chest, under his arms, placing Jason Kelly against J.R.'s chest.

J.R. handed his knife to the Marine who had injected Jason with morphine. "Now, when I say I got him, you cut that strap, and that last chute wire."

"Are you sure, sir?"

"Yes, goddammit! Give Taco the signal. Get him airborne first. And when I say cut, cut it!"

The two Marines waved their arms, swinging free on their ropes, and the two anxious-faced Marines above disappeared from view. The drooping rope excess grew painfully taut as the belaying clips were cut loose. J.R., peeping upward until he could see the chopper's lights approaching the roof's edge, the two Marines above letting go of the ropes tied to the roof, the tension caught again by the rising helicopter, but not before dropping the four figures below a full six feet. The tension resumed, and J.R. screamed into the wind.

"Now! Cut it now!"

The Marine's arm swung in a short, vicious swipe, and the last thread of material holding Jason Kelly from a sheer drop of sixty feet to his death was cut away. Now, only his brother's love and brute strength would provide the measure of survival for the flight to the White House. The chopper moved ponderously across the mall, bending left, staying at altitude, trying to minimize the swaying ropes with their precious cargo.

The Marines watched anxiously as they flew forty feet above the ground, knowing they were safe, wondering how the C.I.A. agent could hold a man as big as the Marine pilot, without dropping him. The face of J.R. Kelly, set and determined, would remain with them both for the rest of their lives. It was very clear that J.R. Kelly was right. Jason was his brother, and he wasn't heavy.

In two minutes, the chopper settled low enough over the White House lawn to allow the two Marines to drop to the ground, where they relieved J.R. Kelly of his burden. Jason was placed on a stretcher and two doctors and a nurse rushed him into the White House, while J.R. sat on the rain-soaked grass, for the first time feeling the muscle pains sweeping across his back and shoulders. The chopper immediately swung up and away, to retrieve the two men left on the Lincoln Memorial roof. It was three hours and forty minutes since the Ace-of-Spades began its attack. It was 8:10 P.M., Monday, stormy Monday . . .

THE WHITE HOUSE
PRIVATE QUARTERS
MONDAY, 9:00 P.M.

J.R. watched as the two doctors bent over his younger
brother. The nurse flitted around the bed, delivering com-
presses, checking the myriad intravenous tubes dangling
from both sides of the bed, suspended from gangly, metal
stands that looked as if they might, given the chance, walk
away, science fiction-like. A sophisticated monitor sat on
a rolling stand. Its green pulse line indicated heart rate,
blood pressure, every vital sign monitored by one, expensive, invaluable machine. None of this equipment had to
be brought in. The White House had housed its share of
sick or potentially sick presidents. Thus, every possible
piece of medical equipment needed was here, at all times.

Jason Kelly was lying on Emily Taylor's bed, the scene
of so much of her personal despair. It still smelled of her,
in spite of the abundant medical potions opened to the air,
including the smell of burnt flesh and powerful ointments.
Thankfully, Jason Kelly was unconscious, breathing under
a rubber mask, the anesthesiologist carefully monitoring
his vital signs while the orthopedic surgeon tried to repair
his broken arm, and the burn specialist stripped away lay-
ers of destroyed, blistered flesh.

J.R. turned away, and headed downstairs, to Rosemary
Hawkins, and her liquor cabinet.

"Thank God for the rain," Rosemary said, holding her
scotch over ice against her cheek, looking out the three-
sided window of her office.

"It's still burning, Rosemary."

"Yes, I know it is. But the weather people tell me it
will continue to rain this hard for the next twenty-four
hours. The ever-lasting sprinkler system, from God and
Company."

"I've heard you don't believe in God."

"I don't. It's a convenient figure of speech, when I can't explain anything in a rational way."

"Well, this is not a rational day, is it?"

"No. It certainly is not. Brian says the troops from the Maryland National Guard are deployed in regiment strength. He says two more regiments will be in place by Wednesday."

"What do you intend to do with them, Rosemary?"

"I've declared martial law. They will maintain order. Shocking as it may seem, Northeast Washington, burning to the ground, apparently is the scene of looting, rape, and murder. There is a wide-open firefight going on between drug dealers for turf control. Think of it, J.R. People shooting it out in the streets of Washington, D.C., while we try to untangle the dead, so we can count them. It all makes me sick." She swept her fingers through her lush red hair, a sign he had learned meant exasperation, or worse.

"It offends your patrician upbringing, I suppose."

"Oh, J.R. Stop it, for Christ sake."

"Sorry. I'm an old cop, that's all. Drug battles are old shit to an old cop. Got any more tequila, Madam President?"

"You should know, you're drinking it all."

"Correct. I am. Regrettably, it appears to have little or no effect on me." J.R. walked to the bar for the latest of uncountable trips, filled his tumbler, and dropped four ice cubes into the glass, causing the tequila to slop over the sides. He held it up, licking around the bottom. Cuervo Gold. Not to be wasted.

"That's glacier ice, did you know that? Conrad thought it was the height of sophistication. Blue ice. Very blue. No taste. Only twenty restaurants in the United States serve it. Very expensive stuff, considering some greaseball in Alaska chain-saws it into shippable pieces at $60-a-pound shipping cost. It takes longer to melt. Some virtue."

"Rosemary, what the fuck are you talking about?"

"I'm the President, J.R., and I can talk about whatever I want."

"Okay. Agreed. But what are you going to do, President Hawkins? The world awaits. It watches. It is, most probably, plotting plots, hatching hatches, supplying supplies, marching marchers. I was just curious to know if you'd bothered to think about that."

"What would you like to know, J.R., who died?"

"I know who died."

"Do you?"

"Yes. The President. The Soviet President, and all but one of his delegation. The entire U.S. Senate. All but twelve of the House. The Supreme Court, total. The British Prime Minister, and her cabinet. The French President. The Italian President. The entire West German Government. The entire U.S. Cabinet, with you being the one exception. Princess Diana. Her husband. China's four top leaders. The Joint Chiefs of Staff, and their aides. Thirty-eight state governors. Thirty-one members of the White House staff. The top eight members of the C.I.A. The Director, and his six-highest ranking staff members, of the F.B.I. Fifty-two nations lost at least some of their governments. Israel lost its coalition government. The Saudis lost fifteen princes. Egypt is without a president, Jordan without a king, and his American wife. Emily Taylor, and her entire family. And many, many more."

"Where do you get this information, J.R.?"

"I'm a spy. I'm supposed to know this stuff. But, truthfully, I get it from Nadine, my section chief, and the best C.I.A. employee ever to pick up a paycheck."

"Good. I'll name her your deputy. I want you to head the C.I.A. What do you think of that, J.R. Kelly?"

"I don't want the job."

"Why not?"

"Give it to Nadine. She's been there thirty years. She's smart. She's honest. She's a patriot."

"And what are you, J.R.?"

"I don't know. But I don't want to run anything. I think I'll just retire, with this little blond I've known for all of four days. She loves me. Wants to make babies, if you can imagine that.''

''Oh, I can imagine that, very well. I would like your babies too, J.R., in a psycho-sexual-intellectual sort of way.'' She gave him a sexy wink, and turned back to the window, resting the cool, glacier-iced scotch once more against her cheek.

The phone rang. Rosemary Hawkins picked it up, and listened, glancing at J.R., her face darkening, turning soft, and womanly, and worried.

''Yes, thank you, Nadine. I wonder if you would mind coming by later, say, in an hour or so? Could you manage that? Yes, I know. I'll try. Yes, I think he's special too. I'm indebted to you. Please come by. Drive the Director's car. There are Marines at the gate. Tell them you are the new Director of the C.I.A. What? Yes, I'm serious. In an hour, then? Fine. Thank you.'' Rosemary put the phone down, very gently, and punched the intercom.

''Yes, President Hawkins?'' A male secretary. She didn't even know his name. The President's and Vice President's longtime secretaries had both been at the amphitheater.

''No calls, please. No interruptions.''

''Yes, ma'am. I'll see to it.'' She didn't know it, but her ''secretary'' was a longtime White House Secret Service agent. He was now the senior agent of the Service still alive.

Rosemary walked from behind her desk, and crossed the lush carpet to where J.R. sat, still sipping Cuervo Gold, still hollow-eyed from lack of sleep, still filthy dirty, still sober and indomitable. He was the sexiest man she'd ever encountered. He was the only man she was afraid of. Afraid of falling in love with him. Real, stupid love, the kind that took away all your sensibilities and knocked you up and knocked you down and submerged what you were. She didn't want to tell him this. Not now. Not tonight. It had been such a terrible, long night, and it wasn't remotely over. She had things for him to do. Things he must do. Yet, she had to tell him.

"Hey, sailor, mind if I join you?"

J.R. looked up and smiled the silly, crooked smile that gave his gruff countenance its abundant amount of charm. "I don't know, miss. My ship leaves real soon, and I may not come back."

"The danger. Is it dangerous?"

"Of course it's dangerous. In fact, this may be my last sight of land for many, many months. All around me, trouble and turmoil, bubbling along, chewing up my only oar, leaving me drifting on the open sea."

"Can I help, sailor?"

"Well, miss, you could stand at the dock, and wave good-bye."

"But that seems like so little to give."

"Well, ma'am, a sailor, off to the sea in the leaky vessel, would, of course, hope to have something to remember, as he goes under for that last, third time."

"A scarf, perhaps."

"A nice thought, ma'am. But I had in mind a gentle touch of a woman, ma'am, if you know what I mean."

"But, sir?"

"Yes, ma'am?"

"Surely, you don't mean . . ."

"Yes, ma'am, that's exactly what I mean."

She drew him into her arms, and lay back, raising her hips, slipping her panties off, while he tried to get his belt unbuckled, and somehow, they were joined, and he filled her in a way she'd never, ever known, and she gave him thunder and lightning and a major portion of her mind, as the horror went away, and the new President of the United States tried to ease the pain she herself would be required to inflict. She locked her legs around him, her slim body dancing under his, feeling the salty tears roll down his cheeks, mingling with hers, even as whatever it was, and it was not exactly sex, bore them away for the briefest of moments. Memorable moments.

They had, finally, removed their clothes, and she had sent him to the shower, to wash away the soot and the fire and the blood of the day. He'd brought an extra set of clothes when he'd been assigned to her on Thursday, and he stepped free of the bathroom, transformed, his face a ruddy glow.

"I never made love to a president before."

"How was it?" She was still nude, sitting cross-legged on the couch, her lush red hair over one side of her shoulder, covering one breast, accenting the other.

"It was. It was special, in a way I haven't experienced before. You did it because Nadine told you something, and, President or not, you wanted to soften the blow."

"You're never wrong, are you, J.R."

"Sure I am. But I figure I'm not exactly presidential lover material, you know? So, in my usual, suspicious way, I figure there's an angle."

"I see. Well, you didn't resist much." There was a hint of anger. And worse, a hint of hurt feelings.

"Rosemary, you are the most beautiful woman I've ever seen. It's not very likely I could resist all that beauty, and all those brains, and all that power. It's all very seductive."

"Well, sailor, can you sail free now?"

"Yes'm. You can keep the scarf."

"J.R., Willy Corchran is dead. Jonathan Bennett shot him, and left him on a taxiway at Myrtle Beach. Nadine just told me."

"God damn!"

"J.R." Her voice lowered, and she came to him, and took his hand.

"God damn! I really liked that guy, with his nerdy clothes and his nerdy glasses and his fucking models and his incongruous, deep-seated courage and patriotism."

"J.R., oh, J.R., I'm so sorry."

"Yeah. I know you are."

"There's more, J.R."

"What? What more?"

"Bonnie, J.R." J.R.'s face registered hurt, and Rosemary steeled herself to go on, hating it, but doing it, because she had to do it.

"Bonnie? Bonnie wasn't even here. I sent her away, with a package of sausage! She's safe. I made sure!"

"Bonnie was killed in a car accident on the way back. Some drunken teenage hayseed in a pickup truck, with his girlfriend. They identified Bonnie by fingerprints, and a note she wrote to you, but you never saw."

"A note! To me?"

"Yes. Nadine found it. She says it said, 'To wherever it ends. Love. Bonnie.' "

She moved to him then, her slim, nude body small in his embrace. Small, but strong. It had been a cheap woman's trick, and she was the first President of the United States who could have used it. It was a hard blow, one of many J.R. had taken this day, but not as hard as it might have been.

Twenty minutes later, when Nadine drove through the White House gates, she found J.R. Kelly and the new President waiting for her. By 10:15 that Monday night, Nadine was announced as the new Director of the Central Intelligence Agency.

The world, at that moment, was growing more and more unstable. In Washington, D.C. the fires burned on, but were beginning to go out. In the Soviet embassy, the senior surviving member of the staff, Joseph, had finally, after a nightmarish five-hour walk, found safe haven. Now, he must find Scorpio.

THE RUSSIAN EMBASSY
WASHINGTON, D.C.
MONDAY, 9:00 P.M.

"Mr. Secretary, are you all right?"

Joseph stared at the receptionist, a look the frightened woman would never forget. "I am alive, Nadia. I feel, under the circumstances, that I am the beneficiary of a major stroke of luck. The embassy staff will not return, because they are dead. Is the code section operable?"

"Of course, Mr. Secretary. Joseph, you . . . you are bleeding." She was looking at his shoulder, the sleeve of his coat torn, the blooded stain on his white-shirted arm very visible.

"It is nothing, Nadia. A small piece of western architecture, embedded, I'm afraid, in my arm. But no matter. I must have the complete text of the Scorpio message. And more important, I must know who Scorpio is."

"Sir?" Her eyes widened, perplexed. Receptionists did not have access to coded messages, under any circumstances. She had never heard of Scorpio.

"Listen to me, Nadia. Yesterday, this embassy received a message. A warning. It stated that the embassy would be attacked, from the air, by a United States helicopter gunship. As it turned out, the President was not attacked by a helicopter gunship. He was killed, with many others, while attending Conrad Taylor's funeral. But he is dead, nevertheless. I must find out who Scorpio is. Do you understand, Nadia?"

"No, sir. I don't."

"Then you are a stupid cow, Nadia. I want the code section to meet with me in the ambassador's office in two minutes. Please notify them."

"But, sir . . . Joseph, you cannot summon the code people to a meeting in the ambassador's office. He will be . . . he will be very angry."

Joseph leaned over Nadia's desk, his handsome, hard face inches from hers. "Listen to me, you stupid peasant! The ambassador is dead. The entire delegation is dead. The President of the U.S.S.R. is dead! Do you understand? I don't care if you understand! Get the code people to me, now, right now! Serve your country, bitch, in its darkest hour!" Joseph stumbled away from the desk, headed for the ambassador's office. The dead ambassador's office. He, Joseph Medvedev, was the highest ranking Soviet official left in the United States. And he must, he absolutely must, talk to Scorpio, or, if the scenario grew even uglier, he must talk to the young marshall in the Fulda Gap. Somehow, he must make sense out of chaos.

K.G.B. HEADQUARTERS
MOSCOW
TUESDAY, 5:00 A.M.

"So, Grenady. What do you think now?" Yuri Popov, "Scorpio" to the intelligence agencies of the West, sender of messages that were half true, and therefore useless, smiled a crooked smile at the young marshall.

"Forgive me, Comrade Popov, but I'm not sure what you mean."

"Oh, come now, Marshall. The President is dead. There is, how should I say, a vacuum to be filled."

"Which president, Yuri? Ours or theirs?"

"Ours, of course. Rosemary Hawkins has been sworn in as the new United States President. Quick work, while the city burns. She is a devil, that one."

"We don't make presidents that way, Comrade Popov. The Party leaders will have to call a meeting. There will be much said. Most of it, of course, will be poppycock."

"You are insolent, Grenady, for one so young."

"I am not too young to be Commander in Chief of the Armed Forces." There was an implied threat in the Marshall's comment.

"I will be frank, Grenady. I believe we must go back in time a bit. We need to retrench. We must put the emphasis on rebuilding our military power."

"Our military power is not lessened, to my knowledge. It is moved back. But it still exists, as always."

"Yes, of course it does. But with the murder of our progressive, charismatic President, I feel the Soviet nation must take a firm stance in the world. Who can say what was behind the mad attack on the U.S. capital? I warned them! But did they listen? Of course they didn't listen. I am an old man. A fossil, about to be retired."

"You created that intelligence, didn't you, Comrade Popov? The American attack. You couldn't have known about that in advance."

"I knew something, of course. Bits, scraps of information, intercepts. I warned the President, as I have said. He chose to ignore me. His plan with Conrad Taylor was all that mattered to him. The Party backed him. The people, although impatient with the slow progress on his promised reforms, they too backed our beloved leader. In his dealings with the Americans, he was giving them all they wanted. He was, in fact, emasculating this country, so the French, and the English, and the rest of the Western nations would continue to put his face on the cover of their magazines." Grenady chose to ignore the polemics of the fifties. Magazine covers. Indeed.

"Rosemary Hawkins was due here, soon, for a secret conference on disarmament and troop withdrawal. Then Conrad Taylor died."

"So, Grenady? This is not news."

"Then William Rodgers became President, pledged to carry on with Conrad Taylor's plans, and promptly named Rosemary Hawkins his new Secretary of State."

"So, young Marshall Malitkov? This also, is old news."

"Now, with two presidents dead, the architect of total U.S. withdrawal from foreign lands is no longer an advisor to presidents. She is President herself. The plans will go forward, Comrade Popov."

"No. They will not."

"No?"

"They will not, because I believe now is the time for this country to assert itself as the leading international power. Of all time, Grenady."

"And how do you propose to do this?"

"With you, Grenady. And the military and spiritual might of the Soviet people."

"And, of course, with you, Comrade Popov, as head of the Party, and its new President."

"That would be a good thing, don't you think, Grenady?"

"Time will tell. You are seventy years old, comrade."

"True. But most of our esteemed younger cadre of leaders was with him in Washington. Therefore, they are dead, these young men. Unofficially, of course. We have no actual figures. But Joseph has been in contact. His opinion is that he is the senior Soviet official still alive in the United States. I authorized him to conduct business, in a normal way, and to consider himself the new Soviet Ambassador.''

''You authorized him?''

''Why not, Grenady? He is a young man, trapped in a city on fire, screaming out for Scorpio. How could I do less?''

''How, indeed, comrade. As for me, I will keep a tight rein on our forces. Our President was right, I believe. And if he was, Rosemary Hawkins will give us a thousand years of peace.''

''Is the destruction of the leaders of our government, at the hands of the United States Air Force, a sign of her goodwill, Grenady?''

''What do you mean, comrade?''

''Rosemary Hawkins, it seems, is the *lone* survivor of the United States Government. How, do you think, she managed that?''

''Coincidence, comrade.''

''Perhaps. But what is required to restore the United States Government? Do you know?''

''No. I'm not a student of constitutional United States Government.''

''Nor am I. But, it would seem, for the moment, the attack on the capital by the so-called madman from the U.S. Air Force, has made Rosemary Hawkins Commander in Chief of the Armed Forces of the United States. In effect, she is, at this moment, a true dictator, with total control of United States nuclear power.''

''So it would seem. Then, comrade, we must walk softly, so as not to make her live up to her red-haired reputation. What I mean is, I will wait to see which way this particular cat jumps.''

''Not too long, Grenady. See to it you don't wait too long. I have called an emergency meeting of all voting members of the Politburo for next week. Seven days,

Grenady. The meeting will cover what is known by then, and, of course, all will be allowed to voice their opinions. I will call a follow-up meeting for early in January. At that time, we will discard the unworkable, and go forward. Can I count on you, Grenady?''

"I will be there, of course, Comrade Popov."

"That is what I asked, and no more. No pressure, Grenady. You understand?''

"Perfectly, Comrade Popov." The Marshall saluted the K.G.B. head, and left K.G.B. Headquarters, his head bent into the wind, a light snow blowing sideways across Red Square. It was going to be a cold winter. He decided, at that moment, to find a way to talk to Rosemary Hawkins, or her representative, sometime before January. He pulled his collar up, walking headdown, his staff car moving slowly beside him through the howling wind and snow. If he didn't take action, he felt the Soviet Union was about to slip back to the dark ages of Stalin. He could not, would not let that happen.

WHITEHALL
LONDON
TUESDAY, 3:00 A.M.

"Well, I can't bloody well say I'm going to miss her. She was, at her best, a complete bitch!''

"Princess Diana?''

"No, you incompetent nincompoop! The bloody Prime Minister. Now, perhaps, we shall get a government that will see to the needs of the British people.''

"And you, of course, Minister, could provide such a government.''

"Do you doubt it?''

"Of course not, sir. You are . . . you're a proven factor. God knows, we'll need that well enough.''

"Of course, the Fleet Streeters will bleed first for the Royals, I suppose, God Save the Queen Mother, and all that rot. Then, we will call elections. Sixty days. And I shall head the party, of course. After all these years of sniffing that bitch's iron crotch, I shall get out from under.''

''Princess Diana's?''

''Lord, Compton, you're even more stupid than I thought.''

JERUSALEM
"RACKET" AIR BASE
UNDERGROUND HEADQUARTERS
TUESDAY, 6:00 A.M.

''We can't wait much longer, Adam. The strike must be flown within seventy-two hours. To wait longer would be suicide.''

''I disagree, Colonel Green. We can handle the Syrians moving toward the Golan. They are exploiting a tragic happening, half a world away. It's not very coordinated. Most of their artillery is in Lebanon. Along with 80,000 of their best troops. Strike the tanks on the Golan. We must limit this, if possible.''

''Have you spoken to the Americans?''

''The Americans who? The President? Yes. The generals? No. They are, I'm told, without the top 10 percent of their most experienced officers.''

''What did Rosemary Hawkins say?''

''She was quite nice. Very tough, that one. She said she understood perfectly our need to defend ourselves. She said the United States would support us to the best of its ability if we were attacked under the present circumstances. She said the Italians have already refused permission to overfly Italy. She told the Italians to, as she put it, 'Put their permission where the Mediterranean sun don't shine.' But she also asked us to exercise restraint. She says the United States's position will be stated more clearly in a speech tomorrow. She was, in fact, very brave. Did you see the TV pictures taken during the attack?''

"Yes, sir. It was a very effective attack."

"Yes. Jonathan Bennett. I met his father once, in the United States, and he spent three days with me, up in the mountains, overlooking the Dead Sea. At that time, he suggested we nuke Syria and Iraq."

"When was that?"

"Last year, General. Just last year. I crossed it off as the drivelings of an old fool."

"And my suggestions, sir?"

"The drivelings of a young fool. Prepare. But wait."

"Yes, sir. But we must be ready."

"Will it satisfy you to put half our Air Force in the air, General?"

"No, sir. It won't satisfy me. But it will make me less likely to be insubordinate."

"That alone makes it worth it. Get them airborne."

"Armed for all contingencies, sir?"

"Yes, General. Arm them for all contingencies."

DAMASCUS, SYRIA
TUESDAY, 6:15 A.M.

"How many tanks can you move against the Golan, Hasid?"

"One hundred and fifty, with 15,000 shock troops, using poison gas."

"And your goal, Hasid?"

"Mr. President. Now is the time. I can lead my brigade into Jerusalem within seventy-two hours."

"Poison gas, Hasid?"

"Why not, Mr. President?"

"Because they will vaporize Damascus, Hasid. You are still of the desert, old friend. No gas. More tanks. More men. And, most important, Jordan."

"But, sir, the Jordanian king is said to be dead, with his wife and family. Jordan is without leaders."

"True, Hasid. But in a month, we shall provide them with rulers. Palestinians, Hasid. Wait. Patience. Restraint."

"But the Golan Heights?"

"Of course. The Golan Heights. In seventy-two hours. We shall bloody their nose, eh? But only their nose, Hasid. Later, soon, Jerusalem. I must talk to age-old enemies to dispel the worst of their fears. But in the end, Syria will rule the Arab world, over the dead bodies of every man, woman, and child in Israel. But you must be patient. Seventy-two hours. Probe the Golan. Kill some tanks. Kill some Jews. Retreat, if need be. We have time. The new American President is a frightened dove. Wait, Hasid. We have waited for centuries. A few more weeks can do no harm."

THE WHITE HOUSE COMMUNICATION CENTER MONDAY, 11:00 P.M.

Nadine and J.R. Kelly watched the information flow across the lines, the printers chattering away incessantly, as the world rolled over, rubbed its collective eye in disbelief, and began to react. The Secure Room in the White House basement hummed with the threatening sound of maximum machine output, a kind of electronic world temperature gauge. And the world's temperature was going up.

"God damn," breathed Nadine.

"Ain't that the truth?"

"J.R., I've never seen anything like this before. It will take weeks just to analyze this information, let alone react to it."

"It do look like a world of hurt."

"J.R.!"

"Sorry. Just whistling in the dark, to keep from hiding under my desk back at good ole Langley."

"Well, we are not at Langley. Langley is here. Rosemary Hawkins told me, personally, that she trusted you implicitly. Why is that, J.R.? You're a flake, and everybody knows it.''

"Sex appeal, I guess. Plus, I did haul her out of the amphitheater. I don't know exactly why she feels the way she does. A lot of it probably has to do with the fact she's scared to death at the moment.''

"No, J.R. Not that one. Rosemary Hawkins doesn't scare.''

"Maybe. Maybe not. She's the President of the United States. We're supposed to pull information out of the air, advise her properly, and provide her with exact facts to make a speech to the world at 10:00 A.M. tomorrow. If that were your responsibility, wouldn't you be scared?''

"Yeah, hell, yes.'' Nadine frowned. "But then, I'm not President. So I says she ain't scared, buster. Now, don't you have something to do?''

"Yes. I do. A lot of things.'' J.R. Kelly pulled loose from the printers all they had printed, gathered a fourteen-inch stack of printouts, and left the room. He headed upstairs, to the Oval Office. Rosemary Hawkins was not there. A Secret Service agent advised J.R. that she was napping until 1:00 A.M., at which time she expected to see Major General Brian Howell. J.R. brushed by the startled Secret Service man, and brushed a stack of papers from the Oval Office desk, plopping his printouts on the desk, and removing his jacket. He had the look of a man about to settle in.

"Now listen, Mr. Kelly, I know what you did and all, but you can't just come in here and take over this office.''

J.R. fixed the Secret Service man with a look only slightly removed from a cave. "Listen to me, whatever your name is. Outside, this city's fires are just beginning to go out. Two presidents are dead in four days, and the third is exhausted in the next room. If she isn't properly prepared by morning, every city in the world could go up in flames within months, possibly even hours. Now, do you leave me alone to do my job, or do we have to shoot it out?''

The Secret Service man glanced at the 9mm slung in the holster under J.R.'s left arm. He thought of the little brother upstairs, fighting for his life. He remembered the C.I.A. agent, carrying Rosemary Hawkins in his powerful arms, gently as he would a newborn. "Ah, hell, Agent Kelly. If you need me, just call. I'm at your service, sir. And I mean that."

J.R.'s face transformed, but only for an instant. A younger face, a brief smile, the weary wave of a burned but still unbandaged hand. The Secret Service man closed the door to the Oval Office. Outside it, four heavily armed Marines, the "roof" Marines who had conducted the rescue of Jason Kelly, remained at their unofficial but accepted post as J.R. Kelly's guardian angels, in Marine Corps green. They belonged to that small community of men across the world who had risked their lives for J.R. Kelly, simply because he'd asked them to.

As J.R. Kelly reached to pick up the coded Desert Flower phone line, it rang. Saying nothing, he picked it up.

"General Howell?"

J.R. made a quick decision. "Go." He'd heard Brian Howell say that often. He considered it a power word.

"We are at the Bennett Ranch, sir, as ordered. We lost a chopper getting in here. A very heavy storm, sir. I'm sure you would want to know. We will, of course, forward their names as soon as possible."

"Who is this?"

"Sir?"

"I said, who the hell is this?" J.R. Kelly, like many Irishmen, had a bit of the mimic in him.

"Why, it's Captain McKauklie, sir. A.S.A. 660. You asked us to—"

"Goddammit, I know what I asked, Captain. Now, get on with it!"

"Sir, yes, sir. The Governor is dead, sir. So is his man-servant."

"Dead. What do you mean, dead? How dead?"

"Very dead, sir, if I'm any judge."

"Captain McKauklie, do you think this is pretty funny?"

"Sir, no sir!"

"Then goddammit, tell it like it isn't very funny!"

"Sir, it appears that Governor Bennett and his employee . . . it appears they sort of . . . sort of shot it out, sir."

"Shot it out? Shot what out?" J.R. was deep into his near-perfect, and perfectly pompous charade. Brian Howell never sounded more like Brian Howell than at this moment.

"It appears, General, that sometime last night, the two gentlemen had an argument, and settled it with gunfire."

"I see. Who won, in your opinion?"

"I'm not a medical officer, General. But it appears to me that Governor Bennett took four hits, three potentially fatal."

"And his servant?"

"Three, sir. All potentially fatal. And the phone was not out of order, sir. It was hit by a .45 auto slug, and basically destroyed. The manservant was holding it in his hand, sir. He is, in fact, still holding it. We can't get him to . . . ah, to . . . let go, sir. He must have been very anxious to make a phone call, sir."

"Yes. So it would seem. Now, what do you intend to do there, Captain?"

"As ordered, sir. Clean up the mess, if any. And you can see, sir, we have a mess to clean up."

"Do you have any press problems yet, Captain?"

"Not yet, sir."

"Good. Good boy. Listen now. You sit tight. You are to secure the Bennett Ranch, until relieved. No one is to get in until you are relieved. This, of course, considering the son's actions, is of the highest national and, more important, international security priority. Clean it up."

"Sir?"

"Bury the servant."

"Sir?"

"Goddammit, what did I say?"

"You said clean it up, and bury the servant."

"Correct."

"How, sir, should I clean it up?"

"Does Adrian Bennett have a self-inflicted wound?"

"No, sir."

"He needs one."

"Sir?"

"I said, he needs one."

"Yes, sir, understood. Sir, who will relieve us?"

"If you can bear it, Captain, a Marine unit will be there in less than eight hours. Until then, you must clean up the mess. And Captain?"

"Yes, General?" The young captain's voice remained calm, in spite of the orders he'd been given.

"By this time next week, you will be a bird colonel . . . *if* you handle this. Do you understand?"

"Of course, General Howell. I understand."

"National security, Captain. That is what we are talking here. Tomorrow morning, the new President of the United States is going to say that Adrian Bennett committed suicide, and that his faithful servant, grief-stricken, did the same. *Do you read me?*"

"I believe so, General Howell."

"Good!"

"Sir?"

"Yes, Captain!"

"Adrian Bennett's friend and lifetime servant was black, sir."

"So?"

"If you recall, General Howell, so am I."

"National security, Captain, is red, white, and blue. And green. When the Marine unit reaches you, you are to disengage and disappear. They will handle the shit details."

"Sir?"

"Yes, Captain."

"If I'm not wearing eagles by Easter . . ."

"Yes, Captain?"

"Nothing, sir."

"You bet your black ass, Captain!" With that, J.R. Kelly hung up the Desert Flower phone, and shut off the auto-tape that had recorded the entire conversation.

Deep in the western snowstorm, A.S.A. Unit 660, under the only black commander in the supersecret unit, began to alter the gunfight at the less than O.K. Corral.

J.R. stared at the Desert Flower phone. He had enough evidence, at this moment, to put the heat to Brian Howell. But he needed more, much more. He walked to the Oval Office door, and invited the four "roofers" inside. He explained what he wanted done. He acknowledged that he had zero power to ask them to do anything at all. Then, in the clearest theatrics, he called Pax River, and requested a C-130. He got it. None of the four Marines in the Oval Office had ever jumped from an aircraft before. By 7:00 A.M., Mountain Standard Time, they would leave the C-130, fully armed, and take charge at the Bennett Ranch. Taking charge, in this case, meant digging up A.S.A. 660's dead bodies, meaning Adrian Bennett and his executioner. It meant, possibly, a firefight between the U.S.M.C. and the members of the supersecret A.S.A. 660 unit of the United States Army, obviously controlled by Brian Howell. As usual, the Marines said, "What the hell," and were airborne from Pax River with fifty-eight minutes to spare.

Brian Howell, alias J.R. Kelly, had, without authorization and, with undoubted taints of treason, set one armed group of Americans, four to be exact, against another much larger group of armed Americans, in the hope that nobody would die, and the country, less Brian Howell, would survive . . . He received only one message from the C-130, and its small detachment, delivered to him by a fresh-faced young man who informed him that he had taken Willy's job, felt he was unworthy, but would do his best. The message sent in the clear was simple. The answer was not.

"J.R. . . . STOP. TURKEY TROTS. STOP." The turkey trots message was padding. "IF OPPOSED,

WHAT?'' That was the message. "TROTS TO WATER, TROTS TO HEAD, TROTS ALL DAY, UNTIL WE'RE DEAD.'' More padding.

The answer showed just how far, and how unreal, the real world had become. J.R. sent it clear, no padding. "ATTACK! REPEAT! ATTACK AND EXECUTE ORDERS. DESERT FLOWER.''

Having imitated Brian Howell, J.R. decided that the best, perhaps the only way, to provide Rosemary Hawkins with what she needed to throw a net over a world mesmerized by the continuing view of the United States capital city on fire, was a spray of fool's gold, liar's powder, or just plain fraud. He picked up the secure Desert Flower phone, and asked the militantly awake operator to locate, and get, Roger Carlyle. The first *personal* call Adrian Bennett had made less than fifty hours ago. It took the operator only seven minutes to reach Mr. Carlyle.

"Mr. Carlyle?''

"Yes, this is Roger Carlyle.''

"Forgive me, sir, for calling at this late hour. My name is Quenton Simmons, sir. I have been asked by Major General Howell if you could possibly be here tomorrow.''

"Here? Where, here?''

"The White House, of course, Mr. Carlyle. Brian, I mean General Howell, feels you should be here, sir, for a . . . how should I say, a private meeting. He wishes to know, sir, if you could find it in your time schedule, and if I may paraphrase him, in your heart, to be here, to once again assist your country in its dire need. If I may say so, sir, he suggested a Senate appointment at the least. Ms. Hawkins, you might well understand is . . . well, how should I say, in need of advice. I'm told that your state governor, the governor of the great State of Connecticut, survived. Fortuitous, sir. Your governor is the sole decider on such matters. I was asked, sir, to advise you that your country needs your vast foreign experience.''

"Ah. I see. And, who sir, are you, if you'll forgive my fading memory for names?''

"Quenton Simmons, Mr. Carlyle. Since today's . . .

unpleasantness, I've been appointed liaison between Ms. Hawkins and those Brian Howell believes are her best hopes for success in a world gone . . . how should I say, discreetly . . .''

"Commie!"

"Yes, sir. A very good word."

"You tell Brian Howell I'll be in D.C. tomorrow, and at the White House at 11:45 P.M. Tell him I am at his service!"

"And the President, sir?"

"Well. Of course. I'm most particularly at her service. Tell her not to worry her pretty little head."

"I'll do that, Mr. Carlyle. We look forward to seeing you. But please, be careful. Washington is a city under siege, as you surely know."

"I'll do that . . . a . . .''

"Quenton, sir. Quenton Simmons."

"Yeah. Well, there will be a place for you when all this settles down."

"Thank you, sir. I'm sure there will be."

J.R. hit the record stop button, a grin, no, not a grin, spreading across his face.

In the next room, the new President slept the fitful sleep of a human being subjected to more than she could bear. More, in fact, than anyone could bear. But J.R. Kelly did not sleep. He cranked up the Desert Flower coded phone, and went back to work.

"Mr. Perry, please."

"Mr. Perry is engaged at the moment. Do you know what time it is?" It was a woman's voice, an outraged, still-sleeping woman. Wife? Mistress?

"Forgive me, madam. My name is Simon Quenton. I'm calling from the White House, in Washington, D.C. I'm afraid, madam, that we are on no particular time schedule here. The city is on fire, madam!" J.R., switching the two names he'd used on his last call, sounded very British, or vaguely British, at least.

"The White House. Oh. I see. Well, that's a horse from a different track, isn't it? I'll get Robert. Please hold."

"Thank you, madam. Time is of the essence."

A horse from a different track? Holy yuppie shit! J.R. drummed his nails on the presidential desk. They were dirty, and the thumbnail was clotted underneath with blood. Jason's blood.

"This is Robert Perry. Who is this?"

"We've met only once, sir. I was a junior protocol officer in the Virgin Islands at the time. Governor Bennett enlisted my aide in acquiring a small interisland carrier you were interested in. I was in the background, you see."

"Oh, yes. I remember that deal. Been a while."

"Yes, sir. 1978."

"Right. Yeah. 1978."

"I'd like to get to the point, sir. Brian Howell, and, of course, others, would like to meet tomorrow, here, in Washington. He suggested the meeting take place at the restaurant you met in earlier this week. Say, at 11:45 A.M., after the new President's speech? She will, how shall I say this . . ."

"The little redheaded bitch needs some help, right, Simmons?"

"Quenton, sir. Simon Quenton. And yes, that is the gist of it. He suggested you might use your own aircraft, to avoid undue publicity."

"Well, we've certainly done that enough, haven't we? Hell, yes. I'll be there. You sure that little place ain't burned down?" Here, Mr. Robert Perry, corporate raider and thief, gave a hearty laugh. J.R.'s grip tightened on the phone.

"Quite sure, Mr. Perry. And the whole Washington area is under the martial law command of . . ."

"Paul Wolfe. Yeah. I know. Sounds fine, Quenton. Do I need to verify anything with Brian Howell? God damn, we got to get this nation back on its feet. Too bad about Jon Bennett. But Adrian's a tough old bird. He can take plenty of hits. Even this. Yup. Poor Jonathan. A sick boy. But a hero! You hear me? A hero!"

"Yes, sir, I hear you. The group will expect you at 11:45 in the morning. Land your aircraft at Andrews, sir. Perhaps Perry Pharmaceuticals might load it with medicine and technicians. What better reason to be here?"

"Brian think of that?"

"Actually, sir, I did."

"You'll go far, my boy. Real far. Well, hell, yes. I'll load it up. I'm a patriot! I'll fill that sucker with two million dollars worth, gratis."

"Your country is grateful, Mr. Perry."

"Yeah. Well, you just tell old Brian and the rest of the folks I'll be there. No problem."

"Yes, sir, I'll do that." J.R. hung up, and switched off the tape.

"Darien Talmage, please. This is the White House calling."

"Hold please."

"Thank you." A sweet, honey-dripping southern voice came on the line.

"Mr. Talmage is on his way to Washington, D.C., sir. He was called there to comment on the political ramifications of the President's speech tomorrow. As you know, sir, he has been a vocal opponent of our government's position on Israel, and arms sales. His radio and television stations will carry his comments throughout most of the South, as will his newspapers. We here at Talmage hope you will listen in. We hope to have Brian Howell, and Major General Paul Wolfe, of the Maryland National Guard, on the radio portions of the show."

"Forgive me, miss, but are you employed by Mr. Talmage?"

"Of course, sir. I'm the head of the public relations department for media events."

"I see. Well then, could you tell us where Mr. Talmage will be staying while in Washington?"

"Of course, sir. He always stays at the Willard. Are the fires terribly bad? It's all so horrible, isn't it?"

"Yes, it's all so horrible. But I think the fires are getting under control."

"The rain. Yes. I heard it was simply pouring in the capital."

J.R. Kelly hung up, switched off the recorder, and loosened his tie. It was time for a drink, and he filled his ever-present tumbler with three fingers of Cuervo Gold. Outside the White House windows, the fires burned on, and people continued to die. It was 11:49, Monday, and true to its reputation, there was still a tiny chunk of blue glacier ice in his glass, unmelted and pristine.

NORTHEASTERN WASHINGTON, D.C. MONDAY, 11:50 P.M.

Eddie LeRoy Jackson, "El Jay" to his friends, moved slowly down the street toward "crack castle," less than 150 yards away now, clearly undamaged, though the entire block was ablaze. Even the downpour couldn't stop this fire, baby. El Jay clutched the MAC-10 .45-caliber machine pistol close to him as he skirted around Primo Pops's burned out Cadillac, its TV antenna scorched black and twisted. He glanced inside. Nope. No Primo, no ladies, no business. He tripped over something and looked down. Melody. Melody Robinson, for sure. Six years old, but she could carry that shit, couldn't she? Burned blacker than she was 'cept for her eyes, staring up at the rain.

El Jay moved along the fire-blackened wall of what had been a TV repair shop and fencing operation a few hours ago. Now, it was falling down on him, and he danced free, just before it landed on him.

The crack castle had been on that corner for as long as El Jay could remember. It wasn't, no way, going to burn down. The outside walls were brick. The inside walls were steel. He'd seen the mayor down here, with that skinny white bitch model he liked to show when he was feeling good, standing at the crack castle door, like any other junkie, just better dressed, Primo covering his ass while he stroked the white bitch's leg, and the little brick window moved, and the mayor came away, a happy man, paying his sleek white bitch with the only thing you could pay her with that she cared about.

The Congress was after his ass, and the reverend kept saying he was a disgrace, but the police didn't say shit, so it just went on. El Jay moved closer to the castle. It looked real dark. Empty? No. Not with 100,000 vials of crack inside. It wasn't empty. But who was crazy enough to be in there? The fire had picked up, and El Jay moved closer, looking up, looking around, seeing everything, like he had since he was a kid. He moved to the door, rapped the brick, discovered the motherfucker was hot! Holy shit! The fucking crack castle was too hot to touch. What did that make it inside? Nothing. He'd been told about the inside. Twenty-four by twenty-four downstairs, air vents, air-conditioned, provisioned for anything. Upstairs, all the bitches, from the little bitches to the old bitches, out of the way, mouths open, like baby birds for a fresh worm, but they ate a different kind of fresh worm upstairs in the crack castle. Course, he'd never been *inside,* but he knew. And now, while it was too hot to breathe, El Jay was going to take the castle for himself. He banged against the door, screaming at the top of his voice.

"Open up, mother fuckers. It's ole El Jay the first, the new king of this particular castle."

And then gunfire had ripped out at him from a hole in the wall upstairs, and he dived into a trench where a house had stood earlier in the evening, a trench filled with the eight charred bodies of the house he'd known, because it was his house.

El Jay fired back, spraying the walls with the MAC-10, and then, looming out of the fiery darkness was a tank, a no-shit tank, like some fucking television advertisement for the Army, and he watched, transfixed as its long gun moved slowly, imperceptibly toward the crack castle, stopped, and then roared once. A screaming, shattering sound more destructive than all the sounds El Jay had ever heard.

The crack castle's indestructible iron door covered in brick was suddenly opened wide, wisps of smoke curling out, and an incredible number of people stumbled out, into the pouring rain and the glowing fires, and they were quickly surrounded by men in battle helmets and body armor, U.S. flags on their shoulders, carrying M16s and looking like a bunch of bad-movie soldiers with nothing to do. They rounded everybody up and marched them off down the debris-strewn street, dodging burning cars and falling buildings, and the tank moved away, obeying the commander's orders to stop the open warfare going on in northeastern Washington at whatever the cost.

And then the street was empty, and the door to the crack castle was standing wide open, or at least the building was wide open where the door had been. El Jay strolled non-chalantly across the barren landscape between his dead family in the trench where his house had stood, and the still-smoking open hole to the crack castle.

He walked inside, and upstairs. The house was empty. Man, he had to get himself a fucking tank! Talk about talking deep shit! Tanks. Whooee!! And turned a corner upstairs, into a small room, and there it was. Boxes of it. Thousands and thousands of tiny vials of crack cocaine, heroin, packages of nose candy like one-pound bags of powdered sugar.

Methodically, he began to carry it downstairs, all of it, until he stood just inside the door made by the tank, with over a million dollars in toilet paper boxes at his feet. El Jay had arrived! He stepped outside, into the light of the fire, flickering lower now under the hammering of the rain, and there it sat, a D.C. police car, doors open, cops rolling out. Well, sure, they'd know, wouldn't they? And he raised the MAC-10 and chopped them down, all three of them, before they knew the great El Jay was there. One of them was crawling away, and El Jay could see him, could hear him, screaming into his portable radio. But fuck it, the man was down. El Jay had put him down, and he swung the MAC-10 over his shoulder on its thin, boot-lace straps. He would just carry this shit away. Yes he would.

As El Jay exited the blown-open crack castle, a helicop-ter gunship swept overhead, its door gunner highlighted for a terrifying instant in El Jay's eyes, just before the post-mounted, heavy machine gun opened up and tore El Jay to pieces, splashing him and his precious cargo back through the castle hole and against the far wall. The gun-ner kept the .50 going, until the castle blew up. It was two days before Eddie LeRoy Jackson's fourteenth birthday. The policeman who called in the National Guard helicop-ter, Michael Raymond Price, age thirty-one, was El Jay's uncle. He too died, less than thirty feet from his sister, Carrie Jackson, Eddie Jackson's mother.

DAY SEVEN: TUESDAY

THE WHITE HOUSE
PRIVATE QUARTERS
TUESDAY, 12:10 A.M.

"Can he talk, doctor?"

"Oh, he's pretty busted up, but he can talk all right. He seems to be trying to get the nurse into bed with him. She protests, saying he's basically inoperative. He makes some ribald remarks about his penis, and it goes on like that. He's hurt bad, Mr. Kelly. And he will be a long time recovering."

"Will he fly again?"

"He says he will. I believe he will. If he lives, of course. But he's young, in all the best ways you can be young. Sure. He'll fly again, and if I'm any judge, he will be whatever he wants in the Marine Corps, up to and including its commandant."

"Can I talk to him?"

"Sure. Good medicine. The best. But don't tire him. He hasn't a lot left to give at the moment. But Mr. Kelly, your brother, in my professional opinion, is in no danger of dying. He has burns, including some slight lung damage. His arm is broken. He has a fractured hip, and a broken ankle. Bones, that's all. They will heal. The burns look bad, but they are superficial, though he is in terrible pain, and we are doing what we can for that. He's seen better days. But he will be 100 percent. It will take a while. But he will. What he needs now has nothing at all to do with modern medical techniques. He needs what all young people need. The warmth of his loved ones. I sug-

341

gest you go in there, and hug him—mentally, of course.
If you physically hug him, they'll hear the scream at the
Washington Monument.''

"There are already people screaming at the Washington
Monument, doc. But I get your point.''

The nurse standing near Jason Kelly's sickbed was one
of the cotton candy, glandular women that used to play
nurses on soap operas. She was really very beautiful, if
you didn't pay a lot of attention to the bloodstains from
Jason's wounds that decorated her once crisp, white uniform. She was holding his hand, and looking at him with
such naked, dazzling admiration and genuine concern that
for the briefest moment, J.R. thought he was looking at
the Madonna herself. He quelled such thoughts by notic-
ing that the top two buttons of her uniform were undone,
and she had ''combat zone'' breasts. Innocence, with nipples. His cynicism satisfied, he brushed her away from
Jason, and took his brother's hand away from her, placing
it gently in his huge paw, flinching at the contact with his
own, still untreated burns.

"A minute, please, miss.''

"Of course, sir. I'll just wait outside. Please, if you
. . . if *he* needs me, call.''

Oh, shit. True love, if he was any judge. But he wasn't.
J.R. couldn't judge true sex, let alone true love. He wondered idly if he'd just met his future sister-in-law, and
would she make him, finally, an uncle?

"Hello, big brother.''

"Hi, kid. How ya doin'?''

"Not very well. I've been trying to get the nightingale
to rub me where it works, but she insists on rubbing me
where it hurts.''

"Smart girl.''

"Beautiful, isn't she?''

"Yeah, kid. She really is.''

"It's very weird to lie here, J.R., in a president's bed,

with about half the medical brass above colonel fussin'
over me.''

"You deserve it, kid."

"No. No, I don't. Did you see him, J.R.? Did you see
that son-of-a-bitch fly? Nobody ever flew like that. Nobody. Von Richthofen couldn't fly like that. Marseille.
Galland. Boynton. Kelleher. None of them could fly like
this guy. I blew it, big brother. I had him, just like we
planned, standing off over the reservoir. He didn't see me,
J.R. *He felt me!* And he shifted, not much, but just right,
and I watched him tear up the bridge. I didn't see his first
pass at the amphitheater. But I saw him coming back. So
quick! Jesus. He came back so quick. And then I got on
him, big brother. I really got on him." Tears began to
flow from Jason Kelly's eyes, mingling with the ointment
on his face, streaking his cheeks with eerie green lines
with black edges.

"I know you did, Jace. I saw you. Taco was up there.
He saw it, but he just couldn't get at him."

"Hell, J.R. I got at him! I hit him more times than I
do a sled towed by the blue jackets off Cherry Point. He
just shook it off! He just shook it off, like I had nothin' to
hit him with. He pulled straight up through that formation.
And I went right up after him. I hate to say this, J.R., but
it was a real trip, that ride up through all those aircraft,
in the rockets' red glow, if you know what I mean."

"I know, Jace. Really I do. I understand."

"And then, J.R., we were up there alone, just the Ace-
of-Spades and me, although I knew that his missiles were
launched, and air-to-air crashes were coming down all
over, and the shit had definitely hit the fan. And you know
what he did, J.R.? He rolled that big son-of-a-bitch over,
and he *aimed* it. *It,* not a weapon. The fucking A-10! But
I could see him, J.R. Jesus. I could really see him. The
fucking A-10, compared to my AV-8B, is like an airliner.

"So I stayed with him, and I swear to God I killed him,
and I shot his fucking Ace-of-Spades to shit. It was on
fire, from end to end. My C.O. would've been proud, J.R.
But it was like . . . it was like he wasn't dead. His plane

wasn't dead. And he was going down, in a sort of controlled tumble.'' The tears flowed more freely now, as Jason gripped J.R.'s hand so tightly he thought his bones might break. The nurse, the soap-opera nurse, had moved to Jason's side and was preparing a hypo, while Jason tried to sit up, his face contorted with pain. J.R. caught him up, held him in his arms, Jason's words muffled against J.R.'s beefy shoulder.

"I couldn't let him do that, bro. I stuck that pretty little AV-8B right into that cocksucker. I don't know why I'm alive. I shouldn't be alive. Jesus, J.R., look outside. The fucking world is on fire!" And then the silky breasted figure in white moved forward, weeping in love or grief or shock, and the hypo thudded into Jason Kelly, a heavy-duty load of "go to sleep" cocktail, and J.R. gently laid his brother back down on Conrad Taylor's bed, the feel and smell of burn ointment plastered to his shirt. He reached out, touched the angel in white on the cheek, wiping a tear with the back of his hand. She clutched it to her cheek, and looked at J.R.

"I love him, you know. I've only known him for two hours, but I love him."

For a bear of a man, J.R. had a gentle touch, when he needed it. It was needed now. He walked around the bed, to the blood-spattered nurse, and held her, very briefly, kissing the top of her honey-blond head. Then he released her, and walked away.

THE WHITE HOUSE
TUESDAY, 12:30 A.M.

J.R. walked across the semidarkened office of the former National Security Advisor/Secretary of State and newly sworn President of the United States. She was on her side, her legs pulled up, her red hair tumbling over the side of her face. She looked very desirable, and very defenseless.

She had taken her suit skirt off, and the round, white of her buttocks against the black of her high-cut panties made it difficult to think of her as President. Of anything.

But she was. And she needed him. He walked away and poured her a small, "wake-up" drink, before returning to her side, sliding down next to her, sitting on the thick-carpeted floor. Idly, he began to stroke her bare legs, starting at her calf. She turned onto her stomach, straightening her legs, her face turned toward the wall.

"Oh, that feels so good. My body aches all over. You're pretty familiar with your President, J.R."

"That's true. But I'm a leg man. And an ass man. You have better legs than most presidents."

Her legs parted slightly, and she groaned, turning to look at him, brushing the long red hair from her face. "God, I really am sore, J.R. Also, you are a tit man. First and foremost. I have hardly any."

"They'll do. Here, drink this. It's time to take care of business."

She accepted the drink and sat up, curling her legs under her, reaching for her skirt but simply holding it in her lap. "What time is it, J.R.?"

"Twelve-thirty."

"I wanted to sleep until one."

"When the going gets tough, the tough wake up. I have something I want you to listen to." He leaned forward to the tape machine on the elaborate ebony coffee table, and punched the play button.

"J.R., what . . . ?"

"Please, Rosemary, just listen." J.R. put his head back against the couch, listening to the playback of his Desert Flower phone calls. Behind him, Rosemary Hawkins swung her sleek legs forward, sitting up straight. J.R. put one beefy paw over her bare foot, gave it a reassuring squeeze. For the next fifteen minutes, the machine spit out its tales of intrigue—and worse: treason. Only the tip of what was probably an iceberg of more people who knew *something* was going to happen, if not precisely what.

"That's Brian Howell?"

"Nope. That's me. But the captain out west believed he was talking to Brian Howell."

Finally, the machine clicked its last. There was a long moment of silence.

"What am I to suppose from all this, J.R.?"

"Brian Howell did not directly participate in, but knew about, the air strike. He sabotaged or delayed key intelligence. He tipped off one or both of the Bennetts about Willy. He placed, or saw to it friends who trusted him were put in place, military personnel that he and he alone can direct. He was not at the amphitheater, which, all by itself, speaks volumes."

"Why? Why would he have anything to do with this?"

"It probably goes a lot deeper than my poor cop's mind can figure. From my standpoint, he's a major-league bad guy, and he's always been a bad guy. He's a black man who made it big and wants it bigger. Hell, call me prejudiced. The others' motives are much simpler. Greed. Avarice. Lust. Power dangled between and in front of men to whom nothing but power counted. Adrian Bennett knew them. He knew them, and, I suspect, despised them.

"As for Jonathan Bennett, he did what his father told him to do, because to do anything less was unthinkable. A hundred shrinks in a hundred years with a hundred computers will never quite decipher *that* part of the story.

"Adrian Bennett was evil, and possibly insane. He knew how to hate. He made Jonathan hate, with a big assist from eight hundred days in a small room with K.G.B.-trained Vietnamese interrogators. Jonathan Bennett is the instrument, but he bears the smallest share of guilt. He was the trigger and the match, but somebody else pulled one and struck the other. The results, as of now, are visible outside the window. It will get infinitely worse, worldwide, unless you use every skill you possess, all the powers of the presidency, and utter, absolute ruthlessness. You must be, for a time, dictator of the United States." There. He'd finally said it all. If she didn't handle it now, he was out of inspirational speeches.

"Brian Howell will be here at one A.M. I asked him,

you know. I told him I needed his advice. What should I do, J.R.?''

"I don't know. I see the world falling apart. The message center is just one threat message after another. Brian Howell is either your trusted friend, or a traitor. How you handle that is up to you.''

"How is your brother, J.R.?''

"He'll be all right. He's in love with his nurse, which, for a Marine fighter pilot, is a good sign.''

"What he did, that boy. Lord. He was very brave. And, of course, he was there because you decided to run the government by yourself, wasn't he?''

"No. Not the government. Just my little brother, and a small cadre of friends doing favors for me, because I asked them to. If I was wrong, I lose a job, or worse. If I was right, and we'd been successful in stopping the Ace-of-Spades A-10, who knows. Doesn't matter, though. He got through, and half my friends are dead, some are promoted, some, no, many, just plain unaccounted for. This puzzle will take months to unravel and solve. Meanwhile, you'd better start doing your job.''

"I'll see Brian Howell, J.R.''

"Figured you would, Rosemary. Figured you would. I'll just take these tapes with me.''

"Leave them, J.R.''

"Bad idea. Brian Howell might get upset, and you want him to *talk* to you. You've heard the tapes. If you need them at a later date, for whatever purpose, they'll be available. I would put on my skirt, though, if I were you. You drive men to distraction.''

"Do I drive you to distraction, J.R.?''

"Absolutely. I'll be next door, if you need me.''

"No.''

"No?''

"You stay here. I'm the President. I'll see Brian Howell in the Oval Office.''

J.R. didn't say a word, simply watched the President of the United States get dressed, pulling on her skirt, tugging on her sleek calfskin boots, dressing with a complete lack of self-consciousness, as she might in front of her lover. Which, when he thought of it, was part of what he was to her. A small part . . .

TUESDAY, 1:00 A.M.

Major General Brian Howell, U.S.A.F., crossed the plush, creamy carpet, stained now by the blackened, soot-covered shoes of the many people who had entered the office since the air strike. He looked, as he always looked, impeccable and the picture of what a general officer in the Armed Forces of the United States should look like. It had been, embarrassingly enough, what had attracted Brian Howell to the newly appointed head of the National Security Agency in the first place, two years before she'd actually held the job. And even tonight he impressed her.

"Brian, how do you do it? You look like you've just come from a dress ball."

"Simple, Rosemary. I changed, to come to see my new Commander in Chief." He gave her a brisk salute, and then, his light chocolate–colored face, so smooth, so young, turned and rolled and opened into a dazzling, old-friend smile.

She walked from behind the massive, oak desk, gave him a brief "old-friend" hug, and returned to the high-backed chair behing the desk, which seemed to dwarf her, stretching a full twenty inches above her head. Conrad Taylor had been six-foot-four, and he had outweighed her by a hundred pounds. It would be easy to take her lightly, in that big chair, behind that big desk, swept clean of all papers, barren except for a phone console and a blank, yellow, lined pad. Easy, that is, if you paid no attention to her eyes, which blazed a cold green, a deep jade of hard, jewellike intensity. Brian Howell, pompous as ever, did not see her eyes.

"What am I up against, Brian. What have you learned?"

"Foreign?"

"Foreign, domestic. What have you learned? I have a speech to give later this morning. I would like to give it without making a fool of myself. What actions have you taken, if any?"

"Actions?"

"Initiatives, helpful hints, whatever. If I can't turn to you, Brian, I'm lost." The voice was submissive, womanly, but the eyes, in the shadows cast by the fireplace, the only light in the room, glowed like hot, green coals.

"Well, Rosemary, I must tell you. The military establishment here in Washington, as well as around the world, has been decimated. I took some of those problems under my wing—in your name, of course. It was necessary to reassign some young officers, move them up into positions they are not really prepared for."

"I see."

"And, of serious concern to us all, the image we project to the world at this time must be one of strength and unity of purpose. I have, reluctantly, agreed to do a couple of radio shows in the morning, after your speech, of course. Perhaps a television show as well. I'm sure you'll agree we must reassure the nation, and the world, that the United States policy is still in the hands of its policy makers."

"I see. Whose shows are you going on, Brian? It's not like you to go public with policy."

"Oh, it's just the Talmage Group, stations primarily in the south."

"Darien Talmage? He owns newspapers too, doesn't he?"

"Yes. A few rather small ones."

"Yes. I see."

"Of course, I will just be explaining what your policy will be."

"But how do you know what my policy will be, Brian?"

"Well, I assumed you would tell me, Rosemary."

"I see. What else have you been up to, Brian?"

"Well, I took the liberty of sending an Army unit to the Bennett Ranch. But they can't get through, apparently. There is a very heavy snowstorm out west. They were to call me, oh, about an hour ago. But so far, I've heard nothing.''

"Why did you order that, Brian?''

"To protect him, Rosemary. His son attacked the capital. I'm afraid for the old war-horse. A terrible policy man! But still, he's rendered much service in the past. I was hopeful we could keep the press off him for a while.''

"That should be easy, Brian. There doesn't seem to be a hell of a lot of press left.''

"Sad. Yes. Very sad. But we will get our message out.''

"I'm sure we will. What can you tell me about the Soviets, Brian?''

"Oh, they're very quiet, Rosemary. No movement there, that I can ascertain. Of course, our forces are on maximum alert worldwide, and the Soviets know it.''

"And how do they know it, Brian?''

"Do you remember the Scorpio message?''

"Yes, but only vaguely.''

"Well, I've let it be known, through N.S.A., that we believe the Scorpio message came from a high-ranking Soviet K.G.B. official.''

"And their reaction, Brian?''

"None, as yet. A few months, perhaps.''

"A few months?''

"Well, they can't organize as quickly as we can, Rosemary. It will take them time. They have no government, no leaders. While they indulge in a little internal bloodletting, we will—how should I say?—fill the vacuum.''

"*We* have no government, Brian. Only twelve members of Congress survived. Thirty-eight governors are confirmed dead. The Supreme Court. The Senate. All of the Senate. What are we to fill our vacuum with, Brian?''

"Well, we needn't go into all that today, Rosemary. Surviving governors will appoint senators. Surviving lieutenant governors will become governors, and appoint senators. You, of course, will appoint a new Supreme Court. In the meantime, the military, under your guidance, will have to step in, and—''

"Run the country, Brian?''

"Well, yes, I suppose you could say that. Of course, I will work tirelessly to assist you. By December first, I will, with your permission, compile a list of patriotic men, both military and civilian, and you can choose from, or add to the list in any way you see fit."

"You're a wonder, Brian. I'm certainly going to need all the help you can give me."

"Thank you, Rosemary."

"By the way, the pilot who shot down the Ace-of-Spades A-10 from Myrtle Beach—you know, Jonathan Bennett's plane?"

"Yes."

"He's upstairs, Brian, here, in the White House. Be sure you put him on your national list of heros up for promotion."

"A brave lad. I saw what he did."

"Did you, Brian? Where were you, during the attack? I expected you, of all people, to be by my side."

"Forgive me, Rosemary. It will always be my deepest shame. Would you believe, my car broke down just short of Arlington Bridge. And the crowd! Then the attack began, and I . . . I must say, I took cover."

"I understand perfectly, Brian. Just think of it! If your car hadn't broken down, you might have been in the amphitheater. You might, in fact, be dead. And then what would I do, and where would I turn? Surely, it was providence. One other thing, Brian. General Wolfe, the Maryland National Guard Commander. How is it, that among all National Guard C.O.s, he wasn't at the funeral either? And how did he mobilize his regiments so quickly? I think it's wonderful. Surely, you plan to reward him."

"Well, I'm very grateful to him. I don't know for sure why he wasn't here, though. Sick, I believe. Stomach ailment of some kind. Yes, you're correct. You might want to consider asking him to come back to the regular service temporarily. Give him a bit broader role."

"Authority, you mean?"

"Well, yes. He's certainly earned it."

"I quite agree. He has. But Brian, he's using tanks, isn't he? So I've heard."

"Yes. I believe he has one, maybe two, tank platoons here. Keeps his troops secure while they try to bring that vicious drug battle under control in the northeast section of the District."

"I want the tanks out, Brian. Tonight. I want them out of this area, and back in Maryland, where they belong. The vision of United States Army tanks in its capital city is contemptible."

"Well, Rosemary, let's not be hasty here. Paul thinks his troops need them, and so do I."

"Get them out. Two hours. Get them out. Now, if you'll excuse me, Brian, I have business to attend to."

"But, Rosemary, I think that—"

"Goddammit, get the fucking tanks out of the capital and do it now! You are dismissed, General Howell." She pushed a button under the desk, and the outer office door opened. A Secret Service agent filled the doorway. Now, in the shadow of her face, he saw the hot, green jade, glowing eyes. She had not moved from the chair. Shaken, Brian Howell left the White House without a word.

"J.R. J.R.!" Rosemary had to shake J.R. awake, and he came awake like a shot from a cannon, sitting bolt upright, nearly crashing into the bent-over, anxious face of Rosemary Hawkins.

"I wonder if you'd like to join your President in a walk, J.R.?"

"A walk. Are you crazy?"

"Yes."

"Okay. I'll get my coat."

"Got it right here, J.R."

"Pretty sure of yourself, aren't you?"

"Nope. Pretty sure of you, though."

They walked out of the inner office, directly into the main floor hallway. Two Secret Service agents, very young-looking, detached themselves from the door and moved after the pair, Rosemary's red hair bouncing as she moved rapidly toward the outer doorway. "Ma'am? President

Hawkins? Ma'am, just where the hell do you think you're going?''

"I'm going outside, with my protector and advisor, C.I.A. Agent J.R. Kelly."

"Can't let you do that, President Hawkins. It's just not safe."

"Can't let me, huh? Let me tell you something, young man. You can't stop me! Now, either come along, or shut up!"

The young Secret Service agent opened his mouth to say something, thought better of it, and shut it with a loud rattling of his jaws. "After you, ma'am. We'll just stay close, if you don't mind."

"That will do nicely. J.R., do you have a hat?"

"Naw. I look even more ugly in a hat."

"We do, ma'am. Umbrellas all over the place."

"Fine. Get us a very large one. I want to talk. Privately, while we walk." In five minutes, unnoticed in the driving rain and general confusion draped on the capital like a black tattered blanket, Rosemary Hawkins headed out across the mall, her arm through J.R.'s, very close to him, her hip brushing his thigh, while the rain came down, waterfall-like, on their huge, black umbrella.

"Oh, Lord, J.R., just look at it. Just look at our beautiful capital." Standing at the edge of the mall, the topless Washington Monument was still the scene of frantic, undermanned rescue attempts. In the darkness beyond the Lincoln Memorial, only a dull glow remained of what had been a raging conflagration. The rain had done what emergency service and equipment might have taken weeks to accomplish. Everywhere, people walked, or worked, or wandered, looking for trouble, or the dead, or loved ones they might never find.

"It's going to take a long, long time, Rosemary, to put this town back together."

"One plane . . . think of it, J.R. One little A-10 from Myrtle Beach."

"Yeah. One plane. Six missiles. Air accidents. Crashes. And poverty, the big fire, the biggest of them all."

In the northeast sky, the fire still raged, defying the rain, flattening the poor. A tank rolled by, followed by two more moving at a pretty good speed.

"I told Brian Howell to get the goddamn tanks out of here. Can't you just see it, on worldwide TV? Washington, D.C., home of the brave, patrolled by tanks, sent by a government too frightened of its own people to allow them even the most basic freedom from fear."

"Brian?"

"He advised against their removal. He said Paul Wolfe needed them to control the rioting."

"Possibly he does."

"I don't care! I'll have no tanks on the streets of Washington, D.C. Apparently, we are a barbaric people, but I'll not contribute to that testimony with tanks!"

"Whoa! I didn't say you were wrong. I just said Paul Wolfe, considering who he is and what his role in this may ultimately be, he might have thought *he* needed them. Not us. *Him.*"

"Point taken."

"Rosemary, why are we out here, walking in the rain and the soot and the grief. I, for one, have had all of this shit I can deal with."

"We are out here, because I need to talk to you. Safely. Away from any kind of listeners, friend or foe."

"Okay."

"When your Marines arrive at the Bennett Ranch, what will happen? What do you want to happen?"

"You heard. I want Adrian Bennett to die of a self-inflicted gun wound. Officially. Unofficially, I'm hoping we can get away with it. Crazy man's father, sick with grief, commits suicide. Faithful servant does same. The gunfight, and I'm sure that's exactly what it was, is bad for everybody, just when everything is already as bad as it can get. Brian Howell sent his 660 unit out to rescue Adrian Bennett. Or to kill him. I don't know which. The

Marines will make sure 'Brian' has his orders carried out.''

"You mean your orders. Brian Howell never spoke to that unit."

"No. And he won't, now. Nadine, at my request, has interdicted that unit's communications."

"He's a traitor, isn't he?"

"Brian Howell? Yes. He's a traitor, and there are a lot more still in the bushes. Sooner or later, we'll root them all out."

"Will we, J.R.? Will we really get to the bottom of this horrible day?"

"Sure we will. It will take time. And *your* time will be better spent dealing with the international repercussions of this day. Jonathan Bennett's air strike, and its consequences to the world's governments, has brought the world very near to anarchy and collapse, economic and military."

"We must arrest Brian Howell. He will continue to stir the pot, he and his shadow government. All those people he's going to bring forward to 'help' me in my time of trial. You should have been there, J.R., to listen to him. Death and terror all around him, and he did everything but jump up and say 'Seig Heil'!"

"You can't arrest him. For what? He hasn't done anything provable. And it will take you a hell of a long time to prove it."

"Then I'll fire him!"

"Yes. You could do that. Then he'd use all his friends to get elected president, probably over your dead body."

"Then what, J.R.?"

"You know what, Rosemary. You know it as sure as your own name."

"I can't do that, J.R."

"Nope. You can't. But I can."

She stopped walking, turned toward him, her eyes searching his face, the umbrella off kilter, the rain plastering her long red hair to her cheeks and shoulders. "Let's go back, J.R. I'm suddenly very cold." She linked her arm through his, her hip warm against his thigh. Their talk was over.

THE WHITE HOUSE
TUESDAY, 2:00 A.M.

"This is J.R. Kelly. Would it be possible to locate Major General Brian Howell? He's needed here, at the White House."

The Pentagon operator said she would do what she could, but under the circumstances, surely even the White House knew that locating General Howell would be easier for *them* than the Pentagon. As it turned out, it wasn't all that difficult. He was with General Wolfe's troops, and his tanks, in northeastern D.C. On his own, given this information, J.R. Kelly headed out into the night one more time. As he passed the Oval Office, he saw Rosemary Hawkins, yellow pad in hand, writing the speech she would give this morning. J.R. walked through the office, kissed the top of her flame-red hair, and left her alone. As far as he could tell, she hadn't noticed him at all.

"So, big brother, where you headed?"
"Into the Valley of Death, kid."
"With the six hundred?"
"Nope."
"Piece o' cake, big brother. Verily, you are the meanest son-of-a-bitch in the Valley. Any fucking valley."
"True."
"See you later, J.R.?"
"Count on it, kid." Jason Kelly went back to sleep, unworried, thinking of large nippled breasts straining against white nurses' uniforms. And she was there, too. One hell of an incentive to get well.

BLADENSBURG, ANNAPOLIS ROAD
LANHAM, MARYLAND
TUESDAY, 3:00 A.M.

"I'm looking for Major General Brian Howell. Can you tell me where I might find him?"

"Hell, mac, he's up with Paul Wolfe, somewhere. The bitch in the White House wants our tanks out of here. Shit. We didn't even know where most of them are. And who the hell are you, anyway, mac?"

The 9mm jumped into J.R.'s hand against the fleshy neck of the overweight major standing next to the National Guard tank. "I'm your worst fucking nightmare, Major. The absolute worst. You get Brian Howell down here, now, or you'll fucking get run over by one of your own tanks. Do you read that, mister?"

"Loud and clear."

"Good. Now, get on the horn, and get him down here!"

The tank column moved down the wide, empty street, far removed from danger, on its way back and into Maryland, and its motor pools and repair shops. The Maryland tanks seemed to be in wonderful shape, on such short notice. Of course, Paul Wolfe had been provided with a bit more than short notice.

Now, with Air Force General Brian Howell riding a sort of "shotgun," Paul Wolfe was reluctantly doing what he'd been ordered to do. Remove his tanks from the District of Columbia. Given a choice, he might have ridden the lead tank onto the White House lawn, to "protect" the new female President of the United States. But he'd not been offered that choice.

Two Marines and a civilian stood in the road, near his initial command post, from which the original tank thrusts had been directed. The Marines stayed in position. The civilian moved forward, one beefy hand outstretched, as if he could stop the rolling tanks in a Moses-like show of parting-the-waters faith. And so he could. The tank column ground to a halt.

"General Howell?"

"No. General Paul Wolfe. What can I do for you, mister?"

"You can tell Brian Howell that J.R. Kelly is here to see him. And then you can continue your armored withdrawal, General Wolfe, as ordered by President Hawkins."

"And just what the fuck do you know about what my Guard units were ordered to do, mister?"

"Kelly, sir. J.R. Kelly. C.I.A. I know more about you than you might want to talk about. However, if you wish, I will gladly arrange a private meeting between you and President Hawkins, sir. I'm sure she would like to personally congratulate you on, first, your miraculous ability to be in all the right places at the right time, and conversely, to have the stomachache required to stay away from the memorial amphitheater."

"What do you mean by that, mister?"

"You know what I mean, Mr. Wolfe. And so does the President. Now get Brian Howell out here, up front and center. And do it now!"

"Listen, you silly son-of-a-bit—" The two Marines in the road moved slightly forward, M16s at the ready, pointed, however loosely, at Paul Wolfe's chest.

"You'll hear from me, mister."

"I have no doubt, but for the moment, shut up. Get Brian Howell out here, and continue the orderly withdrawal of your armored units from the streets of your nation's capital. You are to consider that a direct order from your Commander in Chief."

For the briefest moment, Paul Wolfe, in the embrace of the steel turret of his tank, stiffened with resistance.

"You're an old man, General. Leave now, before you have no further opportunity to age."

The tanks buttoned up, clanked along, picked up speed enough to make them graceful instead of awkward, rattling buckets of bolts, and the wide highway was soon empty, except for the impeccably dressed Brian Howell, exhaust smoke swirling around him, giving him the look of an ancient, dark-skinned genie, appearing from the bowels of the earth.

"Well, Mr. Kelly. You get around, don't you?"

The two men were twenty feet apart, in the middle of the highway. The two Marines were gone. In a city torched, blown apart, and set on its heel by men like Brian Howell, they were, for the moment, alone.

"Adrian Bennett is dead, Howell. Your 660 unit is burying him, at this moment. He has a self-inflicted gun wound, at your order."

"He what?"

J.R. slipped easily into his Brian Howell voice, repeating the order to the young, snowstormed captain who would be an eagle colonel by Easter, or . . .

"I thought you were a fool, Agent Kelly. Someone I could dissuade, or at worst deflect."

"You were wrong, Howell."

"Everything I said to Rosemary Hawkins tonight, everything, was a setup."

"No, General. The words you used were your own. Or Adrian's. Or Carlyle's. Or Paul Wolfe's. But mostly Adrian Bennett's. My beef with you goes deeper."

"I'm not sure I understand, Kelly."

"Okay. Let's start with my little brother."

"Jason Kelly? A very, very brave man."

"I have intercepts that prove you warned Adrian Bennett that a Marine pilot might be waiting for his son."

"Bullshit! Jonathan Bennett flew over D.C. unopposed."

"I also had a friend a Myrtle Beach A.F.B. A nice, nerdy little kid with thick glasses who thought he was James Bond. And he wasn't James Bond. So young Mr. Bennett slopped my friend's brains all over the taxiway at Myrtle Beach."

"Prove that, Mr. Kelly, if you can."

"And there was Bonnie, a confectionery blond of extraordinary beauty and common sense, and you didn't know anything about her, but I was afraid of what would happen, so I sent her away. Away to safety. But she wasn't safe. She was killed, coming back to me, to make babies with a washed-up, balding, potbellied old C.I.A. man."

"Oh, c'mon, Kelly. This is just all a bit maudlin, isn't it?"

"Okay. Stuff what I have to bitch about. Let's talk about your service to your country, and particularly your service to Rosemary Hawkins."

"Sir, I have served Ms. Hawkins, unflinchingly, for years. She herself will tell you that."

"Yes. Unflinchingly. Promoting Conrad Taylor's ideas, through her. They were, after all, her ideas, weren't they?"

"For the most part, yes, though what it has to do with this conversation, I can't imagine."

"Oh, c'mon, Brian, try! What do you and Adrian Bennett have in common? Slaves, right? He kept one, you're born of one. Why shouldn't she believe you were the creamy black-skinned soul of peace and rapprochement with the Soviets, the Chinese, the Arabs. You with your 'I'm above all this black shit' face, and let's us do what the reverend said, without the reverend. She bought it, you sold it, and you, of all people, are a total, complete fascist, a disciple of a slave owner transferred from the deep South only by an act of birth."

"Tell me, Mr. Kelly, do they teach you this socio-psycho babble stuff in the C.I.A., or did you get this from reading books by short-thighed white women with no training?"

"I'll tell you where I got it. I got it from third-grade religion class, from Father Byrne, when I needed him most, from the nuns when I hated them most. I got it from the trusting eyes of my little brother, and the warm thighs of a president shocked beyond a human's ability to accept shock. I got it from dealers in Cadillacs, and dealers in Mercedes, and dealer wanta-be's in dark alleys. I got it from you, General Howell. From the belief that what you stood for *must* be good, and righteous, and American. I got it from a twisted, sad belief in a God, my God, spoken to in Latin, without holding hands while I listened to a

Salvadoran refugee play guitar. I got it all, because, whatever I am, I have always been decent.''

J.R. tried to remember when it had last rained in Los Angeles in August. The wind drove the rain sideways up the street, kicking up a curious mixture of dust and rippling puddles as the parched earth struggled to accept the storm, the ground baked hard as cement by two hundred days without rain. The raindrops seemed larger than normal, hitting harder, erupting in tiny explosions all around him. Then the heel of his cowboy boot was blown off, skipping end over end down the street.

The guy with the Uzi ran off another string, a long, wracking cough, joined by the blistering hiccup of the AK-47 from the guy behind the front wheel of the Cadillac. Pinned down, and rained on, pissed on by the bad guys in the City of Angels. He hurled his bulky frame across the short open space between the overturned police car and the low brick wall, the Uzi racketing after his one good heel. J.R. popped up, fired the Browning until it jammed, cleared it, fired again, popped the empty clip loose, slapping a full clip in, running the brass into the welcoming maw of the chamber, a satisfying chunk as it kicked one in and ready. He peered over the low wall, saw the bad guy aiming at him, centered the Browning, squeezed, saw the bad guy go down behind the car. Hit? Who knew. The AK-47 began to chip away at his wall.

J.R. began to laugh out loud. Holy shit! This was really exciting! He rolled to one corner of the wall. The Uzi started up again. Still two bad guys. He laughed again, glanced once more at the overturned unmarked police car, his partner draped out of the front door, upside down, his legs still in the car, his eyes staring out around the neat hole between his eyes, the back of his head gone and his brains splashed across the interior roof of the car.

In the distance, sirens began to wail. Cavalry. To the rescue. Only who would they rescue? The police car was a dark blue Mercedes, and J.R. undercover, was known as Paul Mason, big-time coke dealer. Who would they shoot at when they got here? He looked once more at his dead partner, the only man he'd ever known that could eat eight Power Burgers in one day and not die. And he stood up, insanely, stupidly, and rushed the two guns, the Browning jumping in his hand.

The first two rounds caught the guy by the Cadillac, the black guy, George, who wore all the chains and beat all his women and who had become one of J.R.'s personal demons. Both rounds hit him in the face. The Uzi chattered as he went down, its trigger pulled by a dead man. J.R. turned, still running, crouched, the 9mm thrust out in front of him.

The distance between J.R. Kelly and the bad guy, in this particular case, Joaquin Perasco Torres (a Colombian by way of Mexico) was less than twenty feet. Culturally, Mr. Torres was a million miles away, and cocksure. He simply stood up, a simpering smile on his face, and dropped the AK-47 assault rifle he'd been using to try to kill J.R. Kelly onto the hot but rained-on street of back alley L.A., the wind whipping his custom-made shirt against his body, his black hair made fuller by the driving rain. He looked impossibly tanned, impossibly fit, impossibly rich. He stared at J.R., his eyes all-knowing and aware. He would walk, he knew it. He'd be back.

Joaquin's teeth gleamed in the dark, rolling air, eighty-eight degrees and wet, the sirens in the distance howling, closer, closer, the grin spreading, the wind and rain lashing at them, frozen in hate, a few feet apart, the bad guy, the good guy . . .

"So, Sergeant Kelly, how did you get to him? Jesus, you were in real bad shape here." A toothpick flicked back and forth in the police captain's mouth, popped inside, reappeared. Hell of a trick.

"Well, like I said, I nailed George by the car. Then the A.K. opened up. I guess I just got lucky. I popped that trigger, and held it down until he stopped shooting."

"Sheesh, I guess! Jesus, even after he was hit, he held on to that AK-47. Died with his boots on, so to speak."

The commanding officer of the Los Angeles Police Department's drug enforcement division smiled at J.R. Kelly, looking down at Joaquin Torres, still clutching his weapon, in spite of the fact that he had six 9mm rounds in his chest.

"Yeah, he was a real bad ass, I guess."

"You did a nice job, J.R. The taxpayers thank you. I thank you. You will do great things one day, I am sure." There was a very hard glint in his eyes when he said it. Eighteen months later, J.R. Kelly was recruited by the C.I.A.

The 9mm went off—once, twice, three times—and Major General Brian Howell, impeccably dressed, fell into the muddy streets of Washington, D.C. J.R. Kelly went to where he lay, shot him two more times, and dragged the body off the rain-swept street. He popped two white-hot phosphorous grenades, set them on Brian Howell's lifeless body, and watched him burn to ashes, just another burn spot on the side of the road.

THE WHITE HOUSE
TUESDAY, 4:00 A.M.

"Yo, J.R.! Been out in the rain?"

"Yes, ma'am. Just making sure Paul Wolfe took his tanks, and went home."

"And did he?"

"Oh yes, he really did. The rain has shut down the fires. I actually think the town has stopped burning. Flights into Andrews are landing every fourteen minutes. The mall will be a massive, medical tent city by dark tomorrow. I think we will soon begin to save more than we lose."

"I'm happy to hear that, J.R. My speech, such as it is, is nearly finished. When will your Marines hit the Bennett Ranch?"

"Two, maybe three hours. Bad storm, I'm told."

"Yes. The storm. Get undressed, J.R. Take a shower. Take my bed, in the N.S.C. office."

"But I'll need to know what the fuck is going on."

"If I run across something important, I'll wake you up."

"And if you don't run across something important?"

"I'll come to see you anyway."

"I'm tired, Rosemary."

"I know you are. But I'll make you less tired. Anyway, sleep. If something goes down, or I want or need something to come up, I'll let you know."

J.R. chuckled, in spite of the heavy weight he bore.

"J.R.?"

"Madam President?"

"I love you, you know." Her green eyes, tired and sad, looked into his.

"Gratitude is not love." Eloquent. That's what he was. In two minutes, still wearing one sock, J.R. Kelly was asleep in Rosemary Hawkins's bed, assailed by her scent, but too tired to let it keep him awake.

THE WHITE HOUSE
TUESDAY, 6:30 A.M.

"J.R.! Wake up! Your Marines are on the Desert Flower line."

J.R. got up, wrapping himself in a blanket, and sort of hopping to the desk, grabbed the phone from Rosemary. "Yeah, Sergeant, this is J.R. Kelly. What have you got?"

"We have the Bennett Ranch, Mr. Kelly, although, if you don't mind, I'll pass on jumping out of a C-130 in a snowstorm again. Bad shit, sir. I'm a Marine. I joined the Marines because I expected to fight in the tropics, not the goddamn snowbound miseries of Wyoming.''

"You have my sympathy, Sergeant. Now what the hell happened?''

''I regret to say, sir, we did have a brief firefight with the 660 unit on site. No casualties, Mr. Kelly. They just sort of melted away. We heard a chopper leave. I don't think their hearts were in it, Mr. Kelly. Two graves dug. Two dead, stiff old men. I'm not sure how to cover this, Mr. Kelly. Self-inflicted wound or not, the inside of that house is wall-to-wall gore. By daylight, somebody's TV or print crew is going to be here. They shot it out, Mr. Kelly. The old black man wanted Adrian Bennett real dead. And that's what he is. Real dead.''

"Can you hear me clearly, Sergeant?''

"Yes, sir.''

"You have about three hours. Send your team through the house, and gather any and all paperwork you can find. After the first two hours, leave the bodies in the ranch house. And burn it to the ground. A chopper pilot named 'Taco' will be in to pick you up thirty minutes before daylight, your time. Load the chopper with whatever records you can find. Blow the safes, if any. Then, burn the Bennett Ranch, all of it, to the ground. Do you understand, Sergeant? Keep the papers. Deliver them to 'Taco.' He'll fly you out of there to Yuma M.C.A.S. where you will catch a Medevac flight back here. Is that all perfectly clear, Sergeant?''

"Hell no, Mr. Kelly.''

"But you'll do it anyway?''

"Of course we will, sir. How's your little brother and Ms. Hawkins?''

"Hanging on, son. Don't you worry. In the end, the good guys are going to win this one.''

"Yes, sir, Mr. Kelly! *Semper Fi*, sir.''

"Yeah, Sergeant. *Semper Fi.*'' J.R. closed down the Desert Flower line for the last time. Adrian Bennett. Suicide, and a burned-down ranch. Hell to pay, maybe, at a later, less critically important time. But for now, at this time, the only way to go. Crazy Bennetts. Grieving Bennetts. And now, no Bennetts.

THE WHITE HOUSE
TUESDAY, 6:45 A.M.

J.R. stared at the ceiling, wide awake, waiting for the sun to come up, lying on his back in Rosemary Hawkins's old office, in her old office bed, with its silken orange and black sheets, its six-foot width by eight-foot length a constant surprise to him.

Upstairs, his brother slept on, drugged, watched over by a lovely young blond nurse who had so far refused to leave his bedside, though she did, according to the doctors, occasionally nod off to sleep.

The office was dark, except for a crackling fire in the fireplace, casting a warm glow through the room that for the first time in fourteen hours was not caused by fires burning *outside* the White House. The wide door to the inner office swung open and, framed in the reflected light behind her, Rosemary Hawkins, wearing some kind of long, nearly transparent smokey-colored gown, paused to look back at him, her lush red hair brushed straight down in long waves that extended below her waist. He could see her body, silhouetted, her feet in high-heeled slippers that appeared to have pompoms on the toes. Then she closed the door behind her, and leaned back against it, only the burnished-copper red hair visible in the light from the fireplace. Somewhere, in the red frame around her face, a pale oval glowed, two green fires at its center. A flash of cheekbones, hair, eyes, but only tiny pieces of the whole. His mouth went dry, and his crotch stirred, moved, betraying him, celebrating her, he had no idea.

"Hello, sailor."

"Isabella of Spain was the last queen to say that. She sent old Columbus off to discover a new world. He found it, I live in it, and it sucks. So don't give me that 'hello, sailor,' line, queenie."

"Oh, but I'm not the queen. I'm the president of the new world. And it is, to say the least, in a shambles. So I have come to you, mighty sailor of old, to see me through the night."

"I've seen you through the night. And the day, for that matter. You did fine, Madam Queen President. Better than fine."

"J.R., in a few hours, I have to tell the country, and the world, what I and the United States can do, will do, under any and all circumstances. Yesterday, I was a scheming bitch, going forth against an inept president, one I could twist and turn my way, to think my way, to do my way. Yesterday. Before the Ace-of-Spades turned the world—and, most particularly and selfishly, my world—to dust.

"I'm in love with you, J.R. And it has nothing to do with gratitude or country or patriotism or manipulation. I'm the President of the United States, and I have a lot to do. I'm going to start by doing you, J.R. Because you don't fool me, anymore. Because I feel you—your thoughts, your ideas, and your gentleness. And yes, right now, your lust. Don't reject me, J.R., because I couldn't bear it."

She didn't exactly walk across the room to him, as much as she floated across it, or seemed to. When she reached the side of his bed, she pulled the garish designer bedclothes away from his body. He was still wearing one sock. She walked to the bottom of the bed, leaned forward, and pulled it from his foot, tossing it over her shoulder, into the darkness. She bent forward, kissing the top of his foot, and then straightened, coming back to his side, very near the head of the bed.

She tugged on a silken bow at her throat, and the diaphanous gown slipped away from her body, and fell in a sleek puddle at her feet. She kicked one high-heeled slipper, sending the gown, like J.R.'s sock, off into the darkness, away from the fire.

The fire. Now, it cast its warm orange glow across her sleek breasts, down into the flat shadow of her stomach, highlighting her full hips surrounding a raging uncut fire of red pubic hair, its light flowing down her legs and vanishing into the rug, before bouncing upward and pulling the light back up her body, a body so sleek and powerful that J.R. could only gape.

"Do I disappoint you, J.R.?"

"I'm afraid to say anything. Anything at all, because I'm afraid you're just a dream, and I'll wake up, with cum all over me, and only a vague memory of how it got there."

"I love you, J.R. Let me help put that cum wherever you want it." She climbed over his body, pulling him deep into her, deeper than she'd ever known a man could go, while she yelped her pleasure, the muscles in her legs quivering as she rode him, bent far back, her shoulders on his upper legs, and then he sprang up, and switched positions, and she was under him, somehow, as he held himself above her, his hips still while she thrashed under him, understanding, loving him for doing it, but not saying it. Here, in bed, he was the president. Here, if nowhere else, the responsibility for each other's pleasure would be given, not demanded. And then he grew in her, and drove at her, all brutal and tender and loving, and she cried out his name, and hoped they had made a baby, a crooked-smiling, funny-faced, bald little hero, like his daddy.

THE WHITE HOUSE
TUESDAY, 11:00 A.M.

"Direct from the White House Oval Office, in Washington, D.C. Rosemary Hawkins, the President of the United States." Sarah Compton, recently a junior member of the Associated Press in Washington, D.C., had accepted, only fifty-five minutes before airtime, the prime job of Presidential Press Secretary to the new United States President. Wearing a bright red jumper, she was an immediate hit. She had announced the new President's intention to speak, and she had not stumbled. She did, however, trip over the mass of cable laid across the Oval Office. But nobody noticed. All eyes were on Rosemary Hawkins. The most critical, cold eye, the camera, about to see, hear, and record every word, every nuance of sound, every facial gesture. The world watched, with considerable apprehension, and gleeful anticipation of total failure.

ROSEMARY HAWKINS'S SPEECH
TUESDAY, 11:00 A.M.

Rosemary Hawkins, dressed in black skirt and turtleneck sweater, looked unflinchingly into the red eye of the camera.

"My fellow Americans. I am speaking to you, and, I'm told, by satellite connection to 98 percent of the world beyond our borders. Less than twenty-four hours ago, I, like 400,000 of my fellow countrymen, had gathered to lay to his final rest . . . no, to celebrate, the life and accomplishments of one of this nation's brightest lights.

"Old, old news now, but it was only last Wednesday that Conrad Taylor's helicopter was struck down by forces only God can marshal. The lightning that sent Marine One into the Fourteenth Street Bridge was tragic enough, devastating enough, for all the hopeful, peace-loving peoples of the world.

"This country, in the gracious ways of its European forefathers, decided to bury this youngest of our chiefs with full honors, inviting all chiefs, if you will permit me the analogy, from all nations. Nations at war. Nations contemplating war. And, of course, the vast majority of nations, contemplating war with no one of his neighbors, near or far away.

"As is the case, under our constitution, a man of vast experience and political acumen became President. Vice President William Rodgers, in his first test as President, pledged to continue Conrad Taylor's policies, worldwide. In the complex and somewhat abstract politics under the U.S. Constitution, I was named the new Secretary of State, an obligation I accepted only after being assured by President Rodgers that he would pursue, with vigor, the initiatives begun and nurtured by Conrad Taylor before him.

"And so the United States asked friend and foe to attend Conrad Taylor's funeral. William Rodgers, in a completely unselfish act, asked those attending the funeral to stay in the United States, for freewheeling talks, no holds barred, no subject out of line.

"The radicals, both right and left, screamed their displeasure. But, to no avail. The leaders came, because the world's leaders believed. And what, now, can I report?

"This morning, I flew a forty-minute helicoptor flight over the capital of the United States. I flew it in a driving rain. And for that rain we should fall to our knees and thank God. I would like to report, briefly, on what I saw.

"Andrews Air Force Base is receiving and dispatching over 150 aircraft per hour. These aircraft are medical aircraft, including, I am happy to say, ten aircraft from Canada, twenty-two aircraft from Great Britain, and six 747 aircraft donated by Lufthansa to ferry special burn teams from our U.S. airbase at Frankfurt, West Germany. I'm told that the Japanese are flying over 185,000 tons of medical supplies and personnel to West Coast bases, where we will shuttle them into Washington, D.C. Regrettably, though given direct clearance, the following countries have declined assistance: the Soviet Union, North Korea, North Vietnam, Syria, Egypt, Iraq, Iran, Mexico, Cuba, El Salvador, Paraguay, Peru, India, China . . . the list goes on, but I shall deal with them in a moment.

"Why does a powerful country such as the U.S.A. need this help? Let me explain, as best I can, what yesterday, Monday, has brought upon the world. All over the world, whatever the time as of this minute, casualty lists have been reported in detail. From Moscow, Idaho, to Moscow; from Delhi, Nevada, to New Delhi, India; from Little Italy, New York, to Italy; from Spanish Harlem, to Haarlem, Denmark. The United States has lost its Senate. *All* of its Senate. It has lost all but twelve members of its House of Representatives. It has lost all members of the Supreme Court, the Joint Chiefs of Staff, the Cabinet, thirty-eight of its governors, thirty-one of its lieutenant governors, 98 percent of its national news staff—television, print, and radio. Two hundred sixty-two members of the Secret Service died. One hundred eighty-seven members of the Federal Bureau of Investigation are dead, including its director and its top twenty-two executive officers. The Joint Chiefs of Staff and fifty-seven of its top staff officers are dead. And most sadly for Americans, Washington, D.C., is dead, or at least badly injured.

"The Washington Monument has no top. The Library of Congress . . . the library is grievously burned. The Folger Shakespeare Library is burned to the ground, as is Fort McNair. Mount Vernon took some slight damage, as did the Washington Cathedral, if you can call the death of an American F-15 pilot slight damage. The Prince and Princess of Wales died in the amphitheater. As did the *governments* . . . yes, the governments of fifty-two nations from around this great, scared world of ours. The British Prime Minister, the Pakistani Prime Minister, role models for women throughout the world . . . gone.

"In this great city, we have hardly begun to count the dead. Oh, I don't mean presidents, prime ministers, ambassadors. I mean the *dead*. The dead who are dead only because they believed in life. Simple life! Marriage, sex, children. And, sadly, sometimes drugs. Why don't we pause here, and quote some statistics that should . . . that had better . . . give our adversaries, anybody's adversaries, pause." Here, Rosemary Hawkins tugged on her turtleneck, and tears formed in the corners of her eyes.

"On the Arlington Memorial Bridge, twenty thousand, unknown, dead or seriously injured. Northeastern Washington, D.C., *minimum* casualty estimate, dead and injured, twenty-eight thousand. Arlington National Cemetery, total, twelve thousand dead or injured. Fort McNair, six hundred dead; one million five hundred thousand books destroyed; two hundred sixty yachts burned to the waterline.

"And how did this happen? The how, we know. One pilot, flying an A-10 Thunderbolt II, better known as a Warthog, attacked the Arlington Bridge and Cemetery at approximately four-thirty yesterday. Six missiles were fired, randomly, causing considerable damage, particularly at the Supreme Court Building and Fort McNair, where the casualty figures are still climbing.

"Three aircraft fell to earth, either shot down or as the result of air-to-air collisions. One came down in northeast Washington, where, much to my horror, I saw tanks! U.S. tanks, rolling down the streets of the District of Columbia, like invader tanks in Hungary, or Czechoslovakia, or Warsaw. But these, these were U.S. tanks, driven by United States tankers. No. Not here. Not under any circumstances. Not under *these* circumstances. I sent them home, to Maryland.

"The A-10 came from Myrtle Beach Air Force Base. Flown by its commander, Jonathan Bennett. We shall never know what caused him to fly so skillful a strike against his country's capital. His father, esteemed former senator and governor, has taken his own life, confirmed only hours ago by a U.S. Marine Corps volunteer team that parachuted into a Wyoming snowstorm under the direct order of Lieutenant General Sonny Flores, Commander of Camp LeJeune, South Carolina. Here, it would be only fair to tell you that the A-10 from Myrtle Beach—and I must repeat here, an A-10 flown by *one man,* not the 354th Tactical Fighter Wing—was shot down by *ramming,* by Jason Porter Kelly, U.S.M.C., VMF 231 Cherry Point, North Carolina.

"I have very few answers to this desperate challenge to world peace. But I have a few words of warning. Warnings, I'm sure that my former political opponents will find amusing, to say the least. Be not amused! My dress was blown from my body yesterday. I'm told everybody has seen that particular piece of videotape. Rosemary Hawkins, in her underwear. Well, listen, world, and listen well.

"I'm not sure who was involved in this terrible attack on our democracy or why. But you cannot attack our democratic history by shattering a few icons, or, forgive me, killing a few Americans.

"Hopefully, we will one day get back to international talks of peace, peace with all who want to create a peaceful world. We, the battered men and women of democracy, have a message for you. And I give it now:

One: An attack on Israel, by Syria, will be considered an attack on the United States.

Two: An attack on Syria, by Israel, will be considered an attack on the United States.

Three: An attack on Britain by anyone, will be considered an attack on the United States.

Four: An attack on the Philippines, by anyone, will be considered an attack on the United States.

Five: An attack, by the Soviet Union, anywhere in Europe, will result in instant, full, and total nuclear retaliation.

Six: Believe everything I have said.

Seven: May I say, finally, that my skirts will remain
         short. But since four-thirty yesterday afternoon,
         my vision is long, uncluttered, and in the final
         analysis, angry, as only an American can be. We
         shall ask our surviving governors to appoint sen-
         ators. We shall ask our surviving lieutenant gov-
         ernors to appoint senators. Twenty-three months
         from now, we, all of us, will stand before the
         American people, to be confirmed, or denied,
         including me.

"The message here is, or should be, clear. We will put
our House, our Senate, our courts, our presidency, in order. Two hundred fifty million Americans deserve it, de-
mand it, and ultimately will get it. But until we do what
we must do, under our Constitution, I, Rosemary Hawkins, have taken a solemn oath to preserve and protect this
nation. I know the American people will help me achieve
this. And this knowledge, I pass on to the rest of the
world."

WASHINGTON, D.C.
TUESDAY, 2:00 P.M.

"You were wonderful."

"Was I, J.R.? Oh shit, I was so scared."

"You didn't look scared."

"I was. My panties were wet."

"That's it? I just have to scare you, and your panties
are wet?"

"Goddammit, J.R.! You know what I mean!"

"Okay, yeah, I know what you mean. The fires are out
in D.C. But they are starting up, all over the world, as of
your speech."

"Alligators, huh? Up to our ass in alligators!"

"Yup. Alligators. But we'll deal with them, won't we?"

"Sure, J.R., we'll deal with them. How long do you suppose it will take?"

J.R. looked at the new, decidedly female President of the United States. "Until the next night strike, I guess."

"Yeah, J.R., and that could come anywhere in the world, couldn't it?"

"Let's just put it this way. We are going to be very busy, keeping us out of war, appointing a Supreme Court, courting new senators, getting nominated, nominating a new cabinet, lengthening your skirts, calling your mom, getting the walls to—"

"J.R.?"

"Yes, Madam President?"

"Why are we going to call my mom?"